FISSURES

CHINESE WRITING TODAY

SELECTED AND EDITED BY

Henry YH Zhao

Yanbing Chen

John Rosenwald

FOREWORD BY

Breyten Breytenbach

ZEPHYR PRESS

Publication was assisted by a grant from
The Massachusetts Cultural Council.

Cover and book design by *typeslowly*
Cover photo courtesy of Bei Dao
Printed by McNaughton & Gunn

Library of Congress Control Number: 00 134751

ISBN 0-939010-59-3

0 9 8 7 6 5 4 3 2 1
FIRST EDITION

ZEPHYR PRESS

50 KENWOOD STREET
BROOKLINE, MA 02446

www.zephyrpress.org

CONTENTS

CRACKED STONE

foreword by Breyten Breytenbach

> *You need to have a window, a form;*
> *then you can look through it.*
> — Guo Lusheng

FISSURES — the title of this collection, would seem to be singularly apposite. It brings to mind the image of a jar starting to leak its precious liquid or a monolithic edifice cracking to let in light. One may similarly be reminded of snaking lightning sundering the heavens, or the first sliver and shiver of dawn on the horizon. It suggests, in any event, the outward manifestation of an irreversible process. Splits becoming visible on the surface are either the advance signals of a new dispensation taking shape, or the result of a center no longer being able to hold the accumulated weight and wear of time. Cui Weiping argues that collapse begins with form, and that resistance to the disorder and darkness of the environment can only take the form of a new order.

The sound of a word (just like the 'sound' of a concept) may set off unexpected resonances. A word also lives in a quite arbitrary field of relations. Or maybe not that arbitrary: sounds, through their shadows and affinities and dissonances, sometimes far-fetched, constitute a history of etymology and thus of thinking. In literature the word and the idea are married in an equal relationship of give-and-take and the offspring will show features of both 'parents'!

Thus I'd be tempted to read around the sound of **fissures: fish** (cold-blooded animal living wholly in water and breathing through gills, with fins for swimming) and remember the proverb — "there's as good fish in the sea as ever came out of it"; **fisher; fission** (splitting of one cell into new cells, or of the nucleus of certain atoms when an atomic bomb is exploded); **fist** (hand when tightly closed); **fit** (suitable, well adapted, good enough — "a dinner fit for a king", right and proper — "it is not fit that you should mock your mother so", the right measure — "the key doesn't fit the lock", "to fit out a ship for a long voyage").

If I allow myself to wander rather aimlessly through the words it is because this collection sets off many bells, both big and small. Perhaps a more apt simile would be to say that the movement of words brings about a wind of shadows.

And indeed, 'shadow' and 'wind' and 'fire' run through these pages of poems and stories and essays, like dark thoughts no less sharp for being muted. Song Lin says, "the skin feels the maturity of wind"; Bei Dao remarks, "it's song that traces the earliest winds"; Duo Duo sings, "to be an extinguished candle in a breezeless night ... to be black wheat, enduring deep thoughts in the wind." It is all about exile. But it might as well be home. Liu Zai-fu writes:

"At that instant the blazing fire became the bosom of our home." Is it the heart which is the crackling hearth? Again and again one encounters through the shadows cast by the words of these writers (the 'Chinese shadows'?) a flickering of light, a lapping of darkness around the edges of beaches and journeys and experiences, the gestures of memory.

The un-initiated non-Chinese reader must be especially careful not to look at Chinese literature through the glasses of his or her own conditioned expectations. We have all been bamboozled by the clichés of exoticism and romanticism, reassured by the security of 'distance' and charmed by the lures of 'difference'. The spectacles piously handed to us were those of dimness, dissolving distances into a pulsating emptiness where 'the ancients' lived as wise but rustic sages. Or else the glasses showed us the fierceness of heroic stances, the abnegation of revolution spewing forth 'school' after 'school' of flag-waving fanatics, where each new generation would stand (or fall) in the sign of contestation. Alternatively — and sometimes simultaneously — we were told that we'll never understand: China is the last Unknown; and since it is so old and so rich and so big and so threatening, it is probably the Unknown Universe. There would seem to be a *need* for us non-Chinese to have a China of the mind.

It is by no means the slightest merit of this collection to be thus wiping clean our glasses in order to give us a feel of the 'ordinariness' of modern existence. It constitutes a horizontal slice of the many expressions of literary creativeness in present-day China. (One should say, in contemporary 'Chinese', since much of it is clearly written from abroad.) In these pages we encounter a wide variety of descriptions of inner and outer lives, of communal life, of history affecting the social and physical environment (without events being capitalized as History), but with nearly no moralizing and little attempt at suggesting how it could be different.

How inclusive and exhaustive is the picture? How would a non-Chinese know? Should it be expected of any group of writers to present a cohesive physical and spiritual depiction of their homeland or even of their condition of exile? I don't think so. Besides, it wouldn't be possible. This volume, in any event, does not set out with the pretense of painting the totality of modern Chinese thought and letters. We catch glimpses (or ricochets) of the swirling arguments which one surmises to be taking place around perennial issues such as ethics, social engagement, the weight of tradition (including its translation into literature), social realism, modernism (and, by now, post-modernism), the 'decadence' of Western influences ... And yet, despite what I noted earlier on, we see little overt reaction to exile or repression or stagnation or nationalism; there is no manifest uprising in thought. But then, since we don't share the reference field of language and literary tradition used by the authors, or the common horizon of a history and of social fabric, one may be missing out on the impact which the unsaid must have under these circumstances. "Silence becomes a lingering theme in our poems" according to Hu Dong. The hollows resonate with sound; 'absence' and 'emptiness' are alive. In fact, they are needed for bringing about movement.

As far as I could see, I repeat, there are no grand gestures, no attempt at a global cure or general condemnation, no revolutionary posturing. The people talked about and talked to are not the powerful, neither in politics nor in culture or philosophy.

What we do get is the nitty-gritty of life, the flow and the flux of words describing life while establishing a (separate) life of their own. For underneath all the translatables there are essential conditions and processes: the same, more or less, for whoever puts pen to paper. We also get an interaction with nature which must be so ancient that it has itself become an all-pervasive culture.

Wallace Stevens wrote: "A poet's words are of things that do not exist without the words." But to effect an entry into "a condition of illuminated rightness ... (that is) poetry itself," as Seamus Heaney asks us to do, or enjoy the "physical emotion" which fulfils the continual need we experience to "recover a past or prefigure a future" — the way Jorge Luis Borges describes the meeting of minds and hearts between reader and writer — we need to move within the same language. In writing, no heart without the blood of word. It might even mean that we need to move among similar confinements and the openings of communal memories.

"When a story is passed around, it changes shape," Hong Ying remarks in *The Snuff Bottle*.

Of course we do not get the *original*: the urgency and the inevitability of a choice of words and sounds and rhythms and references, adding up to echoes discernible only to the native speaker. All of us have 'cultural genes' made up of memory and tone and the transmission of attitudes to 'beauty' and 'usefulness' and 'importance'. These 'genes' give us a profile of specificity, maybe even of difference. But at the same time we all experience, at least sometimes, the desire to revolt against the established assumptions, and the permanent need to find new forms for old facts and fears and fictions.

Is this not a universal feature? A strain in our human condition? Isn't life a 'translation' of the original death?

The opening up of new spaces, the transition from the original to the translated, the maturing of comprehension — leading, hopefully, to a deepening humanism, towards tolerance and curiosity and the enjoyment of differences — these are among the important tasks which we'd like to allocate to writers. Because, before you know it, it's all over. Many of the writers in the present collection convey this sense of passing accompanied by a nostalgia for the ineffable, with delicacy and a perfume of sadness that cannot be modified by translation.

Recently in Paris I met a Chinese comrade, Bian Tong, coming out of the Montparnasse cemetery where he'd been to pay his respects before the tomb of a countryman who died far away from his native soil. Bian Tong has also been living in exile for quite a while now. In a jocular fashion we started talking about the strange seas of old age, and of how one needs to find a place in which to lie down if you don't want to get lost. We both admitted to visiting these boneyards, nearly secretively — not as if either of us could afford a mooring place in a crowded and fancy port like this one!

We compared notes, as it were. In what position would one want to lie? Facing the sun, yes, but surely not to have it in the eyes. And wind? One would wish it to be heavy with birdsong and the fragrance of flowers; one would like to feel the maturity of wind on the skin. What kind of cherry must come on top of the cake? Doves of peace? A jar of mourning? A cross? The Book of Learning? A bell-jar covering immortal petals? Some angel figure with snapped wings folded together like longnailed hands? Would it not be advisable to be put away in a half-seated position under a bump of speechless clods in the shade of a moss-covered tree? Is it that reprehensible to be without a name forever? What about the stake, or the oven? Perhaps, we mused, it would be better to disappear like a sleeping dolphin in the timeless green cathedral of deep waters. Or to be consumed by the fire of stars and the wind of birds high in a tree. Or to be mistaken for future offspring somewhere on an unexplored beach where only turtles still come to bury their stuttering of eggs. Choices! Choices!

And what will the day which comes to fetch us look like? ("To draw a line, as if through a miss-spelled word," was the way Bian Tong described that moment.) Will it rain? Snow?

Perhaps, we agreed (and in any event), it is better to prepare and polish your own stone while you still have hands. Better still, we concluded, to put up a stone of commemoration for the people we feel close to, for those whom we consider as ancestors even though they are our contemporaries.

As I have tried to do in this foreword.

Can Ocells, Catalonia
August 1999

SONG LIN TRANSLATED BY YANBING CHEN

QUATRAINS

Life loses the tenderness of wings
becomes sharp, and dull. In the mirror,
we barely recognize ourselves,
on dream's branches ominous creatures perch.

How much we'd like to walk away, avoiding
expectant eyes. Rest, like dust.
Or sit among reeds, watching under a cloud
wild geese returning in the distance.

Dig earth, water the garden, just like the ancient poets;
pulses echo chrysanthemums' chirps.
Nothing could change us
change our love for the fish-scale bark.

But on the rocks, before the end of the summer,
wind from the ocean lights up clusters of blackberry lanterns.
The alarm's over, we want to go home.
The night descends. The articulation of the galaxy's will.

EULOGY

Flowers and dew, what does their existence mean?
Nature keeps its silence.
Except for happy conjectures,
what grasp do humans have of the dead and the gods?
following rules of the universe,
escaping primordial catastrophes,
modestly breathing the unknown?
The skin feels the maturity of wind,
like waterfalls, forest springs.

In the deep wilderness under the night
the satyr's still roaming.
Free mountain spirits and ocean sirens
are witnesses to human exile.
The song descends with feathers and wings,
and turns in blood into stars.
The earth needs you, partner of the future,
morning of destiny!
Feelings gather and rush underground.

BEI DAO

TRANSLATED BY YANBING CHEN
AND JOHN ROSENWALD

LANDSCAPE OVER ZERO

it's eagle that taught song to swim
it's song that traces the earliest winds

we trade shards of happiness
enter family from different directions

it's father who identified darkness
it's darkness leads to the classics' lightning

the door of weeping clangs shut
the echo chases its scream

it's the pen in despair that flowers
it's flowers that resist the inevitable journey

it's love's light that wakes
illuminates the landscape over zero

KEYWORD

my shadow's highly dangerous
this craftsman hired by the sun
brings the final knowledge
empty

that's the dark nature
of the moth's work
the smallest child of violence
footsteps in the air

keyword, my shadow
hammers the iron of the dream
stepping to that rhythm
a lone wolf walks into

the dusk of no-one's-defeat
an egret writes on the water
a life a day a sentence
the end

UNTITLED

philatelists spy on life
happiness flashes and expires

arrogantly, night kneels
holding up generations of lights

wind shifts, birds run berserk
how many apples has song shaken down?

the relentless lover's hair turns white
I bend and look into the face of destiny

the fountain appeases me
at the moment of futility

VIGIL

moonlight smaller than sleep
a river runs through our room
where does the furniture dock?

not only chronology
but also the recognized front
of the illicit climate
bring us closer to rain forests
o weeping line of defense

the glass paperweight detects
wounds in the narrative
how many dark mountains blocked
1949

at the end of a nameless tune
fists clenched, flowers scream

OLD PLACE

death looks at a painting
always from the other side

out the window at this moment
I see the setting sun from my youth
back again at the old place
I'm anxious to tell the truth
but before it's dark
what can be said

drinking words from the cup
only makes you more thirsty
invoking the earth alongside the river
I listen among empty mountains
to the weeping of a flute player's heart

the tax angels
return from the other side of the painting
and count from those gilt skulls
all the way to the setting sun

AS I KNOW IT

not until those heading for the story
removed a mountain
was he born

setting out from the accident
I've just arrived in another country
the inversion of letters
restores meaning to each meal

standing on tiptoes to reach time's mark
war for him is too far away
yet father's too close
he bends to pass the exam
and steps onto the boundless deck

the wall has ears
I must catch up with him
writing!

he paints the road red
lets phoenixes land
displays dying gestures
those ambiguous road signs
encircle the winter
even the music is snowing
I take extra caution
under each word lies an abyss

when an immense tree
quells winds from all quarters
his garden
grows deserted through fantasy

casually, I look through
his unfavorable record
and can only believe in flowers from the past

he forged my signature
and grew up
switching coats with me
he steals into my night
searching for that which ignites the story
that blasting cap, that fuse

XI CHUAN TRANSLATED BY YANBING CHEN

FROM *VIEWS FAR AND NEAR*

FIRE

Fire cannot illuminate fire; what is illuminated by fire is not fire. Fire illuminated Troy, fire illuminated Emperor Qing Shi's face; fire illuminated the crucible of the alchemist, fire illuminated leaders and masses. All these fires are one fire — element, passion — pre-dating logic. Zoroaster only gets half of it right: fire has to do with the bright and clean, as opposed to the dark and foul. But he neglects the fact that fire is born out of darkness, and mistakenly opposes fire to death. Because fire is pure, it is faced with death; because fire is exclusive, it tends to be cold-blooded and evil. People usually see fire as the spirit of creation, not knowing it is also the spirit of destruction. Fire that is free, paternal, and holy; without form, without mass; neither spurs the growth of any life, nor supports any standing object. Just as those who are full of ambition must give up hope, those who accept fire must accept great sacrifice.

ZHU WEN TRANSLATED BY MAO LIANG

DA MA'S WAY OF SPEAKING

It was the summer of 1989 when I graduated from college and was assigned to work in an electric company in the city of Nanjing. The train arrived at one in the afternoon. With two colossal bags on my shoulders, I maneuvered my way out of the station and was immediately surrounded by a cluster of rustic-looking girls soliciting guests for cheap hotels. Drenched in sweat and in a terrible mood, I yelled, "Leave me alone! I'm not traveling anywhere, I'm going to be stuck in this hole for a while!" A brother-in-law living in Nanjing was supposed to come and meet me at the station, but he hadn't shown up yet. I had told him not to come at all because I was sure that a bookworm would be more trouble than help, but he insisted on coming anyway. I figured in the meantime I'd better find some shade and get something to drink. It was the sort of weather that made you, and everyone else for that matter, feel like a sticky pile of viscera stuffed in the city's sweltering gut, and wriggling around. As soon as I sat down near a phone booth, a few of the more confident girls sauntered over. They swayed back and forth trying to lure some business out of me. What a pain! Who could possibly think about something like that in this sort of weather? Maybe you can, but I just couldn't. They sneered, called me a loser, and then, twisting their huge asses around, threw themselves on the other passengers. Thank goodness, finally some peace. It was then that I noticed a voice behind me in the phone booth.

He was talking rapidly, in an excited and rhythmic way. The phrases he repeated the most were "it's fuckingly good!" and "I'll slash you!" And the way he laughed — an intermittent cackle with gulps of breath, as if he were convulsing — went way beyond the normal operations of vocal chords. All of this instantly brought on a warm feeling of familiarity. I was sure that I had found an old friend in this alien place, but when I turned my head to greet him, I discovered that the man in the booth was a complete stranger. A tall and thickset guy, leaning on the side wall with one hand, he continued his conversation in the same animated way. I continued observing him through the tinted glass. The more I listened, the more unbelievable it became that I didn't actually know the guy. By now he had already felt me watching him and responded by throwing me an angry and hostile look. Ignoring his threat, I continued staring. A few moments later he hung up, came out of the booth, and charged straight at me. As he shoved me hard on the chest, I caught sight of a coiled snake tattooed on his outstretched arm. But the guy in front of me was much more terrifying than the snake, and it only then dawned on me that I was in trouble.

"What the hell are you looking at?" his tone was now unfamiliar, not the same one he had just been using on the phone. In fact it was so strange that it almost seemed as if he had suddenly put on another face.

"Well, I was just thinking that we might have a mutual friend."

"We do?"

"Yes, I'm sure you must know him, Da Ma."

"You a friend of his?"

"Yes, we were classmates for a while in Beijing, I'm sure..."

"Okay, I'll let you go, but not because of him. I don't give a shit about that sonuvabitch!"

He reached into my shirt pocket and took a cigarette, lit it, and then hurriedly walked past me to Bus stop No.1.

"Wait a second! Could you tell me where Da Ma lives?"

"I'm looking for that sonuvabitch myself! He's a fucking good liar, if nothing else. He's going to pay!"

This all happened on my first day in Nanjing. I've now been here five years, but have never once come across Da Ma. Not that I've gone out of my way to track him down. Da Ma was not the kind of friend I really needed to find, nor was he for most of my other classmates. You'd be happy enough to run into him on the street, but that was it. He was the restless and agitated type, which you could feel in the way he spoke. I suspect he might not live in Nanjing anymore, but I'm certain that he did live here at some point. Three of the people I've met since coming to Nanjing definitely knew him. They all speak the same way he does. It's amazingly easy to pick out, even in a noisy crowd. Everyone's impression of Da Ma is basically negative. They've all been entangled in his snares, and none of them knows where he's at. Talking to them is exactly like talking to Da Ma; at first my interest is piqued, and then I'm thrown for a loss. I actually feel as if I've come across Da Ma several times since graduation. And that's exactly what it is: it's Da Ma's way of speaking. It's a contagious disease, a kind of spreading fungus. Once you pick it up you're doomed. Whenever you're upset, you exclaim naturally: "I'll slash you!" and when you're feeling good, "It's fuckingly good!" Isn't that amazing? I can still remember the narrative rhythm Da Ma used most often, it goes like this (you can wave your arm the way Da Ma would to get a better feel for it)

$$4/4 \quad \text{x xx} \quad \text{x xx} \quad \text{xxxx} \quad \text{xx} \mid \text{x xx} \quad \text{x xx} \quad \text{xxxx} \quad \text{xx} \mid$$

It all began in the university. The day after registration, all the freshmen were packed and sent off to a Liberation Army station in Baoding, Hebei Province, for one month of military training. Freshmen now have to undergo three months of training because they are a more pampered and disruptive group in general, and military training has proven itself to be an effective method of strengthening discipline and organization. From the first day of training, I couldn't wait for the final chapter — the firing range. I wanted to really show them what I could do. I had been a master bird shooter since junior high, though that had been using a bird gun. The sun was ferocious that day. Dressed in combat fatigues, we all sat in formation on the ground, waiting for the company commander's order to line up and be led to the shooting range. We were led ten at a time, because there were only ten shooting positions in the range. It was then that I first noticed the short figure in the front row. He seemed even more anxious than I, and was talking incessantly to a reluctant audience nearby. When the first group's shots sounded, this short figure gave out a loud cry and jumped up from the ground where he should have been sitting, turned around, and shouted at us:

"They're firing! They're finally firing!"

His hysterical yelling brought a wave of unrestrained laughter from all over. As soon as he was done yelling, he began to sprint toward the firing range. A dark-faced soldier who was in charge of maintaining order caught him in time, lifting him up by the collar like a chicken. He reluctantly sat back down in his original spot, murmuring to himself the entire time. That brought on another round of laughter. They tried to taunt him, but he remained silent. He sat there motionless — one leg folded on top of the other. So, please allow me to introduce you to the main character of our story. This short figure is none other than Da Ma.

As luck would have it, our section was the last to shoot that day. We had been roasting under the sun, listening to shots that we weren't firing for more than two hours. Our heads were spinning and stars were flashing before our eyes. If it had been permitted, I would have left. But, when our turn was finally called, I was instantly brought back to life. Da Ma was in the same group. He was at the fourth position and I was at the seventh. The company commander was stationed behind the first position. He hollered: "Lie down!" and we all lay at our respective positions. As I loaded my rifle, I felt my hands shaking — out of excitement of course. Guns loaded, we all waited motionless on the ground for the final order to pull the trigger. I took several deep breaths of the pungent odor of gunpowder lingering in the air. I loved that smell.

It was then that Da Ma scrambled up from the fourth position and aimed his semiautomatic rifle at everyone on his left.

"Freeze! Or I'll slaughter you!"

In first and second positions were two girls. They gave out a loud shriek, and hands over their heads, shrunk into a trembling pile on the ground. In third position was a boy from Shandong, who stammered, "Damn you...that gun is loaded! D...D...Damn you."

"I know that. That's why I told you not to move. Put your hands over your head!"

The face of the company commander — who was standing behind the first position — lost all color. Pointing at Da Ma, he said, "Careful! You bastard! This is no joke, no joke!" He walked slowly toward Da Ma as he spoke.

Suddenly, Da Ma turned his rifle and pointed it at the commander, shouting in a stern voice.

"That means you, too! Stop right there!"

The company commander stopped. Viewed from my position, Da Ma, semiautomatic in hand, seemed the perfect image of a Children's Corps member during the Revolutionary War. It was a pity I couldn't see the expression on his face at that exact moment. I could only guess at it by the reflection of the commander's frighteningly white face. They remained in that stalemate for quite some time. Then Da Ma suddenly started to laugh. It was that special cackle of his and gulps of breath, like he was convulsing. He laid the gun down at his position and got back on his stomach, ready for the order to fire. For Da Ma, his joke had come to a smooth end, and everything was supposed to snap back to normal. But it was far from the end. The company commander charged over, dragged him up by the collar of his uniform, and shoved him out of the shooting range, cursing incessantly. I remember that Da Ma left the range with great reluctance, complaining all the way — "Why? Why are you doing this to me?"

When military training was over and we returned to the campus, the final punishment for Da Ma's misbehavior on the shooting range was publicized. The incident was recorded as a Serious Offense, which according to our teacher was already lenient treatment. We didn't know what Da Ma thought about it; after all he had his own ways, his own way of speaking. He was seen wandering from one dorm to another, always engaged in an endless stream of babble. Before the end of the term, Da Ma's roommates all picked up his special way of speaking, which they then used to accuse Da Ma of his various misdemeanors. Before the end of the school year, most of us in the department seemed to be hopelessly under the sway of his speech's eccentric rhythm. To me, however, Da Ma appeared to be someone under the constant torture of an agonizing anxiety, hands wringing in an amorphous desire to grasp something, but what — with such small and pitiful hands — could he grasp? To tell you the truth, no one could possibly deal with him every day, for he had this excruciating habit of bedding his small gleeful head of happiness on your pain and embarrassment at the most unexpected moments. For us, Da Ma was out of tune; a wretched and stray black sheep. When he realized that he was being avoided, Da Ma started hanging out with the guys out on the street, taking part in their nefarious operations. During those days, a scar on his face or a new, expensive jacket would become a most heated topic of discussion and conjecture.

His next felony happened on a Saturday afternoon during the first semester of our junior year. He had just returned to campus and, as usual, was wandering through the dorm. Seeing a classmate sitting on the sill cleaning the windowpanes, he stalked his game on tiptoes and gave him a push. Taken completely by surprise, the guy fell out of the window. He was fortunate enough to break only one leg due to the fact that he had been on the third and not a higher floor. Da Ma tried to explain, in his own unique way, that he had meant for it to be a joke, and only a joke, and that he had no idea that he wouldn't grab hold of the sill. I really did believe that Da Ma was only joking, but we all knew he was done for this time.

When Da Ma packed up and was ready to go, our teacher tried to comfort him. The conversation went, as I remember, in Da Ma's way of speaking, and concluded with Da Ma saying, "It's fuckingly good!" Then he hurled his bag over his shoulder and marched out of the dorm. But as soon as he got out of the building he stopped, sat on the ground, and started weeping. Our teacher went after him and told him that he could stay around for a few days if he liked; that no one would chase him away, but that he would eventually have to go. Hearing this, Da Ma wept even harder. It was a sad sight. Da Ma was expelled from the university and sent back to his hometown. After that his name came up frequently in conversation, not that we missed him, but because he still owed some of us money and meal tickets that he had never paid back.

The second year I was in Nanjing I met Xiao Chu, my current girl friend. It was a summer day in a fast food place called *The Big Three*. I remember hearing a girl at the neighboring table chatting excitedly to a young man who — chopsticks frozen in mid-air, enchanted — was listening to her humbly. I went over and told her that I had to ask her something very important. That was how Xiao Chu became my girlfriend. Before that she had been going out with that fair-skinned, gentle-looking young man over there. But ever since then Xiao Chu and I have been seeing each other. That alone, I'm sure you can understand, has not been an easy thing to manage. And in the end I have that bastard Da Ma to thank, because he was the one who really made this relationship possible — which sometimes makes me feel like I'm in the middle of a swamp.

"Miss, You must know a guy named Da Ma."

"Da Ma — Big Horse? What do you mean?"

"No, Da Ma, it's a name. Da as in MADA — motor — and Ma as in MADA."

"OK. But I don't know anything about motors."

"No, the guy's name is Da Ma."

"I don't know anything about Da Mas, either. Did you want something else?"

That was the beginning of our love. For a long time Xiao Chu insisted that Da Ma didn't exist; that it was a name I'd invented in order to start up conversations with good-looking girls. But I continued to trust my instincts. Xiao Chu must have known Da Ma. I searched for traces of Da Ma in the Advertising Company she worked for, her family, and even her ex-boyfriend, but found nothing suspicious.

"Xiao Chu, have you always talked like this?"

"How would I know?"

"Trust me, you must have met Da Ma at some point! Maybe you just didn't know his name."

"Will you drop this Da Ma thing? I won't dump you if you don't mention his name again."

"No, I'm serious. You must have..."

"Shut up! One more word about Da Ma, and I'll slash you!"

I was determined to find out how she had been "infected"; I needed to map out completely the disease's route — this "Da Ma's Way of Speaking." You think I'm crazy? No, not if you've ever heard Da Ma speak, and not if you've heard her speak. Just as my investigation seemed to be going nowhere, things took a rather unexpected turn. That is, one day I realized that I had fallen in love with Xiao Chu, this very girl who often gave in too easily to her impulses. That naturally diverted my attention, and I had to forget about Da Ma for a while. But not completely. Our love grew more intense through our frequent quarrels, which occurred, if not daily, then once every two or three days. To let you in on a little something, I'm not a lightweight when it comes to this sort of fighting. I can guarantee that you wouldn't last a round with me, but I was no match for Xiao Chu.

The moment she opened her mouth, I saw Da Ma descending from the ceiling, arms thrashing in the air. Fighting with him was like playing squash — the harder you hit, the faster the ball bounces back at you, and the more unpredictably it bounces. Repeated defeat taught me humility. It was in this way that the ship of our tender relationship sailed through yet another turbulent storm, entering a stretch of water that was deeper and calmer than our treacherous sea of emotions.

Xiao Chu loved photography — not that she loved to take pictures, but rather loved having pictures taken of her. Each time a fight ended, she would straighten her hair, drag me out to the eastern suburbs of the city, and force me to take pictures of her. I had never known a girl with such a morbid desire to pose in front of the camera. Xiao Chu had had three boyfriends before (not including me) and each of them had left at least one entire album of photos. It was a good opportunity for me to appreciate their vastly different aesthetics, as well as the different degrees to which they understood Xiao Chu. Xiao Chu had a confidante named Lian Xiang. They had been close friends since childhood. Lian Xiang worked in a photo studio, and over the years had provided logistical convenience for Xiao Chu's photo craze. I didn't like this friend of hers at all. She would have been pretty if not for the grayish complexion that she had acquired from her perennial sullen and cheerless mood. But the worst thing was that she was a loyal co-breeder of all of Xiao Chu's bad habits. She was my biggest headache. She'd never let me get near her the entire time I'd known Xiao Chu. She told me she studied self-defense. How could I be sure? But I'll tell you right now, you're better off giving her the benefit of the doubt. What I really couldn't stand was the way the two of them lay crammed together in the same small bed, gossiping for hours on end. They had an inexhaustible list of topics to prattle on about, of which I was sometimes one. Lian Xiang's intelligence was indisputable, and she kept teaching Xiao Chu all sorts of dirty tricks to try on me. Of course that's the way I saw it. I should have hired someone to kidnap her and sell her off to a distant mountain village. Only then could I have a stronger hold on Xiao Chu. But was this really an option? Even this idea was thought up by Lian Xiang, and then passed on to me through Xiao Chu. She was a real pain. There were times when I wanted to say to her, "I'll slash you!"

But what am I telling you all this for? What happened between Xiao Chu and me belongs to another story. I should say that I normally have a great deal of restraint. The reason for my temporary loss of control is due simply to the inextricable shadow of Da Ma.

Sometimes I felt real pity for Da Ma. One day when I was washing my clothes in the laundry room, I saw him wandering aimlessly from one room to another like a stray dog. No one would even acknowledge him. I called his name and he gave me a friendly smile. He quickly walked over to me. Only later did I realize that this had been a salvation to him, but an unwise move on my part.

"Do you consider me a friend?" he asked in a grave, serious tone.

"Well, up until now, yes."

"And in the future?"

"In the future — I have no idea." What I was trying to say was that if Da Ma would be kind enough to leave me alone, so that I could wash the clothes that had accumulated over the last six weeks, I would still try to be his friend.

Da Ma nodded, closed his eyes, and drew several deep breaths. Then he suddenly opened his eyes and fixed me with an intense gaze.

"I'm going to tell you something. I have to tell someone about this right now. If not you, then someone else. Anyway, I have to tell someone today. I have to. I slept with Li Yuyu last night."

"With who?"

"You heard me."

"What? You and her? How could..."

Li Yuyu was our English teacher. She had just graduated from Beijing Foreign Language Institute, was tall and strong, and had a ridiculously high notion of herself. Most of her male friends were foreigners. And Da Ma was such a thin and short guy — not even the right size....

"She thought the exact same thing at first — and that's why I went. I talked at her almost all night, and I was standing the entire time. We were in her dorm room. I knew I'd break her. Finally at about five in the morning, just before dawn, she couldn't take it any more. She yawned and then said to me, "Oh, what the hell, come over here. And that was that."

Before I was able to recover from the shock of his stunning narrative, Da Ma, cackling in his usual way, executed a perfect about-face, just as we had done many times before in military camp.

"That's all. Now wash your clothes." That was his final sentence.

To tell you the truth, the real truth, I hadn't believed a single word. Was there some jealousy involved? Maybe, I don't know. But Da Ma did have an amazing academic quarter. He slept in his dorm room whenever we had English class, he never did any of his homework, but at the end of the quarter he still got full credit for class. No one was too surprised. There were a lot of other things about Da Ma that caused a greater amount of curiosity. It was just, how do you say, fuckingly good!

In those days, forensics was very popular and contests were being held all over campus. At the time it seemed like there were quite a few things worth debating, and the rules of the contest were not as refined and strict as they are nowadays. I seriously recommended Da Ma to our teacher to represent our department in a debate contest sponsored by the school Communist Youth League Committee. We all figured Da Ma was the right person, and he accepted the post readily. In exchange for his effort he bribed our teacher to lend him ten Yuan's worth of meal coupons. Our first opponent was the Department of Marxism. You could tell by the name that it was going to be a hard fight. Before the contest began, I saw Da Ma huddled up at the rightmost seat of the forum, his shoulders hunched. He seemed a little maladjusted to the setting. Students were bustling about the noisy room, making endless preparations — a line here, a microphone there. When the judge announced the start of the contest, Da Ma was almost asleep. Someone poked him. He jumped up. Then, slowly and somewhat wretchedly, he stood. It was a completely unforgettable night. He talked, and he talked, and he talked. He stood there and went on and on all night, pausing only briefly when the judge interrupted him with repeated shouts. His opponents were furious, the audience was in turmoil, even members of our own side were in a frenzy. Everyone was yelling by the end of the competition. The judge had realized much too late that there was absolutely nothing in common between the given topic and what was being hurled across the room, except for the fact that they were both in Chinese. Wiping the beads of sweat breaking out on his forehead, the judge stood up and walked around the table to where Da Ma was standing. Young man! He patted Da Ma on the shoulder. No response. He patted him again. Extremely irritated, Da Ma turned around and hissed at him,

"I'll slash you!"

Needless to say, we lost the contest. It was our fault. It was too much to expect Da Ma to fit into any set of rules or regulations. When it was all over, we found him soaked in sweat, nervous and ashamed, without the heart to face us. Though he did know just how brilliantly he had performed that night. His way of speaking would soon be popular all over campus. Let me show you the rhythm of his speech:

X XX X X X XXXX XX0X | XXXX 0 XX XXXX X X· |

Isn't that a forceful, heroic delivery? And at the end of a paragraph he would conclude, unexpectedly, with a series of triplets, like this:

XXX XXX XXX XXX

If he was in a good mood or if his audience happened to be a girl, he would then throw in some syncopation:

4/4 X X X 0 X·X | X X X XX X |

When he was begging the chair of our department not to throw him out, he drummed like this:

4/4 0XXX 0XXX 0XXX 0XXX | XXXX XXXX 0XXX X|

It was not an easy rhythm to handle, especially the brief pauses before the semiquavers. Try it yourself. You know, I really am beginning to miss Da Ma.

I was distressed to see that Xiao Chu was getting more and more out of line. One day in a clothing store she wanted to try on a red T-shirt, so I went looking for the fitting room. When I turned back around she had already taken off her own T-shirt in front of everyone and was putting on the red one. People were shocked by her exhibition, and I, of course, was the most embarrassed. On April Fool's Day, she made me wait for her at Sun Yat-sen's Mausoleum the entire afternoon. It would have been all right if she had stopped there. Foreigners have their Fool's Day just once a year, but I had the luxury of celebrating one whenever she was in the mood. I was forced to use intuition to examine each of her invitations, to figure out which one was just another April Fool's trick. But I was often wrong, and as a result, she would come to me in tears, throw a tantrum, and reiterate her innate repugnance at anyone who stood her up. You can see how this couldn't continue. Her condition was making me seriously uneasy. But, where had it all gone wrong?

"Listen, Xiao Chu," I said to her. "You have to … all right, all right, take it as a request: please, please stop talking this way!"

"Which way do you mean?" she kept wriggling in her chair.

"The very way you're speaking right now, Da Ma's way of speaking!"

"Again! Again about this Da Ma! What is it? Is it male or female?"

"It used to be male, but if you keep this up, I'm sure there'll be a female one very soon."

The other day, in order to prove my earnestness, I ransacked all my cabinets, cases, and cardboard boxes for a photo with Da Ma in it. In the end I did find one. It was a group shot of four people including me and Da Ma. The photo had been taken in our freshman year at the Summer Villa in Chengde. In the photo, Da Ma's hair is tousled and his eyes are looking off god knows where. The baggy white undershirt he's wearing dangles loosely by the shoulder straps. It was indeed very impressive. On the far right, a young man with a crewcut beams in his revolutionary vitality. That's me.

"You looked fuckingly good back then, like a peasant-worker new in town."

"I want you to look at him! Him! This is Da Ma!"

"You could easily point to any of the three and tell me this is Da Ma. It wouldn't make any difference to me, would it?"

"No, no. Look carefully. This and no one else is Da Ma."

"Oh … yeah, now that you mention it, he does look slightly more interesting than you."

"Slightly! Get real! A lot more! All he'd have to do is stand right here and open his mouth, and girls like you would run away with him on all fours."

Xiao Chu stopped and lowered her head. We were hurled into a silence, a dreadful silence. She slowly raised her head and stared at me, and then the tears began streaming down her face. "How could you say such a thing!" Oh, God! Tears, what the hell are they! The incident that afternoon ended with the precious photo being torn in half. But thankfully, both Da Ma and I escaped unscathed. Xiao Chu had intentionally spared the two of us. From this action I surmised that she was not completely beyond salvation. Even in her anger she hadn't gone over the top, but instead picked, as her point of attack, a guy with a flat face whom I couldn't care less about. Yes, I've always been an optimist. From then on whenever I was with Xiao Chu, I restrained myself from speaking as much as I possibly could. For all communication that I could manage with gestures, I used gestures. All of this was to reduce her chances of speaking, which was a key step in the treatment I had planned for her disease.

Nevertheless, Xiao Chu was never short of company for chatting. Lian Xiang, for one, would never reject her. I decided that I needed to talk with her, to bring her over to my side in this operation. I was aware that it was probably not the best way to go about it, but I had no other choice. So I invited both Xiao Chu and Lian Xiang over for dinner one weekend. You can imagine how painful it must have been for me. I had seen Lian Xiang on a couple of earlier occasions, but it was that night that she left the deepest impression on me. She seemed to be a girl of an incomparably serene nature. Her wispy voice and soft, gentle steps reminded me of a vulnerable kitten — before you heard anything she was already there standing next to you. As a matter of fact, she seemed a better match for me than Xiao Chu. I figured if I revealed this to Xiao Chu, it might get her jealous enough to lose Da Ma's way of speaking. That of course would serve as a backup plan. But for the moment I decided to get right down to business. I brought up the topic of my concerns quickly with Lian Xiang when Xiao Chu was busy in the kitchen. Xiao Chu might have heard something, because she called out from the kitchen: "I'll slash you if you dare say anything bad about me!"

Slash me or not, I had to get on with it. I went through my script in a most summary fashion. A faint smile flitted across Lian Xiang's face; even when smiling, her face was pale and gloomy.

"That Da Ma's way of speaking, is it really such a mystery?"

Yes. I reiterated my conviction several times, but felt a little weakhearted without any persuasive evidence. As a last resort, I dug out the half-torn photo and handed it over. She stared at the photo for a long time. Slowly, I saw a dark cloud move into the clear sky of her eyes.

"What did you say his name was?"

"Da Ma."

"That's Da Ma?"

"Yep, that's him."

A week later, Xiao Chu found me at my place. She appeared to be exhausted and asked for a cigarette as soon as she stepped in the door. I watched as she smoked intensely, leaning back on the sofa. The usual worry and agitation was gone. I wasn't prepared for such a transformation. I liked the way she smoked, and almost felt the pleasure she was drawing from the cigarette. She drew a second one from the pack when she had finished, and said,

"I never guessed you were telling the truth."

"What do you mean?"

"There really was a guy named Da Ma."

"Of course there was! You should've believed me."

Xiao Chu lit her second cigarette. I lit one as well. The gentle and smooth way she spoke revealed something new about her, a certain tenderness that I had never seen.

"Lian Xiang, you know, she knew Da Ma. Aren't you shocked?"

"She did?"

"She met him and ... they spent a night together, but just one night."

"She told you this?"

"Yes, she told me. But that night he wasn't Da Ma, he was Li Jing. That was how he introduced himself. And the address and the phone number he gave her were all false. Lian tried contacting him later, and of course she couldn't find him. That was a year ago. Where's the bastard now?"

"I really have no idea. He must be somewhere. But I don't know."

"Maybe he's already dead."

"Not necessarily. But it doesn't really make a difference, does it?"

"I hope he's dead. Let him be dead."

Xiao Chu stubbed out the cigarette in the ashtray and remained silent. I didn't quite follow her. I wanted to ask her something else, but her silence hushed me.

"I can't believe it." Suddenly she started again, tears in her eyes. "How could Lian have gotten involved with that kind of guy? How's it possible? I just can't figure it out. This Da Ma guy, he's not worth feelings like that."

I disagreed, but restrained myself because I didn't want any more trouble. Please, no more. But by then the solution to the other matter seemed to have emerged. I had finally sniffed out the origin of Xiao Chu's strange way of speaking. It all started with that one-night stand. Mysteriously, Da Ma had planted the disease in Lian Xiang; then from Lian Xiang, Xiao Chu picked it up in a way that seemed to me even more mysterious. That's all I know. Therefore, on this matter, which is quickly becoming dated, I can tell you only this much and no more.

Author's Note

Da Ma was killed in the autumn of 1993, on the trucking route from Sichuan to Tibet. A quick-tempered native stabbed him with a dagger, which cut right through his liver and killed him on the spot. I learned about this through an electrical engineer named Chen Ran. He and Da Ma had set out on a hiking trip to Tibet from Xi'an that summer. He told me that Tibet was not their planned destination. They had decided to go as far as possible until they used up all their money. Somewhere on the road Da Ma told him that he might not go any further if they reached Tibet. At this point in his story, Chen Ran came to an abrupt stop. I could see he was sinking into his memories, which he must have tried hard to erase but had failed. He was aging visibly in front of my eyes.

"Actually," he said, about half an hour later, when he'd recovered from his depression, "no one killed Da Ma. He killed himself."

"It was late in the afternoon, and it was still light, but there were very few travelers or vehicles on the road. As we climbed up a slope, we saw a man walking down the other side. I suggested resting a while, and Da Ma agreed. We took off our packs. Then all of a sudden, I saw Da Ma dashing toward the man up ahead. Seconds later he was at the man's back. He yanked out a dagger and shouted, 'Give me your money! Or I'll slash you.'"

"That was the third time he'd pulled this prank on the road. He enjoyed it so much, and I had no idea it was going to be his final act. The man turned around slowly, and then before I could see his face, the dagger, Da Ma's own, was stabbed into him beneath the ribs."

Sometimes I thought of writing something more detailed about my friend Da Ma, but it wouldn't do him justice. I actually know so little about him, which is the way most of his companions end up feeling. But we all remember his peculiar way of speaking, his thin lips, his black teeth, and the few words that were jammed in there, trying to get out: I'LL SLASH YOU!

Finally, I would like to pin a photo here of Da Ma, so that you might gain a deeper impression of him.

CUI WEIPING   TRANSLATED BY SU GENXING

GUO LUSHENG

It was an evening in the summer of 1993 — the curtain of darkness already drawn — when I heard someone call from outside. I opened the window and looked down: Mang Ke was the only one in the group vaguely recognizable. "Come on up!" I called.

"Guo Lusheng." His head inclined somewhat to one side and his jaw jutted slightly upward as he made his self-introduction. "We have come unannounced," he said with an apologetic smile.

I felt a sudden warmth — I had not, as a hostess, heard people talk with such politeness for a long time. Most of the "vagabond" poets, whom I'd had the fortune of receiving, appeared as if they all had bombs under their arms, which they would not hesitate using to level my whole family along with themselves.

Also in the group were Huang Xiang from Guizhou, and Hei Dachun and his girlfriend from Beijing. After making tea, pouring water, and seating my guests one by one on the sofa, I began to size up this legendary figure of the poetic circle. "Speaking of tradition," Duo Duo once remarked, "Guo Lusheng is our own small tradition."

He appeared to be too big — head, hands, feet — at least that was my first impression. In fact he was very thin — not someone who'd been born frail — but as if part of his body were purposefully hidden somewhere, or that after undergoing repeated omissions and deletions, what was now left was only this hollow, capacious frame. He tended to smile as he spoke, and when he did his eyes became a single line. He slipped into his role in the conversation with such rapidity that there was hardly any transition. The tone of his speech was a mixture of resolution and ambiguity. He talked about Whitman, Hemingway, Eliot, and many others. Mang Ke mentioned a novel he'd just finished, at which point Guo inquired with considerable interest, "How does one write a novel?" Mang Ke spread out his hands. "Well, you write from beginning to end." And that, perhaps, was the most succinct and interesting exchange on literature between these two contemporary writers.

A patch on the knee of his pants caught my attention. It was an old pair of pants whose color had become difficult to identify. The patch was of a slightly darker shade, but still quite in consonance with the rest — apparently a product of his own sewing skill. It was extremely rare in Beijing nowadays to wear clothes with patches.

He asked for a pen and a piece of paper and began to concentrate on his writing. The conversation, however, continued, and people did not bother to lower their voices for his sake. After a while he looked up and asked if I should put the child to bed first. I waved with a smile, telling him that it was the holidays. "Then I'll read you a poem." There was a certain determination in his tone. "One I wrote in the hospital."

Reading the poem, he became almost a different person. All those elements in him that were out of harmony with each other all of a sudden grew compliant. He read with ease and composure, extending to its limit every single syllable, as though he were trying its endurance and attempting to unfold all its beauty at the same time. While he indulged himself in such intoxication, a kind of rhythm gradually took hold and quickly spread itself among the rest of us.

We applauded. "I'm in there, I'm not free." This he repeated a number of times.

His departure that night threw me into a long contemplation of the differentiation of various degrees of mental disorder made by modern medical science. A person like him could certainly live a normal family life, whereas many others around us were in greater need of psychotherapy. I did not see why he had to go to the mental hospital. My suspicion was later confirmed in part by my friends: that is, he is essentially a "large-sized" man willingly bound by chains, with or without form.

To understand his poems and his person, one must first understand the meaning of these chains.

This must be rare for poets: Guo Lusheng's poems were first widely circulated in handwritten copies. These include his "Believe in the Future," "Beijing, 4:08am," and "The Ocean Trilogy." His readers were thousands of ordinary people, most of whom did not show any particular interest in poetry but were simply fascinated and touched by his lines, which struck a sympathetic chord. This is a far cry from what happens to some of the "poets" these days. I've mentioned this on more than one occasion: certain "poets" of today appear to be known more for their physical existence than anything else — their bodily accomplishments have long resounded in people's ears before readers are able to read or remember any of their lines. And their lines have little chance of going further than their anecdotes. Apparently, the emergence of Guo Lusheng was not without particular historical reasons, which have indeed been the subject of some analysis. What I would like to point out is a much neglected aspect — in a time when everything was turned on its head, Guo Lusheng demonstrated a rare faith — the faith in poetry. Under no circumstance was he oblivious to what was required by the form of poetry, nor did he go beyond the limit allowable for poetry as an art. In other words, although life may be disorderly or broken, poetry must create harmonic forms so that it can bring under control what is shrill and ferocious; although life itself may be twisted and obscure, poetry must provide a solid and beautiful order, wherein people may find support for their depressed souls; and although life may be fraught with ugliness and pain, still poetry is ultimately beautiful, being the source of the sense of beauty and the driving force of progress. Such faith, demonstrated through the faith in poetry, is the embodiment of the heavily devastated conscience of that time, as well as an indication of brightness, of the courage in conquering an adverse environment. On this point, Guo Lusheng differs from numerous avant-garde poets of a later age. The so-called split begins always with form, about which Guo Lusheng has never surrendered a step.

When the spider's web ruthlessly seals off my blast furnace,
When dying smoke from the embers sighs over the sadness of poverty,
With the same old stubbornness I smooth out the ashes of disappointment,
And write down in beautiful snowflakes: Believe in the future!

When my purple grapes turn into dews of deep autumn,
When my flower snuggles in someone else's arms,
With the same old stubbornness, I pick up a withered, frost-coated vine
And write upon the cold gray earth: Believe in the future!

—"Believe in the Future"

Unless you keep reading these lines out loud, you will not be able to appreciate the balance, the connotation, and the beauty of their sound. There are six full feet in every line of the Chinese, which is rather unusual in either ancient or modern Chinese poetry. It is precisely these prolonged moments that serve as the elaborate vehicle for such heavy sentiments (yearning, disappointment, and the recovery therefrom). They are released slowly, and gradually. In order to read these lines in one breath, the reader has to further extend the pause after each foot, thus producing an illusion of endless extension. Meanwhile, some great effects are also attributable to the four-line stanzas, the strict parallels between the feet of adjacent lines, and the rhyme scheme. These are but artificial elements, but it is precisely such artificial assembling that creates on the whole a different kind of space and time, effecting a self-sufficient world of poetry. Those heavy sentiments are rendered clear and accessible, here and now, as if they were objects hanging before one's eyes, perceptible and touchable, so that they lose the oppression latent in human beings and acquire a sense of emancipation and liberty. For people of that time this was undoubtedly a luxury of intellectual enjoyment. Through Guo Lusheng's harmonious and beautiful meter, what was obscure is elucidated, and what was frozen released. Lin Mang once wrote, "His poems cast a ray of warm sunlight into our vast and empty spiritual world."

At a certain point in my life I began to have suspicions about those "artists or poets for survival's sake," a small army in itself. For these people, the primary concern is the fact of their own existence; what they experience in and out of art is nothing more than the pains and worries of their individual lives, including the anxiety of not being recognized. All these flow like mud into the brain and blood of the poet so that what comes out finally is a "poem of survival," in which the experience of survival, raging and tearing through the fabric of the poem, making it as cacophonous and hysterical as this world, greatly undermines the experience of poetry. The other category of artists (I dare not call them "artists for art's sake") do not exclude the fact of their existence in this world — only they dare not place its importance above art. What they are concerned with is how to produce a harmonious and balanced artistic whole and how to obtain and transform the contents of life into objects to which art can refer. Their conscience is expressed above all in their respect for and love of the art with which they are engaged; it is reflected in their professional ethics. The resistance to the disorder and darkness of the environment can only take the form of a new order. Otherwise, one disorder would replace another, and a new disintegration an old one, which is ultimately meaningless. In this sense, the modern metrical poetry to which Guo Lusheng has devoted nearly thirty years of concentrated experimentation could perhaps always be a starting point and an example. For the avant-garde poets of China who have had so many painful lessons, this is a point particularly worth taking. I always contend that in this field, collapse begins with form, and is deepened by the disorder thereof. Hai Zi and Gu Cheng are two such examples.

One chilly, windy day this spring, a few friends and I paid Guo Lusheng a visit in the hospital. Very soon the topic shifted to He Qifang. Guo recalled the latter telling him years ago that poetry was the "thousand-year-old snow on West Mountain outside the window." "You need to have a window," he said, gesturing with his hands, "a form, then you can look through it." He appeared far more clear-headed than many of us around him.

The following question is more or less puzzling, something I don't know what to make of.

"Mad Dog" is one of the pieces in *A Collection of Lyric Poems by Shi Zhi and Hei Dachun,* an anthology published in 1993 (Shi Zhi — Forefinger — is Guo's pen name). It is said that he once wrote a statement about "Mad Dog" to the effect that when the poem first appeared in *Today,* it was dated ahead of its actual time of composition, that the poem was actually written in 1978. Apart from this correction, we've also noticed a subtitle for "Mad Dog" in the *Collection* "To Those Who Indulge Themselves in Mere Talk of Human Rights," which had never appeared on any previous occasion. That ten years later Guo Luosheng insisted on its restoration should not be without reason. Indeed, every line and every word of Guo's poems are the result of careful consideration. What does Guo Lusheng intend to say through this act? Why did he want to break away from the society of the then avant-garde, of which he was one (Jiang Qing once singled out his "Believe in the Future" in her condemnation)? Reading over the entire poem "Mad Dog" again, what, can we say, does Guo Lusheng wish to express, if not the sense of irony that people suspected it of?

> After being duped mercilessly time after time,
> I no longer think of myself as a human being,
> As though I've become a mad dog,
> Roaming the world, aimless.
> I'm not yet a mad dog,
> Not having to take risks for hunger and cold.
> Yet for that very reason I wish to be a mad dog
> So as to experience fully the hardships of survival.
> I'm less than a mad dog!
> In desperation a dog can still leap over the fence,
> But I can only endure in silence,
> More miserable than a mad dog.
> Only if I could really be a mad dog
> Could I then break the invisible chains,
> And then I would, without the least hesitation,
> Give up my so-called inviolable human rights.

"Mad Dog" is the central image upon which the whole poem rests. Yet what is built around it is a logical framework with distinct gradations: as if a mad dog; but not quite one yet; even less than a dog; if really a dog. To compare oneself to a mad dog apparently implies a grieving sense of self-mockery, yet self-mockery is not self-pity. Behind such self-mockery is an unexpected leap: the poet laments that he can not break away from all the chains, inside and out, with and without forms, that he cannot roam farther in the world and apprehend life at a deeper level! Guo Lusheng obviously sympathized with the other side of the vast world, with those who led a harder life, who are the unfortunates. The "mad dog" is intended to signify both such a world and the unfortunates, for whom there certainly existed no such thing as "human rights," of which they had not the least comprehension. What seems to be implied here is such a premise: that "human rights" is still a sort of restriction in reality, an operation within the existing order; and that there is within the concepts it emphasizes a sense of superiority; though it appears to involve everyone, it is in fact not the case. What I've chanced to see in him, which is not often seen in people of this generation, is that Guo Lusheng would rather regard himself as one of the unfortunates than style himself as "avant-garde," or compare himself to a "swallow," or "Prometheus" or the "disseminator and spokesman of truth." His posture involves lying back rather than leaning forward; it begins with a low pitch rather than a high one; and is inclusive, tolerant, rather than aloof and discriminating. Note that the imagery he frequently uses includes "among people," "life" and "people" instead of "world" or "sky," which are favorites of other avant-garde poets, and are abstract and condescending. More often than not, Guo Lusheng "places himself back into it," although what he receives there is the same unfair treatment.

Thus, Guo Lusheng has escaped from a cruel age characterized by power and strong voices. He does not participate in its game, nor is he concerned with its rules. Hence for him the question of withdrawing oneself does not exist, neither does that of martyrdom. He keeps away from the battleground resounding with reports and thick with gun smoke. None of the various new weapons — ornate diction, color, and packaging — indispensable to many, is part of his vision. He had no umbrella for protection, not even the skill of self-preservation. Such a state cannot be free of danger. He does not go ashore or work for some small change for survival. There were no navigation guides or lighthouses on the sea where he wrecked his boat. He is indeed "aimless," as he puts it himself, for which he has paid a dear price. The critical point where he constantly positions himself defies language's power of description — there, he has nothing and would keep nothing: wealth, fame, all those small comfortable conventions, not even a voice in his own defense. What he is able to give he has given. What then has he got in return?

> My heart is overcast with black heavy clouds
> Inside it the chill blustery wind blows
> At its bottom rests the sediment from brine
> From its head rises a mountain covered with unmelted snow
> …
> But still it is a heart
> And it still beats right in my chest
>
> —"My Heart"

He repeatedly mentions this "heart." In fact the "wounded heart" is an image that appears frequently in poems he turned out during his stay in the hospital the past several years. He appears to be a mute, who cannot help pointing from time to time at the part of his chest that is still beating. "As stormy waves subside from the heart/only emptiness and desolation remain at the bottom"("In the Mental Hospital"). "I have no choice, but to open my chest/to let you take a look at this wounded heart—/it is covered everywhere with pried-off caps of beer bottles/and scars left by cigarette stubs" ("Wounded Heart"). These lines evoke in the reader such a fearful bleakness that the poet must have exceeded a certain limit, otherwise he would not have experienced such pain and bitterness. You may call such a heart humble and impoverished, where nothing is left but throes, but it is also lofty and self-restrained, irreplaceable and incomparable. To this world, it looks worthless and negligible, yet since it is completely aware of itself — it knows its own pains — it is at the same time full of self-respect. Nothing else can measure its weight. It is independent and expansive; detached but sentient; misty, amorphous, but undoubtedly at once determined and faithful. Its past madness can be viewed as having risen out of a courage that approaches religious fervor, such as allows one to "challenge the law with his own person," but at the same time it is also so cautious that it seems to "hover over an abyss" or "walk on thin ice." Anyway, it is not like what it is perceived to be. You may feel your own heart is similar to this, but not before taking off various masks.

We may now try to understand from another angle why Guo Lusheng takes such gingerly steps with form. A heart as expansive, amorphous, and sympathetic as his not only needs, but loves the small shackles of form, and through those delicate chains it beats out a rhythm, a breathing, a steady pulse of the spirit.

May 5, 1994, Jinsong

HONG YING TRANSLATED BY JOHN CAYLEY

PREPARING HIS BIOGRAPHY

I didn't realize that he was deployed like this. If I'd known
I wouldn't have squeezed the handle of my umbrella tighter in the rain
pouring down   because he was walking on the other side, his face clouded,

in silence. If the rain had stopped
I would have had to bend low   crouch down, and let the edges
Of his jacket lightly brush the top of my head   the roses he was holding
All at once shifting the position of this island

I saw clearly that he would crash through the warning line
after getting into the white car   cutting round a lamppost on the corner
like a tongue.   And he made me let go of my umbrella,
made me drop my scarf, trembling feverishly. Yes, Yes….

he was only able to go on, straight on, a bit more surely than I   That white car
the heavy blood around the square formation
tapping and tangling all of the lines of my palms.   What did he and I
do wrong? But this is only a first chapter, unfinished….

October 18, 1993

Duo Duo   TRANSLATED BY GREGORY B. LEE

IT'S JUST LIKE BEFORE

walking in a night when snow flutters on the forehead and it's just like before
walking over from a blank page and it's just like before
walking into that invisible field and it's just like before

walking among words, among wheatfields, walking
among discounted shoes, walking up to words
eeing home, that moment, and it's just like before

straightening western clothes in the wheatfield, and it's just like before
kneeling on kneecaps cast from a gold shield, and it's just like before
his world's most resounding, most resounding

just like before, just like before is the earth

a time when a ray of autumn light shone between the grass mower's legs, it is
a burst of wild laughter within a stretch of golden corn, is it
a burst of firecrackers spurting out of the red pepper patch, it is just like before

No arrangement whatsoever can reproduce its gilt
Its order is a burst of furious growth in the prairie on an autumn day
it has ubiquitous powers of persuasion, it is just like it was before

A September burst of cold cow dung shoveled into the air and it's just like before
October's stones moved into ranks and it's just like before
November rain passes through a place where you aren't and it's just like before
Just like before seventy pears on the tree smile a crooked smile

Your father just like before is your mother
a fit of coughing in the midst of laughter
The ox's head jolts along the vanishing road
and just like before a whole family rides the ox cart watching the snow
licked by an enormous ox tongue

    so warm, warm like before

it's snow come from memory, increasing the weight of memory
it's snow's debt, at this time not yet covered by snow
it's snow that has turned over that page

    turned over, and it's just like before

winter's wheatfields and burial grounds have already joined up
four desolate trees grow right here
light of former days gushes into the narration, crumbles beyond discourse

    crumbles, and it's just like before

your father turns your mother's death into his sky
turns his death into your mother's tombstone
your father's bones walk down from the high hill

    and it's just like before

each star is experiencing this life and world
each shard of broken glass buried in the backyard is talking
for a reason that will not be seen again, says

    it's just like before, it's just like before

1993

FIVE YEARS

Five glasses of strong liquor, five candles, five years
Forty-three years old, a huge sweat at midnight
Fifty hands flap towards the table top
A flock of birds clenching their fists fly in from yesterday

Five strings of red firecrackers applaud the fifth month, thunder rumbles
between five fingers
And four parasitic poisonous mushrooms on four dead horses' tongues
in the fourth month
       do not die
Five hours past five o'clock on day five five candles are extinguished
Yet the landscape screaming at dawn does not die
Hair dies but tongues do not die
The temper recovered from the cooked meat does not die
Fifty years of mercury seep into semen and semen does not die
The fetus delivering itself does not die
Five years pass, five years do not die
Within five years, twenty generations of insects die out

1994

THOSE ISLANDS

are toes that have really left shoes
they take shape in flight, yet they retain the soil
they are real tumors that remain in the brain
and they retain time
in the motionless landscape go through changes
at every crash of the waves say: no
their loneliness comes from the sea bed
comes from remains of sailors' faces left over by fish
comes from those who crave stormy seas

The cries of the toothless have once reached there
loneliness, have once there been judged salvation
when I follow travelers, like false pearls
flowing swiftly to their jetty, I
stare at the shadow I cast to the seabed
a plough hung all over with pearls
ploughing up the burial ground that has remained in the brain:
over there, midst the laughing sand of the naval base
still there is, still there is a beneficial wasteland providing for the growth of words

1993

NEVER A DREAMER

to be a cake on the other side of the human world, using
teethmarks left by children in a piece of toast
as a bed, pulling over the other nipple
to be a bird that only likes to circle
not weeping, not buying insurance
not the product of prayer
not in this order

never a dreamer

to be an extinguished candle in a breezeless night
to be starlight, shining on the nape of the horserider's neck
to be grass that sprouts but for one season, to be a poet
to be a pear frozen on a tree
to be black wheat, enduring deep thought in the wind

never a dreamer

to be wind, yelling loudly at the earth
to be a water drop, silently dripping
to be the convulsion rippling along the horse's back
to be an egg from which father might hatch
from eerie time
sleepless time, commemorating stars
at the moment perfect for gathering riddles!

1994

RETURNING

Recognizing the ocean from the deck
in an instant, make out its enormous peregrinations

From atop the sea recognize a plow, in an instant
making out the courage we had

at each instant, coming only from
each solitary fear

forehead against forehead, standing on the threshold
saying goodbye, in an instant five years have passed

hand tightly grasping hand, saying let go
in an instant, the sand in the shoes has come entirely from the ocean

just now, by candlelight learnt to read
in an instant, the weight of the backpack lessened

just now, while swallowing coarse bread began to feel
in an instant, the water in the bottle had been returned to the ocean

stared at by an ox from the home country, clouds
make me weep, in an instant I weep

but whichever direction I go
in an instant, it turns to drifting

scrubbing an ox's back benumbed by a clarinet
memory, in an instant has found its source

words, in an instant make their way back to dictionaries
but within words, navigation

renders those who have not yet begun navigating
forever — incapable of returning

1994

Hu Dong
TRANSLATED BY JENNY PUTIN

THE DEATH OF ZILU

A man opened the shop door and quietly strolled up to the counter from where he proceeded to inquire about the provenance of an ancient official's hat — this incident did not warrant all the fuss my stingy customers went on to create. Yet pretending that they had been scared witless, they dubbed the new arrival a black-bearded knight-errant-cum-outlaw, dressed in a brightly-colored ancient official's uniform. According to them, the boor who barged his way into the shop (their description) greeted me and exchanged a few words, then reached under his coat and, instead of pulling out a checkbook or cash, most unceremoniously placed a black handgun on top of the bare glass counter. Then there was a sound of voices, which immediately attracted the attention of those present who thought that a good business deal had just been clinched. But instead they saw me blanch and abjectly produce the cashbox and key as instructed, handing them over to the burly thief in front of me. Even though I made it plain, repeatedly, that these details were fabricated after the event by those cowards who had scampered — the real incident unfolded just as I shall explain later, and as I have already told the people who claim to have my best interests at heart, though no one will believe a word I say — the sand in the hourglass did not trickle through for nothing this time. Seen from this perspective, your story gives us an insight into what really happened that day — the affected listeners could barely conceal their disappointment as they gave me a token pat on the shoulder all the while laughing at me — it's just not possible! You know, when people have had a terrible shock, they sometimes react by denying the seriousness of the incident. We know how it all came about: our antiques dealer, who habitually cheated us with fake goods, wouldn't be able to extract himself this time from his own fanciful tales. Behind my back, they flaunted their misguided little minds.

I was utterly fed up with their little games and gibberish. At the end of my tether, I was forced to make an announcement — I could have accepted it if they had come clean and openly branded me a liar. And as for my supposedly intelligent, close friends, I had hoped that my resentment in itself would have been sufficient to persuade them to abandon the psychoanalysis which was obviously only adding to my distress. "It's a rare condition (my story), a product of a repressed imagination (corrupted by childhood stories told by a nanny from the countryside)." They were already on to this. Their investigations developed into a predetermined diagnosis. And then there were the policemen and journalists with trained eyes. I put it to them that if they thought a lunatic could tell tales of this sort as coherently as I, then all the more reason to leave me alone and let me get some peace and quiet. Given that I am not a storyteller, I would hardly change my story to pander to those fools itching to hear some cock and bull yarn — raiding classics such as the *Yanyi* to embellish it with bits here and there just to keep them happy, cooking up some plot that would not be out of place in the movies — would you believe it! — even though I probably would have been tempted to say as much to the last nosy bastard who came to me begging for an account of the event — compared with me, what evidence could this shifty bunch advance when at most, all they could have overheard were a few lines of the prologue, and even then they were whispering among themselves and not paying attention? They shot off like a bevy of ferrets escaping to the great outdoors. They left me behind. Only I and the boor remained in the shop. For a while it was so quiet it almost made me want to laugh — and, unless one's vision were faulty, a pistol had indeed appeared on the counter. However, closer inspection revealed that it had been very badly maintained and in a few areas had worn to a shine, so that it was no longer completely black; and the rumors were also true in claiming that the new arrival made a request, except that his apparently belligerent tone was in fact extremely unassuming. His bearing, dignified even in the direst of straits, convinced me that he was a cut above my crass, pretentious contemporaries. He had won my esteem even before I withdrew to get the cash box and key. "You have obviously been expecting me for some time," he apologized. "Now if you wouldn't mind giving me the hat and a bag of money for my journey." His substantial bulk remained still. After a while, his long slender eyes seemed to discern something in my vacant expression. He was unequivocal in his explanation: "It is I, Zilu. I am Zhong You, former body guard to Confucius."

He made no attempt to use his illustrious position to intimidate me, neither did I display any condescension by dismissing him as some impostor. "Yes, I understand," I answered swiftly. It was neither out of indifference, nor studiedly casual. I sensed that we were like two guys hitting it off at a first meeting, like old friends, as soon as he walked through the door. This then developed into a rush of restrained excitement running throughout my body. I went to grab the things he needed right away with almost unconcealed excitement, but grew embarrassed, because it was almost the end of the morning and yet the cash box was practically empty — there was of course the month's rent which, according to the lease, was due that day. Before leaving the house that morning, I had put some money in the inside pocket of my jacket and was intending to pay my young landlady-cum-sweetheart after finishing at the shop in the early evening. Now, to avoid a mix up, I was anxious that Zilu in demanding money from me did not spot this chink in my armor — luckily, when he glanced at the cashbox, he seemed unfazed by the lack of money. He gave me a knowing grin, returning my bashful smile. At the same time, he stretched out his other hand and grabbed the key which I had just produced.

Ever since the business opened, the hat had been locked in the display window of the antique shop. According to legend, it was made by a late Ming craftsman who detested the ways of the world. The original on which it was modeled, a special headdress worn by a minor official in the Spring and Autumn period, is no longer in existence. I had acquired it from a declining Manchurian family in exchange for a chipped knife (a copy) which had been used by their Manchurian predecessors, and had brought it into the shop and displayed it prominently in order to attract customers. I must confess that the fact that it had not been sold was thanks to my customers' total unawareness of its presence. People walked around the shop, but no one had ever asked about the hat. I viewed this with incomprehension and relief. For whenever I thought that I should make an effort to sell the hat for the sake of the business, I was always reluctant — admiring the hat had been my pastime for many years. The material was simple and natural, the workmanship fine, the appearance neither obsequious nor supercilious. The hat had a felicitous air that induced a quite artless sense of reverence. This entirely fitting ornament, while it made my shop seem shabby, also enhanced its *gravitas*. Hence my decision to display it in the shop window. Alongside those moribund wine cups and brash jade objects, it was unique. Thus when I was engaged in penny-pinching haggles, I never lost sight of my original resolve. It consoled me that I could extricate myself from the indignity of defending my exorbitant prices at a moment's notice and return to my former life of noble impecunity. But to return to the main point, the hat was unusual. In the past, I had kept it hidden away at home, but I always felt that this was somehow inappropriate. It had seemed different then, not delicate and agreeable as it is now, but burdened with an excessive bulk and awkwardness. Only when it was exposed to the public and to the light of day did it bring me a sense of greater ease. Like a swan, the hat longed to spread its wings. Every time I looked at it, like someone who has given up all hope of catching up, it was like seeing a patch of clear sky after a shower of rain — it was that sort of all-pervading yet not overbearing feeling, fresh but moist. Moreover, it clearly had no adverse effect on my dirty dealings, which I continued to pursue between the ample garment of history and the skeletal body of coins and bank notes. Neither did it deter me from continuing with my marital infidelity, which had me wavering between trembling carnal desire and token shame.

The hat was a stimulus for free association. It had me conjecturing about the human bodies that had sported it. Imaginary skulls appeared in my wineglass. During a particularly inebriated session, my butterfly imagination formed an adoring attachment between the hat and a person. In 480 BC, there was a coup at the court of the state of Wei. The perpetrators had been plotting it for some time. Kui Kui, who had been in exile for some time, colluded with Minister Kong Li and deposed King Chu of Wei who had reigned for twelve years. Kui Kui set himself up as monarch, King Zhuang of Wei. At that time, Zilu, a city magistrate (a minor official) under Kong Li, heard about the incident, returned immediately from another part of the state and asked Kui Kui if he could kill Kong Li. Kui Kui refused, so Zilu committed an act of arson. Alarmed, Kui Kui ordered his men to attack Zilu. Unfortunately, during the ensuing battle, Zilu's hat was dislodged. He put down his sword: "A gentleman should die wearing his hat." So he picked up his hat and went back into battle only to be killed by a sword.

"Yes, this is the hat that was dislodged from my head," the guest who had come uninvited to the shop spoke as if relieved of a heavy load. "However, there is a slight inconsistency. I did not die a violent death in the skirmish, but as I went off in pursuit of my rolling hat, I escaped through a door into the present day."

The antique shop occupied the ground floor of a two-story building on the main street. I rented it from an old friend, an utterly disheartened draper. One day, he made a special point of stopping by my house. Thoroughly fed up, he lamented: "Human beings are no longer worthy of their noble skins." Fewer and fewer customers were going to his shop to buy his silks and satins. The enormous variety of synthetic fabrics had corrupted their tastes and had become synonymous with sartorial elegance. He was most ardent in averring that it was distaste for this trend rather than considerations of profit that had upset him and influenced his plans for the future. He felt ashamed for everyone, because no one seemed to care that he had gone out of business and planned to move overseas soon.

It was out of consideration for our friendship that he, bitter and disillusioned, persuaded me to give up struggling with my historical writings (I had been a history teacher at a secondary school) and use the worthless antiques and fakes that I had mostly inherited from my family to open an antiques business in place of the silk shop which he had already closed. He said that bringing out my old objects was more

in keeping with the zeitgeist than writing a book. Writing had become obsolete. Nowadays, to earn money from selling a bolt of fabric or a pot was to engage in a fruitful way with the rewriting of history and to drive the workings of the times forward. He exhorted me to merge hobby with bread-winning. The draper despised mismatched careers: "It's like an expert in chemical fertilizer going into the cosmetics business and a fine perfume specialist taking up fishmongering!"

As I knew that this draper had always loved silkworms, I couldn't really argue with him, although I was not entirely sure what he was getting at. He was probably highly delighted, because he handed over the business to me at a very low price. Smugly, he explained that the inception of my great enterprise was due to his influence, and he had no intention of hitting up an old friend for any money in the process.

So it was that I rather hesitantly joined in with the times and became a businessman. With much ambition, I laid my collection out in front of my customers so that they could nitpick and engage in absurd discussions. At first I thought that I could make enough money from the sales to dress warmly and eat my fill and thereby insure that I could also get on with my treatise on the nature of history. Gradually, it became clear that it was not to be — there was no real demand for the objects I had. And I was not inclined to drop the prices. In order to keep going, I had to do as others and bring in a few fashionable, salable lines such as jade ornaments and *sancai* horses, even Mao buttons. Luckily this incontrovertible business psychology did not drive away the more discerning customers. They hung around the shop, superciliously engaging me in conversation, flaunting their superior education by bandying aliases of the sort like Huan Zhu Lou Zhu and Lan Ling Xiao Xiao Sheng. They examined each object painstakingly and exhaustively, huffing and puffing for long periods over defects that other people would never have noticed. I actually found this rather comforting. But it was not long before I realized that they were quite different from me. My love for the antiques was unadulterated: they were fixated by one issue in particular and they pestered me incessantly. And the issue? Whether the object in hand was really as old as it purported to be, and whether it

was really worth the price. Faced with hassles of this sort, I answered: it depends where you are coming from — from the past or the future. Obviously, objects that you are looking at today will be considered old in the future. In our snobbish eyes, even the Mao buttons could have an antique patina, and resonate dully like an ancient tiger tally in response to a covetous rap. Conversely, if you transport yourself back to the Ming dynasty, you might consider a Xuan De incense burner a worthless ashtray. My pricing policy was subjective and not based on the objects' pedigree (which I regard as superficial anyway) — A Han dynasty terracotta burial figurine could have been fired only a few years previously, while a *Shè* inkstone presented to an imperial examination candidate could have originated with the beginnings of calligraphy. Whether discoveries can be made among an array of beautiful objects rests on the reliability of a customer's power of discernment. During my business negotiations, I was continually at odds with my customers. Of these connoisseurs who sought to censure me with arguments about mixing the spurious and the genuine, I would ask: How is a superb, remarkably true-to-life reproduction deficient from the original? In respect of its faithfulness to the original? In respect of some truth that we need to determine? No, absolutely not. In reviving the original features, not only is there no obfuscation in the reproduction, it actually holds greater historical value, for historical value — if it exists — is based on incessant reproduction and revision (continual oral and written retelling). And I maintain that the endorsement of this process of reproduction lies in the artist paring away all distractions to produce a reproduction that is historically highly accurate and a powerful representation of the original. Moreover, if this process produces another truth which in my view is worthy of acknowledgment (my customers, of course, disagreed totally), then in comparison with the original work, the reproduction lacks only one element — the original work's air of inauthenticity. The customers contested this disdainfully, claiming that what reproductions lacked was value, the kind of perverse value dealers such as myself (sadly, I was no longer a historical writer) labored to cook up.

But although they despised me, they kept coming into the shop. Perhaps they were on a mission to weed out the undisguised authenticity (expensive reproductions) only to seek out the only marginally cheaper fakes (antiques)? It was infuriating — skillfully crafted works of art were being relegated to second position for no good reason. Of course, they were incapable of understanding that one could appreciate the original work in a reproduction. "Fakes are fakes!" they cried. Their stubbornness was irremediable.

So you see, I was already starting to feel resentful, just like the draper before me. In their conversations, the customers were probably saying that I was just like him, a self-seeking, greedy dealer, stupid enough to enjoy being derided and lampooned. On the one hand, the customers were disappointed by my unprofessional approach to antiques dealing, on the other hand they came along to buy up what they considered to be real treasures. After the deals were struck, they never forgot to refuse the epigram that I used to trot out free of charge: it is not in the value, but in determining the value that people in their unawareness are devalued to the level of spiritual fakes.

And yet, my business had its sweeteners. First, I left behind being unable to make ends meet. I had moved from being an indolent good-for-nothing, totally dependent on my wife when I left my employment as a teacher, to an industrious fellow, 'entrepreneur' in common parlance. My wife had given up work and become a housewife. After a while, she felt relaxed enough to consider starting a family and was now at home awaiting the arrival of our first child. What's more, with the opening of the shop, I had managed to establish a reputation for myself, and more people were coming to see me from near and far. Every social encounter was a boost to my vanity (before it had never occurred to me that I had any). Apart from this, people heard that I had been a history teacher, and this produced an incessant influx of people asking advice on knotty problems and questions of general knowledge. In going out of my way to help, I used the opportunity to market the concepts I was developing in my unfinished book. When I was found out subsequently, people began to make associations with my unscrupulous pricing procedures and concluded that my historical research was unreliable. When I ridiculed Li Shimin, I was by definition showing my distaste for Li Zicheng, and in lionizing Qiu Ranke, I was also putting Emperor Chong Zhen on a pedestal. People said that my arguments were specious, just like my attitude to fakes, that I was putting Zhang's hat on Li's head — that I was reinventing the sacred deities of Shen Nong and Fu Xi as foreigners, that I was turning the opprobrium directed at the coup of Xuan Wu Men and the An Lushan ethnic rebellion upside down. In my riposte, I cited the example of the *Shi Ji*, pointing out that there was hardly a like work that had not been touched by its craftsmanship. At the same time, however, its dispassionate narrative had opened a can of worms; in later derivative works, interpretation and opinion had been obscured by received wisdom; widely-promulgated, false reputations had damaged the ability of writers to present a direct critique of people and events. The authors had been reduced to spineless sycophants. The gleaming independent spirit of historians of the pre-Christian era, their totally spontaneous individual will, had been castrated just as Sima Qian had been. This terrible trauma had produced a line of impotent works that celebrated castrated desire and established the accompanying 'Castrato School' of history — this debate, which flared up frequently, filled my antique shop with an atmosphere that disturbed and delighted me more than money ever could.

A businessman's sleight of hand which succeeded in killing more than two birds with one stone yielded another, most attractive return — a mistress, my sweetheart, the draper's coquettish niece — she and her husband had moved into the area from a remote province to look after the family's investment on behalf of her uncle after he had moved overseas. As a reward for their efforts, her uncle had arranged that my monthly rent would go to them. While meager, it was enough to cover the couple's expenses. Before long I noticed that my airhead of a land-lady was spending her days dreaming quite naively that her uncle would come back and take her away — I found this both laughable and stupid, but I swear on the reputation of the hat, that her alien accent was extremely pleasant to the ear, and only her oaf of a husband didn't realize her beauty. Her husband liked to loaf about; he was the sort who liked to go gambling with a bunch of friends, perhaps even mess about with other women. But that was none of my business. After a few months of stopping in to deliver my rent, I seduced her under the peacock and silver canopy, on the bed adorned with silks and satins, where the draper used to sleep. In the beginning, I found excuses to stop by the house, bringing one or two small gifts and downing aphrodisiacs with the sole purpose of whetting her appetite for some rough and tumble. Eventually she succumbed to my charms. The draper's former house became my pleasure dome. Even if her feckless husband had guessed that something was going on, he knew it was in his own interest to keep his eyes as well as his mouth shut. Even though he ran into me occasionally when he was out and about with his friends, the money his wife had given him jangling around in his pocket, he behaved as if nothing improper was happening. To avoid embarrassing him openly, I never allowed my charming little sweetheart to come to the shop. In my letters to the draper, I never referred to the affair. For a while, I even suspected that his benefi-cence was a deliberate ploy to drag me down into the mire. If this were the case, there was no need for me to put on a hypocritical show of surprise, nor to decline a friend's tacit gift. In bed, I had elbowed out his niece's husband, to whom he could not refer without contempt. If he had got a whiff of something improper from his residence overseas, he would probably have laughed his socks off.

So the shop was the one place where I could enjoy unadulterated blessing — without a bed or a woman. It was like a temple, with me, a virtuous Buddhist acolyte, making money out of the worshippers. I would go to the shop early every morning and sweep up, in order to experience cleanliness for myself. I calculated that this peace and quiet was one of the lucky blessings that the draper had passed on to me. Included in the premises he had rented to me was an upstairs store-room about the same size as the showroom and at the back a small patch of land surrounded by walls rather like a courtyard (in one of the walls there was a door that had been sealed up). At first, I had racked my brains to think of a proper use for these two empty spaces which were basically unnecessary to my purposes. I had imagined a few bonsai, a fishpond, card table, a reception area for guests, even tatamis. I had also thought of taking someone on, an indispensable female shop assistant. In the end, however, I discarded all these ideas. All I did was put a chair and desk upstairs together with a few historical tomes that I had planned to flick through when there was some time to spare. The empty storeroom made me rejoice that I was not holding on to stock I did not need, and made me consider that to waste space was actually to have space. An unused courtyard was actually worth more to look at than one with a fish pond or a few bonsai. And not taking on a female assistant (I had thought originally of having one with short eyelashes) had saved me a great deal of unnecessary hassle. Recently, I had had enough work to keep me busy, but if I had had her as well and had been paying for an extra salary, it would have seemed extravagant in the light of my current circumstances. In addition, I needed to be on my guard, for there was a danger that the empty storeroom would have become the locus for a bit of hanky-panky between myself and the assistant. This could easily have set tongues wagging and led to disaster. I am not a cavalier person who dismisses danger lightly. Besides, the more lovers one has, the more money one spends; this is something that all men who play the field while supporting a family should understand.

So being empty, they were left empty — but the extraordinary thing was that when the man in the funny clothes who was standing in front of me insisted that he was Zilu, the one who had escaped death at the sword of one of Kui Kui's powerful guards, my mind suddenly went blank, leaving a space as large as the upstairs storeroom and the courtyard put together. His few words of introduction took over, totally filling the space. Feeling rather claustrophobic, I considered going upstairs: grabbing some books and discussing his revealed identity presented no difficulty for me. But just as I was beginning to think this, he wandered off in the direction of the shop window. Immediately I began to feel a sense of regret, because here for the first time, quite unexpectedly, was a man of the type who, on being reminded that it (the hat) was a fake, seemed not to hear. I watched him in fear and trembling — he picked up the gun, held the key in his fingers, undid the lock, took out the hat, stroked it, and put it on his head. Then his delight became apparent. He searched in the light coming off the window for his taciturn reflection, and smiled again.

It must have been at this point that a white police car appeared, sirens wailing, and screeched to a halt on the opposite corner. Armed policemen surged from the car, dispersed quickly and fired one bullet that skimmed the edge of his hat, ricocheted off a square tripod on my left, and made a few turns before embedding itself at great speed in the leg of an eight-immortals-table. Refracted bright sunlight, dispersed by the glass from the broken window, came down in huge dazzling sheets.

With my hair standing on end, I realized that the revengeful policemen had already surrounded the building both from the street and the larger buildings on all four sides. The incident a moment earlier suggested that they had probably planned to use the moment he walked away from me to finish off this undesirable character who was examining his reflection in the window. But, as the highly-trained marksman pulled the trigger, Zilu — what else could I call him? — began to move back towards me. He dived behind the counter with me. "Is there an escape route?" He grabbed hold of my shoulder amicably, and said these words so nonchalantly he could have been joking. But he wasted no time taking in my descriptions of the structure of the building, gave me a push, and directed me to take him upstairs.

The chair, desk, and books were just as I remembered in their original positions. Apart from the dust, nothing had changed. On re-examination, it did seem as if the space in the storeroom was being wasted. As if already familiar with these surroundings, Zilu told me that he used to memorize poetry and the rules of swordsmanship in a room similarly bare and sparsely furnished. He was up and about immediately, feeling not the least bit sorry for himself. He searched out a hitherto undiscovered hole in the floor which had been stopped up with a small piece of wood. He stuck his pistol in and rattled it about vigorously; a clump of wood chips fell through exposing a larger hole. "Now we can see the shop door and the broken window below. If the police are rash enough to invade from the front, we'll finish them off."

There was another round of gunfire, this time into the air. Then someone shouted through a loud speaker telling him to release his hostage and give himself up. The command was repeated several times. Zilu fired several angry shots through the hole in the floor by way of a response.

The police fell silent. It was getting on toward midday. There was no sound of pedestrians going up and down the main street or the roar of traffic. All around was a calm, like an afternoon siesta. I guessed that all those faint-hearted people would be standing outside the police line waiting for the incident to conclude. But they would have to wait. For upstairs, a conversation which seemed predestined to take place between myself and Zilu, now unfortunately a criminal, was about to begin.

The discussion grew out of the hat. First of all in a manner befitting a knight, Zilu respectfully thanked me as one who happened to have recovered a piece of lost property — I asked him not to go to such trouble — "But haven't you been kidnapped by the owner, who ought to feel indebted to you? At least that is how it will appear to people on the outside. Your worries about the unexpected are already upon you," Zilu retorted not without a degree of satire. A rather disagreeable tinge appeared at the corner of his mouth.

My skillful argument had already taken shape when I heard the police shouting. My response came quite naturally. "I don't know whether you have kidnapped me or not and it's not important, because my current plight is no different in essence from the one you were in just before you arrived. Just as the hat was awaiting its owner, so I, in my private reflections, have been awaiting a character and a conversation that could not and yet would take place. In this conversation, the sentence structure and the words are everything, to the extent that the outcome of the conversation is unimportant. The crucial point is the form of the conversation, a form that after hundreds of years can be applied by kindred spirits without first being put to the test."

"A conversation under siege." Zilu was congenial and clear — it was like an extended march where my presence had been forgotten, as if

he were living through the siege of time itself. As he spoke, he dug out a scroll, and handed it to me as if to a colleague or a traveling companion. It was crisp like a roll of white meat. Only when I unfurled it did I realize that it was a wanted poster. I devoured the text like a starving man, and only when I pondered it afterwards did I realize how familiar its mendacious and ridiculous content was. A revolutionary war veteran, militia company captain Huang Tianbao (also known as Huang Niu, the Bull), who, resentful after a dispute with the upper ranks, took advantage one day of a lapse in security and stole four or five guns together with a certain amount of ammunition. The very same night the newly-constructed district offices were destroyed in a fire and two officials attending the scene were shot dead. In fear of punishment, the culprit fled and committed a series of crimes. He has been traced across a number of provinces and has killed and injured a great many policemen attempting to intercept him. This man is an extremely dangerous criminal ... There is no need to quote further. It was not stated whether this multiple murderer had another name, the most serious omission from the circular in my view, for there in the upper right-hand corner of the document, quite unmistakable, was a clear, half-length picture, which upon examination proved to be my companion Zilu.

"But what has all this to do with me?" Zilu was sitting on the chair. He was vexed. "I escaped the sword, fled Kui Kui's shameless administration and watched the sword in my hand change to a pistol. I reappeared in a huge burning compound and had hardly found my feet before two devils lunged at me out of the raging flames on the burning mosaics. I held my breath, but the pistol rushed on at them, commanding them to fall to the floor. Terrified, I retreated, leaving the place which was now thick with smoke and engulfed in flames. What followed is just like a nightmare — night and day, I drifted from one hiding place to another. I crossed I don't know how many rivers, roads, plains, and mountains, was forced to associate with all sorts of people. People looked me up and down in a quite humiliating fashion as if I were a sorcerer who had lost his charms. People were quizzical in their greetings. Their silence divulged their suspicion, which made it difficult for me to se-

quester myself among these degenerate people. I fled north, south, east
and west, taking buses, trains, and tricycle rickshaws across cities, towns,
and villages, but to no avail, there was no escape from the prying eyes of
the authorities. One day, I limped into an apparently quiet compound
(in actual fact it was the general office of a small newspaper), where-
upon I immediately attracted the attention of some editor who singled
me out, shouting loudly (the ugly report of the pistol had not deterred
him). I picked up the wanted circular that was lying on his desk — but
who on earth is going to believe this? Here was my image that I had seen
floating on the surface of a clear forest stream appearing now on the
surface of the paper, like a ghastly specter. I had taken on someone else's
identity complete with some garbled murder charge and now I was about
to be arrested. While on the run, I learned from an illiterate old woman
who was selling eggs that my teacher and all my fellow pupils had al-
ready turned to dust, that they were all now orbiting stars (quite by
chance, the old woman mentioned one of her ancestors, Duan Muci,
who was actually a fellow junior disciple who particularly loved dia-
logues with Confucius). In the course of all those irrepressible sighs
and nightmares, at least two thousand years have gone by. And the
spookiest thing is that one day, in a moment of exhaustion, in the midst
of a confusing and complicated daydream, I saw this shop and there,
sitting in the window like a paper sparrow hawk in a cage, was this hat
that I had been worrying about day and night. Looking around, I could
see the hoards of policemen hot on my tail. Of course, they are still the
same men Kui Kui had gathered. It is as if I, who once was Zilu, am
being punished. Time has quite mercilessly given them exactly the same
features, each and every one.

The wanted poster slipped out of my hand onto the floor. The
fugitive's faltering, unfinished confession produced in me a longing to
retort, but I found that the retort did not come easily. For, if he was
really the person who had been on the run for a thousand years, the Zilu
I had imagined, then my doubts were like my contemporaries whose
easily roused suspicion he despised. If he wasn't, my protestations were
irrelevant. In truth, I already believed him unconditionally — this man

had fought against unlimited adversity and loneliness only to be exposed as a historical flaw. The tribulations he had suffered had convinced him that the turmoil in the state of Wei had continued from the pre-Christian era into the present day. In other words, for a thousand years, the story remains the same — the police are the lackeys, the ordinary people are the informers (my customers for example), the officials are Kong Li, controlling affairs in the capital, and the person issuing the orders is, of course, Kui Kui, the imposter monarch whom Zilu infuriated. On his thorny journey through to the present day, Zilu had been declared a contemporary person without any opportunity of redress — this was not a printing error on the wanted poster, but the vicious machinations of generations of schemers and plotters, and the establishment's open eradication of dissent — at this point I was shaken suddenly by a fear I had never before encountered. It made my blood run cold. It wasn't a fear of the coordinated force of the legal authorities, but history, flexing its evil talons, ruthlessly tossing aside my queries, mercilessly annihilating this bold, spirited fellow who had had the audacity to slip through the net and escape to the present.

Zilu's arrival was therefore a scandal — whichever way you look at it. To get under the skin of history and cause an irritation by not conforming to the chronicles of murder is unforgivable. But sympathy aside, I, with all the research I had done in historical records and Confucianism, had one reckless question. I had pondered repeatedly, which I could not help raising with this man, who was a misfit today as in any other period, a question that is simple and crude yet could prove crucial and fundamental; that is, why did Zilu court the trouble by asking the newly enthroned Kui Kui if he could kill Kong Li? Although it is said that Kui Kui and his cronies hid in Kong Li's house where they later attacked the completely undefended King Chu and snatched the throne, thereby committing the shameful crime of insurrection, this apparent rebellion had a tortured logic of its own. First, Kui Kui who had spent many years in exile was actually a former prince of Wei, King Chu's father, and he wished to exercise his rightful claim to the throne. In reality, after Kui Kui's father, Duke Wei Ling, died, Kui Kui's son succeeded to the title because

Kui Kui was in exile. Applying Confucian principles — by this I mean, *jun jun, chen chen, fu fu, zi zi* — on returning to Wei, the elderly Kui Kui wanted his son to concede the title to him, an expectation that was perfectly justifiable; but King Chu was a covetous man with a poorly developed sense of filial piety who ended up being deposed by his elderly father, championing a popular cause; with regard to Kong Li who had served King Chu, it could be argued that, bound by ties of friendship, he had always been under the influence of the exiled elder prince. So, taking the position of father as the anchor stone in the sequence of relationships, when he came to weigh his priorities, he felt he had no choice but to participate in the insurrection.

Ignoring Zilu's shake of the head, I once again suggested that, on careful reflection, Kui Kui and Kong Li's actions were also decided in accordance with certain rituals. I selected a copy of the *Zuo Zhuan* from my small print versions of the *Shi Ji* and *Zuo Zhuan*, dusted it off, opened it and read aloud one of Zuo Qiuming's passages — there it was stated that Kong Li was not himself responsible for the insurrection, but was forced to collude with his mother and crown Kui Kui. Leaving aside for a moment the complexity of the whole incident, as long as Zilu accepted that Confucius had underlined the supremacy of filial piety in his writings, it would be difficult to pick fault with Kong Li, and unspeakable to kill him, for deferring to his mother's will. If this statement could establish that Kui Kui was not a total impostor (and very likely he wasn't), then it went without saying that Kong Li could not have been a vile character. In which case, I was very much afraid that it was Zilu who, fired up by some unrealistic, one-sided cause, had been compelled at some juncture in history to play the role of the impulsive character. In my view, as a subordinate of a subordinate, as an outstanding city magistrate and, even more importantly, as a disciple of the great Confucius himself, Zilu had only seen a change in part of the world which went against his ideal principles, but ignored the fact that the world was, for the most part, operating harmoniously. The rest of the world was probably operating according to broader Confucian categories. I venture that if it had not been Zilu, that loyal and brave minor official, returning like lightning to the capital, but Confucius himself, he certainly would not have placed his conduct, so extreme that it invited the admiration of others, at odds with his teaching and cultivation of all time as a result of some incidental confusion between right and wrong — at this critical juncture, I assumed that Zilu was a Confucian, but once again I sensed from his bearing that there were differences between him and Confucius. Otherwise, how could Confucius have predicted so accurately Zilu's imminent demise when he heard that there was turmoil in the state of Wei? All the great thinkers have advocated flexibility in dealing with events, but Zilu, it seems, was of the opposite view. According to my reasoning, flexibility is the essence of Confucianism.

"It is true to say that Confucius' regret that I had only gone so far in my profession, and no further, was directed at this." Zilu took up the thread. "Even though the master himself did not conform entirely to this pattern, he hinted to me that we should act in accordance with circumstances, in order to respond to trends, squeeze out other factions, and promote his great thinking. Frankly, I am not a qualified Confucian disciple. A great many true Confucians have abused the concept of 'flexibility' and in doing so have become people who say one thing and mean another, always going back on their word. In the months that I was companion and bodyguard to Confucius, he never let up in instructing me both verbally and by personal example. Our friendship — I should stress that there was no one closer to him than I — was mostly harmonious. In his critiques of me, you will discover he thought from the start that I would come to a sticky end. He was convinced that just as one is powerless during periods of collapse, he would never change me — human beings are willful. In Confucius' eyes, although I am no longer the Zilu who insulted and attacked him, I am still extremely dangerous. I differ from those Confucian scholars who believe they will make their mark through long, painful scholarship. When I asked Confucius for advice on etiquette and scholarship, I refused to become embroiled in the contradictions of Confucianism — that is, to be forced to accept "flexibility." The code that I follow as a human being is not one of complex unintelligible concepts such as loyal ministers and filial fathers, but one that is much older and simpler."

When Zilu got to this point, perhaps unable to bear the unpropitious silence outside, he approached the window and, under the cover of the wall, took a look outside. Our conversation continued. I sat on the chair he had just vacated and waited for him to return. In an uncharacteristically depressed tone, I put it to him that if one were to conclude that his conduct were at odds with the rigorous and exacting tenets of Confucianism, would he be able to tell me what his guiding principles were. I confessed that I had worked them out to some extent but was still not entirely clear.

"A world in its entirety (the universe) is something people cannot grasp." Zilu moved his hands to illustrate. "At most, people can only take responsibility for a part of the world, for the things that are closest to them. This part often shrinks to the point where only we ourselves remain. We are guided by a sequence of personal rules and use individual beliefs to ward off the chaos of the universe. The philosophies for dealing with the world, which have developed out of these personal codes, are clearly demarcated and solid, not complex and elusive. They are incisive and direct, not puny and winding. So, things are clarified. These philosophies become articles of creed through pithy, meticulous wording enabling us to experience and practice them throughout our lives. Sometimes the words will ascend on high and shine brightly like stars. My creed values promises more than anything else! Today it is called keeping one's words — But in the lifetime of my ignoble existence, swallowing one's words to gain weight has become rather fashionable. Imagine if you will, a person who has given his pledge, how can he use words to cover his embarrassment and ingratiate himself with two sworn enemies? A failure to deliver on a promise is a great shame. Kong Li actually aided and abetted Kui Kui to attack King Chu who had put his trust in him. Even to Kui Kui, who took no shame in associating with him, Kong Li's act of trampling on his pledge (surely more precious than gold or life and death) should not be exonerated. The lesson of the state of Wei is that people are accustomed to establishing lofty ideals in order to justify themselves and manipulate the concept of flexibility. This is how they have led the world into the present day which is even more chaotic than before."

Zilu's resentment intensified. Again he used a reference to 'parts' to make me feel inadequate. "History is confused and difficult to distinguish. However, its individual parts — segments — are distinct. It is in these individual parts that we exist and are defined as human beings. If we step outside these areas, we go beyond the reach of our own power. What Kui Kui found unacceptable in my request was the fact that I had stepped outside the confines of my relationship with Kong Li and into the territory defined by the relationship between Kui Kui and Kong Li (difficult to quantify and grasp). My intention was not focused on Kong Li, but in persuading Kui Kui to kill me. He did not understand, so in order to force his hand, I started the fire."

"Why?" I asked, stupidly. Zilu responded in his own time. "My opinions differ from my teacher in the following respect. I believe that the qualities of a gentleman are nurtured in the context of a very simple relationship, and are not extracted from complicated arrangements of power. Today there are no knights and hermits, and yet that band of mutually mistrustful Confucians remains. After the incident in Wei, how could a self-respecting person such as I derive any pleasure from staying? I saw it as a timely opportunity thwarted by an unexpected bump, which has delayed my chance of winning until today."

"Now what you mean by 'bump' is surely the hat you could not afford to be without?" I deciphered this from his arcane ramblings. "You were demonstrating that though wearing a scholar's garb, you were not really a true follower of Confucius; serving under Kong Li, you did not want to sink to his level. Politics, like etiquette and scholarship, are just stage props for your only entrance — your few meticulous words were like diamonds, clear, tangible crystals, steadfast and beautiful." "No! Like a burning star," Zilu painfully and fervently agreed. " So, have you used up your one and only opportunity?" "Of course!" Zilu picked up the copy of the *Zuo Zhuan* that I had replaced, "When I was killed by that sword."

"I cannot believe that you have lived solely in order to die." I had got to the bottom of the matter, my voice was loud with excitement. "Your obsession with language, with "quality, not quantity," made you realize that order (on the local level) is already gone, and people have made words their business — cashing in on the chaos, so to speak. You have been waiting all along, waiting for this fashionable business to develop in a way that suits your abilities — when you, sharp-eyed and clear-headed, came rushing in from another place to the scene of the incident, you were already taking up an unique opportunity to allow the star of your pledge to break through the darkness. Your stature bears no resemblance to a peer of the realm, an official or a great thinker, but simply shows a faithfulness to yourself — in order that words can be words. What is startling is that in that remote time when there were no trains and telephones, apart from yourself, there was only one other person, Confucius, who understood that in the end you would commit suicide under the broken sword of time."

Whether in tacit recognition or lost in reflection, Zilu stroked his hat (it was only then that I understood that it was really an extemporaneous embellishment). Then, he moved over in front of the window again. There, apparently bored by the discussion, he fired the gun at random — bang bang bang. The shiny yellow bullet casings rolled onto the floor like dying bees.

A certain gentleman, leaving behind a crisis in the spiritual world, with loose hair and clutching a pistol (probably holding a sword when he set off), arrived in my hitherto uneventful antiques shop, robbed me, and held me by force. I never recovered from the distress the event caused and, as a result, lost some of my marbles. I have already stated that this all stemmed from the nonsense peddled by those troublemakers who delighted in others' misfortune. They were the ones who brought in the police, who completely ruined my shop (this development, like the damage to the leg of the eight-immortals-table, caused me considerable distress). And it did not stop there. They kept coming to my house, and using all sorts of doublespeak to bring me out of my shock. When I mentioned Zilu, they could barely suppress their laughter as they explained that as a person, Zilu no longer existed. Instead, it was an animal — out in the country, it was the name given to a bear who was invoked to frighten unruly children who did not eat all their food. They said that my imaginings were all to do with my nanny because country people were always telling stories about bears. Behind my back, they used references to madness to frighten my already petrified wife.

But even these humiliations and the incident combined were still not enough. For after I had shelled out a huge wad of money to restore the shop, and as I was preparing to open again, I received another fat letter from the draper. Contrary to my expectations, it was a most vitriolic attack on me. Not only did he announce that he wanted his business back, but also that he wanted to sever all contact with me. I shall not detail his insults here. Anyway, I surmised that he had received a letter from his niece's husband behind my sweetheart's back. The letter must have reported all the changes in the antiques shop and my recent circumstances and then exposed the relationship between myself and my sweetheart. This sent me into such a turmoil that I could barely carry on, because the draper stated quite explicitly that he would be returning immediately to put right what he described as total chaos and to settle the score with me. In the middle of the night, deceiving my heavily pregnant wife, I slipped down to the kitchen and burned his letter, which was full of quotations from Confucius. Of course, this was of little use, I told myself. Since I had already hurt him deeply by thwarting his designs on his pretty niece, I was very much afraid that my attempts at rescuing the situation would only fan the flames of his anger. In order to escape the imminent arrival of punitive forces (in the name of Confucius), I started to plan my escape, just like Kui Kui — who, after an affair with his father's favorite concubine, a beautiful woman called Nan Zi, fled fearing execution — now, the angry Duke Wei Ling was the draper, and his niece, Nan Zi, while I, facing imminent disgrace and ruin, was tormenting my mind with self-inflicted worries: as you wandered dissolute from place to place, Kui Kui, did you ever wonder whether there wasn't also an element of love that was struggling to stay afloat on the surface of that insatiable river of desire?

I had no answer, and having no answer was one of my retributions for having accepted for no good reason the goodwill of the draper. In the gaps in my severely impaired mind, I actually thought of my book that I had picked up and then abandoned again and again. I did not know whether I would get tangled up again in the thousands of superficial strands and loose ends, if I were to take up writing once more (anyway, what else could I do?). In my imaginary work, I would investigate meticulously the intimate links that lay buried in between appreciation of cultural relics and the whole historical truth. I would take Zilu as an example to prove that a masterpiece, which might be a reproduction, can be truer and have greater value than the original work — let the words be the witness, what a conversation we shared between us! Like the hat which had rolled down through the millennium, our words had traveled through each and every one of those centuries all the while there was a reward on his head, through each and every substantial yet superficial work, and arrived at the present day, achieving the highest status accorded to a fake. In the storeroom, where we were holed up together (it was like a sacred, fortuitous vacuum), in the twilight that we greeted together, I changed the subject again and again — from the origin of the antiques shop to my fascination with the complex ins and outs of three generations of the Kui Kui family, from the non-existent female shop assistant to my perceptions of space. I had stopped playing for time and dallying with him. I was anxious and frightened, afraid that as soon as I stopped talking he would disappear from the revolutions of the crystal ball. The oblique rays of sun beamed in warmly through the window, falling on the desk and books, and for a moment, I felt we were like two old friends chattering away in a large bright hall, whiling away our leisure hours.

Contract, income, mistress, and what a special day it has been today! In order to defy the police's inauspicious silence, I had no choice but to continue the flow of words. "She must be wondering where I have got to! As usual, the bath will be full of hot water, the scented candles burning." Zilu seemed to smack his lips in appreciation of the topic, but in fact he did not really understand what I was saying, and listened in near cruelty. He conformed to no conventional pattern and existed in a purely self-referential, eternal structure and therefore had no interest in contemporary life. I was forced to change my approach and ask him questions instead — from Zi Gong to Yan Hui, from Confucius' skills in martial arts to the city magistrate's salary, from the quality of chariots and horses to the infantry, from popular sentiment in Wei to the customs of his hometown in Bian — in the end, I once again returned to Confucius and asked him whether the real Confucius was like those images I had seen in the temples, a man fond of an ascetic look. Zilu laughed. "No, he had the look of a man who has been bowdlerized by subsequent generations." His speech over, he began to sigh with emotion. "When Confucius and I were together, swimming the backstroke or practicing archery, he would often refer to today. The present day is just as I saw it, Confucius' morbid anxieties have become reality — people have become painfully entrenched in complex relationships."

My words dried up. I had to stop. The conversation, which Zilu likened to a long march, had already gone as far as he could take it and had reached its terminus. An embarrassed silence (which was unbearable) was broken by the police launching their frontal attack. The gunfire, like an awesome loud bell, began to resonate right on cue, announcing that the end of the conversation was upon us. The police would not be as cautious again out of consideration for human safety. The window exploded catastrophically. The shards of glass sprinkled into our faces. A gas canister came hurtling in, quickly bringing tears of farewell to Zilu's and my eyes. Zilu brandished his pistol wildly, jumping back and forth in the seemingly no longer empty storeroom. The foul odor of the invisible gas brought on an unending volley of curses. I grabbed hold of him as he hurtled down the stairs. There we could look down into the courtyard from the window in the back wall, not yet a target of attack it seemed. "Go! Go!" I dug the money out of my inner chest pocket and forced it on him, but my throat was on fire and while my mouth moved, no sound came out. I pointed to the sealed-up door in the courtyard wall — May the gods strike me down! I was convinced suddenly that if Zilu were to launch himself at the door, and were able to break it open, he could resist a fate which sought to return him to a book, and escape into a time where there were no written records.

When he appeared in the courtyard, his substantial physique was facing away from me, like an elephant Xeeing the battleWeld in an ancient war. No, it was more like an anxious yellow ox, muddleheaded and careless lurching forward into a dead door. But something seemed to strike him, dislodging his hat which fell to the Xoor. Muttering, he put down his pistol and carefully picked up the hat. My eyes burning at the sight of this, I suddenly noticed a sepia tinge Xooding over this all too familiar picture.

The remainder is not imagined or exaggerated. The people who had listened to my story were unanimous in saying that only the Wnal event could be taken as true...

When he placed the hat on his head, the bullets, like a swarm of bees returning to the hive, penetrated him from all sides.

Translator Notes

Zilu (559-420 BC), also known as Zhong You, was one of Confucius' 72 disciples.

Yanyi is a historical romance. It has a traditional format with each chapter headed by a couplet summarizing its content. The stories are based on real historical events and are popular with storytellers and their audiences.

Ming dynasty, 1368-1644 AD.

Spring and Autumn Period, 770-476 BC. China at this time was divided into separate states. It is also regarded as the golden age of China's culture.

State of Wei was one of the states of the Spring and Autumn period that straddled present day northern Henan and southern Hebei.

Sancai is a glazed terracotta horse produced during the Tang dynasty. There are numerous reproductions.

Apart from being known by their real names, literati in China also have a number of aliases. *Huan Zhu Lou Zhu'* and *Lan Ling Xiao Xiao Sheng'* are the aliases of the author of the famous martial arts novel "Swordsmen of Shu Mountain" and the erotic novel "The Golden Lotus" respectively. The real names of these authors are not known.

Tiger tally is a tiger-shaped, bronze military tally used in ancient China.

Imperial Examinations were the selection procedure for officials and civil servants. They were introduced in the Sui and Tang dynasties and continued until the end of the Qing dynasty in 1905. The inkstone is so-called because it came from *She* county in the province of Anhui.

Li Shimin was the founder of the Tang dynasty; *Li Zicheng* led the popular uprising that overthrew the Ming dynasty. *Qiu Ranke* was an obscure mythical figure of the same period as Li Shimin; *Emperor Chong Zhen* was overthrown by the uprising led by Li Zicheng.

Shen Nong and *Fu Xi* were two of China's most legendary figures.

The *An Lushan Rebellion* was started by two Turks, An Lu shan and Shi Siming in the mid-Tang dynasty. The *Coup of Xuan Wu Men* was instigated by Li Yuan at the beginning of the Tang dynasty.

Shi Ji is China's first official history written by Si-ma Qian of the Han dynasty. It exerted an enormous influence over historical writings of later generations.

Eight-immortals-table is a large square table that seats two people on each side.

Duan Muci was another of Confucius' disciples.

jun jun, chen chen, fu fu, zi zi is one of the tenets of Confucianism. Confucius believed that rulers (*Jun*) should be rulers, ministers (*Chen*) should be ministers, fathers (*Fu*) should be fathers, and sons (*Zi*) should be sons. He considered that social relationships should be conducted according to these categories and regarded these relationships as fundamental to the structure of society.

Zuo Zhuan is one of the Confucian classics written by Zuo Qiuming, an official of the state of Lu during the Spring and Autumn Period.

Zi Gong and *Yan Hui* were two of Confucius' most famous disciples.

GAO ERTAI TRANSLATED BY H.BATT

MY SISTER LAN'S SPECIMEN BOOK

In 1944 my big sister married Jianbao and went to live with his family. It always confused me — when had they gotten to know each other? I could never figure it out.

My big sister's name was Shulan. She had the fairest complexion of the four daughters in my family. The darkest was my youngest sister, whom we all called "Third Black." Shulan was the most elegant, the most spirited and imaginative, the one whose feelings were most easily moved. She could recite poems by heart, she would sing and sing, and burst into tears as she sang. Then as soon as something cheerful happened, for example, if someone showed her a lifelike locust woven from grass, she'd burst out laughing. She called herself "Mistress Lan." When she walked in, she always said, "Mistress Lan has arrived." Father said her calligraphy was better than mine and Second Sister's, because there was a certain freshness about it. One of her shortcomings was that she was afraid of hard work. She never did well with dirty or difficult chores, and Second Sister always had to clean up after her. She had very little courage, wouldn't dare pick up a grasshopper or touch a silkworm. Whenever she saw a worm she'd scream. She was twelve years older than I, but whenever she had to go outside in the dark, she always took me along with her. Lastly, she was headstrong. One time Zhao Shihong showed her the *Anthology of Qing Poetry* that he'd hand-copied. One of the poems was by Zheng Banqiao:

> I tell you, new bride in the red sedan-chair,
> Don't burst out in anger like a spoiled child
> At your old in-laws, their hair white as silk.
> In their home you are no daughter.

She hated the poem and started shouting, grabbed the page and ripped it out.

Her mind was active from morning to night. She took an interest in everything. Picking out the different stars at night, watching a chance autumn snowfall, flying kites, hanging lanterns — she was passionately serious about everything, but especially about the strange, exotic leaves of plants and trees. As soon as she spotted one, she'd pick it, classify it in her big, thick notebook, and note down where she'd collected it. According to what she'd learned in her field observation class, she divided different leaves into seven categories: pinks, carambolas, mustards, beans, colzas, asters, and roses. She took the first syllable of each category and turned them all into a sentence: "Pink cars must be cold as roses." She said this helped her to remember them. "This isn't just a word game. I'm going to write a *Study of the Plants of the Lower Yangtze*."

But this notebook of hers wasn't all plant specimens. There were paper-cut designs, prints of kitchen gods and door gods, painted faces of Peking opera characters, and other colorful, bright and gaudy drawings, with the date she'd collected each one written beneath it, together with a simple explanation. For example:

"A curtain-flower with a frog inside it...."

"A child's vest with vipers and toads and in the middle a rooster eating the vipers and toads..." "The bay tree in the moon and the rabbit in the moon grinding medicine to keep you safe..."

"The doorway-guardians Yu Chigong with the black face and Qin Shubao with the white face, mandarins of heaven."

Her favorites were the "Ox in Spring" drawings because she was born in the year of the ox. I've never seen any other drawings like them.

Big Sister never let me look through this notebook by myself. When I wanted to look at it, she turned the pages for me, one at a time, slowly and carefully, because the notebook was made of grass-paper and tore easily. Sometimes I got impatient because she turned the pages so slowly, and I'd insist on turning them myself. She'd call out, "Mother!" As soon as I heard that cry, I vanished to avoid any trouble. After, she'd come looking for me, and say, "Want to look at the notebook? If you want to look, I'll turn the pages for you."

The year she was married to Jianbao, my oldest sister was twenty-one. She carefully wrapped the notebook in a piece of cloth and took it to Jianbao's house in Baocheng. Jianbao's was a big, old-fashioned family, "Old in-laws, their hair white as silk." She went to Baocheng in a red enclosed sedan-chair, borne along to the sound of horns and drums. As the sedan-chair started uphill, she insisted she wanted to get out. She always liked climbing hills, and this time she insisted more forcefully than ever on walking. She absolutely would not ride. Everyone insisted that it was not permitted. Even Jianbao tried to persuade her. "It's not the custom," he said. "I've never heard of such a thing." Big sister started crying and beating her fist against the sedan-chair, but all in vain. The sedan-chair continued on, rocking and swaying.

There were lanterns and streamers hanging everywhere, gongs clashing, drums pounding, people going in and out — such a commotion it made me dizzy. Before the house was a deafening uproar: a dozen tables, with the hosts urging everyone to eat as much as they could, guests playing finger-guessing games, the loser drinking a cup of wine.

I was sitting beside Second Sister. I turned and asked where Big Sister was. She said she was in the "bride's room." I pushed my way out of the parlor and went to look for her. In the confusion I tried the wrong door. Finally after a great deal of trouble I got to the bride's room, but my sister wasn't there. A crowd of boys swarmed around the door, peering in. Inside were four or five girls sitting in a circle on the newly-oiled floor, playing a game of "sheep-shin." The furniture was all new, the table was covered with mirrors and glittering glass utensils. The smell of the fresh tung oil from the floor filled the room, strong as in a ship's cabin. On the edge of a bed decorated with carving was an opera singer in an embroidered red satin dress, wearing a short sleeveless vest covered in ribbons and glittering jewels, and a sparkling, tottering hat in the shape of a chandelier all covered in pearls. She sat with her head down and her back to the door. I felt terribly anxious and disappointed — I didn't know where to look for my sister. Without even realizing it I cried out, "Big Sister!"

The opera singer turned around. From deep within the jangling jewelry and ribbons I made out my sister's face. It was covered in tears, her eyes and nose all red. It was obvious that she'd been crying. I walked over and said, "Big Sister!" She said, "I want to go home." The girls in the room all stood up and stared at the two of us, eyes wide with amazement. The boys outside the door seemed to relish the scene even more, and stared with mouths wide open. One of them turned around and yelled, "Come look at this!" just like when visitors at the zoo see a rare animal that's been asleep stand up and start moving around. I don't know why, but I became embarrassed, as if I were giving a bad performance in some comedy. And so I turned around and ran out. Ever since, whenever I think of this moment, I always feel that by not staying and talking with my sister, I made an unforgivable mistake.

Second Sister and I, together with our dog Lion, often walked across Journey Mountain to Baocheng to visit Big Sister. Every time we saw her, Big Sister cried and said, "I want to go home." Lion always ran around her wagging his tail, and jumping up onto her. The school needed teachers, and father asked her back to teach, but the Zhao family wouldn't allow it. They always said, "There's too much housework here. We can't get by as it is." When my grandmother died, Big Sister came back for the funeral and stayed on, unwilling to go back until it was time for her to have her baby. After she went back, Zhao Zhongxiang, the baby's grandfather, chose its name, "Xuexian."

After the war against the Japanese was over, we came back home to Chunxi. Big Sister had to return to Baocheng. It was a long way to go to visit. We only saw her at Chinese New Year. She and Jianbao would come pay us a New Year's visit, bringing Xuexian with them, and stay for a few days. Xuexian was the portrait of the suave little gentleman. He called me "Uncle," and Second Sister and Younger Sister he'd call "Auntie." He even brought his books along and played very little during the day, spending his time instead on reciting from books in his prattling voice. Every evening he repeated what he'd memorized to his father Jianbao, who held the book. He stood, facing away, hands behind his back, legs wide apart, reciting in a loud voice as he raised and lowered one foot, then the other, his whole body rocking back and forth. My father said, "This is not suitable at all. It is the style of the old household academies." Jianbao said there was nothing he could do about it: the boy's grandfather always examined him in this fashion at home.

After the Communist land-reform, Zhao Zhongxiang and his two brothers, Zhao Zhongyou and Zhao Zhongde, were condemned as "landowners and industrialists." Zhao Zhongde was shot, Zhao Zhongyou was imprisoned, and Zhao Zhongxiang, after suffering through several public accusation sessions, died, together with his wife. When the three families' estates were confiscated, my big sister again and again requested permission to keep her grass-paper specimen book, but they took it away despite her protests. She ignored everyone's warnings, and kept pestering members of the Peasant Union and Workers' Team, until finally her persistence moved someone, and it was given back to her. It was terribly battered, many of the dried leaves had fallen out, but she was still excited, as if she'd had some rare piece of luck. The village committee assigned Big Sister's family a bit of land and found them a couple of rooms in a grass hut. This hut had three rooms. Big Sister and her family lived in two of them. The third room was left to the peasant family who now lived in the house of their former landlord. They used the room for their oxen and sheep. Big Sister was born in the year of the ox, and Jianbao in the year of the sheep. It was hard to say whether living with cows and sheep was a coincidence or preordained.

They lived in this grass hut for over thirty years. And when Xiaoyu and I went to see them more than thirty years later, I didn't recognize them. It was hard to believe that these two listless, apathetic old people with their turbid, dull expressions had been my life-loving sister Lan, interested in everything, and the lively, energetic Jianbao. Xuexian was already a middle-aged man, had never found a wife, had forgotten everything he'd studied, and had become completely illiterate. When I mentioned him, both old people burst into tears, saying that he ate too much, "till there was nothing left." "Nothing left" was right. There was nothing in the room but a couple of beds, a bamboo couch, a stove with pots and pans, a water jar, a few farm tools, and a wooden stool. It frightened me to look at them. I couldn't imagine how they managed to survive.

Everything, including the old mosquito net covered with patches was the same old stale dark brown. The only thing that was new was the glistening yellow rice-straw in the loft. It was their fuel for cooking. There were no animals in the livestock pen next door. In the daytime they were all out in the pasture. The powerful stench of cattle dung and urine along with the odor of rotten straw invaded their little dark space morning and night. They said after thirty years they were used to it.

When I asked about the specimen book, Big Sister said she'd kept it wrapped, up in the garret. It had been confiscated again during the Cultural Revolution. They said it had all sorts of feudal superstitions, wanted them to explain what they were keeping it for, and she and Jianbao had been summoned to many public accusation sessions. At this same time they had a daughter. They named her Zhao Xiangtou. She was clever and quick. When she was still little she used to go through the fields after the harvest picking up stalks of wheat and rice and bolls of cotton. Quick with her hands, quick on her feet, she gathered much more than other families' children. When she got older, she took in everything she saw and helped other families spin yarn and weave cloth, make shoes and clothes, weave baskets and nets; all fast and nimbly. She grew up more and more beautiful. Everyone who saw her praised her. She married a demobilized soldier and went with him to work at the Qingshan Tea Farm. A devoted daughter, she often came to see them and to look after her old father and mother. The old couple said Xiangtou was the only joy and consolation they'd had their entire lives. I asked why Xuexian didn't take up a trade. They said he couldn't. "He'd studied himself dumb."

When we left, Big Sister accompanied us part of the way. The burning sun high in the sky was too hot for her. We kept urging her to go back. Finally she stopped. We walked on until we could just barely see her. She was still standing there, gazing after us.

Later on I lost my freedom and was forced to flee abroad, never to see Big Sister again. In 1995, in a little cabin in a forest on the shore of a lake in New York State, I received a letter from Second Sister in China telling me that Big Sister had passed away, from poverty and illness, at the age of seventy.

ZHANG ZHEN   TRANSLATED BY YANBING CHEN

THE FOREIGN BEACH

A naked woman
walks onto a foreign beach

The Leaning Tower of Pisa, scars all over
breathes the silence after a disaster

The sun grills her hair
and crackles
She runs, arms clasped around her body
lost on the outskirts of the city of time

More domes, ever-more striking
like hollowed-out balls of ivory
Sick with a disease, history comes flooding
She weeps, face buried in her hands

These uninhabitable towers
This unswimmable water
This smoking land
This moth-eaten hill

Crisis has become routine
Grass swiftly withers
By the end of this mistaken journey
she'll have lost her gender

The bus has just carried away a crowd of old tourists
As the sunset dissolves in water
everything has changed, and turned —
soft, and tender

July 1992
Revised, November 1993

JANET TAN   TRANSLATED BY THE AUTHOR

ADAMS RIVER

American sockeyes usually mature in their fourth year. In early summer the impulsive mating instinct drives them out of the deep ocean on an uninterrupted voyage back to their birthplace. The mysterious compass inside each body helps them navigate the Pacific storms to arrive at the northwest coastline of the American continent. In early September, from the smell of pulp and traces of mountain snow, they find the rivers that sent them down to the ocean a few years before. They gather around the river 's mouth — a five-hundred-mile no-return upstream journey starts from here and ends at the narrow streams in the high mountains. By the end of the trip, the foot-long body of each sockeye turns into a golden red.

Rong's voice came to a sudden stop, like a tape run to its end. Every time she went through this part of her lecture on the life cycle of the salmon, she felt as if she herself were a party to this suicidal journey. She didn't know how much the young students sitting there really understood, but she felt herself carried away by her own voice — there was something irrational in it, something that had nothing to do with science — to another place: a quiet forest in the Kakuwal Mountain valley, the sockeyes in their mating season flirting with each other in the shallow water with their dazzlingly red bodies and golden-green heads.

The summer was just over, and the intense pleasure his kisses and caresses left on Rong's body was already a distant memory. Pleasure was always the first thing to go, and the moment's happiness was hardly ever enough to fend off the loneliness and doubt of the following eleven months. Any suggestive detail would set her off into a stream of consciousness about love and desire. But that, he said, was not the whole of life.

The spike on the sockeye's back is its sexual organ. The first time Rong stood with him by the river, they did not know that what was happening in the water was a matter of life and death. It would be more accurate to say that they themselves, having to part again, were going through the pain of life and death. They had left the world behind and come to this valley where few had set foot. They did not know this was the home of the sockeyes. They walked aimlessly along the river valley, spreading out the blanket to rest when tired. But that always led to a hopeless situation in which they would roll into each other's arms, until the last piece of clothing came off, the last breath of passion wrung out of each body. The old Indian man who watched the forest told them they would be safe all twenty miles upstream along the river. The bears were well fed from the sockeye bodies on the riverbank. Besides, bears do not like the smell of men. Therefore they left their tent in the Indian's small cabin, and carried with them only one blanket. They watched the snow-covered mountain peaks, the mist gathering around the valley strewn with yellow and red leaves — strangely it was not cold. Their shoes felt the moss-covered ground spongy under the falling leaves. Her skirt, caught on grass stalks, picked up black thorns and burrs. Getting up from the ground after making love, their bodies were decorated with crushed red and yellow leaves. If one body woke in the middle of night, the other would, too. It was like making love in a dream, but which part was dream and which part was real seemed no longer important after a separation of more than ten years. What amazed them, though, was that the sealed memory, once reopened, showed no trace of time. That night, he didn't say it was not the whole of life. Nor did he mention his wife, a woman who had fought with her life to be his wife. Sometimes, when Rong was lonely, that woman would emerge from her memory. With a smile on her face, she had been trekking in Rong's loneliness for more than ten years.

They had not spoken to each other after they left San Francisco, using their hands, lips, and bodies to communicate. They ate very little, slept very little. Only later did she learn that in the last twenty days of their lives the sockeyes also ceased to eat and sleep. By the time they washed up on shore, they were mere skeletons.

The air was permeated with the odor of dead fish. Yet in the midst of that odor, Rong could smell the cool refreshing scent of autumn maple leaves, of pine needles, of the icy water of the river, but not of death and corruption, even though on every pebble lay the corpse of a sockeye. She found no sign of pain or struggle in their open eyes — as if death were only a pronoun, a word not appropriate to describe the extravagance and splendor of their ending. Yet those smells and sensations Rong captured only later when she revisited the place. Every fall from then on, during the sockeyes' spawning season, Rong would drive alone from San Francisco to the Adams River. She would walk upstream along the river for two miles, past the old Indian's cabin, and then back. She noticed many things she had overlooked at that time: swarms of dead fish, the odor, and the pair of empty sockets in the fish's head where the eyes had once been. For years, those eyes haunted her, forcing her to confront the fear of death in her subconscious. When a woman decided to prove her love with death, who could challenge her determination? Rong knew she did not have such courage, such heroic strength. Death was too real, and it smelled: empty sockets, rotten body, and all. Rong knew that he, too, was afraid of death.

After years of study, Rong had developed a mixed feeling toward salmon. With instinctive longing, the sockeyes returned to the Adams River. They had no painful memories of their home. They sailed through thousands of miles from all parts of the Pacific back to the Adams River to mate and procreate. When thousands of obsessed salmon crowded into the narrow stream looking for mates and spawning beds, a war broke out below the limpid current. Females used their strong tail fins to sweep away rotten leaves on the bottom of the river, used their sharp teeth to prohibit other females from getting closer. They tried to protect not only the spawning beds, but also most importantly, the males that were attracted by their coquettish tails. At the moment the female sprayed eggs, a male had to fight over from the crowd and accurately ejaculate thousands of sperm toward the descending eggs. After four hundred miles of travel and more than twenty days of fasting, the sockeyes were in their final sprint. Their skins were peeling off, their energies leaked into the water together with their sperm and eggs. But their instinct did not weaken; on the contrary, it reached its peak, the sign of which was their vermilion bodies and raised, golden green heads. Strenuously, they twisted their bodies to attract the attention of the other sex, decorating their desire with the most magnificent colors. On the bodies of the sockeyes, the end of life achieved an extravagance and splendor which was the exact opposite of the life-and-death struggle underwater.

Rong knew they had never thought about this when they came to the Adams River. They had taken the Kakuwal valley as their shield against the past. Once they came here, there was no need to question their awkward fate. When language becomes limp and incompetent, it automatically loses its function. Several times, the irrepressible thrill convulsing her body made her scream. The fractured cries sliced through the valley. Shaken by the momentum of their own bodies, they stopped to listen. What they heard, however, was the echo of despair, bearing no connection whatsoever with the harmonious chords of their lovemaking. Rong swallowed the fluid coming out of his body together with the limpid water. Only later did she realize that thousands of salmon sperm and eggs floated in this water.

Of course that was not the whole of life. It was only an instant's happiness followed by eleven months' loneliness and doubt. By now Rong was accustomed to such doubt, a mental exercise nobler than those practiced by the fish. In the ten years Rong was absent from his life, he had two children with another woman, and built a home; though he and his wife quarreled constantly, they also licked each other's wounds. He could not think of any reason to change a script everyone had already accepted. He simply needed to adjust his mood occasionally in order to rise above the situation. Luckily, in this type of drama, all the dialogue is performed only in one's own heart, with no audience, no critics.

From time to time, Rong had a strong urge to pick up the phone and call his wife. Please, come and watch the sockeyes with us, she would say.

In her moments of doubt, Rong thought of him as a man who drew a strict line between his desire and his responsibilities. While desire waned with the passing of time, responsibilities formed an integral part of life, allowing one a sense of fulfillment. In a web in which desire was held at bay by responsibilities, the task of procreation could be fulfilled easily without the mad and savage instincts of salmon. Yet Rong was just a fish that had escaped through the mesh of such a web. In the sublimation of her aimless migration, she embarked on a pilgrimage. Every autumn she would come to the Adams River, where the desires of summer were sustained in the recollections of fall.

He told her that he might not be able to see her again next summer: the children were older and needed their vacation, and so the family needed to make travel plans. Perhaps he could think of an excuse to get away in winter. There was an echo of guilt in his voice that she could hear even over a long distance call. She did not know if he felt this same guilt making love to his wife. Then I'll go to the river this summer, Rong said. It wouldn't be so bad to go alone and relax a little bit, he said, not realizing that summer was not the season to go to the Adams River.

Summer at the Adams River was, in fact, quite beautiful. No bloody, noisy scenes of spawning salmon, no bears groping for food on the bank, only the peaceful mountain valley and shallow water. Rong took off her shoes in the warm sunlight and waded upstream on the pebbles. Sailing through the ocean storms, through the warm and cold currents, the sockeyes with their spawning instinct probably never realized they were bidding their farewell to the ocean. Possessed by the enormous changes that were taking place inside their bodies, they flaunted the magnificent colors of their scales. They crowded into the shallow stream, leaving behind the once deep and wild ocean life forever. A life of such courage and resolution made Rong envious. If procreation was indeed so important, then perhaps he was right; he had already found his migratory destination.

The Indian cabin appeared on the right. The cabin had been empty since last fall, and the door and windows were starting to fall from their frames. During those years, there were only a few occasions on which they had spoken to the old man. Only twice, perhaps: once when they left their tent in his cabin, and he told them that keeping a fire on the riverbank at night would keep the animals away; another time when they came back to retrieve their tent, and he asked them if they had seen a child playing barefoot in the forest. Obviously, he was telling an Indian legend, but in a way unfamiliar to English speakers. Unable to make himself understood, he turned and walked away. Afterwards, whenever she passed the cabin and saw the vacant eyes of the old man, a strange feeling overcame her, as if she shared his loneliness, a loneliness in which there was no need for language. An iron pot covered with cobwebs now hung on a tripod outside, under the steps. Inside, a sleeping mat chewed up by invading animals lay on the floor, its fabric and stuffing everywhere. After all, one could spend his life in such a way.

You need a family, a child, a normal life. His words fell like snowflakes onto her palm and melted immediately. Rong would like to press this palm to his chest. Like you? Like everybody else? Then why did you come to the Adams River?

In summer, the Adams River was full of inch-long salmon. Rong used her straw hat and caught two struggling little lives. For a long time, she looked at them in the sunlight, contemplating their fate. The survival rate of these fish was one in a thousand, the majority of them perishing on their migratory journey. When these little fish left the Kakuwal valley, tumbling down the waterfalls all the way from the Adams River to the ocean, they didn't know that four years later they would have to retrace every one of their strenuous steps. Following the law of nature, they left the valley; answering the summons of nature, they returned to the valley. It had all been arranged — life and death — no matter how broad the ocean separating the two, no matter how deep the valley.

Rong put the fish back into the water, and lay down in the shallow stream. The water coming from the snowy mountains was cold, and she soon turned numb. She thought about the city she had come from: theaters, libraries, cafés full of people reading newspapers and magazines. The City Lights bookstore was probably holding a reading and the Firehouse Theater still performing excerpts from *Ulysses*. She also re-

LU DE'AN TRANSLATED BY JOHN CAYLEY

THE HARD-WORKING GLAZIER

Earlier than you would have imagined.... He'd
made a visit a few days before, but forgot
his tape, and using only his hands to measure
could still work out and recall the dimensions.

But then a whole week went by
with no news of him, silence.
Those windows, I'm afraid, sooner or later
he'll have to come back and measure again.

The same size, two panes in all,
that was me calling out loudly.
I was in the rear courtyard garden
and he'd already climbed up.

But now ... it's his turn to call to me
from outside the glass
making all kinds of gestures
as if needing some help

a mute, with his hands full
as if frozen stiff
as if someone from another, different season
with a car behind him, parked in the snow.

Years later, I recalled the scene:
that day, I was still sleeping
and he'd already fitted the last piece of glass, without a sound,
and the room was suddenly clean and new and warm.

January 1992

NOVEMBER'S GUIDE

TRANSLATED BY YANBING CHEN

I told you I was just a stranger
who only knew the destination was an island.
The residents later called it a village.
A few trees grew into woods,
and beyond the woods, more woods,
and the sea curls and tumbles beyond these few acres.

House after old house stood, as if pausing on its way to somewhere else.
You can see this from a distance sitting in a car.
Only most of the owners do not live here,
and it'd be rare if any of them showed up more than once a year.
Such a waste, such a good place.
And the sea curls and tumbles beyond these few acres.

So quiet around here it seems almost like a story,
the conclusion of a story, and an enviable one at that.
It says a hundred years ago
a hurricane swept half of the village houses
to the bottom of the sea, and among them there was a church.
And the sea curls and tumbles beyond these few acres.

Real estate developers dropped off, like scattered leaves
the locals dropped off, like scattered leaves
but before long they all returned....
the same way they left.
The houses were restored, according to memory.
And the sea curls and tumbles beyond these few acres.

More people came, and that's how he got to know
what was going on outside … only now
they built fences, and a better church,
and fishing poles stretch out from the yachts —
those who have money like playing that way.
And the sea curls and tumbles beyond these few acres.

Because there are birds during the day, and stars at night,
because those who have money have money, and can afford it.
The locals are growing old.
Only they always come to the seaside in the evening
to listen to the sound of bells from the sea,
listen to that church at the bottom of the sea....

And the sea curls and tumbles beyond these few acres.

November 1991

Xu Xiao

TRANSLATED BY H. BATT

A MAY THAT WILL LAST FOREVER

It was autumn when I chose my husband's grave. The cemetery was in Beijing's Western Hills, surrounded by green pines and cedars against a background of smoke-trees. Their purple flowers and green leaves tinged the atmosphere with a simple dignity. The friends who had accompanied me thought it was a suitable place, so I said, "Then let's arrange it."

I knew it was not what he'd wanted. Before he died, he'd said he wanted to be buried under a Chinese scholar-tree, simple and serene, with a drooping crown covered with unobtrusive, scentless, tiny white-toothed blossoms in spring. If I could have lived in a courtyard, I'd have planted a scholar-tree and buried him beneath it, watered it, pruned it, watched it grow thick, tall, and sturdy, year after year, until I was old, until I died.

At these times such a simple desire is nothing more than a dying man's extravagance. So once again, keep your regret to yourself.

I first met Zhou Meiying at the home of Bei Dao. It was the winter of 1978. Zhou Meiying saw the first issue of *Today* on The Democracy Wall. He left his name and address and passed word of the meeting around to his many friends. That first day, except for Bei Dao, I knew nobody. The people who left me with the deepest impression were Zhou and Cheng Yu. Cheng Yu had been jailed because of his involvement in the "April 5th Tiananmen Incident," and we had both been in the Half-Step Bridge Detention Center, although we hadn't been tried together.

What made the deepest impression on me about Zhou was his beard, which covered only his chin, leaving both cheeks bare. At first I thought he was being unconventional, trying to start a new fashion. Only later did I realize his beard was too thin to shave. In the hospital, the nurses called him "the old goat."

He came almost every day after work to the meetings at Liu Qing and Liu Nian-chun's — Number 76. He said little, but gave the impression of having great depth of character. The men usually drank. Some routinely got drunk and made such a spectacle of themselves that one didn't know whether to laugh or cry. His capacity for drink was by no means inferior to fellows' like Bei Dao, Mang Ke, Huang Rui or Hei Da-chun, but he never became inebriated. Like so many deities of the cup, he never got drunk, but always played the role of the big brother who picked up the pieces, took the drunken one home or sat with him out on the street until dawn, listening to him pour out his heart as he sobered up.

I clearly remember one Sunday afternoon. We were at Number 76 every Sunday to print and bind the current issue of *Today*. Although conditions were terribly difficult, we enjoyed the task, which everyone felt was a sacred one. In the evening we went over to Zhao Nan's for meetings. We read to each other from our novels, poetry, and plays — whether we knew each other or not — and sometimes we read to each other from famous works. It was here that I first heard the poetry of Yevtushenko and Octavio Paz, it was here that I got to know the name of Marguerite Duras, and came to adore her after reading her short story "Moderato Cantabile."

That Sunday afternoon the sunlight was pale and languid, broken into jumbled fragments by Number 76's chaotic, dilapidated courtyard. He stood in the sunlight, long-legged, pigeon-toed, slightly stooped in a pair of shoes that had lost their shine, trousers with frayed cuffs, and a long beard on his chin — the portrait of dishevelment. I don't remember who he was talking with at that moment, or what he was saying, but I do remember his gesture, his expression. Arms crossed in front of his chest, stern, as if there was a thought forming in his mind ... his usual appearance. In the endless days and nights after he died, I tried my utmost to recall the days we'd spent together after we got to know each other. Many inessential details I can't remember; only his features, his gestures, his movements, his expression stand out in my memory, ineradicable. Sometimes, when I wasn't expecting it, he'd suddenly appear, pushing his clattering, beat-up bicycle, leisurely walking up with that old, worn yellow school bag over his shoulder, one shoulder higher than the other; walking up to me with a serious expression in his green coat. I felt his gaze, his breath, the scent of him was an indescribable sensation. Whenever I felt that sensation, I knew my every past use of the word "despair" had been rash.

He stood there that Sunday, and at that moment, in the afternoon light a strange thought came over me: if I wanted, he would fall in love with me. I could make him fall in love with me.

The idea first pleased me; then frightened me. At the time I was in love with someone else, while he, urged by people around him, was giving in to a certain girl's love, not to mention the story that was circulating about his attempted suicide due to an earlier love affair. It was only several years later that we truly fell in love, and several more years before we were married, had a child, experienced all of love's joys and fears, the hope of life, the despair of death ... but it all began that afternoon, the instant he turned around by chance, reached out toward a girl with his usual stern expression — as if there was some thought in his mind, and touched her.

A little more than a year later, *Today* was suppressed, but we met more frequently than ever.

His work unit was downtown. His friends would drop by, stay a while, then wouldn't feel like leaving, so his office became his parlor. There were often unofficial meetings after work. Whenever someone came it was always a bowl of noodles, make it two, maybe a five-cent fried wheatcake. The conversation ranged far and wide: national affairs, family affairs, there was nothing under heaven we didn't discuss. Sometimes little was said ... the silence that follows the resolution of every problem when there's nothing left to say, and everyone's satisfied. The poet Tian Shao-qing describes his feelings about those days like this: "No matter when we met or how long it had been since we'd seen each other, just to sit down with Zhou, drink a glass of beer and chat gave me the peaceful feeling that the world hadn't changed." In an essay on Hei

Da-chun, Wei An calls Zhou "the nurturer of poets." I don't like this description. The praise is overdone. Although it proceeds from good intentions, it doesn't correspond to the facts, though I believe the restless soul of an eighteen-year-old boy could become peaceful and silent in the course of such an all-night talk.

This kind of conversation between soul mates became his style of life, his mode of existence. The mutual understanding between him and other men, knowing and treasuring each other's strengths, knowing and forgiving each other's weaknesses, became the fulcrum of his existence, his life's work that continued unbroken to the very end. I believe that if so many friends cherish his memory, it's because by remembering him, they remember their youth, their naiveté, their sincerity and their dreams. Where shall we go now to find the Old Summer Palace where we met in those years? What shall we do to set out again on those country outings with bottles of beer and dried bread in our backpacks, playing our youthful games in the open fields?

I became his regular guest, coming to know more and more of his experiences as well as who he was.

In 1956, when he was just ten years old, he went to the hospital with serious stomach problems. After exploratory surgery he was diagnosed with lymphosarcoma, a condition as dangerous as a malignant tumor. It required surgery and then radiation. Our country's medical technology and treatment facilities were primitive back then. In the course of radiation treatments his back and stomach were burned to sheets of scar tissue. For decades afterward he suffered from radiation enteritis. The internal scars adhered to his intestines. He missed a year in primary school and another in middle school, and when the cultural revolution began, he was in his third year at Beijing Number 65 High School.

On account of his health, he wasn't sent to the countryside towards the end of the Cultural Revolution, and so his home naturally became the transfer center for other educated youth who had been allowed back to the city. Returning from Shanxi, Shaanxi, Inner Mongolia, Northeast China, from the villages, from the army, his classmates, and his classmates' classmates, his friends and his friends' friends, his relatives and his relatives' relatives all brought back vast quantities of local news. Though he didn't experience them in the flesh, he heard with his own ears the heartrending tales of those political movements: public criticisms, struggle sessions, suicides, imprisonment of educated youths he knew, and of those he didn't know. Their accounts made him feel as if he had suffered them himself. In those years, he was always busy calling on the mothers and fathers of classmates and friends, making phony phonecalls and sending false messages for those who had come to see their parents and didn't want to leave Beijing immediately for the countryside, busy seeing someone off at the station, meeting someone at the station.

At the same time, he read an enormous amount of literature. Sometimes he spent days on end at the library. Galsworthy, Dostoyevsky, Tolstoy, Hugo, Dickens, the exposure and analysis of good and evil, and the depression, indecision, resistance, despair of the educated youth, all mixed up together, were like a profound spiritual baptism for him. In a letter to a classmate assigned as a worker to Inner Mongolia, he wrote: "This morning I went to a friend's wedding, and I felt happy for him. When I got home in the evening I learned that another friend had been condemned to death. What could I do? That's life." One can imagine his feelings seeing off friends, and his feelings afterward, alone in Beijing.

In 1975, one of his high school classmates, who'd been sent to Inner Mongolia, was suspected of being involved in a murder because he'd helped put up political posters on behalf of ruralized educated youth, some of which, in attacking Lin Biao, contained the expression, "Gang of Four." Many educated youth were jailed. He actively involved himself in the case. He was going off everywhere, advising, planning action. One of his classmates who worked on it with him recalls that whatever materials for the appeal passed through his hands became clear, organized, forceful. The appeal soon had results: the Beijing Military District assigned investigators, the case took a sudden turn, some of the young people were quickly released, and those actually involved were dealt with leniently.

Heedless of the risks, he helped countless friends avoid investigation. Unable to endure their sufferings, he took up their cases. At other times, he patiently acted as mediator, helping friends to resolve love affairs and marital conflicts, sympathetically listened to friends as they poured out the bitterness in their hearts. I often heard him tell of love triangles, suicides in the name of love, personal accusations, disputes settled in private, disputes brought to the police and to the courts. He couldn't avoid getting entangled in misunderstandings and grievances. It was as if there were a public meeting, an invisible moral court where he was the judge, resolving *gratis* an endless stream of cases.

They all said he was a good person, that he created himself — or rather that everyone created for him — the following reputation: if you have a problem, he's the first one you think of. He focuses his entire attention on you, he can follow your train of thought, complete what you start to say, doesn't jump to conclusions, and doesn't simply say what you want to hear. He tries to get you to stand in your adversary's shoes and examine the problem over again from their angle. Even if you're wrong, he'll never make you feel rejected; when you need help, he'll sympathize and understand, give you his time and his money, and won't let you refuse; but when everything's going your way, he won't gild the lily with offers of unwanted help.

He once told me about a worker in his factory who had three children. The husband and wife made less than sixty *yuan* a month. In winter the family ate cabbage and pickled vegetables, in summer they bought heaps of cucumbers. He often helped them out with money. Once at New Year's he gave the worker twenty *yuan*. When New Year's was over, he was displeased to see him wearing a new coat and trousers and couldn't help saying, "The money was to improve things for the children. If you'd bought twenty *yuan*'s worth of meat and eaten it in one meal, I wouldn't have minded. If you needed more, I'd have found a way to help. But I didn't give it to you to buy yourself clothes." A few days later, the worker simply paid him back. When he told me the story many years later he still got upset over it. "You don't know how much I hated myself at that moment, how I wanted to slap myself in the face. Other people wear new clothes. Why shouldn't he? Just because he was poor. He was a person, too. He was a man, a father of three children. Didn't he have the right to decide to buy new clothes? Just because the money was somebody else's — mine. Just because I could still pull out another twenty *yuan*, that gave me the right to lecture him, attack his self-esteem. What kind of a person had I turned into? But you don't know how miserable his three children...." He told all this without any beating around the bush. I don't know why, but at the time it reminded me of Montanelli's confessions. I felt terrible for him, but there was nothing I could say. He'd been wrong and I couldn't think of an argument to comfort him. I understood how he felt when he saw those children. This wasn't the usual case of good intentions gone awry, of ineffectual sympathy. He'd gotten trapped in a conflict between two good purposes and couldn't pay attention to both, and so I felt all the worse for him.

The best example of his character was his unrequited love. She was divorced and worked in a factory in another city, with only her aged mother to help bring up her young daughter in Beijing. And during the Cultural Revolution, to come from a "five black" family, and with relatives living abroad ... no need to say how hard it was for her. Before she'd managed to get transferred back to Beijing, he came once a week for several years to fetch her old mother's water and coal, and run errands all over the city for her. I can't really say whether it was sympathy or love between them, whether sympathy led to love, or love engendered sympathy, but in the seventies, to choose a relationship like this took courage. He used to compare it to carrying a cross. The reason they were finally unable to marry was not because he found the cross unbearable, but because his mother, tied to tradition, couldn't accept his marriage to a divorced woman with a child. He loved his mother so much, and didn't want to hurt her, that he carried a double cross and no one got what they wanted. Three swords piercing three hearts. His mother was heartbroken that he was getting old and still unmarried, and he finally parted forever from the woman he had been unhappily in love with for so many years. For a while all this cast a shadow over our relationship. A love story's first chapter is romantic, but the conclusion can't help being humdrum. One hopes to make everything come true, but the result is never what one dreamed.

Maybe he began to feel that what one can do for another is too little, and gradually revised his creed to "Do what I must, do what I can," but no matter how tired he was, no matter how difficult things got, however much he suffered, he never grumbled and never complained. More than once I heard him say, to me or to someone else, "If you're hurt, there's nothing else to do but just crouch in the corner, lick your wounds, then stand back up as if nothing's wrong."

On New Year's Eve, 1985, we were finally married: no ceremony, no apartment, no money. We didn't even tell our families. Our entire household furnishings consisted of two, fifty-cent aluminum pots. We cooked our meals with those pots in the apartment of a friend who was temporarily out of town, using a five hundred watt electric hotplate. That's how we spent our honeymoon. All I could think was, as long as I have him, I have everything. Twenty days later he was taken to the hospital with an intestinal obstruction.

When he came out of the hospital, two months later, we moved into a borrowed apartment. It was only a little more than ten square meters, but it felt like home.

In winter, the pot on the stove and the cold outside conspired to cover the windows in ice. When he got home the first thing he always did was take off his steamed glasses and say as he wiped them, "Our place is warm." We toasted steamed bread or fried pancakes on the stove, talked about what had happened at our work units, discussed our mutual friends, and recalled stories about the old days in Beijing. If it happened to be a snowy day and friends came over, he was like a kid. He'd change the line "old friends come visiting on a stormy day" to "old friends come visiting on a snowy day." He'd fuss about, drink with them, then we'd all eat Mongolian hot pot. In summer, he liked to drink new beer. In those years, new beer wasn't easy to come by in Beijing, and I often stood in line with two mismatched plastic buckets, because I knew that when he got home from work, if he didn't have some new beer to drink, especially if friends stopped by, he wouldn't be able to sit still.

Our little apartment was never dreary. Someone would always drop by unannounced. Shi Tiesheng often visited. We had no sofa and no armchair in our little room, so we had a folding chair specially ready for him. Tiesheng would turn into our doorway on his wheelchair, give a shout, and Zhou would go out and carry him in on his back. Afterward, when Zhou's health got worse, Tiesheng wrote a sign and stuck it up on our cupboard: "The host isn't well and needs rest. Guests will please limit their visits to fifteen minutes." Guests would start to get nervous after fifteen minutes, but Zhou always insisted, "That wasn't written for you, take it easy."

I'd always been against drinking. After I got to know him, I often heard him say, "Someone who doesn't drink can't understand the land of 'Meeting soul mates over wine ... a thousand cups are still too few.'" He always said, as long as something impels people toward the good, whatever it is, there's no reason to oppose it. He more or less convinced me, and from then on I wasn't blindly opposed to drinking. Though he was never choosy about what he drank, or what he ate with it, he was quite exacting about his drinking partners, and never drank with people of the sort, "When words are out of tune, half a phrase is too much." The conversation topic and the conversation partner were his favorite snacks with drink. It was not as accurate to say of him that he liked to drink as to say he liked to meet friends over drink, not as true to say he was a connoisseur of beer as to say he was a connoisseur of people, of life.

He certainly had refined taste, and could bring out the savor in bland things, bring out the sweet in bitter people. By taste he could accurately tell whether one dish needed onions or if another had too much Shaoxing wine. To others a soup without pepper was tasteless, for him it was inedible. If fried instead of boiled with salt and pepper, shrimp was no longer shrimp, peanuts no longer peanuts. He didn't care what there was to eat, but how it was cooked, and with whom it was to be eaten.

He liked eating tree-of-heaven leaves, and Shi Tiesheng liked eating them, too. Every year when the leaves came out, they both picked the tenderest leaves from the trees near their houses and brought them to me, and afterward, when the leaves were for sale in the market, they brought more. It became a kind of ritual for him. When he lay in the hospital as this season came, his face took on a pitiful look because he couldn't eat tree-of-heaven leaves with Shi Tiesheng. In his last year, his mother boiled him up some peanuts mixed with tree-of-heaven leaves. He saved half and had me take them to Tiesheng. He knew, of course, that on every street there were tree of heaven leaves for sale, and I was horribly busy, but still he pressed me over and over to take them: if I couldn't take them today then put them in the refrigerator and take them tomorrow. Tree-of-heaven leaves were no longer tree-of-heaven leaves in his mind; they had become a symbol. Eating, in his mind, was no longer eating; it was enjoying things we love together with those we love and who love us.

He was particularly concerned that nothing materialistic, nothing profit-oriented should be discussed in gatherings with his friends. Whenever they met, I used to call his invariable smile his "parentheses" on his thin face. When he was enjoying himself, he used to sing Beijing opera, local opera, Shaoxing opera, folksongs, foreign songs, any kind of song so long as it was authentic. The song he sang most movingly was the northern folksong "Little Cabbage":

Little cabbage, withered in the field,

Three years old, mommy's gone....

He wasn't a good singer. His voice was thin and wavering, but it was exactly right for this song.

I was quite willing to cook and buy drink for these gatherings. I was used to preparing for them. I don't know if I'm like all wives in this, but that's how I was, and I was happy to be that way. At times like that, I felt lucky. Maybe my understanding of luck is a superficial one, and I ask too little. Maybe I'm ignorant and ill-informed, but I felt that this was a woman's genuine good fortune, my good fortune. Now, with his photo hanging in my room over my bed, the first thing I see of him in my mind is the way he was among his friends: laughing, singing, now speaking with fervor and assurance, now muttering to himself, his happy expression when he started to laugh, his "parentheses," the nervous excitement of his lips. He used to point to me and tell everybody, "This is my wife. My wife pickled these mustard greens.... This is my wife's fishhead soup ... such a good cook ... nothing like it anywhere else...." As I remember this, I think that if time could flow backward, and I could love him anew with a twenty-year-old's fervor and a forty-year-old's understanding, even if his illness had been dragged out longer, I'd be there, doing what I had to, doing what I could. I truly think this, whether others believe me or not. If only time could flow backward....

He generally disliked commotion, even more so because of his poor health. After 1989, he became more taciturn than ever. When there were no guests, he often sat silent for long periods of time. He could read for hours on end, and read quickly. He read so extensively that he made me, with my degree in Chinese literature, feel left in the dust. He liked to be alone, and even when he was with people he still spoke little. His reticence was both his means of attack and defense; convenient and effective. Once, when someone attacked him in conversation, he gave no reply for three hours, absolutely nothing, until his adversary was utterly discomfited.

Many of his friends who'd emigrated sent him a New Year's card every year, but they never got a single reply. He persistently refused to send one. They couldn't figure him out.

After he became ill, I helped him put his papers in order. These included love letters, all in the same handwriting, from southern China. They were written to him when he was young, from an amateur writer of some reputation, romantic and full of deep feeling. Putting the dozens of letters in order, I discovered there was only one common theme from start to finish: his failure to reply.

I could understand the helpless frustration of a woman in love never receiving a single letter in response. Before we were married, there was one argument that almost led to our breakup. He wasn't like most men who tried to make up with their lovers. His face was constantly pale, he gritted his teeth, he didn't plead, he never snapped, he never made a scene, he didn't use sweet talk, he just stood waiting outside the gate where I worked, keeping out of sight. Finally I couldn't take his silence any more.

After we were married, I experienced even more of his "tongue of steel." If he decided not to talk, all threats and promises would be to no avail, and if you tried to deal with him with a cold shoulder, then you would be playing right into his hands: if you could stick it out without a word for ten days, he would pay you back with a silence of twenty. With his friends he could forget himself and be infinitely tolerant; to me he was ruthless.

Our first fight after we were married was over a little ball of dough. I'd finished making dumplings and cut the leftover dough into noodles. I didn't have a chance to boil them over the next few days, and since it was hot they started to turn black, so I threw them into the garbage. He accused me of wasting food. I thought he was making a fuss over nothing, and in the end we had a bitter quarrel.

His simple material needs and lack of interest in wealth and fame won him many people's respect, and I myself thought there was no difference between us on this point, but in the little everyday affairs of family life, they became an obstacle. His frugality reached the point where I couldn't bear it.

Six years after we were married, we were finally allotted a two-room apartment. I hoped to make our home a warm and beautiful one. As a wife and mother, I wanted to spend all my energy making my husband's and son's lives as good as other husbands' and sons'. What was wrong with that?

But he said, "As far as I'm concerned, living in an old one-story cottage or an apartment building is all the same. What's the difference? Either way, I can have my friends over. I can read, play chess, listen to music."

We didn't have a color television, and before we had our son I didn't mind. But as our son gradually got bigger, and wanted to watch cartoons, I thought we should buy one.

He said, "When we were young we didn't have television, and we were able to expand our minds all the same." He objected to my dressing up, "Whatever you wear, it's all the same to me. If I cared that you're not beautiful I wouldn't have married you." I had to admit I wasn't as detached from material possessions as he was. I was more ordinary. But I was a woman, a woman who wholeheartedly looked after my husband, my son, my home. If no one acknowledges your effort, no one understands your dreams, in short, nobody acknowledges your feelings, you feel wronged. I resented his eccentricity and lack of common sense. I hated his coldness and indifference. I felt his stinginess and his generosity, his prejudices and his extremes were all an attack on me; an attempt to torture me.

If I place his body, his experiences, his character down in this manuscript when his life is past, and it's all history, and I read it all through carefully from beginning to end, I find it's not hard to understand. If he'd tired himself out for fame, power, and money, would he still have been the same old Zhou his friends knew and loved? If he hadn't emphasized to the utmost the things he valued, in a time when society was being torn apart, how could he have preserved himself from being torn apart? How could a man, weak from the torments of illness, without a strong body, without brilliant accomplishments, have gained people's honor and won their reverence? Why, again, would I have worshipped him in those years, loved him, married him? Of course he wasn't perfect. He followed the bright light in tradition, and was shrouded by the shadows of tradition. He despised custom, but wasn't able to change life. If someone who thought he was perfect was disappointed, that wasn't his fault.

For four years, from 1991 until his death, he was so ill he couldn't leave his bed.

What did two failed operations mean? It meant that a man who appreciated the color and flavor of the most ordinary things in life would now be bound to a bed, forced to endure a hopeless course of treatment. It meant a man who could not endure troubling others had now lost the power to care for himself. It meant a frugal man now had to spend hundreds of *yuan* a day to stay alive — and all this was the result of a misdiagnosis.

After thirty years, it's impossible to know whether the sample was taken improperly, or if the lab test was botched, or if there was a problem with the microscope. Later, when a preserved sample of the biopsy was reexamined, it showed that the so-called lymphosarcoma that they'd made so much of was nothing but an inflamed lymph node. But whom to question, where to protest? All he could do was submit to fate. The glucose, the albumin, the plasma, the transfusions flowed drop by drop, bottle by bottle, day after day, year after year into his body, unable to arrest its gradual decline, with every nerve abnormally sensitive and fragile, every cell dying.

He kept saying, "I'm tired, I have no strength." This wasn't exhaustion in its usual sense. When his condition reached its worst, his shoulders, his legs, his neck, even his eyelids and fingers lay motionless; a burden to him. Without nutrients, his weight fell to ninety pounds. A five foot seven inch man unable to support the weight of his own body, lying there as if he were about to float away. I massaged him constantly, from his head to his feet. I thought it was the only way for him to feel his own existence.

Before the operations he wasn't allowed to eat, which of course left him famished. For nearly half a year he ate nothing, couldn't even suck on a piece of fruit candy. I squeezed watermelon juice through a piece of gauze and gave it to him in a spoon. After the operation he was permitted food, but he had no appetite. When he ate he became sick and vomited. Then there was the diarrhea, every day, seven or eight times, whether he ate or not. I'd help him to the bathroom, holding his bag of glucose. I couldn't tell from the sound whether it was urine or feces.

Then there was the dropsy, the dizziness, the rapid heartbeat, the open scars on his stomach, like blood-red eyes always oozing pus, always filthy even after several changes of dressing a day ... so horrible the nurses couldn't bear to look at them.

Most unbearable of all was the inexplicable fever, constantly higher and higher, until in the final six months it hardly ever went down. In the morning it was 37.5°C or 38°C degrees, by afternoon it was 39°C, sometimes 40°C, day after day, until everyone was used to it. Even I got used to it. It became routine. I'd bathe him in ethyl alcohol to cool him, then call a nurse to give him an injection to bring his temperature down, then sit by him until he burst out into a sweat and his temperature went down to 38°C, then sponge him off with hot water, then leave the hospital; not that it bothered me to stay overnight in the hospital. In the last year there were many nights I never went home, but at some point I began going home no matter how late it was. I didn't know what I could do for him by staying, but in the end I regretted it.

The most depressing thing for me were all the tubes sticking into him, long and short ones, as many as five at a time. The tubes in his major veins brought on the risk of septicemia and pneumothorax, both of which he was getting constantly. After the second operation the infection and the pneumothorax sent him to the emergency room. I watched the doctors insert a needle as big as a knitting needle into his chest. My legs went weak under me. I wept. He'd been ill for three years then, and I thought I was beyond crying. But I wept. It was unfair to him; it was unjust. Why did every disaster have to fall on him, just because he was so strong? God was unjust.

Nothing could change all this; money and medicine were equally impotent. No one who saw him imprisoned on that hospital bed could help or console him. A healthy person stands empty before one who faces new sufferings, new tortures, new decisions every day, every month, every year. If many of his friends seldom came, it was not from lack of sympathy; it was that they didn't know how to express their sympathy to a person who accepted no sympathy. Not that they were indifferent, but that they could not stand indifferent before one who, thirsting for life, was dying.

He lay in the hospital for three years, fully conscious, with full use of his limbs, but without strength and in terrible pain. Endurance had become his daily ritual. Between an easy death and his struggle with illness, he had chosen the latter. When his spirits were good he could read a bit, when they were not so good he would listen to the radio with an earphone; when things got worse he lay with his eyes closed. He was always quiet. Nobody ever heard him shout or groan. He was born with the ability to "grit your teeth and take it." He was good at using a blank stare to make people leave him quietly. One reason I kept running three times a day to the hospital was that I knew he would never call a nurse or a doctor; often his fever was over 39°C and nobody knew. He took tubes down his stomach like he was eating noodles. No matter what the treatment, no matter whether it was a new intern or a nurse-in-training, he always said, "Come on, it's all right, try it again, try it again…." His arm was black and blue. New nurses thought it was strange — why was this patient so special, why was there no need for instructions before giving him painkillers? The assistant head who operated on him said in forty years of practice he'd never seen a patient so tough.

We never discussed it, but we both knew that there was no hope. Still he couldn't help wanting to live. On New Year's Day, 1994, I bought him the biggest red balloon I could find and hung it in the window. When New Year's was over, it was covered with dust and I threw it away. He lost his temper at me, said we could have used it next year. I said if I kept the balloon it would be no good by next New Year's anyway, and besides, who knew if we'd celebrate New Year's in the hospital, so why worry about it so much. I never imagined my words could hurt him. He angrily replied, "Yes, next year you don't know if I'll be dead or not, right?"

In April, when the weather was at its best, we went out into the hospital courtyard to get some sun. A milk-white intravenous bag hung from the wheelchair our son pushed. It had been a long time since he'd been outdoors. He kept saying how nice the flowers were. That day I'd brought our son's jump rope. I bought him his favorite melon seeds and some ice cream for our son. He sat under a cherry tree and watched the child skip rope until his face was all red and he was covered in sweat. He mumbled some encouragement to the child, told me to be sure he got enough exercise. For our little family, that was a real holiday.

The only time we'd ever gone to the park was on our son's first birthday. That was in spring too. He sat him on his shoulders so that the child's eyes were wide with fright. A one-year-old remembers little; that day in the hospital courtyard was our son's last and only memory of a spring outing with Daddy.

A few days later it was his birthday. I'd talked with our son about buying a small television as a birthday present, but Zhou was resolutely opposed to the idea. So I had to forget about it and instead bought some red chrysanthemums and brought his son to see him. When he took the flowers he cried. I'd never bought flowers for him before because I knew he didn't like cut flowers. Several times when friends had bought him flowers, he made them take them home. But this time he was happy, and kept saying how nice they were, put them into the tin vase himself, kept rearranging them.

Six days later the flowers were withered, the leaves turned yellow, the petals curled up, dejected, defeated. The next day I got an emergency call from the hospital. By the time I got there, his pulse was already gone.

I washed his body, shaved him, changed his clothes, held his hand as it went from red to white to gray; that hand, semi-transparent as a candle. It was so familiar to me, that hand, pale, dry and hot, the bones and arteries visible beneath the skin — he was often so restless he couldn't fall asleep until I would stroke it. When I'd been sick ten years before, he'd spread towels on my forehead, he'd helped me turn my father in his sickbed and help change his clothes ... we weren't married then ... but I already knew those hands, already completely knew him.

Did he die calling my name? Was there something he wanted to tell me he hadn't had time his whole life to say? I believe ... I'd rather believe ... if I'd been there, he'd already have been at his last gasp, but if he'd still been alive, my wish would have been fulfilled. Maybe his voice would have been so faint that nobody else would have been able to hear, but I would have been able to hear. I simply can't get over the fact that I wasn't there. May is not merely a month of sorrow. It is an infinite abyss.

For several years after, I imagined myself wandering in a desert. With almost self-admiration I watched this woman — lonely, desolate, but sure of herself — withering in the best season of her life, breaking, scattering, and dying, moment by moment, but believing with her whole heart that someday she would achieve a perfect beauty through her self-destruction, and rise in her own creation.

No one understood the beauty, the profoundness and ingenuity of silence better than he. For someone who truly believes "silence is golden," to say nothing is better than to say everything.

But when all is said and done, it's no longer silence. He is no longer paralyzed, no longer blind, no longer deaf, dumb ... his life is over.

Sometimes looking back on that year, I feel as if I was watching events happening at some other time. I had experienced death before and thought I knew what it meant to be the living left behind: a void that life would soon fill up. But for a family, one person more or one person less is not a matter of numbers. The disappearance of one is the disappearance of everything. And time cannot ease everything. A person, once a part of your life, is your blue sky, your sunlight, your air. Once they are gone, life becomes overcast forever.

March 1995, Beijing

GU XIAOYANG   TRANSLATED BY DUNCAN HEWITT

TRUANT DAYS

It must have been sometime around 1968 when our school set up a "study group for hooligans," to which, without a moment's hesitation, our teacher sent me. I was twelve and in fifth grade.

The "study group" consisted of some twenty pupils — the most notorious students in school. There were the ones who were always getting into fights; the compulsive vandals who broke light bulbs, wrecked chairs and desks, smashed doors and windows; the pickpockets and petty thieves. Most of them were troublemakers who had been a disruptive influence in the classroom. My offense was: "smoking, drinking, singing dirty songs, and fraternizing with dubious individuals."

The first time I smoked was when I stole one of my father's "Great China" cigarettes. My friend and I hid in the doorway, as if plotting some great conspiracy. He taught me how to draw the smoke into my lungs. I smoked two in a row and my head started to spin. By the time I got home I was feeling a bit sick ... I lay down on my bed and started eating an apple, but I'd barely taken a couple of bites when I fell into a deep sleep. Later we used to go to a house that had a dressing table and do our smoking there, so that we could practice holding in the smoke in front of the mirror.

My dad was a serious smoker; when he was reading he'd go through one after another. I'd sit somewhere where he wouldn't be likely to notice me and watch him closely. He could inhale a quarter of a cigarette in one drag — and it was only a long time afterwards that a faint puff of smoke would slip from his lips or nostrils. I could never figure out where the rest of it went. At first my friends and I assumed there must be some kind of trick to this, and we practiced again and again, but we could never get it right; however long we held the smoke in our stomachs, when we exhaled there'd still be a thick white cloud, more or less as much as we'd breathed in. Needless to say, everyone was full of admiration for a seasoned smoker like my dad.

We were actually extremely careful to keep our smoking a secret. Most of the time we did it at Dali's house, listening to records. Dali's place had just been ransacked by the Red Guards, and all the rooms had been stripped bare — but by some fluke the one thing which had escaped unscathed was an old Russian gramophone. One time we were listening to *Love of the Butterfly* when Chicken Xie came charging in all flustered, shouting: "Quick! The cop's are coming!" The words had barely left his lips when in walked the policeman. "What's this you're listening to — *Love of the Butterfly*?" he asked in an expert tone. Then he marched over to the gramophone, picked up the record and walked out. We were left sitting in a cold sweat. "Shit," said Chicken Xie, "the moment he heard it he knew it was the *Butterfly* — the guy must be an old pro."

My experience with drinking goes back a bit further than my smoking. There was a period of time when it was extremely fashionable to sell off old, used things. I sold the 1964-66 editions of *The People's Daily*, with hardly a day missing. Dali's elder brother lugged out two copies of *Das Kapital* — they were bigger than the stones in the city wall, but they turned out to be worth next to nothing. I can't remember what the others managed to get their hands on. We took our things to the Salvage Station at Gongyuan, exchanged them for cash and then headed straight for the Dongdan Restaurant; we squeezed around one table and each ordered a big bowl of draft beer, as if we were in one of those gatherings of the heroes in *Outlaws of the Marsh*, where "downing the liquor, they flung their silver pieces on the table and yelled to the inn-keeper's lad to come and fetch them."

My teacher's name was Mr. Wa, otherwise known as "Old Cow." He had a small head, a body of solid muscle, two slits for eyes, and a mouth that never shut quite properly. He'd been sent to us fresh out of his final year at high school. As far as I can remember, that was the time when all the middle school students were about to be sent into the mountains or down to the countryside. How he managed to stay in Beijing as an elementary school teacher I never figured out. From the very beginning Old Cow saw me as a thorn in his side. When I think back I can't recall a thing he taught us, or what methods he used; all I can remember is how he used to make me stand up in class, and how he criticized me and forced me to write self-criticisms again and again. When we went on rallies — to celebrate the publication of Chairman Mao's latest instruction or China's successful detonation of the atom bomb, or to protest against the Soviet Union for annexing Zhenbao Island, and so on — he used to take advantage of the darkness and the crowds to give me a good kick in the butt.... I guess the fact that I can write a bit today is not unconnected to Mr Wa's cruelty back then in making me write all those self-criticisms. I remember one day when class stopped for lunch, he wouldn't let me go home, and insisted that I write a thorough self-criticism while he went to the cafeteria to have his lunch. There was no one else in the classroom, and after I'd written two lines I laid my head on the desk and fell asleep. Eventually a teacher happened to come in and see me there, and asked me why I wasn't going home. My reply must have sounded really pathetic, because he thought for a moment then said: "Leave it, you don't have to write it. Go home and get yourself some lunch!"

In those days the Beijing Public Security Bureau often held "Public Show Trials" in the Workers' Stadium. They were called trials, but in fact the verdicts had already been written long in advance. First the official in charge would make a speech: "At the moment the situation at home and abroad is broadly positive, but the class enemies are up to such and such…" and then he'd read out the verdict. There was always a batch of people who'd been given the death sentence. The convicts were always trussed up, their legs in shackles, a signboard around their necks. There were three policemen, one on either side and one standing behind, gripping the prisoner by the collar. When the official in charge read out: "X's crimes are great and have caused extreme outrage. In accord with the law you are sentenced to death, to be carried out immediately," the policeman behind kicked the prisoner to the ground, and the crowds started chanting "Down with X!", "If the enemy doesn't surrender he'll be wiped out!", "Long live the dictatorship of the proletariat!", and "Long live the all-conquering thought of Mao Zedong!" The atmosphere was one of high excitement and drama. The people sentenced to death came in all shapes and sizes. There were active counter-revolutionaries, fugitive landlords, rapists, murderers.... I still remember the name of one of the condemned men, he was called Xia Du'ke. He couldn't have been more than a few years older (he was also still a minor); his father was an official in a government ministry, and the family lacked nothing. But this young man had been breaking into houses. He had fallen into a life of petty crime, and for this he was taken away and executed.

What I found hardest to understand about Old Cow was this: when I was in the Hooligans' Study Group, whenever there was a public trial and people were going to be executed, he always insisted I go along and watch. I asked him what the point was. He said he wanted me to go for "educational purposes." But what did executing people have to do with me? What sort of education was I going to get from that? Just because, at the age of twelve, I'd sung a line from a "pornographic song" — "You ripe flower bud ... suddenly you open up, oh, what a beauty" — that was still a pretty far cry from committing a capital offense! Could it be that he realized my "crimes" weren't "great," and the "outrage" wasn't "extreme," and so he wanted me to learn a few more tricks from other people, so that I'd soon be trussed up and dragged out to the execution ground myself?

Later there was one time when we were supposed to be meeting at the north gate of the Worker's Stadium. That day there was a huge rainstorm. As I was riding there on my bike I suddenly made up my mind to head for Guangxumenwai to buy vegetables. That was the first time I ever played truant.

One day not long after, I went to play basketball at the Dongdan Stadium with a bunch of middle school students; by evening we were starving, so we walked over to Taijichang — to what's now the "Pine and Crane House," but in those days was a small Shanghai snack shop — to get a bite to eat. For some reason the "innkeeper's boy" realized as soon as he set eyes on us that something wasn't right; after we'd ordered our food, he came back and asked us whether we wanted anything to drink, so we ordered a few bottles of "petite champagne." The moment we'd finished our feast, still clutching half a steamed bun in my hand, we headed for the door. But as soon as we got outside we were stopped dead in our tracks — lying in wait outside the door was a whole squad of police, lining the road like a crowd of well-wishers; we were trapped in the middle. In those days the Beijing Public Security Bureau was diagonally across from that snack shop, on Righteousness Road, so it was extremely convenient for the police to mobilize, but to this day I can't figure out why they bothered to mobilize just to arrest us. Even if it was our own fault for provoking them on their own doorstep, was helping ourselves to a nice dinner really such a big crime worthy of disturbing so many of our dear officers of the law? I've forgotten the details of our lockup, or what they questioned us about; all I do remember is that after our interrogation was over, a long time passed before a man finally came in. He said they'd already been in touch with each of our schools, and told us we must each go to our school's "Workers' Propaganda Team" the next day to explain what had happened. Then he picked me out and marched over to me, wagging his finger at my nose: "You may be the youngest, but you're the worst of the lot," he said. "I've heard all about you. Tomorrow Team Leader Zhang and Teacher Wa will make you pay for this."

We set off back down the road, none of us saying a word. I couldn't stand another mouthful of the half-eaten steamed bun I was still clutching in my hand; as we passed Dongdan Park, I flung it into the trees. I thought of Old Cow's body of solid muscle, of his slit-like eyes. Those two slits and I had stared at each other for two years, but try as I might, I could never figure out what was concealed behind them. I thought, I've had enough of the kind of education you get from public show trials. All of the capital crimes: writing reactionary diaries, rape, sodomy, adultery, illegal seduction, gross indecency — I know all the details by heart. All that's missing now is for me to put them into practice. So there's really no need whatsoever for me to go to school anymore.

At the start of my formal truant days, Old Cow was still determined to save me. He got many of my classmates to pass messages to me, saying they hoped I'd pull back from the brink. He often made a special diversion when he was cycling home from school so that he could pass right in front of our door in the hope of catching me. In those days the subway was being built nearby, and the construction site was piled high with an endless supply of stones. I stockpiled large quantities at the corner of the street, behind trees and in our doorway. Whenever Old Cow came down the lane I would pelt him with a hail of stones. The last time, once he'd managed to calm down, he slammed on his brakes, put one leg down to balance and yelled at me: "Just you wait, young Gu! I'll make you pay at graduation." But the stones were raining down on him from all sides now and as soon as he'd finished shouting he jumped back on his bike and scuttled off. That was the last I ever saw of him.

My truant days were the happiest days of my childhood. I hated school and despised my teachers. And even though I did go back to school later on, skipping school had already become a regular habit. All of the useful things I know now, I either taught myself or picked up from friends when I wasn't in school. School reminds me of the public show trials — at least in those days there really was a certain similarity between the atmospheres. And even though I played truant, it was an atmosphere I could never completely escape. And that's true even today.

November 1993, Los Angeles

ZENG HONG TRANSLATED BY YANBING CHEN

THREE SHORT-LIVED POEMS FROM YESTERDAY

No. 1: The song recalls
generations of grief, and speaks out loud
today's misery. Who else is it for
if not for you?
No. 2: I live in the weakest spot in your heart
beating a drum with a bone, awakening the small spirits in your body
We want you to wake up.
No. 3: Tonight, footprints
of defeated consciousness on a piece of paper turn into smoke.
Through it, bluish jack-o'-lanterns
blink on the bookshelf; where are you,
my lonely nothingness?
— these three broken stanzas
are like three floats on my fishing pole
tiny white bits from a goose quill
strung to float on water.
They are willing to sink, but the fish
only touch them, not biting.
I'm going to spread my anxiety over the water.
Wait and see, you who are still struggling....

11/25/93 20:00

LU DONGZHI   TRANSLATED BY DESMOND SKEEL

THE STAGE

The stage towered high above.

The play had finished. The actors were taking their bows, the audience had started to leave. They were waving their arms high in the air like surrendering troops. Their waving seemed to be driving the audience away. It was as if they were shooing away a flock of crows gathering on desolate sandbanks. My seat had been at the back, far from the stage. I was still sitting there. Most of the people in front of me had stood up. There was a lot of commotion in the theater. Those bodies that had stood up and were now moving blocked my view. On stage the actors were still bowing. I could only see their arms raised high in the air. I gazed at their arms as though gazing at a lotus pond in late autumn, until two short men about half a meter tall closed the curtains. They seemed to be closing two quivering red gates. I stood up and watched them close the gates tightly shut. Then I gazed at the two closed gates for a while. Afterwards I roused myself and followed the mass of bodies moving outside. I was tired. It was as if a number of my internal parts were aching as they expanded and contracted. There were a lot of people. The jostling crowd moved very slowly. For some reason I turned my head a few times to look back. I saw countless pallid and blurred faces that seemed as exhausted as I was. They were like a line of troops who had been walking for ages, enduring hunger, hurrying on in the moonlight.

Once outside the theater we were immediately immersed in sunlight. It felt as though we had climbed out of the water onto the bank. The sun was so bright that I felt a little giddy. I'd only been to see a play — but it seemed as though I'd been parted from the sunlight for months.

Crowds of people surged along the street bathed in sunlight. I was among them. I had to get to the southern end of the street before I could get a bus home.

Somebody poked me gently from behind. I looked around, thinking at first that I must have bumped into somebody I knew, but found an unfamiliar, somewhat furtive face looking at me. Actually it wouldn't be quite accurate to say it was an unfamiliar face. I had the vague impression that I'd seen this face somewhere before. It was just that I couldn't remember where. I had the feeling, however, that there must have been some connection between this person and myself.

"The deal's about to go through this time," he said smiling at me.

"Is that so?" I replied, taking the opportunity to have a good look at him. I still couldn't remember who he was, but somehow I had the feeling that there really was a deal between the two of us, and that it really was about to go through.

"I heard the news at lunchtime," he said.

"It's been so long. I suppose it must be about time."

"You're right. It's taken them so long. It's really outrageous the way they've dragged things out."

"I agree. I thought there might be some news today."

"Well then, my friend," he said, taking me around the corner to a quiet and secluded spot, "why don't the two of us go now rather than waiting until evening — in case they left earlier. You never can tell these days."

"You're right. I was just thinking the same thing," I said hastily.

"Okay. We'll go now."

"Okay. We'll go right now."

We hurried on our way. The roads all seemed familiar. We hardly spoke another word on the way. The roads really were familiar. We seemed to be going to where I used to work, or to a friend's home.

We walked into a courtyard and then into a house. The house wasn't that large, but there were about ten people sitting inside. I seemed to know some of them. They all looked displeased, as if something serious was about to happen to them, or as if they had been waiting for some time.

"You are the last two to get here. Where on earth have you been? It's outrageous!" A fat man shouted angrily at us. I couldn't remember who he was, but I knew he was in charge.

"Okay, that's enough. They're here now," somebody interceded for us. I looked at him gratefully. He seemed to be one of the characters in the play I had just seen. I knew that his words carried some weight.

"Forget it. Let's get a move on!" said a tall man standing up. He seemed to have authority.

"Somebody comes late every time, but never this late! What were you two up to? If you're going to be this late next time, don't even bother showing up." The fat man turned around to look at everyone. Some of them looked very nervous. They must have been late as well — or at least had been late in the past.

"Let's go, everyone. And be careful on the way," said the fat man.

We walked out of the house, across the courtyard and out into the street. The dozen of us walked on in silence towards the road that led to the outskirts of town. We must have looked like a band of robbers or a group of laborers.

We soon reached the outskirts and before long walked into some woods. None of us was as nervous now as we had been at the outset. We began to relax, our pace slowed down, and we said a few words to each other. It was as though we had crossed a police line and had now entered a safe zone. I looked all around me. Apart from us there was not a single soul nor any movement in the woods. We walked along a small path. Then I noticed that I was dripping with sweat. I felt my chest and found that my clothes were wringing wet. I looked at the others. Their backs were also wet.

It was afternoon and the sun was moving lower in the sky. Its light carved up into fragments by the poplar trees. I knew these woods and this path very well indeed. I must have come to these woods and walked through them when I was young. It seemed as if I'd been walking through them for years.

A large expanse of sandbanks skirting a river came into view as we came out of the woods.

We must have arrived, I thought, and sure enough just as I stepped onto the sand I heard the fat man say: "It's still early. Soon everyone will have to exert themselves for all they're worth."

"That goes without saying. We'll do whatever you say."

"We'll give it all we've got."

"That's right! We're bursting with energy, aren't we, brothers?"

Everyone agreed and made clear that they were ready to pitch in and work. I couldn't help feeling a rush of excitement. It was as if a moment I had been yearning for for ages had finally arrived. I knew that they were all old hands, but this was the first time for me.

We walked along the sandbanks. Pits of varying depths dug into the sand and large piles of gravel gradually came into view. Most of the pits were filled with water. I knew these were abandoned mines and that we had come to pan for gold. I seemed to have known for ages that I had always been in this line of work. They were my partners and we had always panned for gold.

I stood with two others at the edge of a large abandoned pit looking down into it. The others had already gone on ahead. The fat man, who seemed to be the foreman, turned to us and shouted: "Come on. Let's go. This spot is no good anymore. We'll go a bit further on this time."

"Keep up, everyone. Don't waste your time looking around. This spot is no good," called out one of the others up ahead.

We hurried to catch up with them.

We walked along the sandbanks for ages. I was very tired and my head was dripping with sweat. The others also looked exhausted. They were panting and appeared almost unable to go on. The whole column had clearly slowed down. I realized that the column was now very long, and there seemed to be more people than before. There may have been more than twenty of us. The men carried bundles and bags on their backs and tools on their shoulders. Some of them even carried shoulder poles. I was carrying a large, bronze-colored bag. It was full and very heavy. The twenty or so in the column walked sluggishly along the desolate sandbanks. We must have looked a lot like a group of rural laborers fleeing to another region in search of casual work, or like a circus troupe. I realized that the middle-aged guy with the beard behind me was a famous itinerant artiste. There was a zither in his bag. Part of it was sticking out. I had seen this zither somewhere before. I seemed to remember hearing him somewhere playing his zither melodiously and mournfully. I turned to look at him several times. He seemed older than before. His face was wooden and expressionless. His eyes were sad and tired, as if he were grieving over something. I looked carefully and realized that among the group there were some poet and artist friends of mine. There were also some of my former classmates. Each of them looked exhausted. I wondered why they had all come, but it seemed as though they had always been part of the group.

The troops at the front eventually came to a stop.

"We're here! We're here!" I heard someone at the front say. It seemed as if we'd arrived.

"We're here."

"We're here at last," said the men at the back.

"I was beginning to think we'd never get here. I don't think I could have walked another step."

"You're right. I can't go any further."

"I'm going to sit down and rest." A chubby man plonked himself down on a sandbank.

"I need to rest as well."

"I've got to rest before I can carry on." Some of the others dropped their things and sat down.

"I'll sit down and rest," I said, also sitting down. I saw that most of the others were lying on the sandbanks, as though paralyzed. Only the foreman and the two other bosses were still standing. They were far ahead gesturing and muttering something.

"Get up. Get up everyone. Who said you could lie down? Don't you want to get on with the job?" shouted the foreman loudly as he turned to see the men lying in disarray like corpses on the sand.

Most of them stood up one after the other, but there were still a few who lay motionless. I also struggled to get up.

"We're really exhausted!"

"All that walking's tired us out."

"Aren't we allowed to take a rest after walking all that way?"

"We're too shattered to keep on working!"

The men muttered under their breaths, but most of them still managed to pull themselves up.

"None of you can slack off. It's getting late now. We have to start at once. If we waste any more time we'll never get finished," said the foreman in a loud voice.

"Get to it. Get to work at once. Get to it, everyone!" said the other two bosses, busying themselves.

The men started to work. Some of us began digging up the sand with shovels, piling it to one side. The rest of us gathered rocks, putting them into baskets. I shared a basket with a skinny guy. Everyone was working as best they could. I found some coins on the sandbanks. My skinny partner and I both picked up several coins. We both looked at each other and laughed.

"So soon!" he said.

"You can say that again!" I said.

We started to be more attentive as we gathered the rocks. We lifted up rocks and looked for gleaming silver coins beneath them. I noticed that the others were doing the same thing, and they seemed to have collected more than we had. Suddenly we were all full of energy. Many of the men ran back for another turn after depositing their rocks.

I realized that the men digging in the sand were frequently uncovering copper coins and silver dollars which were much bigger than the one- two- and five-cent pieces we were finding. They were digging up the sand desperately, stuffing the coins into their breast pockets one after another. The foreman and the other two bosses were also sparing no effort. Before long those of us who had been gathering rocks started to dig into the sandbanks with our bare hands. I knelt by a sandbank and dug with all my might. My fingers ached. I dug out copper coins and silver dollars. I also found a host of much older coins. I found five *zhu*, half a tael, fifty *daquan*, coins from the Yuanyou period, Shensong ingots, coins from the Qianlong period, and treasures from the Xianfeng period. I also found a number of Yan Dynasty daggers and one from the Qi. When all my pockets were crammed full, I ran over to fill up my bag. The others didn't seem to have as much as I did. I was just about to chuckle in satisfaction when I saw that two guys were showing off what looked like a silver ingot as large as a fist. One of them said: "Look how big it's grown!"

"Who'd have thought they'd have grown so big!" the other said.

I was just about to go over and take a look when the foreman called out: "Come here. Come here, everyone. We've almost got enough rocks."

At this everyone hurried to pack their things away and then carried over the empty baskets. The two guys hurried to hide their big find, almost afraid that the bosses might see them.

I'll probably never find something quite that big, I thought.

"We've almost got enough rocks. We should pile them together," said the foreman.

"I think there's enough. Quickly, pile them up."

"Okay, don't just stand there, we're not doing this for the fun of it," said the other two bosses.

The men all came over and started to build a wall of pebbles around the sandbank.

"Take some of the men over to fetch the poles," ordered the foreman.

Several of us were sent about forty meters away to carry over the bamboo poles as thick as ricebowls that were piled there. I kept on searching as I carried over the bamboo poles. I kicked over a few good-sized pebbles to see if there was anything big hidden underneath. Although there were a few things that were quite large, none of them were nearly as big as the one the others had found.

By now the sun was about ten meters above the horizon. It bathed the sandbanks in a red glow. They looked like they were bleeding. We feverishly busied ourselves like a band of ghosts building up a grave for someone.

"The sun is about to set. Quick, let's get the stage built! It'll be dark soon," said one of the bosses.

"Okay everyone, one last push. Let's get this stage built," ordered the foreman.

"Come on. Get to work, everyone. Bring the rope over," said the other boss.

One by one the poles were erected. Some of them were laid horizontally and tied firmly in place.

The stage slowly began to take shape.

We started to cover it with canvas.

It was gradually getting dark. Two men who seemed to be electricians were installing lighting cables. I noticed that one of the electricians had once been to my house to repair a tape recorder. I knew he was good at his job.

One cluster of lights came on.

Another cluster of lights came on.

Lots of lights came on.

"How's that? Will that do?" asked the foreman smiling.

"Of course it will," said one of the bosses.

"We've done a good job building this theater," the other said.

"It *is* a good job. It's got style. Look how large and splendid the auditorium is," said the secretary.

"Yes. Yes. Much grander than I'd originally imagined," said an old fellow who seemed to be a cadre.

"There's quite an audience today," said a man in a suit.

"Naturally. That goes without saying," said a man in glasses.

Only then did I realize that there was an audience below the stage. A mass of dark heads and gray faces waited in silence, looking like a field of crops at night.

There was a commotion below the stage.

"You should bow to the audience. Come forward, everyone," the man in the suit turned around and called to everyone.

"Bow to the audience. Come on, quickly now," shouted another man in a suit.

A lot of people moved forward from the back of the stage. I advanced a few steps nearer to the front. The stage was soon filled with people standing. Some of them jostled their way forward to a more conspicuous position. We all raised our arms and started waving. Then we smiled and clapped our hands. Then we raised our arms and waved again. Then we clapped our hands again.

The commotion continued below the stage. The audience was applauding. Some of them were even cheering and whistling. Everyone stood up and a sea of heads began to move.

We were still standing on the stage waving our arms in the air. The audience was leaving the theater. There was a great amount of noise. Just then two men in thick make-up and green costumes came from behind the scenes. They went to either side of the stage and slowly closed the two large curtains in front of us.

CHEN DONGDONG TRANSLATED BY YANBING CHEN

FROM *LEXICON, NOUNS*

34. Lily

I lack any concept or knowledge of *lilies*. I use the noun more or less the way one drives on ice — the wheels slip and spin, but the car doesn't move. For me, the signified of *lily* is a nonentity. When I write down the word, I don't know what it means; it fails to kindle the torch of imagination, which I use to illuminate the fragrance permeating memory's valley. So much so that, one day, in a glass-fronted flower shop on Nanjing Road, as I stand in front of a bouquet of flowers that the owner points out as lilies, my eyes still cannot reach the plant itself. What I see is still nonentity, an exclamation in the form of a noun.

40. Anteater

Hard to predict against what backdrop it will appear. Its figure defies the imagination of this world. Its body, which violates the laws of evolution, should prove the irrationality born out of nature's spirit. For me, the anteater is a fantasy come true; for insects, the theoretical basis of pessimism and despair. As for a line in a poem, it is a dark noun which can never find its proper place. It might pass under the lintel of a verse, it might have lingered in the cold moonlight of an ode, it might poke its curious snout — which has nothing to do with snouts — into one more nest of rhymes. But essentially it is outside poetry. It comes at unexpected moments, casting its queer shadow on the words I have just written. . . .

57. Camera

The importance of the camera lies in the fact that it has taught me another way of observation, one that is limited and repeating, that leaves out unnecessary things; that focuses on parts, expands distance, and achieves better clarity and precision due to its reduction of scale. Observing through a camera is like caressing without stirred emotions. It might be mechanical, but it's active. It brings structure to what is being observed, and modifies it through an analysis of and an emphasis on minute details of light and shadow. It becomes a not necessarily indispensable extension of my vision; as a nerve fiber it stirs my brain. Eventually, it might become the composite organ of both thinking and seeing, and live independently beyond life and death, approaching eternity. When a body is reduced to dust, the camera (once possessed by the body, and having almost become a part of the body) breaks free, and lives on. Through the camera, someone will discover what I see and think at some particular moments. It is an organ that arrests and ignores time.

ZHANG ZAO

TRANSLATED BY YANBING CHEN

NIGHT VIEW OF NEW YORK

> *I will go to the bank by the wood*
> *and become undisguised and naked.*
> —Walt Whitman

Holding a red trout you climb the dark night
New York is just like New York, dangling
    in a hot tear, drifting to an abyss

Heartbeats of the zodiac dart about like cockroaches
Stuck in fat, the burglar-proof lock sows along its route
    ears, diamonds, escape

and you; holding the arms of your New York King
you stroll down Fifth Avenue
    Automobiles, like ghostly creatures, pass over a bewitching scent

Stories about agonies over body shape
succumb to deep eye shadow
    Yet, what can be more erotic

than success? In the night sky
a cloud drifts past, an occasional consolation
    from eternity. The invisible you

walks alongside the absent New York King
Inside the Future Bar with its gilt interior
    men and women suck like bats at the bright mirror

With a lighter you summon the flame
one petal of flame, the waiter's water bows
    you fail to locate history's cigarette butt

left or right, so flick it offhand into
the ashtray of the Third World
    Half of a lover lingers like an echo

and kisses the other half, Sylvia Plath
how proudly she hated nakedness
    A whole body is like a raw onion

Peeling it to the heart, you hear only the weeping skins
disintegrating into revolving doors, the killer passes
    you have no way out, like the world wearing

the underwear of the subway, unable to stop
Death, this steel gatekeeper punching tickets
    blocks the way again and again, like a scum

Holding a red trout you walk into the dark night
seeking the trail of your most intimate friend
    a dreamer who dreams about sex changes —

lodestone dance girl, Mona Lisa of
promises, a distant look on her face
    scattering the Empire's objective sticky stuff

in her dance, spattering Utopia
The fantasized mystery of identity
     runs in her nerves green wine, red lights

How can she feel your presence? You, liberator
with a shapely body, who's just come in, the outdoors disappears
     the fragmented outside tossed to a suicide like a tip

He falls, hyper-real, nowhere to be found
or he could be fine, abducted by the thumb, a junkie
     hovering over the remote control, to the foam pads of images

the TV set, the distribution center of survivors' thoughts
inside which the Tarot
     is revealing its hand, waiting to be claimed

Card exchange: an awkward man who looks
a teacher, is prophetically breaking through
     the French word riddle: fish, *poisson*

"If you drop an *S*
then it turns to poison," the New York King thinks,
     "No wonder Parisians are fussy eating fish."

A sharp bright beep: he, the fake fisher King
leaves a message, bald, wearing a nonexistent cloak
     comes out of his evening bath, water dripping from both ears

"I will go to the bank by the wood
and become undisguised and naked."
     But would the world turn for the better? It is possible

Whitman, humming the Song of Myself
driving a taxi, the most evanescent creature of the night
    picks up a few satellite men in distress

crossing the Brooklyn Bridge—
the black clouds are putting felt caps
    on male skyscrapers, the angels are cleaning windows

crossing the Brooklyn Bridge—
sees you in the rear view mirror, blood oozing from all five apertures
    beaten again and again, inevitably, by a few dark

shadows. You stand there, looking calm
Where, where is my muse?
    Loving, enduring, asking, I

holding a red trout, sink into the dark night
while you, a fountain erupting in your mouth, unfold
    above the statue the daybreak "why"

Hong Ying TRANSLATED BY JENNY PUTIN

THE SNUFF BOTTLE

The afternoon Fuzzy fainted, the sun was white hot. Every breath he sucked in felt like a puff of fire from a charcoal furnace. As his body began to sway, he held on to the telegraph pole for support, but it was too smooth; as everything in front of his eyes went black, he fell to the ground. After a few minutes, maybe less, he was aware of someone bending down and picking him up. He felt his feet knock against what seemed to be a door frame, and then he was laid flat. Someone pried open his tightly clenched mouth and poured in a bitter liquid. After that his mind went blurry and he drifted to sleep.

The door banged shut. Fuzzy stirred. His limbs were weak and floppy, his throat was parched. He opened his eyes: on a windowsill was a stack of yellowing, thread-bound books like broken bricks. A pungent smell of medicinal herbs permeated the room. Fuzzy knew immediately that he was in the old hermit's house down the flagstone slope. The old man knew how to take pulses and diagnose illnesses. Most of the people in the area went to him when they were ill. When they were well they never gave him a second thought, but he never turned anyone away, the stupid old fool.

Fuzzy put one foot on the floor, then slipped on his sandals. The room was dark. Pieces of wallpaper, grubby and torn, were coming away from the wall. The few sticks of furniture — a bookcase, table, and bed — were old and the varnish had worn away except in the cracks, but everything was clean and neat. Fuzzy had a good look around. Next to the bookcase were several large shelves fixed to the wall. At the very bottom were bundles of medicinal herbs. The second shelf was covered with large and small bottles, some empty, some full of what looked like seeds. His hand alighted on a two-inch high, mud-colored bottle. Fuzzy polished it against his shirt, leaving black dust marks on his clothes, but at the same time exposing the shiny, rich smoothness of the bottle. He poked his finger into the neck of the bottle. It was such a tiny hole only his little finger would fit. The stopper, which had dropped down onto the bundles of herbs, was like a small marble, crystalline and translucent. The more he looked, the more he liked it. He pushed the stopper in, hemmed and hawed, and then put the bottle into his trouser pocket. On tiptoe he gently pushed the door open. The kitchen was on the other side with two long benches against the wall where the old man did his consulting. There was no one in the street. The sun still hung up in the sky like a ferocious face. Hitching up his trousers, Fuzzy set off in the direction of his home keeping close to the walls under the eaves.

Fuzzy had been counting on his fingers the days until his big brother came home from the boat: he knew the school term would begin about the same time. That day he had forgotten how many days he had counted, but his brother appeared anyway. Hui was there too, helping him sort out his sailcloth bag with his toothbrush, hand towel, clothes, and other things. Scattered in among these were some peanuts and red dates. Hui had had her braids cut short. They just reached her shoulders. She was very lively. Her brows, eyes, and lips were so fine they looked as if they were drawn.

In his heart, Fuzzy called her sister-in-law.

After seeing Hui off, his brother told their mother not to do any more baby-sitting or laundry for other people.

"But with only your father's pension and your wages, how are we supposed to make ends meet?" Mother was washing the dishes as she spoke. "You would need money if you were going to get married. I can manage OK. There's life in me yet."

His brother opened his mouth to speak, but thought better of it. It would be a while before he could get married. Hui's father didn't approve of the romance between his daughter and her classmate. Stuck up old git, lounging around all day drinking tea. He was no better than their father working in the engine room on board ship, but he thought his daughter pretty enough to marry above herself, too good to be a female worker all her life.

The usual meeting place was by the nursery school wall. There was a clump of bushes by the curve in the wall. In amongst the thickets of weeds was a profusion of smelly white flowers. Fuzzy was late. He squatted down at the foot of the wall. The nursery school was opposite the middle school separated by a pond, littered with rotting cabbage leaves and carrot tops.

Three shadows scuttled past, the tall one in front was Liu Yun. Fuzzy stood up quickly and told him that his brother was back from work but that he was being closely watched and had been unable to get away.

To his surprise Liu Yun did not shout at him. He was clutching a pile of books which he tossed down to the edge of the pond. The book at the top of the pile bore a picture of a big bearded foreigner. Fuzzy had been coveting this for a long time. But he concealed his eagerness: Liu Yun didn't like books, he just liked to steal them. And he liked girls too.

Liu Yun was three years older than Fuzzy. He had not finished middle school but he was already hanging around on the street all day, smoking, drinking, and singing dirty songs. He was behind all the local pranks, but he looked just like any innocent, pale-faced schoolboy. In addition, he had become quite a fighter and liked to side with the underdog. He had made quite a name for himself on the streets. Suddenly the cicadas began to whir as if they had just realized that people were there. Fuzzy went to swat a long-legged mosquito that had landed on his arm. He missed. Liu Yun dragged him over to the street lamp. Fuzzy saw that Liu Yun had curled his hair into two waves, his shirt was clean and neat, not like Fuzzy and his friends who went about bare-chested when it was hot. It wasn't Liu Yun himself who broke in through the library window; he was always some distance away, giving orders.

"Who's visiting your house?" Liu Yun asked.

"My sister-in-law," Fuzzy replied.

"What nerve! They're not even married! Aren't you a sweet-tongued devil! Any more tasty tidbits where she came from?"

Liu Yun's tone was playful, but the look on his face was serious. He had had a string of girlfriends, barely finishing with one before he went on to the next. Fuzzy was worried. He wanted to run, but his hand reached into his trouser pocket for the bottle. He fingered it. He looked at Liu Yun, gritted his teeth, and handed it over.

Liu Yun took it half-heartedly in his hand. At first glance, under the dull yellow street lamp, the bottle was nothing special.

"Shine your light on it. Look there, two fish!" said Fuzzy.

Liu Yun didn't need the flashlight, he had already seen them. The bottle gleamed exquisitely. He gave it a good look.

"I'll take it."

"Only if you promise not to go after my sister-in-law." Fuzzy's words were muffled, but his meaning was clear enough: leave Hui alone!

Liu Yun was the local heartthrob and all the girls were after him. He could have whoever he chose.

"What do you mean? OK, I'll stay away from her!" Liu Yun switched on the flashlight. The beam shone on the bottle. "Those can't be fish. It's a couple screwing. They've got old-fashioned haircuts, and there are trees, mountains, and a river." Liu Yun shrieked, "They're all naked!" He showed Fuzzy. Fuzzy was shy, and Liu Yun shouting at him made him even more embarrassed to look. Liu Yun pointed to the scatter of books at the edge of the pond. "All yours, sunshine."

During the holidays, Fuzzy's brother did odd jobs on a building site during the day. His evenings were spent flirting with Hui. No matter how bad Fuzzy wanted to get out, he had to pretend to be good. His mother, under orders from his brother to rest, busied herself with the cooking and housework. With more time on her hands, it was as if she had grown an extra pairs of eyes. She went about supervising Fuzzy's homework, what time he went to bed and got up, his meals and trips to the toilet. He was like a caged monkey.

That day Fuzzy had been sent out to buy soy sauce. As he emerged from the shop he caught sight of the old hermit heading up towards the crossroads. His clothes were even scruffier than usual and he kept looking from side to side, obviously worrying about something. A woman who was buying vegetables grabbed hold of her fat lollipop-sucking daughter and intercepted the old man. She told her daughter to stick out her tongue for the old man to examine.

He waved them aside and kept on walking.

The woman jumped up and hurled a mouthful of abuse at the old man over the vegetable stall. Her language was colorful.

"So, go to the hospital. Go on!" the old man retorted coolly, and staggered off up the steps.

The woman shut her mouth in astonishment. People on the street were taken aback: the old man never had a good word to say about hospitals and was always such a softie. What was going on?

Fuzzy's face went pale then red. He hadn't stolen it exactly, the little bottle, and besides, the old man had so many. It wasn't because of that. Nevertheless, he slipped into a doorway and waited until the old man had gone past.

"Look at me, son." His mother put a bowl of fried bean sprouts on the table. There was not a drop of oil in the bowl. She wiped her hands on her apron. "What have you been up to?"

"Nothing." His voice was feeble.

"You're lying. How dare you lie to me!" Mother was onto him.

Fuzzy buried his face in his book. Mother grabbed the soy sauce. "Just wait till your brother gets home. He'll have a few things to say."

"What things?" Fuzzy wasn't scared of his mother, but he was terrified of his big brother, just as he had been scared of his dad. When his dad was out of work he used to take his big brother and him fishing in the stream or pond. When his dad was in a good mood he used to laugh and joke. His big brother was just like him, strong, dark, and lively. Fuzzy was fine and delicate. Even though he ran around in the sun all day he never got brown, just pink. He felt like a wimp because of it.

"The police were here earlier. Cases of cigarettes are missing from the cigarette factory again. Some workers on the night shift saw the culprits, a bunch of half-grown kids apparently." Mother was mixing the dressing for the cold noodles. "If they own up, they'll be let off lightly, otherwise they'll end up in the coop like chickens!"

Fuzzy breathed out slowly. He put the book down and beamed. He went over to his mother and fanned her gently. He swore that he hadn't had anything to do with it. He was all charm and sweetness. His mother couldn't make heads or tails of it. But Fuzzy knew who was behind it: it must be Liu Yun.

After dinner, everyone in the neighborhood brought their chairs, mats, and bamboo beds outside to cool down. They would wait until the temperature had dropped before going back into the house to sleep.

A neighbor called over to his mother: "They caught the hooligans who stole the cigarettes."

"Have they?"

The neighbor had a long, thin neck. He was wearing a pair of wooden-soled slippers. He nodded. "They took whatever they could lay their hands on, not just the cigarettes. They've got them, though."

Fuzzy, who was sprinkling cool water onto the bamboo couch, glanced at his mother. As he lowered his eyes he seemed to say: "See, it wasn't me!" She smiled. Liu Yun had got his just desserts. Fuzzy was sad about the bottle. The clouds and countryside on the bottle moved in front of his eyes. He regretted giving it away. Water from the basin splashed over his feet.

His brother came in followed by Hui. Fuzzy poured them each a cup of cool water. Someone called his name.

He looked out the window. His heart missed a beat. Liu Yun was standing by the side of the street. He wasn't behind the cigarette job after all.

Liu Yun marched in uninvited, saying he wanted to borrow a book from Fuzzy. Liu Yun never read books. Fuzzy said he would grab it. Hui offered him a seat. Fuzzy's brother was in the kitchen filling a basin with water to wash his face. Hui asked Liu Yun what kind of books he liked.

Liu Yun said he liked reading stories. His face was deadly earnest.

Hui beamed a brilliant smile. Fuzzy thought he detected a change in her voice. Liu Yun looked very mature, much older than seventeen.

Fuzzy grabbed two books and stood outside pointedly. "Here are your books."

Liu Yun said goodbye to Hui politely. Fuzzy's brother came back into the room carrying the basin. He brushed shoulders with Liu Yun as he went past.

Liu Yun walked on ahead quickly. Fuzzy followed closely behind. When they got to the edge of the pond, Fuzzy had still not spoken when Liu Yun swung round and gave Fuzzy a shove. He fell backwards, sitting down in a puddle. Water seeped in, soaking his vest and underpants. The books he was carrying fell into the mud.

Liu Yun said, "You're sneaky and cold. I only came over to borrow some fucking books."

"You lying bastard!" Fuzzy surged up and butted Liu Yun with his head. He caught him off guard. He staggered, almost falling into the pond. "Give me back my bottle!" Fuzzy shouted.

"Your what?" Liu Yun, who had recovered his balance, exploded. "You can't give someone something then ask for it back!" He laid into Fuzzy. "And don't you ever speak like that again to someone bigger than you, or you'll be drinking out of that sewer."

Liu Yun had held back. He had been lenient with his fists. Fuzzy hated him all the more.

When his mother saw his bloody face she panicked, worried that the neighbor had seen him. She reached out and pulled Fuzzy into the house, shutting the door tightly behind him.

Fuzzy didn't say that it was only a nose bleed. He just kept moaning. From the other side of the table his brother asked, "Who did this to you?"

Fuzzy didn't flinch, as if he hadn't heard his brother's question. His mother stuffed cotton wads into his nostrils and wiped the blood from his face, then told him to look up. "It's a sin, my boy. What on earth did you do to get messed up in this?" Fuzzy couldn't bear to see his mother cry.

Fuzzy ached all over and he stank of sewage, but his mother and brother couldn't see the real cause of his pain.

His mother opened the chest of drawers to find some clean clothes. Then it occurred to her: "Wasn't it Liu Yun who had come looking for Fuzzy this evening?"

Fuzzy neither shook nor nodded his head. It was enough that Mother had said it. His brother would be after Liu Yun for sure. He wouldn't forgive him.

His mother cleaned Fuzzy up and rubbed alcohol and gentian violet into his bruises. He lay on his mother's folding bamboo chair while she fanned him gently.

The stars, large and small, were like flying insects darting in and out of view, as if playing hide and seek with the clouds. The wind had cooled. The streets were deserted and peaceful. Fuzzy and his mother went back into the house.

"Where's your brother?" His mother peered out into the moonlight.

Fuzzy sat up on the bed ready to go off and look for his brother. His mother held him back.

That night Fuzzy had a nightmare. He woke up shouting. It was already morning. He couldn't remember what time his brother had come home the night before or what had happened. There was no one at home. Mother had probably gone to the market to buy the vegetables fresh in from the suburbs, and his brother had gone to work.

Fuzzy scooped a ladle of water out of the pot, drank two mouthfuls, then spat the rest out. He noticed a half sheet of paper on the windowsill weighted down with a broken brick.

He picked it up. The writing was clumsy and crooked. It was Liu Yun's. It was all settled, he had written, and he wouldn't be coming over to Fuzzy's house again provided that Fuzzy didn't come after him for the bottle. Fuzzy had not expected this. This wasn't at all like the proud Liu Yun he knew. His brother must have given him a good beating.

Strange, Fuzzy muttered. The ache in his limbs had disappeared. He rolled the paper up into a ball and threw it out the window. Deep down he forgave Liu Yun. He should be even prouder than Liu Yun.

He gulped down a bowl of rice porridge, hesitated, then walked out of the house. He wouldn't have an opportunity to get away once his mother was home.

Where should he go to play? With no particular destination in mind, he jumped up and down a few times at the crossroads then ran off down the hill.

Passengers who had just disembarked from the ferry walked in small clusters up the old abandoned cable car tracks. They were a long way off and not clearly visible. Fuzzy stood facing the backwater. The gently sloping beach was bigger than the school playing field. There were no strange stones or submerged reefs, the water was calm and warm, and the sand soft and fine. Every few days the body of a drowned man or woman floated down into the backwater where it would linger whirling around. Fuzzy didn't care. Anyway, water is water. He dog-paddled for a while then turned over on his back, his fourteen-year-old frame supported by the murky river water. The sun had not yet reached its full ferocity. Some young boys about the same age as he were having a water fight. There were not many swimmers this early in the morning. From now on he would make sure he always came down at this time. He narrowed his eyes. The cloudless sky dipped down to within an arm's length of his face. It was heavy and he couldn't push it away. His ears picked up the rhythm of the waves lapping against the bank. If Dad hadn't gone back in four years earlier to save the others from the fire, he could have jumped off the boat into the river and swum across in one breath. Fuzzy made his way over to the bank. He parked himself on the spongy, soft beach, his face nestling into the sand. The cool river water lapped around him. He was like a fish.

A hand grabbed hold of the back of his neck and squeezed lightly. Fuzzy screamed.

The hand let go. Fuzzy turned over and looked up. It was the old hermit. Fuzzy trembled.

All the way back to the old man's house, Fuzzy did his best to get away, but the old man held on to him tightly. His beard was gray, but he was still very strong.

The old man lifted the lid on his teacup and blew the tea leaves to one side. "Give me back my bottle."

Fuzzy shook his head as if he hadn't understood what the old man was saying. It was like being summoned to the teacher's office. His arms hung straight down by his sides and his head was bowed. He was used to being kept behind by the teacher.

"You're too young to be liar!" the old man went on, saying that he had been looking for Fuzzy for several days. He'd taken Fuzzy in after he had fainted and looked after him, and in return for his trouble all Fuzzy could do was steal from him.

"That's not true. I didn't steal it!" Fuzzy curled his lip and leaned back, perching his bottom on the edge of the table. He pointed at the bottles sitting on the shelf. "They're only medicine bottles anyway!"

"Those are. But the one you stole is different."

"It's not at my place," Fuzzy blurted out. He wanted to carry on but his tongue twisted into a knot: "You ... stupid old git."

The old man stood up and paced up and down the room. He picked up the teacup and put it to his lips, then all of a sudden smashed it on the ground. Tea and shards of porcelain shot across the floor.

Fuzzy watched the old man, his mouth agape. Now that the old man had let out his anger, he seemed calmer.

Imagine a city moat and a cloudless sky, the capital city stretching out beneath the intense blue firmament, the Forbidden City resplendent like an enchanted palace. Once upon a time, there was a foreigner with a fine nose who possessed a very special trinket. To restore his breathing, he would pour a drop of magic potion from the trinket, inhale gently and sneeze. The potion could cure all manners of ailments. The foreigner adored opera. He fell in love with an opera singer who played women's roles. He became a regular opera goer and an amateur performer. The broken-hearted hero longed for love, his tears flowed like rain as the melancholy refrains rang out. Vainly he searched for a beautiful soul among the blossom sprays. The fairy maidens performed the dance of Chu. The Wu River overflowed with regret. When the foreigner came to leave, he gave the trinket to the singer.

The opera singer made himself ill, pining for him day and night. He saw a host of doctors but none could cure him. Then a young doctor who had come to the capital to visit relatives prescribed a concoction of herbs that saved the singer's life.

The doctor took the place of the foreigner. Time went by imperceptibly to the start of the Republic. The warlords went into battle. The doctor had to return to the south where his wife and elderly mother awaited him.

"Endless wanderings over mountains and rivers, farewells come easily but meetings are hard." This poem by Li Houzhu is written on the inside of the bottle. The calligraphy is the work of the great Master Ma, as the signature and seal testify, to complement the intrinsic pattern of the clouds, the rolling landscape, and the embracing couple, a union of heaven and earth! A pair of eyes that many a mortal would be eager to die for.

The old man went on. After the singer and doctor separated, the fighting intensified. Their letters never arrived, and after a year without news, the singer disappeared. Some people said that he committed suicide or was killed in the war.

Fuzzy was completely baffled.

"Hurry up and give me back the bottle you stole!" The old man snapped out of his reverie and fixed his eyes on Fuzzy. "Ill-gotten precious things are unlucky. You're too young to understand these things."

The old man rambled on incoherently: the bottle is a most exquisite light honey color. Your imagination could roam forever around the lines of the natural grain. The person who traced those lines was exceptional indeed. It's a rare work of art handed down from generation to generation. The hollow at the base of the bottle complements the undulating line and movement of the two bodies. Not to mention that it was a work of art labored over for many years, commissioned by the foreigner for a fortune, on a precious piece of jade.

Fuzzy heard the last sentence loud and clear. What was he saying? That the pretty medicine bottle was a precious stone? Give me a break! The old man was wacko. All he had was that pile of yellowing broken brick books. He's pulling my leg!

"Please bring it back," the old man was almost pleading.

"I didn't take it." Fuzzy decided to deny everything.

The old man broke into a long laugh. It was a couple of minutes before he regained his composure.

Fuzzy was petrified. The old man patted his shoulder solicitously. "You go home and think it over. Take your time. When you've thought it through, come back and tell me."

Hui had not come round for ages but Fuzzy's brother didn't seem bothered. He had never mentioned the evening when he had stood up for Fuzzy. It must have been ugly. Liu Yun was a head shorter than Fuzzy's brother and must have taken quite a beating. Even though Liu Yun was a mean puncher and kicker, he wasn't a seasoned gang fighter like his brother. Otherwise why would Liu Yun have kept his promise? In fact, there had been no sign of him for some time.

Fuzzy needed to consult the calendar. Only one more week before his brother had to return to the boat.

"Are you still going to the building site?" he asked his brother.

"No. Do you want to go fishing?"

Fuzzy nodded. "Shall we tell Hui?" He felt stupid. Why did he have to ask?

"No. She's busy." Fuzzy hadn't expected this answer. His brother didn't seem eager to talk about Hui, or at least that's how it seemed to Fuzzy. If there was a problem with Hui, it was that Hui's father didn't approve of them getting married — the same old story. What could they do about it? Fuzzy was worried.

The two brothers set off, one behind the other, fishing rods in hand, bait, little bugs, and earthworms in a small plastic bag. The hot spell had passed and the temperature was much cooler. Flecks of sunlight pushed through the branches of the trees, searing the patches of ground where they landed. The shaded areas were cool and dark. Neither spoke as they followed the stone path up the hill. The rear mountain reservoir offered a good vantage point. As you fished you could watch hundreds of boats in full sail going by. Pictures of the days they spent with their father reappeared before his eyes. Fuzzy felt happy and began to hum a tune, the words were unintelligible. Suddenly he stopped in his tracks: on a slope under some trees sat the old man cross-legged, nonchalantly yet purposefully there, in close-fitting cotton trousers. His hair was completely white and neatly combed and shining as if smoothed with honey locust oil. Fuzzy could not help walking over to the old man.

"Oh Fuzzy!" his brother called gently, yet forcefully. He seemed angry.

Fuzzy turned around and walked silently to his brother's side.

"What's your interest in him? He's got a bad reputation," his brother scolded.

"He's a healer," Fuzzy explained.

"He's under surveillance, an evil element from the old society."

Fuzzy picked up his fishing rod and whipped the tree. The leaves shook and began to drop one by one.

After they had climbed the hill, they came to a wide, steep road. In one direction lay the cigarette factory, in the other the textile factory. They crossed the road to the textile factory and took a small path through the fields. His brother told him that there was a whole basket of stories about the old man. Fuzzy was curious and pestered his brother to tell him.

His brother didn't really know. He remembered the grown-ups talking about the old man when he was little, but the stories were not considered suitable for children's ears. "He was from the lower Yangtze region. Before Liberation, sometime around 1949, his wife left him, apparently taking the children with her. She couldn't stand him. He was taken very ill. After he recovered, he told everyone that he could cure the sick and people believed him. It's best to keep your distance from people like him, the further away the better." His brother warned him not to get involved.

But I am involved, Fuzzy thought. The old hermit had given medical advice to so many people. He never turned anyone away, even when he was woken up in the night. All those big mouths and lazybones on the street preferred the convenience of seeing him to lining up in the hospital and shelling out for medicine. And he didn't even demand a thank you. Fuzzy cursed the lot of them. He dodged the night soil collectors, holding his nose against the stench of shit.

The pond was controlled by the production brigade. There were new rules: twenty cents per fisherman. That was forty cents for Fuzzy and his brother. It was only five cents to see the film, *The Guerrillas on Hong Lake*. With forty cents you could see it eight times. Mother couldn't bear to part with so much money. Fuzzy had been to the movies with his father. His brother paid and they were admitted into the bamboo enclosure around the pool. There were quite a few people fishing, a bunch of nondescript kids sitting and squatting beside the pool whiling away the hours. Two little girls sitting under the locust tree with their picture books were particularly conspicuous.

Fuzzy filled a plastic bag with water and put it in a stone hollow. He sat down next to his brother. The places where you could watch the boats sail by were all occupied. His father seemed more distant now. Disappointed, Fuzzy stretched out his legs and dangled them over the edge of the pool.

When they set off down the hill several hours later, Fuzzy carried the plastic bag cradled in the frame of the fishing net. In the bag were three silver carp just bigger than the palm of his hand, swishing around in the water, their mouths gaping and closing as they gasped for breath. "Those peasants from the production brigade must have taken all the big fish," Fuzzy muttered, then swore out loud.

His brother handed him the two fishing rods. "I've got to go check on something. You go ahead." Fuzzy saw that they were not far from home. They were almost at the crossroads.

His brother disappeared around a corner of two wooden walls. Fuzzy was happy. The fishing had been as exhilarating as ever. At least it had revived his brother's spirits. He was off to look for Hui at last.

His mother scaled and gutted the three fish, put them in a bowl, sprinkled them with salt, ginger, and garlic, and drizzled on a few drops of oil. She stood the bowl in the pan to steam. Fuzzy twisted his mouth.

"Oil is rationed, and it's expensive." His mother rolled her eyes. "Oh, here's Hui." His mother's voice softened.

"My brother's gone to look for you. You two must have just missed each other."

"Why would he go looking for me?" Hui's shoulders twitched and she began to cry. Fuzzy and his mother were dumbstruck. His mother gave Hui a damp cloth. When she'd stopped crying she wiped her face. She said that our brother had been avoiding her for two weeks and when they'd spoken he'd been very distant. Mother said that wasn't the case and that she was the only one he thought of. But Hui was not faking. Fuzzy was angry. He didn't know whether to sit or stand. He wanted to say something to comfort Hui but was afraid he'd say the wrong thing. He simply strode out of the house.

Fuzzy wandered aimlessly along the street. The shadows at the foot of the walls were dark, the houses run-down. In the street, women, their shirts crumpled, were calling their children home for supper. There was the smell of oil and peppers, and sounds of coughing spluttered through the narrow windows. He hated all this. A poster on the wall had been washed away by the rain, leaving only a corner. Fuzzy tore it off gently and threw it onto the ground. That's it. He would go and find Liu Yun to see if the bottle was real jade. In truth, Fuzzy could not tell real jade from imitation. Not any wiser, he found himself halfway down the flagstone slope.

The door to Liu Yun's house was locked. Fuzzy asked the neighbor to tell Liu Yun he had stopped by.

The neighbor promised to pass on the message. She looked Fuzzy up and down and glowered. Fuzzy glared back at the skinny woman. A duck puffed out its chest and nuzzled her toes. She kicked it. The duck squawked and flew off. She gave it an angry stare and swore. Fuzzy had never heard such explicit yet sophisticated language. He was awe-stricken. He lowered his head and walked off, the words going round and round in his mind.

The following afternoon, Liu Yun burst into Fuzzy's house, his face beaming. Although Hui wasn't there, Fuzzy had kept the piece of paper bearing Liu Yun's promise. But seeing Liu Yun agitated him. He hadn't been very smart giving that bastard an excuse to come to their house.

His brother came in and they greeted each other with a martial arts salute. He and Liu Yun seemed to have patched up their differences and there was no sign of a grudge. Within a couple of minutes they were calling each other brother. Fuzzy's fears had been groundless.

After leaving the house, they found a quiet spot. Fuzzy asked if he could have a look at the bottle.

"I haven't got it on me," Liu Yun replied. There was a new brightness and sparkle in his eyes. He seemed a different person.

Fuzzy felt the hairs stand up on the back of his neck as if the old hermit were shadowing him in pursuit of a debt. "I stole the bottle from the old man and now he wants it back. He says it's a snuff bottle." Fuzzy didn't dare tell Liu Yun that it was made of precious stone.

"Are you finished?" Liu Yun was ready to go.

"The old man wants it back!" Fuzzy could see that Liu Yun was uncomfortable and his voice began to rumble.

"You tired of living?" said Liu Yun in a half-mocking tone.

Was it that serious? Would Liu Lun kill him if he asked for the bottle back? Fuzzy sensed something vicious in Liu Yun's words. Otherwise he wouldn't be so scared. His mother had collected pig bristles from a workshop and had brought them back to the house for sorting, black with black and white with white. Fuzzy gave his mother a hand, but he was too quick and often mixed them up. Everyone around him seemed strange.

The day before his brother was due to return to the boat, Liu Yun and he were caught red-handed at Liu Yun's house by public security officers. It was cut and dried; they were handcuffed and led away. Everyone said that it was Hui's father who had reported them. Fuzzy ran with a neighbor all the way to the road. As the police car pulled away, Fuzzy heard his brother shouting, "Hey Fuzz, take care of Mom!"

Fuzzy had barely taken stock of what had happened, when everyone, adults and children alike, began shouting at him. They seemed to be repeating what his brother had said and laughing loudly. Someone said that Liu Yun had confessed to having been seduced.

It rained lightly during the night. All the houses were quiet.

Fuzzy climbed out of the window and made his way to Liu Yun's room. The snuff bottle was in the secret place in the brick wall where Liu Yun hid things. Only Fuzzy knew where to look. He tucked the snuff bottle inside his shirt. Liu Yun was not a bad guy, at least in his mind, but whenever Fuzzy thought of him, he felt uncomfortable. He had walked quite a way along the road when, unable to resist any longer, he took out the bottle and looked at it under the street lamp.

"Don't look at it!" an elderly voice echoed behind his back and a hand grabbed the bottle. "There's already been one seduction, and you go looking for another. There's already been one mistake and yet you want to go off and make another?" The old man let out a long sigh.

Fuzzy jumped in front of the old man and grabbed for the bottle. He could clearly see the white beard and long white hair. The old man's grip wasn't tight enough and the bottle slipped away into the bushes as he fell to the ground. Fuzzy ignored the old man and dived into the bushes to retrieve the bottle.

On the day of the trial, it was cold even in padded clothes. Mother kept close to Fuzzy. She was in a daze. Everytime her son took one step away from her side, she called out hysterically: Fuzzy, Fuzzy! The announcement was posted on the wall facing east at the crossroads. It said that his brother was the prime culprit and that he had committed a grave, despicable crime, which had resulted in an attempted suicide. The People could not deal with him leniently, and therefore, in accordance with the judgment of the court, the death sentence had been passed. In front of his brother's name was the word "Sodomite," and over his name was a large red cross. As Liu Yun was younger, he was considered an accessory to the crime and was sentenced to a labor reform camp in the Far West.

Fuzzy and his mother sat motionless holding the tweezers. Some of the pig bristles smelt of urine and rotten fish. Fuzzy stared at the small heap of pig bristles on the table. He thought that one of the tufts looked like his brother's hair. The image of his brother with a shaved head was unfamiliar, particularly surrounded by all those people. A single bullet pierced his brother's chest. He swayed a little then stood still. The second bullet hit him in the head. He fell to the ground. The way he stood there was unlike the others being executed, but Fuzzy couldn't say exactly how.

When a story is passed around, it changes shape. The neighbor thought it was odd that Fuzzy didn't cry. His mother held her palm in mid-air never letting it come to rest on Fuzzy's narrow, thin face. Not only did Fuzzy not cry, he began to laugh.

Time passed like water through sand. Fuzzy ran into Hui only once in the street. She was no longer the sort to try and kill herself by drinking pesticide. She'd married a worker from another province. She had put on weight and seemed unfamiliar. When she called out to Fuzzy, he stopped in his tracks and didn't budge. She talked on and on, her breath was pungent with garlic. Then she noticed one of her friends and left Fuzzy standing there alone. She started up a conversation with the friend. Further down the street her voice was still audible.

Fuzzy donned a red armband. He was the first in his school to adopt the revolutionary cause and join the Red Guards. He kept it from his mother. He didn't want to go home, so he banded together with his classmates and they caught the train to Beijing to see the Great Leader. He pushed and shoved for his life, and finally managed to squeeze his way onto the train. His friends were thrown back into the sea of people on the platform.

People were everywhere, in the corridors, on the luggage racks and window-sills, underneath the seats and even in the toilets. In the middle of the night, Fuzzy curled up and went to sleep.

He walked and walked. Eventually, he reached the old man's house. The old man was lying in bed already half paralyzed. Why should he care about this man? The dunce's hat in his hands required a head. Who? Fuzzy threw a stone at the window, glass splintered and flew everywhere. All he heard was the sound of the glass breaking, but no one came out. He pretended he didn't know Hui's parents. He was simply watching others smashing the house of counter-revolutionaries who had slipped through the net. Hui's father was beaten to a pulp. Fuzzy sat on the windowsill throughout. He didn't lift a finger. He just gave the orders.

They were running short of dunce's hats. They would have to make a new batch. Perhaps they could use the slogan posters.

Fuzzy tossed and turned, then woke up. The train trundled on, kacha, kacha. It felt as if it were running over his body. The dream and reality converged in a mush. He pushed the person sleeping against him away, and stretched out his aching legs.

Having rearranged himself, he reached into his purse for the little piece of jade. Excitement coursed through his body. He felt very lucky to be experiencing such a thrilling revolution. The train was speeding across a starless plain. In the expansive darkness, only the dim lights of the carriage glowed. They outlined the contours of other pale faces, just like Fuzzy's: a grass-green uniform, a burning red heart, and a gently swaying body.

HU DONG   TRANSLATED BY YANBING CHEN

FROM *THE SORCERER'S BOOK*

1.   Upper Nine   The Arrogant Dragon Repents.

At the mother tongue's line of defense
a strange homesickness
a dying rose

In exile, someone wrote these lines of solitude. They touched me and made me recall my own departure from the country. A cold morning, the train stopped on the border of Manchuria. I was shaken awake from a nightmare by my wife. Repressing the sudden rush of panic (which excited me like a heavy fog), I went through the exit formalities.... Finally they all got off. The train started to rumble again, and slowly moved to the other side with the speed of someone dragging along in an art gallery. Under the gaze of the Red Army officers and soldiers, I suddenly felt relaxed and cheerful. The reason was simple: As I looked out the window, looking over their hefty shoulders, over the frontier they guarded and defended, the majestic and glorious autumn of Siberia dazzled like a human organ.

2.   Six Four   Empty the Bag, No Fault No Praise.

The last day of the year, the wind's mumps worsen; the clouds compete
with each other to pile the pillows higher. I'm not immune either. On
the double bed, I live on strenuously. I wrap myself in a white sheet, my
eyes devouring a sky as gloomy as my age, devouring the desk, which I
intrude upon from time to time — what is it that deserves all the time I
have squandered there? I turn the question over in my mind. The whole
morning, my heart laughs out loud like a fool. Too cold, we can only
keep warm by taking walks — I recall another winter, a friend who was
later sentenced to jail said to me: "There are three ways to destroy a poet
— loneliness, poverty, and unfair criticism." I replied that one had no
need to worry about such things, and furthermore, I thought there were
two types of poets: the literati and the artist. The former carry with
them dreams of tradition, apparent ambition for their profession, fame-
seeking opportunism, and longing for immortality. The latter know deep
in their hearts that artists are nothing but creatures of humility, and pay
no attention to the various kinds of catch phrases that spread like a
plague. I notice they usually come and go as they please, ignoring their
surroundings. They also seem to have no companions, not even a pet-
phrase. They are like those gloomy faced musicians in London or Paris;
in public squares, subway stations, and on street corners, they stand in
the midst of strangers, playing their solos.

4.   Six Four   In Distress, Be Thrifty.

Writing requires that we maintain silence. Silence is our sole pleasure.
Snowdrifts decorate mountain peaks, headstones stand in graveyards:
amidst alpinists' cheers and boisterous funerals, they remain silent. Ex-
cessive excitement and sorrow leave some of us speechless. Silence be-
comes a lingering theme in our poems. Yet in some people's poetry, the
fear of losing one's voice, the fear of being mourned by survivors who

only pretend, exaggerates the erection of the headstone into an unbearable blow, and since the blow is fatal, it receives naturally no praise. To rid themselves of such fear, or embarrassment, their writing metamorphoses into a trampling of the thousand-year-old snowdrifts, into a protest against, and a refusal of, the primordial silence — just like backroads farmers suffering from a harvest-complex, they drag out their tractors and bring out their hoes, all for the purpose of weeding out the pitifully scarce beautiful flowers of silence in the fields and around their huts. They are determined not to let them take root in the sterile soil, in our exercise books which yield mere grain. What resolution and persistence! Unfortunately, what they weed out are not the words of slander and praise, which they are constantly anxious to carve into the stone.

6.　　　Nine Five　　　　　　　Litigation, Prime Auspices.

A motley crowd, each and every one worried that he might be a better writer than the other. Yet all of them, under the premise of having no qualms about lying, trained themselves to do numerous dirty tricks, and hand-in-hand built an age of depravity. Everyone was quickly infected with the habit of imitation and the custom of quotation, and compares and competes with each other. Such a phenomenon reveals the tension among ourselves. In the absence of natural relaxation, culture has become for us a spiritual burden. Nevertheless, it is a step forward. Compared with the benighted era we've just survived, we are now braver and smarter, weak minds having replaced total idiots. Perhaps in this mouth-watering self-complacency, we have only neglected one virtue, that is, the virtue of being fed up.

SHI TIESHENG   TRANSLATED BY DESMOND SKEEL

BRIEF NOTES ON WALLS

Things that didn't really seem important at the time have now taken permanent root in the memory. They have been there all the time, sleeping peacefully. Occasionally they wake up, open an eye, look around, and on seeing that you're busy (being promoted or withdrawing from the world), go back to sleep again. They are so quiet for so long it's as if they're not even there. Thousands of lucky chances slip by. Eventually, one day they emerge again. Time seems to have completely worn away the so-called important things in life. But they were always there, keeping a resolute watch, heavy with an almost incomparable weight. Just like an old photograph: you failed to pay much attention when you took it, tossing it somewhere, forgetting for years that it even exists. Suddenly, one day while sorting through old things, you come across it, wipe off the dust, and get the strange feeling that this represents both where you've come from and where you're heading to. Meanwhile the occasion and reason for many photos you took in earnest to remember a place have escaped you completely.

In recent years I have often found myself recalling a wall. It was built of piled-up broken bricks; the wind could dislodge the fine dirt that had collected between them. It was a very long wall — or at least it seemed long in the eyes of a child. After a fair distance the wall turned a corner into a much narrower lane. There was a street lamp on the corner of the lane, just in front of which was the gate to a courtyard. A good friend of mine from school used to live there. Let's call him L. It's not that important whether L and I could have been good friends forever. What is important is that at one time we were inseparable. A section of my life's path was paved as a result of this friendship. We walked together to and from school through these dense lanes, summer and winter, in bright sunshine or under starry skies, accompanied either by the sound of the wind or the cicadas droning in the trees. At the age of nine (or perhaps ten) L told me that he planned to marry a girl (M) in our class when he was older.

L turned and asked me, "Well, who do you want to marry?"

I wasn't at all prepared for this question. I thought about it and then agreed that M was really pretty. L also said that he intended to earn a lot of money.

"What for?"

"Do you think you'll still be spending your dad's money when you're older?"

When I think back now, there's nothing that could improve the childlike innocence of that friendship.

I once gave L something I treasured. I can't remember what it was. Then one day we had a fight. Exactly why we fought I can't remember, but what I do remember clearly is that, after the fight, I went to ask L for the thing back.

In all honesty, I wouldn't have dared go and ask for it on my own. Perhaps I wouldn't have even thought about going to ask for it. A number of friends, who at the time had an ax to grind with L, egged me on. They slapped their chests and said they would be happy to go along with me. So we went. As we walked along that very long yet familiar wall, the setting sun shone brilliantly. Yet, as we got to L's front gate, it seemed like the street lamp on the corner was dimly lit. The wall couldn't possibly have been that long. My memory must be playing tricks on me.

I was a little scared as I stood in front of the gate. My friends, who stood at my side, did their best to inspire and encourage me. They reminded me that it was even more contemptible to turn and run than to surrender. I couldn't shirk my responsibility or shift the blame onto someone else. Why had I gone and told anyone about my fight with L, and that I'd given him something? This is what had given rise to my friends' advice. I walked into the yard and shouted for L to come out. L came out, listened to why I had come, stared blankly at me for a while, went back inside and brought the thing out. Without saying anything, he placed it in my hand and went back inside. All in all the conclusion of the ordeal was extremely simple and passed more quickly than the clicking of a camera shutter.

Under the street lamp on the corner, my friends and I broke up for the night and went home. They looked at the object in my hand and asked, "What did you give it to him for?" Their tone and expression lacked the intensity they had when we set out. Their expectations had been crushed.

I went home alone, walking close to the wall. The wall was long — very long and bleak. My memory seems to be in error here as well. The street lamp couldn't have been lit, for the features of the passers-by approaching me were unclear. The evening breeze was soft, but still made me feel grumpy. It seemed to carry my soul, as well as my body, high into the air, where it floated in the twilight and then disappeared into the wall. As I walked I picked up a twig and gently brushed it against the wall, dislodging the dirt between the bricks bit by bit.... Whatever was sent on its way in that instant, as if with the click of a camera, took root in the memory, evolving into future problems.

That is possibly my first memory of walls.

Afterwards, other walls began to wake from sleep.

While out for a "walk" one evening, I maneuvered my wheelchair into the alleyways where I often played as a child. Actually, I had never strayed far away, often passing close to them, just too busy to go in and have a look.

I can remember that there had once been a short, red brick wall there. A group of eight- or nine-year-olds would always disturb the family who lived on the other side of the wall. We climbed up a small tree, clung to the edge of the wall and begged them to throw back our soccer ball. Although the wall was hidden in a cul-de-sac, the width of the alley entrance was, unfortunately for them, just the right size for our goal. The stretch of open land outside the alley was our soccer field. It was inevitable that the ball would be kicked towards the goal, and if anyone kicked the ball into the air near the goal, there was an eighty or ninety per cent chance that it would land behind the wall. We clung to the top of the wall asking over and over for our ball back, promising never to do it again. We were anxious that the daylight was gradually slipping away. Our "soccer mania" would have to be put on hold overnight. One day, the ball went over the wall and landed smack in a pot of noodles. It had been behaving more like a basketball than a soccer ball. When we climbed up the small tree to take a look, we saw snowy white noodles rolling into the coal ashes amidst a plume of steam. It happened during the so-called "three years of hardship." In view of what happened, losing the ball seemed fairly insignificant. Like rats, we scurried away under cover of darkness. A few days later, led by our parents, we came to retrieve the ball, but only at the cost of closing down the "soccer field."

The small lanes remain unchanged, perhaps a little older. And the "soccer field" has long since been crushed beneath a restaurant. The family who lived behind the short, red brick wall is certainly much safer.

I wheeled my way through the streets and down the lanes. The gray wall started my heart thumping. I knew that if I went further along the road I would come to my kindergarten. The gray wall was very tall and behind it the trees were even taller. Once there had been a bird's nest at the top of the tree. It was no longer there. I passed along this wall every day I went to kindergarten. As soon as I caught sight of the wall, any hope of slipping back home was immediately extinguished. The gray color was a cruel omen that filled my childhood with terror.

This "conditioned reflex" was established one afternoon in the middle of summer. The reason I remember it so clearly is that at the time the cicadas were droning their loudest. That afternoon Mother was going to some faraway place on business. At best I hoped that she would change her plans. At the very least I hoped that I wouldn't have to go to kindergarten and would be able to stay at home with Grandmother. But both motions were rejected out of hand. Bursting into tears as a means of vigorously arguing the case also proved ineffective. As I think back on it now, all Mother wanted to do was to establish a set of rules that were firm and impartial before going on her trip. When I didn't stop crying,

Mother had no choice but to offer to take me out for a walk.

"I'm not going to kindergarten!" I restated my position as we left.

Mother took me for a walk through the streets, buying things for me to eat on the way. Although it all seemed very suspicious, as we had walked so far along a road that didn't seem to lead to the kindergarten, I loosened my tight grip on Mother's dress and felt a little bit more at ease. But! No sooner had I popped into my mouth the sweet things that Mother had bought, than the high gray wall appeared before me. It was only then that I realized that all the small lanes led to this place. I burst into tears, even though I knew it was no use. But as soon as we had stepped through the gate into the kindergarten my wailing automatically stopped. I knew deep down that I had no more tricks up my sleeve and that the only plan for saving myself was to be on my best behavior. The "disaster" within the kindergarten walls had to be endured — or perhaps it was just because I was an innately timid and emotional child.

I moved three years ago. From my window I could see a kindergarten. Often, while sleeping late some mornings, I could hear the children shouting as they went into the kindergarten. I made a point of going up to the gate and taking a look. The children who refused to go into the kindergarten all exuded a kind of heroism, which suggested they would rather die than surrender. As soon as they found themselves within the walls, they managed to swallow their cries immediately. Dread turned into injustice and teary eyes looked towards the sky desperately hoping for the evening clouds. I don't think there was anyone who sympathized with them more than I did, but to encounter walls at such an early age isn't necessarily a bad thing.

I recall clearly the sight of Mother disappearing behind that high, gray wall. Of course, she walked around the wall and out onto the road to some faraway place, but to me it seemed like she had actually walked into the wall. There was no gate; Mother had gone into it. Cicadas droned loudly in the treetops. Mother cut a very small figure beneath the tall trees. My fear was already somewhere far away.

Now I have a lot of time to sit by the window and look out at walls, whether they are tall or short, near or far, standing in great numbers like precipices. Where there are people there are walls. We are all within walls. There aren't many things we'd be happy doing in broad daylight. Tall buildings in neat rows remind me of library card catalogues. Only God can open every small drawer, look up the billions of secret spiritual histories, and see each dream of breaking through the walls hesitate within the sealed wall. Death arrives promptly, stretching its hand into the wall to snatch some of them away, as if drawing lots.

Sometimes we travel great distances, on buses, trains, or planes — God forbid they fall out of the sky and find someplace without walls: wastelands, oceans, grasslands, or even deserts. But we are not necessarily ever able to escape. The wall is always in our mind, constructing fear and stirring memories. Whenever we travel to some faraway place, there is always a Robinson Crusoe returning from some faraway place. A boomerang sets out from the wall only to return.

At first, philosophers said that labor created man. Now they say that language created man. Did walls create man? Language and walls share fundamental similarities: an endless number of walls stand before an endless number of gates that cannot be opened. Structuralism, deconstruction, "post-something-ism" ... and so on. The enthusiasm for games can never be dampened, but we are still surrounded by four walls. The desire to demolish all walls has always been with us. Is it possible? I sit by the window fantasizing about a magic trick, such as chanting "abracadabra" until presto, the walls are gone. And what about that then? I suppose that everyone would definitely be thrown into utter confusion (just like hot oil poured onto an ants' nest) not knowing where to go. What should be done? Should we seek food over hill and dale and then go to sleep? But at the end of the day that's just not interesting enough. Then they all bury themselves in thought: perhaps it would be better to have walls after all. We build walls and houses not only to protect ourselves against the wind and rain, but because everyone has secrets and, of course, a little wealth. Secrets? If you don't believe me, sit and think about it. They are the mother and father of curiosity.

Actually, secrecy is a wall in itself. Stomachs and eyelids are both walls, as are false laughter and crocodile tears. Because these walls are soft and tired, we also need solid and durable ones. Even if we suppose that these spiritual walls can be easily removed, mountains and rivers are walls, as are heaven and earth, and time and space. Destiny is a boundless restriction. God's secrets are an endless wall. What God possesses is more than likely the wisdom to build walls. And if we really got rid of all walls, even though a long-standing ideal would be seen to be coming close to realization, just wait and see. The whole world, I'm afraid, will start to snore in a sleep brought about by a lack of curiosity. We wouldn't even know what to start talking about in our sleep.

Curiosity is the most important thing of all. Secrets must be kept.

The desire to discover secrets will eventually lead to the wall of meaning.

Life has to have meaning. This platitude cannot be overthrown by any "ism." It's also useless to add the prefix "post-." Take love, for instance. It can be abducted for a time by material desire, but we should not believe that therefore it can be wiped out. The days of "nothing is that amazing" will have to come to an end. The dance of "take offense at nothing" is likely to collide with the wall. If you're not dead after the collision, the next step is to lift your eyes and see the writing on the wall: Hey, where're you going? What're you up to? You can't avoid it even if you want to. With a creditor's face, meaning has come to your doorstep.

The reason for meaning is probably meaning itself. Why does there have to be meaning? Why does there have to be life? Why does there have to be existence? Why does there have to be? The reason for weight is gravity, but what is the reason for gravity? It's weight. Someone who studies physics once told me: whatever you do, don't attempt to explain motion and energy or time and space as separate entities. It became clear to me immediately: don't attempt to explain man and meaning as separate entities. It's not that man has desires, but that man *is* desire. This desire is energy. If there's energy then there's motion. If there's motion then there's definitely movement forward into the future. What and why are forward and future? This obvious question causes meaning to be born. And on the sixth day God created man. God was stronger than Mephistopheles. No magic or incantation can delete the achievements of the sixth day. In all the time since the sixth day, you may have been able to avoid certain kinds of meaning, but you cannot avoid meaning altogether — just as you can avoid a single journey, but you cannot avoid the journey of life.

If you don't associate yourself with one kind of meaning, then you do with another. If you don't have any meaning, then you fall into what Kundera has termed "the unbearable lightness of being." So what are you? What kind of thing is life? If it's so light that there isn't the slightest weight to it, then you're bound to disappear. When I asked for that thing back from L, I was too young to describe the anxiety I felt on the way home. Thinking about it today, clearly it was because of the word "light": in the wink of an eye a treasure had been treated like garbage. A section of my life was so light that it floated off and was no more. Actually it was never really anything, just light and insubstantial like dust or smoke floating in the wind. The lightness of one part of my life threatened the weight of my whole life. Anxiety seeped into my soul: will all phases of my life end up like this? Man's fundamental fear can be summed up by the word "lightness": such as discrimination and indifference, such as mockery, such as the worthless stock certificate in the hand of a pauper, such as lost love and death. Lightness — the most fearsome thing of all.

To seek meaning is to seek the weight of life. There are different kinds of weight. Different kinds of weight are only truly measured when they hit the wall. But many weights are still light on the scales of Death. The weight pivots on the balance point of absurdity. A weight stems from this, one for which you're willing to live and die, one whose burden you are willing to bear, whose gravity under which you are willing to wear away your life. It's not stubbornness when I say there're no regrets; it's sober obedience. God's measure of the soul is sacredness. Sacredness is the acknowledged weight of the soul. There is a ritual when death pays its visit, dust to dust, earth to earth, and you watch the past evaporate, but you can hear that something heavy still remains, if not in the real world, then at least somewhere beautiful. Could my friendship with L still be heavy enough to have weight at a beautiful place?

Don't let the desire to break out of walls die — otherwise the snoring will begin again.

But you do have to accept walls.

In order to escape their influence, I once went up to a wall. Near my home was an old garden that had fallen into disrepair. The surrounding wall was in ruins but still solid. During the years when I was at my most despondent, I would wheel myself up to them. There was nobody around, only an age-old silence. Wild flowers grew and blossomed between my silent self and the silent wall. Injustice also grew and blossomed. I struck the wall with my fist. I hacked at it with stones. I wept and muttered curses before it, but only a little dust was gently dislodged. Nothing else stirred. Heaven doesn't change. The Way doesn't either. The old cypress tree stretches out its branches and leaves for a thousand years as if it were only one day. Clouds move across the sky. Birds fly through the clouds. Wind tramples the grass. Weeds take root generation after generation. I turned to pray to the wall, putting my palms together and inventing a prayer or prophecy. I chanted aloud, pleading with it to let me die, or at least to give back my legs so that I could walk ... but when I opened my eyes, the great wall still stood there. Beneath it to some god-forsaken person sat blankly. The setting sun, vast and empty, walked into the garden. If I fell asleep, I fell into a dried-up well of dreams. The well walls were high and slippery. My calls from inside the well merely buzzed as they collided with the sides. No one could hear them. Silent injustice blew in the wind above the well. I woke up to find myself still alive. My shouting had startled no one; it couldn't startle anything. There was green and moist and dried-up moss and delicate spider webs on the walls. Behind the body of a snail that had died halfway through its journey was a trail of scale-like footprints. Some child had written 3.1415926 over it....

On a particular winter night I saw an old man beneath the wall. I always have problems with memories and impressions: my memory tells me that the old man was not necessarily beneath the wall, but I've always had the impression that he was there. So let's say he was. It was a snowy night bathed in haze and moonlight. My wheelchair creaked its way over the snowy road. It was the only sound in the garden. As I went along I could hear drifting from afar the drawn-out strains of a bamboo flute. It seemed to be there and yet not there among the snowy mists swirling around the old cypress. Although I was unable to distinguish the tune, the drawn-out music seemed to fit my mood perfectly. As I listened carefully with bated breath, I made out the tune, "Su Wu Tends the Sheep." When the music ended I felt miserable. Then I sensed movement in the shadow of the wall. Only then did I realize that an old man was sitting cross-legged on the stone bench beneath the wall. He looked mysterious in his black clothes and gray hair. The snow-covered ground bathed in moonlight seemed extraordinarily peaceful. The bamboo flute played again. It was the same piece of music, expressing grief at having been exiled to a desolate place. The flute music was not actually drifting from afar, but coming from the old man's lips. Perhaps it was his lack of energy or perhaps it was that this old tune had traveled a bumpy road to the present day, but the music kept stopping and starting without ambition. The old man's trembling breathing could also be heard clearly. When he finished the tune a second time, the old man laid the flute across his legs and put his hands on his knees. I couldn't see whether he had closed his eyes. I was startled, even grateful, and listened again and again to both the flute-playing and to the intermittent silences. I took it to be instructions from Heaven or spirits coming to guide me.

The old man and his flute remained on my mind for many years, but I was never able to guess in which direction they were leading me. It needn't have been anything mysterious, perhaps just something urging me to go on living. Then one day while I was speaking to the wall again, I realized the flute that night had been singing "accept": Accept limitations. Accept incompleteness. Accept misery. Accept the existence of walls. All that crying and shouting, it's just for escaping the wall. All that anger and cursing, it's just for escape. All that flattery and kowtowing, it's just for escape. During the years when I was at my most despondent I would go and talk to that wall. Yes, I spoke to it out loud, thinking that was the better way to show my devoutness and solemnity. Out loud, I beseeched and interrogated the wall. Afraid of angering it, I also apologized and repented out loud. But either way, it had absolutely no effect. The negotiations inevitably broke down, for it was unable to agree to any of my conditions. The wall wants you to accept it, proclaiming this one meaning over and over again until you hear it, neither obsequious nor supercilious. And only when you stop asking questions, but can hear it asking you many more questions, can the conversation be called a conversation.

I've been writing all along, but always felt it would never amount to very much — regardless of the work, the author, or the "ism." Writing with a pen or on the computer are both conversations with the wall. It's as essential as eating, drinking, going to the bathroom, and sleeping. Eventually I moved far away from that old garden and could no longer drop in whenever I wanted. Before I moved I had a feeling that I would miss it, but I never would have guessed that what I would miss most would be the four surrounding walls. They crossed no one's mind for many years, though I do remember several saplings having turned into trees in the broken tiles at the top of the wall. But no matter what time of day or where I am, all I have to do is close my eyes and I'm instantly there beneath the wall. Wild flowers swell into buds between the silent wall and my silent self. Endless paths stretch between endless walls. There are many things I need to say to them slowly, so I note them down and call it writing.

You Ren TRANSLATED BY YANBING CHEN

OCTOBER'S WRITING

In a time of fake jewelry, my face is more fake.
Autumn deals out its blow not through broken branches
but through the swing, it swings out past the abyss of October
and swings back as a different look in someone's eyes.

Who witnessed darkness, and lit the oil lamp in the skull
in pitch-black? Who returned by bus and then was carried by his feet
to the day's apex? Slipping twice in one day does not
point in the same direction; starting at night, they end at night.

Only self-disguise saved the skin.
My old distant bones, slapped by the wind, showed marks of water.
Lonely, and cold, even the swallow can only get close to them in spring
carrying earth in its mouth. O, a heart covered

by leaves, the visiting footsteps avoided it
like frequent avoidance in a life, which I understand.
How hard life is when no one cares about you.
The cold dew is forming again, the frost-wind blows out the oil lamp.

In a darkness this deep I cannot keep myself
from secretly being replaced. Fake body, fake mind
climb over elaborate fences. Essential details of yesterday migrate
to today: tired of speaking, afraid of speaking.

Look at the yellow flower, autumn's blood relative, pressed
between book leaves, surrounded by words of sorrow
which it does not understand. Aimless earth, a sheet of paper bearing
an oath; tell me, should I read out loud my self-redeeming words?

When the splendid sunlight of autumn moves close to the crowd
who extracts his own body?
It is not flying, but grasping from visible flesh
an invisible body, another face in the time of fake jewelry.

— it was you who gave birth to her, my mother and elder sister.
It all really started from my reading eleven years ago; now
I keep quiet, like a cicada in a cold wind. Those bone-piercing cries
bounce off into darkness, not through words, but through meditation.

                                                    October 1994

HAN DONG TRANSLATED BY DESMOND SKEEL

TAKING ADVANTAGE

1.

Ma Wen grew up in poverty. His family didn't buy a television set until very late. However, more than a year of university life had seen him change in many respects. For example, he no longer considered watching the news after dinner every day a luxury. He arrived at Duan Hui's house at the start of winter vacation. While he had only just gotten used to television, Duan Hui's parents were already starting to worry about the frequent disputes which arose between themselves and their children due to differing tastes in television programs.

Ma Wen's arrival coincided with the unveiling of the second television in Duan Hui's family. He couldn't remember whether he had, in fact, come to witness this spectacle. The television, which had an orange casing, was installed in Duan Hui's sister's room. It was her sixteenth birthday present from the whole family. Cardboard boxes and polystyrene were strewn all over the floor. Like the television set, she too seemed to have just emerged from the pile of rubbish on the floor.

That year's Spring Festival was instantly forgettable. After returning home, Ma Wen shut himself away in his room. It was, however, impossible to avoid greeting those friends and relatives who came to pay their New Year's call. He usually exchanged pleasantries with them before locking himself back in his bedroom, which was actually a storage closet. The buzz of conversation came from the living room on the other side of the wall. Outside the window, firecrackers flew into the air with loud bangs. They exploded into powder at a height parallel with his eyes, red and yellow scraps of paper falling thick and fast.

Situated as he was at the mid-point between the sources of the two sounds, Ma Wen remained silent. He fantasized that Duan Hui might come with some cakes, bringing his dazzling sister with him. Ma Wen went nowhere, just waiting for the two of them. He tempered his sense of hearing amidst the usual festivities of the New Year. It really was a kind of torment, training his hearing to be as acute as that of a mouse — especially if, in the end, his guests never showed up.

The main problem was neither the worn-out voices of his relatives nor the firecrackers outside the window. It was his sister and prospective brother-in-law in the room next door. Like Ma Wen, they too had locked themselves in their room. The number of times they opened the door was fewer than the number of bowls left in the corner of the room. The flat consisted of two bedrooms and a sitting room. Their mother remained in the sitting room both day and night facing the two secretly locked doors. Comparatively speaking, Ma Wen actually preferred it when the house was as noisy as a train car all day long. He was scared of his mother's senile fumbling and his sister's coquettish laughter which were exaggerated in the silence.

"Disgusting!" His sister Ma Fang's shrill voice negotiated the corner and came in via the south-facing balcony. Ma Wen did his utmost to close the open balcony door. As he did so, he also closed the door on his mysterious precognition. Not once did Duan Hui and his sister come as he had willed. And when he no longer actively willed it (due to a lapse of memory brought on by a martial arts novel) they still didn't come.

2.

Then something happened: Duan Ai ran away from home. Three days later she came back of her own will. This gave Ma Wen the opportunity to pass openly and legally into the inner sanctum of the house — Duan Ai's small room — during the next vacation (summer vacation).

She welcomed him with a tin of sweets, whereas Duan Hui — his classmate from high school — merely nodded to him from beside the flowerbed in the yard. At last he was her friend — or mainly her friend. This change didn't necessarily leave him feeling unhappy, it was just that he wasn't really used to it.

If he could have stopped her at the dock and brought her home, things might have been even better. But she had never been on that snow-white boat. She'd never been on any boat. He'd never seen her appear among the crowds spilling onto the quay. The reason for his persistent imagination was that he wanted many more people to see her together with him — two eminent pinpoints of light rapidly drawing closer together against a dark background.

As he had these thoughts, she was fast asleep at a classmate's house. She had sealed herself in the wondrous land of dreams. In the real world images and doubles of her were everywhere. She had been totally doted upon that day. The image of a young girl, continuously duplicated upon the emotional screens (or in the narrow minds) of the friends and relatives who had been mobilized into action by the family. At the stations and ports of all the important towns within a thousand kilometer radius of the city where Duan Ai lived, those entrusted with the task of finding her opened their hollow eyes. She became such a lovable explosion of youth in the eyes of those who considered themselves detectives.

Three months earlier when Duan Ai had run away, Ma Wen had been one of those hollow people entrusted with finding her. He sat on the stone breakwater eating seven loaves of bread, following the dubious routes of many ferries with a line of vision like that of a water bird.

Her mysterious disappearance was apparently the result of a difference of opinion on an exam. (The family had maintained that she should go to technical college while she had an inordinate amount of ambition, which exceeded her intelligence, to apply for the university.) Perhaps it was just that she had reached the age when one runs away. Her leg muscles had developed over the years and had to be put to use at once. It was nothing more than a covert rite of passage into adulthood. Even if this was her reason for running away, it remained mysterious.

Duan Ai welcomed the first formal visitor to her own small room (it was different from the get-togethers with and visits from her classmates). The topic of her conversation with him failed to touch upon the extremely important subjects of her running away or their correspondence after she had been found. Nor did it touch upon the alliance which had only been brought about through a need for resistance — Ma Wen had resolutely stood at Duan Ai's side, raising his arms in respect at her courage in applying to the university.

They only talked about food that day, further developing their shared aspirations on the subject of taste.

She liked chocolate, "White Rabbit" toffee, and sour plum candies. So did he. As for fruit, she liked oranges and watermelon, while he preferred watermelon and peaches. They shared a mutual disgust for the most typical of fruits — the apple. She ate no meat other than pork (and it had to be lean). He was nowhere near as fussy as she was on this point. They also discussed cold drinks, cakes, and noodles. It would have taken several afternoons if they had continued the discussion. And had they tasted everything one by one, then it would have taken many more afternoons. For the months that followed they scheduled a meeting almost every afternoon, with a plethora of different tables, spoons, and paper bags. Among the illusory piles of scattered resplendent rubbish (made up of melon skins, fruit peels and candy wrappers), she heard him say that he had eaten raw birds' eggs and mercury (he had bitten the thermometer while his temperature was being taken).

"So you've eaten glass as well?"

Ma Wen nodded resolutely.

"Brilliant!" said Duan Ai.

However, he had taken almost none of the tablets she had taken since she was small. She had been afflicted by many more illnesses than he had. She enumerated the names which have become immortal in human history: otitis media, rhinitis, tonsillitis, bronchitis, pneumonia, arthritis, enterogastritis, scarlet fever, whooping cough, mumps, dysentery, measles, caries, the common cold, and a sty. She had dislocated a joint, had had an ulcer and worms, had suffered from heatstroke, had burnt herself (on a hot water bottle under the covers), had been bitten (by a centipede) and had pricked herself (on a thumbtack). She dwelt at great length on the subject, taking enormous delight in it, as though she were enumerating family treasures. It was hard to believe that this lovable person had been afflicted by so many ills, and yet had become a rare and expensive fruit preserved by all the different medicines she had taken.

"You haven't even had chilblains?" she asked, disappointed.

During the course of the discussion he gradually lost the upper hand, and turned against her by criticizing her for having been pampered since childhood. She appeared to have been waiting for this admonishment for some time, and listened immediately and with bated breath to his fervent lecture. He thought he could hear the rustling of her long eyelashes brushing together as she blinked. If nothing else, they had found the fundamental pattern for their future relationship. Both of them had assumed their rightful positions. The sun now shone clearly down upon them: one was a pure girl unaware of the ways of the world and accustomed to being pampered; the other was a steady young man who had grown up in adversity but was a future pillar of the state.

3.

Although Ma Wen was only twenty years old, his seven roommates still treated him as someone who would never find a wife. They all had their own "wives" — legal spouses or lovers. They all had a sense of superiority because of this and failed to show even the slightest mercy towards the twenty-year-old virgin. The total combined age of the seven of them was not far from two hundred. It was therefore a battle between two hundred years of experience and a mere twenty. Ma Wen had no choice but to draw on the explosion of youth that was Duan Ai.

After lights-out the young men's dormitory resembled an animals' lair. Moreover, they shared an insatiable hunger. The imaginary dining on the seven women (their "wives") was a practice that had to be carried out each night. The most important condition was that each of them had to bring a dish in order to take part in the potluck. Ma Wen therefore always tried his best to delay his return to the dormitory, or he would be condemned to spend the whole night with earplugs. Despite this, he was still regarded as getting his meal for free, and faced discrimination. As a result, his self-respect was dealt an unprecedented blow.

So, when he mentioned Duan Ai, Ma Wen was immediately welcomed as warmly as vegetables that had just come into season.

What was special about the imaginary potluck? A single illusion could be broken up infinitely into countless other illusions and served to every diner to enjoy at length. Each diner, however, needed to enjoy many such illusions (otherwise there would be no point to the potluck) — the more the better. Though illusions are different from the substance of life in that they are not durable, they can, nevertheless, be disassembled and re-assembled at will according to individual needs. Ma Wen served Duan Ai up to the bestial banquet, placing her onto the filthy and greasy dining table. "She is my girlfriend," he said, and immediately, she was chopped into pieces, ladled on a china plate with a shining gold rim, and served.

4.

Wang Yi was one year ahead of Ma Wen. They met by chance at one of the many unremarkable weekend parties. After that, events developed with amazing speed. The place where the two of them rendezvoused moved from the cinema, into which light leaked at every corner, to Wang Yi's home (oddly enough, she didn't live on campus). She taught him to use some sort of spray. That evening he tried many things for the first time.

He started doubting her status and chastity. The only way of understanding her was through her devotion. The following morning he therefore accompanied her again to her home, where there was no father, no mother, no brothers or sisters. This time he insisted that they not go by taxi. (The evening before he had taken a taxi for the first time and was locked inside unable to open the door.) She assumed that walking slowly along the street would be romantic, and agreed with pleasure. That night he didn't dare repeat any of the things with which she was strangely familiar.

He wanted to talk about something else, about her room, about her dancing, and ... about her experiences. But she just wanted to prove herself.

As far as Ma Wen was concerned, this had been a long apprenticeship — lasting three to four months. He left the animals' lair and came to a warm land of soft lights and gentle fragrance — Wang Yi's abode of plenitude. Consequently, the illusion of Duan Ai failed to tickle anybody's tastebuds for the time being. She floated far away from Ma Wen's field of vision, returning to her own silence, awaiting the next time she would be summoned.

Ma Wen had never seen Wang Yi's enigmatic foster father. His getting together with Wang Yi was a chance holiday, an occasional moment of secret happiness, coming at a time when her foster father had gone away for some reason. They had now both transgressed. He had treated the academic year during which he had to spare no effort as a chance holiday, and she had treated this chance holiday as a destiny.

Amidst danger and trouble, and at an ambiguous point between an oppressive past and a hapless future, they fell in love. They were inseparable. On the eve of her foster father's return (two or three times every six months she would receive prior notice) Wang Yi had to clean the room thoroughly. (The heavy mattress was highest priority among other priorities.) Everything belonging to Ma Wen (his textbooks, his dirty clothes, the small presents he had given her and his odor) also had to be disposed of.

She wrapped a scarf around her head and tied an apron around her waist. Clutching an aerosol can much larger than the one in the bathroom, she wildly sprayed everywhere. He was like a cockroach that she had killed and swept out of the door. But such was her capability that, as soon as her foster father had gone downstairs dragging his bamboo cane (his chauffeur would be waiting outside to take him to the airport), she would immediately be able to resuscitate the cockroach waiting in the dustpan.

If she had once shared her bed with a foster father she did not love, then couldn't he have a girlfriend, a soul mate?

Duan Ai therefore became a pivotal piece on the chessboard of their mutual slaughter. She was one of the red pieces belonging to Ma Wen. Apart from the "king" who symbolized the one playing the red side, the only other piece which could be brought into play to defend against Wang Yi's vast army was Duan Ai. She was not only intended to offset the existence of the white-haired foster father, but also had to cope with the disastrous romantic life Wang Yi had led before her foster father had appeared on the scene. Didn't her foster father possess an unflappable demeanor perfected in the business world? It went without saying that Duan Ai's tranquillity was virginal.

Sometimes he (she) would destroy her (him) in order to express that loyal tendency so essential in love. The old man, who was "at death's door," and the young girl, the "little minx," were knocked onto the floor in one fell swoop. At Ma Wen's instigation, Wang Yi threw out a large bundle of things her foster father had given her: a make-up box, some clothes, jewelry, and letters. Of course, his house stayed, so did the contraceptives, which were as indispensable as Wang Yi's body.

It was then Ma Wen's turn to throw something out. He really couldn't think of anything worth throwing out. Eventually he found a tangerine that had been locked away in the drawer for ages. It was black, dried up to the size of a ping pong ball, and hard as a walnut. If his memory served him correctly, he was convinced that it was part of a bag of fruit that Duan Ai had given to him when he left home last term. He acted as though he had found a treasure, taking it to Wang Yi's place and handing it over to her to throw out personally.

He also found two notes from Duan Ai which said things like: "I came over to your place but you weren't in. I had a great time with your sister. She's such a good laugh!" He was in no hurry to hand them over, deciding instead to retain them for later use. Ma Wen knew that Wang Yi's tape recorder, watch, perfume, and embroidered slip had all been given to her by her foster father and she hadn't exhausted them yet. Although he was poor, he had to play along in this game with her to the very last — because he loved her.

It was because she also loved him that she had the following deeply moving idea: they would no longer blindly throw things out. She would hand over to him for safekeeping everything that her foster father had given her. And he would lock everything that Duan Ai had given him (no matter how much) into her trunk. The quality of the things exchanged clearly differed, but from the point of view of feelings they were certainly of equal value. Ma Wen thereupon exchanged the two notes and a copy of *The Selected Poems of Shu Ting and Gu Cheng* (Duan Ai had lent the book to Ma Fang, but Ma Wen had discovered it at home and had secretly brought it to college) for a large trunk of things.

The trunk itself was also part of the exchange, because later they suddenly realized that it too had been a present from Wang Yi's foster father.

The high quality leather trunk thereafter became a veritable props basket. On the eve of her foster father's return, Wang Yi would always "borrow" it, taking out the dazzling array of objects and putting each in its rightful place. As soon as her foster father had left, she would immediately return it to Ma Wen. Because of this constant fuss, Wang Yi's home didn't seem quite as comfortable and pleasant as it once had felt.

The place was completely empty apart from the mattress which couldn't be moved. (The things that weren't able to fit into the props trunk were also disposed of.) It really looked like a prison cell. Wang Yi was as plain and unadorned as a prisoner. Her complexion was pale and she wore the cheap slippers that Ma Wen had bought from a street stall. She smiled contentedly as she stood by the wall on which hung only the hand-woven straw hat that Ma Wen had given her. (Apart from the symbolic head and feet, Ma Wen didn't have the economic means to masquerade as her lover.)

Could she now be compared on a fundamental level with that girl with inherent beauty? Essentially she didn't own a thing in the world — except for him. She took ten rolls of photos of him, decorating her room with his image: one real wall and the four walls of her soul. Afterwards she would either hand over to him her foster father's camera or place it in the black props trunk.

He was deeply moved and began advocating that faded beauty was the best kind of beauty. He no longer believed in innate beauty, purity or innocence. He believed in weakness brought on by suffering and a pallor which remained even after removing make-up — just like Wang Yi, his only lover. He gave her his final keepsake — a photo of Duan Ai's back. (At the time Duan Ai had oddly refused to enter the picture, or

had she perhaps some premonition about today? He had feigned inter-
est in the cockscombs in her garden and, as he took the picture, he se-
cretly included her childlike back in the shot.) She gave him a yellowish-
brown stone about the size of a thumbnail in exchange. It was her foster
father's gallstone. It was the last of the treasures they had kept secret
from each other.

5.

The following summer holiday Ma Wen and Wang Yi returned
home as a couple. They openly shared the bed in his sister's room. Since
her marriage, Ma Fang had lived separately from her husband. She moved
to the storage room, which had once been Ma Wen's room. Their mother
remained in the sitting room as always

It was only later that Ma Wen realized the reasoning behind these
arrangements. It was not only due to his sister's generosity and his
mother's enlightenment that they had been given the only room with a
double bed, it was that this room could be observed conveniently, as
though a transparent glass case. In the darkness and quiet his mother's
and sister's antennae rose into the air, probing their every move. The
following day the information they had intercepted would be delivered
to Duan Ai along the regular channels. They would tell her how Wang
Yi ground her teeth, snored and talked in her sleep, and how she (Wang
Yi) had, shamelessly, dealt with Ma Wen in both the soft and hard way.

Initially they were biased towards the one they approved of (Duan
Ai) and in broad daylight nitpicked the other's (Wang Yi's) posture,
facial features, table manners, accent, and the way her buttocks moved
as she walked. They never pointed this out to her face, but merely re-
ported their impressions to Duan Ai, and in the course of their conver-
sations they made new discoveries. Since Wang Yi's arrival they had
become much more intimate with Duan Ai; since Wang Yi's arrival their
eyes and ears had become that much more important to them.

For her part, Wang Yi took every advantage of the opportunities
she had while preparing vegetables or making dumplings with them to
inquire about the name "Duan Ai". They became indisputable notaries,

judges, and brokers enjoying a certain amount of authority, always siding with the weaker one out of the kindness of their hearts. They knew a lot about Duan Ai, but told Wang Yi very little. They knew very little about Wang Yi, but told Duan Ai a lot. Their method of accumulation and filtration was very odd. However, their pride prevented them from gaining many more opportunities to understand the situation, even to the extent that they knew absolutely nothing about Wang Yi's home or her foster father. They knew several things about Duan Ai that even Ma Wen didn't know, and became complacent because of it. They maintained the appearance of having a good idea of how things stood and of being calm and collected, almost as though they wanted Wang Yi to beg them for the information.

One day, seizing the opportunity while Wang Yi had been in the bathroom a long time, Ma Fang said to Ma Wen, who was busy fetching toilet paper, "If you have the time you should go and see Duan Ai, she..." She seemed to hold back her words.

"You're constantly on her mind," his mother interjected.

"Mm," Ma Wen responded, unwilling to hear the entire story (he reckoned it would be as long as the pink toilet roll in his hand, and Wang Yi was shut in the toilet and might be suffocated by her own cute feces at any moment). "Okay," he said, interrupting their florid narration, and then added concisely, "She just wept when she heard I had a girlfriend, that's all. Lots of girls wept when they heard I was going out with someone — some even threw themselves from tall buildings!"

"If you don't hurry up I'll jump out of the toilet window!" Wang Yi's voice came through the slatted vent at the bottom of the toilet door.

Although it was actually quite despicable, they had made up their minds not to let him past until he had listened to the end of that extremely moving story. However long it took to recount the tale, Wang Yi would not be able to come out until she had wiped her bottom, unless she really jumped out of the window — and they didn't care if she did.

Later that day Ma Fang said to Duan Ai, "She doesn't even bother checking how much toilet paper there is before going into the bathroom. She just gets Ma Wen to fetch it for her." For his part, Ma Wen had convinced himself that Duan Ai had wept bitterly when she discovered he was going out with Wang Yi. Though he only really savored the details after loyally confessing all of it to Wang Yi.

The couple had picked up the habit of taking afternoon naps while at the university. One day, when they were lying next to each other on the double bed, Ma Fang called Duan Ai.

They had arranged to meet by the police stand at the crossroads. Ma Fang accompanied Duan Ai upstairs, suggesting that she take a short rest on the mat by the door. She went in by herself to make sure that they were asleep (they both had read several pages of a book before falling asleep, the open books still covering their faces and their stomachs, moving up and down as they breathed gradually and evenly). Stealthily, she beckoned Duan Ai into the apartment, getting her to sit on a high-backed sofa in the sitting room.

The sofa had its back to the south-facing room and served as a screen. By peering around it, one could observe everything in the bedroom. If the observer turned her head back around, the only thing the couple could see would be a tuft of unrecognizable black hair above the back of the sofa. If she slouched slightly, they wouldn't even be able to see her hair. Ma Fang's mother sat on a small stool opposite Duan Ai and, like a small girl, covered her smiling mouth with her hand. Everybody was in good spirits.

The day's proceedings had been masterminded singlehandedly by Ma Fang. She had worked out the time and was keeping to a strict schedule. Having set her plan into action, all that remained was for her to coordinate and participate in it. Her mother was not to be outdone. It was the height of the summer and appetites were dulled by the sickening heat, yet she had still prepared an extremely appetizing lunch. The lunch had been sumptuous enough to make almost all of everybody's blood rush down from their head to the stomach so as to aid digestion and promote sleep (hypnotizing them). Furthermore, at her daughter's suggestion, she had put four ground sleeping pills into the wintermelon and dried shrimp soup that both Ma Wen and Wang Yi loved.

As speaking was out of the question, they could only exchange their intense feelings by means of meaningful glances and gestures. Their movements appeared exaggerated and comical. They had every reason to give a free hand to the stage fantasy they had hidden deep in their hearts. What did Duan Ai actually see in this imaginary atmosphere that was both simultaneously stimulating and terribly stifling?

She saw the doorframe that had been painted red (it was the first time she'd noticed that the doorframe was red, and what was revealed to her behind the door seemed remarkably like a mirror image with clearly-defined borders). There were four naked feet protruding from beyond the edge of the picture. Two of them were large and two of them were small — doubtless part of two bodies of the opposite sex. Then she focused her attention on the two rather small, evidently female feet. Looking upward, she had not, for the moment, seen any bedclothes. Therefore she couldn't help imagining her (Wang Yi's) naked body (like the two naked feet with yellow soles) lying there. The feet twitched as though reacting to the stares. Duan Ai quickly averted her gaze.

Ma Fang insisted that Duan Ai move a step or two closer to the left side of the door so that she could observe the whole of the nap-scene more clearly. Duan Ai could now see everything except their heads. The shape of the bodies beneath the blanket resembled a willingly abandoned wilderness. She saw the mountains which were their bottoms, the dams which were their arms, and the rich and populous plains which were their bellies. Duan Ai really didn't dare look up at the features of Wang Yi's face, as if therein lay concealed an artillery battery which could launch a barrage of shells against the spies in the clouds at any time.

When she got home Duan Ai locked herself in her small room. In the lonely mists and heat she removed all her clothes. She wrapped herself in her bath towel and looked again and again at her own headless body in the aluminum-framed mirror on the wall.

6.

Perhaps it is time I reveal the present situation and future of the two key characters in this story (More often than not, this is something that the author deliberately neglects).

First of all there is Ma Wen. After all those happy academic years and meaningful holidays, he graduated and was assigned a job. He neither remained in the city where Wang Yi lived (which was also where their college was) nor did he return to his hometown (the city where Duan Ai and his mother lived), but went to a place in the south which was between these two cities. He worked in the planning bureau in a coastal town (he had graduated in architectural design). This town was about the same distance from both the other towns he had lived in during his life. If one were to connect the three places with straight lines, then he would have an equilateral triangle (coinciding with the shape of a love triangle).

In reality his capacity for social interaction was average, his work was average, and the state of his health and fortune were also both average. Average implies passable, fair to middling, nothing remarkable. In addition, apart from one letter every day (sent out separately from either end of the straight line), the nature of his relationship with Wang Yi consisted of holidays pieced together bit-by-bit and an interminable period of waiting.

And what about Duan Ai? She now has a much longer jaw than when we first saw her. The bridge of her nose now protrudes proudly. There are now fine and closely-knit fishtail wrinkles at the corners of her eyes. Her voice has become coarse and wild. Of course, she never made it to university and was therefore recruited by a factory as a worker. Since her family was upper middle class, even though she worked in a factory, she still had some room to maneuver and was given light duties in the less busy departments. Outside of work she seemed to be a typical unmarried woman. Her favorable family background and her exceptionally good looks meant that she could take her pick as though on a merry-go-round. Comparisons, rendezvous, break ups, meeting, listening to the opinions of her family, waiting for the other party's reply, staring at the furniture, and being difficult — all of these things made complete a life style particular to her age, at the same time pleasing and dispiriting, inescapably hollow.

7.

She became Ma Fang's closest friend. The pair of them took every opportunity to see each other. It was like a festival whenever they met. They went shopping and to restaurants together. They dressed provocatively to attract the attention of the young men who had nothing to do all day long but lean on the pavement railings. They winked and whistled at them. The more courageous of them would walk up and block their path: "What do you think of my mustache? Is it like Stalin's?"

"Who's Stalin? How come we've never heard of him?" They had learnt to handle the situation with ease a long time ago.

Ma Fang particularly liked going shopping with Duan Ai. As they casually strolled down the street, they immediately became the center of attention. Ma Fang couldn't remember ever having been so popular. Although her husband had helped her overcome the frustrations and dissatisfactions peculiar to an unmarried woman, he was not an especially good-looking man. He wasn't able to make her feel proud and exuberant in certain public places (that is, at a dance organized by his place of work, or on a stroll through the streets, which was sort of a national pastime). Duan Ai gave her this opportunity. One was pure and angelic and the other an easy-going and graceful married woman. They complemented each other well!

She would never admit to being only a foil for Duan Ai. In fact they were doubtless foils for each other. They would emerge only together on the unprotected streets plagued by thousands of unforeseen dangers. There was a trace of protective softness in her concern, whereas the young girl always followed and heeded her, regarding those young men on their trail with equal contempt, regardless of their looks, wealth, or age. It was in this respect that they appreciated each other.

People gathered around them as they walked from north to south and from east to west (depending on the length of the shopping street), nurturing their beauty, encouraging their cruelty, and exuding a distant sense of inadequacy. She was not a foil for Duan Ai. It was more that the whole world was a foil for them (her and her).

For a while they absolutely loved photography. One of Ma Fang's classmates owned a darkroom with supposedly the best equipment in town. He took care of all their developing. They weren't at all interested in the scenery on those enlarged, dripping wet photos. The subject was always the same: either Duan Ai or Ma Fang. They were both photographer and model. While the dresses were the same and the style and type of shoe always similar, the faces were different. The professional photographer thought that they must have changed their clothes either in the bamboo grove or behind the ruined adobe wall in the background. It would certainly have been wonderful had somebody taken a quick picture at the time.

Later on he actually became their exclusive photographer. Not only did he unconditionally do all their developing and enlarging, but he would follow them everywhere with a camera slung over his shoulder. Another disciple of the opposite sex therefore appeared at the side of the sisters who "showed disdain for all males." He would run behind and in front of them, climb up high and crawl along the floor, kneel down and lean over at the waist, and lie down on the ground. He would capture all of their flirtatious expressions: their arrogant strut and their occasional unwitting grin. The twosome became a threesome and was more alluring than before. If Ma Fang still suspected she might be a foil for Duan Ai, there was now somebody who was genuinely a foil for her: she was being set off, as was Duan Ai.

If Duan Ai was identified as the first seed, then Ma Fang was the second. Together they formed a top-seeded team which was highlighted by the photographer's presence. In this collective (threesome) Duan Ai's radiance was unmistakable. Naturally, Ma Fang resembled this radiance more than the photographer in both appearance and essence. They were both female, for instance. However, therein lay a danger, for it just so happened that they compared themselves with each other. For his part, the photographer was ugly and wretched, and in a league of his own.

In addition to the photographer, their other acquaintances included the manager of a fashion boutique, a third-rate poet, and a philistine who had started practicing martial arts at the age of five. This ring satisfied their basic needs. They were later surprised to discover that the manager of the fashion boutique had a Stalinesque mustache and that the poor poet had once blocked their path. They hadn't seen them for several years and had walked unsuspectingly into the trap they had laid. As their conversation grew deeper they realized that they had come to this conclusion much too soon.

On those days when they habitually roamed the streets throwing hearts into turmoil, the lout went into business with a fierce determination and became the manager of a fashion boutique, carrying a pager at his waist. His boutique was situated on the shopping street where they often walked. And who could deny that the painful successes of the poet had nothing to do with beautiful women? The strong and brave philistine never had the opportunity to become a rapist, so fate instead pushed him into becoming the protector of two tender young women who were as beautiful as flowers.

How did this ring — or wheel — roll down the road in the bright sunlight? A riotous profusion of time scattered like the fragments of a vase through the bowing and bending buildings on either side of the street. This was how the crucial years passed. firstly, Duan Ai lost her virginity in the photographer's darkroom. Later, in a hospital operating room filled with screams, she aborted the child of the fashion boutique manager. With Duan Ai's assistance, the poet eventually proved to himself the fallacy of his doubt regarding his own sexual prowess that he had harbored since childhood. In the end the philistine came over to pick up the pieces, knocking the other three out. Together with Ma Fang, whose eyes were filled with sympathetic tears, he attempted to rebuild Duan Ai's life.

8.

At the time, Ma Wen was living in the indescribable loneliness of a strange town. The postman was the person with whom he was perhaps most familiar. Every day he handed him one of the letters that had been sent by Wang Yi hundreds of miles away. As a result of the long period of waiting, Ma Wen was becoming more and more sensitive towards the length of the letters, the form of the closing greetings, and the time they took to arrive. They argued with and hurt each other in the letters. It wasn't like before when they were together and problems could always be solved before the end of the day. The time and the distance between them became additional burdens. Everything was down in black and white, and was unmistakably clear. There was no means of carrying out prompt changes or making the necessary supplementary explanations. And they (the hurting or begging words) time and again greeted those loving eyes like some sort of compulsive disorder. Afterwards a knife would engrave the words, including those characteristically cherished by lovers, onto his head like flies settling on brain-splattered inner walls. The venomous words resembled stains that had formed over the years, and could not be removed with the repeated washing of their thorough examination of the past.

Ma Wen constantly smelt the pale blue lined paper. An indistinct yet fragrant perfume left him at first intoxicated, then aroused his apprehension, and finally made him simply shudder. Was that brown stain soy sauce or blood — or something else? In the folds of the letter paper he once made out the smell of smoke. He shook out a tiny shred of tobacco from the envelope. Sometimes there were hairs he didn't recognize, or an eyelash that was too short (compared with the image in his memory of her dark eyes). He feared one day he would tear open an envelope and find a love letter she had meant to send to somebody else (he knew she had always been careless).

The time she was together with her foster father, which coincided with the time she was together with Ma Wen, had come to an end (Ma Wen had insisted upon taking away the props trunk). Who was she with now? Another problem made him terribly upset: why hadn't she come away with him? Why hadn't she married him before he left? Although she was no longer together with her foster father, she and Ma Wen were still at opposite ends of the earth. This was her finest hour, yet she remained in a place he could neither aspire to nor encroach upon. Had he become another foster father to her? He could neither take a holiday nor had the money to go and visit her.

He mentioned these concerns in his letters. Her reply was very straightforward: "Think of me as another Duan Ai!" It was a game of counterpoint that they knew by heart. However, once her foster father had actually gone, Duan Ai was unable to resist the thousands of troops that had amassed behind him. Ma Wen understood. For the past few months they had simply been carrying on a symbolic battle. Wang Yi's foster father was as much her patron in real life as a representative and symbol of all her loves and pasts. Duan Ai, on the other hand, was merely the homologue and the counterweight of that symbol. Apart from this, she wasn't really anything.

Out of pity, Wang Yi established for him two lines of defense: the symbol of her foster father was a banner restraining the disorganized rabble behind him, and Duan Ai, as a corresponding banner, formed a second defensive screen preventing the enemy troops from charging in. After her foster father had left, however, all the defense installations had crumbled and disintegrated.

That night, the troops belonging to Ma Wen's rival in love galloped out of his body and rushed to and fro. There were ear-splitting calls for blood. Sparks flew from their knives and swords. Horse hooves as large as rice bowls trampled on the lantern of his heart. He was woken up from the nightmare by his roommate. He turned over and got out of bed. His roommate returned to his own bed, pulled up his quilt, and went back to sleep again. Ma Wen turned on the desk lamp and, in the light, pricked up his ears to listen to the indistinct howling of the waterpipes in the washroom on the other side of the corridor. He blew out a mouthful of smoke. The cracks in the windows immediately absorbed the blue smoke, as though constantly pulling a thread from outside the window.

Ma Wen opened the props trunk for the first time in several years. He searched for the image of Wang Yi's foster father among the variety of presents. He picked up a gemstone necklace, looked at it under the lamplight, and then poked his head into that circle wavering in mid-air. He saw his superfluous Adam's apple in the oval hand-mirror: otherwise, the neck encrusted with constantly glistening jewels looked exactly the same as Wang Yi's. The stones were light yet heavy. Their owner remained calm and contented in the middle of the night.

As he further explored the image in the hand mirror, he discovered his dozing roommate in the distance — those feline eyes between the top of the quilt, long hair radiating a green light that immediately dimmed. Ma Wen simply swept the ink bottle, the desk calendar, and water cup to one side, laid the treasures from inside the trunk onto the table-top (his desk was placed next to his roommate's), and then spread them out on the bed. He shone the lamplight on them. The intense aroma of face powder immediately filled the room, covering up the stench of the permanent pile of rubbish lurking behind the dormitory door.

His roommate was certainly stupefied. Although he was educated and knew what transvestism was, he could do without such a shock at close proximity. There were dozens of beautiful bras and different types of make-up among Ma Wen's collection. In this crude and impoverished environment, he was stabbed by the radiance of their nobility and magic. Or was he just affected by Ma Wen's unreasonable actions? In any case, he couldn't help sighing.

Ma Wen decided not to torment the poor man any longer, called him over and explained the whole thing from the beginning. Through loneliness and pain Ma Wen gained a friend. After a week or so, his roommate was no longer curious when he opened the trunk and routinely inspected its contents every night. After saying a few words of comfort to Ma Wen, he would finally go off to sleep calmly. But Ma Wen's inspection went on for a long time (perhaps three months?). Every night he opened the props trunk and lined up the expensive junk on the table. He stared in silence, occasionally changing the position of one or two of the objects. His expression was like that of a chess master poring over the board. In the end, every object had a fixed position. For several nights running he put them on the table and didn't move them. By means of his intensely arduous correspondence with Wang Yi, Ma Wen learned when almost every one of the objects had been presented to her and in what context. Wang Yi therefore referred to him as "despicably narrow-minded."

Wang Yi deliberately revealed to Ma Wen all the new developments in her life. Apart from her foster father she mentioned others, mostly men he didn't know. Ma Wen preferred to view this move as absurd blackmail. Even when he wrote a letter requesting a photo of her foster father (if she didn't have one, she could describe him in words or tell him which one of their mutual acquaintances her foster father resembled, or even which film star, just to give his imagination a workable focus), and she sent a photo of herself with another man, he still thought it was a photographic effect, a deliberate piecing together of pictures in the darkroom. Regardless of what Wang Yi told him, he insisted on believing that the foreigner whose hairy arm was around Wang Yi's shoulder was her foster father. She had never revealed her foster father's ethnic background or age (the guy on the photo was a young foreigner still wet behind the ears). He only knew that he was male.

In her next letter, Wang Yi drew Ma Wen's attention to the date in the bottom right-hand corner of the photo. Actually he had turned a blind eye to this the last time. Even if this date were correct, it wasn't impossible that her foster father could have staged a comeback after Ma Wen had left, taking his former lover along the road to the coast. A photo of two half-naked people with the azure sea (the beach, snowy waves, and the blue sky) in the background.

"Only if he had been reincarnated and had found his way into Davis' body," Wang Yi's shrill voice resounded from the stationery as though from an empty beach.

Ma Wen had been forced into a dead end.

He then thought of something and hurriedly wrote down with a fountain pen: "Who was the photographer who took the picture of you?

Presumably it was that respected foster father of yours!" He turned his probing gaze beyond the edge of the photo and imagined the ghostlike existence of the person holding the camera. Even if he stared at the photo for a long time he couldn't become jealous or feel pain at not having been on the scene himself. Slowly, he melted into one with the person who had once stood before them and taken this picture. They laughed coolly at the camera. Under his protection and at his instigation they conveyed a sense of dissolution. It was all to please his numb and decrepit eyes. Through that old man's bones Ma Wen discovered Wang Yi's incomparable sexiness: her toes tightly biting the sand and her dress blown by the wind like a piece of flowery cloth floating by chance onto her curvaceous body. Her partner looked like a clumsy ham-fisted animal, desperately trying to escape her scorching beauty (the arm around her shoulder was not pulling her closer but seemed to be doing all it could to push her away).

"Poor Ma Wen," thought Wang Yi, and wrote as always: "My foster father is the last reality you are able to accept."

9.

She brought her weapon — a mop handle — downstairs to greet him. She stared at him through sleepy eyes for ages before calling out, "It's you!" Her body had fully developed by now. Those parts that had only just started to grow when they last met were now trembling as though they didn't know what to do (they seemed to have received chaotic orders and wanted to run out of the other side of her dress). Ma Wen heard the sound of their struggling and twisting. Then all subsided, like the peacefully drooping branches of a fruit tree in the aftermath of a gale.

She really was happy. Ma Wen looked at her disheveled hair and her sleepy eyes, and couldn't help laughing out loud at the way she held the mop handle tightly in both hands. She hurriedly explained, "Security's lousy around here. I didn't know it was you."

He felt completely at ease because of her panic and even made some impudent comments, "We haven't seen each other for years and now you look at me as a mosquito, a criminal, huh…." For as he pushed open the green screen door a moment ago, her voice immediately called out from inside, "Close it quickly, don't let the mosquitoes in." He wondered whether he was as unwelcome as a mosquito.

She said, "I like to read in bed. I'm getting more and more near-sighted."

They sat down in her small room. Ma Wen rubbed his hands as he examined with full interest all the changes that had occurred (as if this were his only reason for coming). It was the same bed, the same desk, the same bookshelf laden with all sorts of dolls, but their positions had totally changed. There was a grass-green carpet he had not seen before. The casing of the black-and-white television that dated from their first meeting was cracked, and the scotch tape used to fix it had become filthy. But it still worked. The picture was still clear. This was further evidence of the passage of time.

The television had been new once, but in the acid rains of time it had corroded and melted. The girl of those days now sitting next to the irretrievably old television was using all her effort to charge towards a new apex. It was not unlike a strange yet deeply moving face gradually emerging from a stone. Duan Ai was rushing into the extremely suitable arrangements nature had reserved for her, a most excellent nose and most beautiful chin, as well as other similarly incomparable parts; as luck would have it, she reached there in the half-hour following Ma Wen's arrival. Afterwards everything would go downhill. Her destiny from now on would be similar to that of the television.

Luckily she realized none of this. She was hugging an animal cushion (a pig or a frog) as she tilted her head and stared at Ma Wen with fixed eyes. The only thing different about him was that he had lost some weight. Apart from peeling some skin from his cheeks, the sculpting knife of time had done nothing. His frown was not the result of apprehension over coming here, but due to his efforts to hide the stabbing pain of her beauty. It was the frown one gets when suddenly faced with a bright light, and you instinctively turns your face to the shade.

"I've split up with Wang Yi," he said.

"You can't have. Weren't you happy with her?"

She didn't move, merely inclining her head to the other side. Her dark hair fell forward from her forehead. She moved her hair back and forth like this, as though drying it. Was this her only reaction to what happened to him? It seemed she was conserving her energy. Now, whether he was willing to or not, the only way forward was to tell her it all.

He told her about the foster father, the props trunk, and Davis. She learned a great deal. By chance, she now knew much more than Ma Fang had gone to great lengths to peddle to her. It was much more important and stranger than what she had gradually forgotten. By way of an exchange, he lured her into speaking about her own love for him. He lured her into telling him that story his sister had long since told him. He wanted her to tell him herself. Recklessly, he had dished up everything about himself, leaving behind a deep pit waiting for her to fill.

Ma Wen pressed forward steadily and, not totally unexpectedly, trampled on himself with odorous sweat and spit — he even cried. Eventually, he could see her red eyes through his misty tears. She wept tears of sympathy and love for him. Once the tension had eased slightly, Ma Wen happened to notice the brilliant sunlight outside the screen door and the shadows of trees dancing. He saw a corner of the flower-bed and the rear wheel of a bicycle. It really was an enchanting summer's afternoon. How he wanted to stay here and become a son-in-law in this pleasantly cool family.

The reunion dinner didn't even take place beneath a secretive atmosphere or have an ambiguous meaning. Out of a sense of family courtesy, Duan Ai's parents entertained him — and didn't have the slightest ulterior motive. They prepared an extra plate — Duan Ai opened a tin of braised chicken for him. Her mother immediately stated that she hadn't bought the supply of tinned food with her own money. Duan Hui's (she purposely didn't mention Duan Ai) father had accepted it in exchange for some work he had done for somebody. Apart from Duan Ai's mother, none of the others spoke directly to him. It seemed as though she were a representative they had sent.

During the meal Duan Ai's mother casually asked after his "wife." Duan Ai chipped in, "He's not married yet!"

"Anyway it's all the same. I mean…."

"Mom, he's split up with Wang Yi."

Her mother suddenly fell silent. The atmosphere around the table grew tense. There was silence for several minutes (which was filled with the sounds of food being swallowed and soup slurped) after which he heard Duan Ai's mother say, "You youngsters should be more careful."

Her next words amounted to a rebuke of Duan Ai.

Then she turned to him. "You haven't split up yet, have you? If you haven't split up, then … (her wording was quite self-conscious) you're still a couple. You can discuss and solve the problem no matter how large it is…."

After the meal everyone retired to their own rooms. Duan Ai's mother was slow to leave, remaining in the sitting room with them. She had a legitimate excuse: cleaning out the cupboard. It had been placed in one corner of the room beforehand as though part of a conspiracy. Duan Ai's mother removed countless bowls and plates, the leftovers on the second shelf, and the supply of tins on the third shelf. These were the sorts of things that needed to be cleaned. She wrung out the cloth and wiped the inside walls of the cupboard. Ma Wen was simply captivated by the dexterity the fifty-year-old woman exhibited in climbing up and down, and by the unnecessary clatter of dishes knocking together. He stared fixedly at every detail of this unexpected cleaning ritual. He could only agree with the earnest words which Duan Ai whispered endlessly into his ear.

Suddenly, he pointed out what was clearly a cockroach to Duan Ai's mother. Once again she removed all the bowls and cups she had just put in, and lifted the cupboard high into the air. Eventually, with Ma Wen's assistance, she finished the cockroach off with a slipper on the unpainted back of the cupboard. Then she sprayed several bursts of insect spray. She sought out several old newspapers to cover the crockery and protect it from that drifting cloud of insecticide. She then sat down on a chair by the table quietly waiting for the poisonous gas in the cupboard to disperse completely.

Duan Ai led Ma Wen hesitantly into her room. The door was left unlocked. This monitored conversation (they switched on the television for interference) lasted for six hours. Duan Ai's mother waited outside the whole time guarding her daughter's non-existent virginity like a foolishly loyal soldier.

During that time Ma Wen went out three times to relieve himself in the toilet opposite the sitting room. He saw Duan Ai's mother reading the old newspaper covering the dishes through her reading glasses. The second time the bowls, cups, and other crockery had been put away and she was sitting at the table eating a plate of leftovers. She finally fell asleep next to a pile of duck bones. At four o'clock in the morning when he came out to take his leave, Ma Wen discovered that somebody had put a gray blanket over Duan Ai's mother's shoulders. That meant somebody else had been there. Could Duan Ai's mysteriously unfathomable and shyly introverted father have been the one who had come out to check up on the "sentry"?

10.

He invited her out again the very next day — anything that was hindered by her mother had to be carried out to the very end.

They went to a park with rocks overlooking the river. It was a place known mutually by her, the photographer, the boss of the fashion boutique, and the third-rate poet — she used means other than language to discuss her life. They groped their way along the dark mountain path (he didn't need to take advantage of the situation like someone harboring evil intentions) before finally climbing to the bare summit above the shade of the trees.

The bracing river breeze that was supposed to bring with it a sense of exhilaration and satisfaction was not there. The motionless river exuded the heat it had absorbed during the day, and every rock was baked by an underground fire. They took shelter in a nook worn down by bodies. It forced them closer together, flesh touching flesh.

Ma Wen realized that he didn't object to touching her for the simple reason that her cool skin made him happy. In his imagination he preferred to erase all those feelings associated with volume and elasticity. By not taking in every part and all possibilities of her, could he guard what was left of his loyalty towards the other woman?

Due to the strong impression left on him by the existence of Wang Yi, the totally different body offered by Duan Ai frightened him. When the second woman didn't live up to the standards of the first, he started to refute her. She (Duan Ai) was both superfluous and deficient, both rigid and yet at the same time excessively soft and inappropriate. She was sick, either crippled or mutated — abnormal, backward and ignorant. In this stifling atmosphere, he was only able to accept her cool body out of a sense of extreme utilitarianism. He was only able to experience it in this dimension of existence — otherwise he thought he would certainly die from the heat.

Therefore, even if she were brimming with warmth, bold or unrestrained, her function was nothing more than a lump of ice preventing rotten meat from giving off a stench — that was not a bad thing in itself. In a series of unreserved actions, she had tried to inform him about what she had learned over the years and about the nub of her existence. She was also eager to accept what he could teach her after she had confessed everything — for it would certainly be genuine, natural, and to the point. She would always remember it with gratitude and never forget it. But he had stopped forever.

Amidst the lingering music she broadcast for herself in her mind, she stuck closely to him. Then there was a kiss, intensely emotional but blind. His attention was moving away from them and was doing its utmost to eliminate all kinds of fanciful thoughts about volume and substance (he had agreed with himself only to retain memories of the refreshing coolness among the sweltering heat). He felt that the rocks behind him were gigantic and hard, that the river water below him was smooth and boundless, and that the night sky was extensive and submissive (he penetrated his right hand into it). Time vanished in succession like the lights stretching for many miles on the opposite bank.

That same evening they returned to the city and enjoyed the air conditioning for a few hours in the all-night cinema. It was three o'clock in the morning when the third film finished. They left the cinema, returning to the scorching hot street outside. Duan Ai went to fetch her bike from under the billboard. They both ate a bowl of wontons at the stall at the crossroads, the solitary light of which shone like a one-eyed person. He put all his weight, a mere sixty-five kilos, onto her bike and they set out.

She took him from south to north across the whole city. He counted that in total they had passed seven intersections busy with traffic and were now crossing a tranquil square. He couldn't help praising her physical strength and her ability to bear hardship. In all fairness, she had developed this step by step following his criticism that she had been pampered since childhood. She had started by practicing washing a handkerchief.

From his seat on the back he said that he could no longer remember his criticism of her and that he no longer held this point of view anyway. Suffering hardship didn't really mean anything. And a good home was a very fortunate thing for a growing child. He was obviously referring to something. Was he going out of his way to curry favor or to explain away his errors? The head wind blew his words behind them along the streets through which they had just passed, solidifying them onto the signs above the shops on both sides of the road or altering the wording on the banners which straddled the road high in the air.

It was almost daybreak by the time they reached the dock. The boat responsible for taking him to the west could be made out vaguely on the river. Perhaps, many years ago, it had been snowy white, but now it was only a pale dusty gray. Close by, some other boats were fast asleep in the harbor — their guest house. Just when he was lost in thought she handed over a bag full of tangerines. Three days later, retaining sufficient moisture, they would be taken to another woman. He would derive the nourishment and strength from the fruit to leave her, leave them. He would neither stay anywhere nor come back. That fateful triangle renowned for its stability had disintegrated completely in the first glow of morning light.

Ma Wen and Duan Ai sat on the concrete wall by the river staring hollowly at each other. Their faces gradually became larger and brighter until a redness drifted between them like traces of blood. Oh, the rosy dawn! They were saturated in its unequivocal insignificance and its mediocre dye.

WANG YIN   TRANSLATED BY YANBING CHEN

WHO IS THE SON GOD NEEDS

Who is the son God needs
Who is cold water, icy tears
a dark old house
a rebellious code

Who is the master of youth
Who is the gloomy dagger
a scanty confession
a worn out scheme

Who is the memory of poppies
Who is the skin of ruins
clock fingers
day lips

Who? Who? Who is the lullabying skeleton
the aching wisdom tooth
Who is the Judgment Day halo
Who is the son God needs

July 1992

GODSEND

How will you thank the sunset, genius
How will you view these political roses
these wimpy springs

How will you listen to the revolt of clock hands
How will you deal with fire in paper
rivers rushing under the city

The mirage up my sleeve
transcends reason and credibility
The glances of patients mimic the flag's
crackling laughter
How false are promises
how swift, those secrets

Bones of sadness, heart of summer
fragrance of sorrow, and yet more,
children weeping beyond the heavenly river

How will you be able to answer

February 1, 1992

SUN XIAODONG

TRANSLATED BY HOWARD
GOLDBLATT AND SYLVIA
LI-CHUN LIN

BLUE NOTEBOOK

It's been a long time since I last read a novel. I have always felt that the novel is an unnatural art form, a fabrication on paper created by the author's mutterings; plots and characters in print have no place in our real lives. The other arts, such as music and painting, at least have some direct, sensual contact with human beings. But novels! An invented story, no matter how well crafted, is still a feeble compilation of words; it has no connection with our daily lives, nor is it in any way related to the sorrow and happiness we experience.

But last night I read novels all night long. I often have trouble sleeping at night, especially when Liang Fen works the night shift at the hospital, leaving me alone at home. Usually, when I can't sleep, I either review lecture notes and prepare for classes, or turn off the light and listen to music until Liang Fen comes home from work, when I drag him off to bed to get a few hours of sleep. Luckily for me, as a teacher, I don't often have to get up early. It's been two years since I stayed on to teach after graduation, and I'm very happy with my job, for, among other things, it gives me a lot of free time to do whatever I like.

But time passes, little by little, leaving no traces, like an ocean that has lost the shore or its islands. Maybe last night will leave something behind; dramatic events like those of last night remain in the current of time like boulders, always visible when we look back. What happened last night may well have been prodigious, transcending daily experience. I could hardly comprehend it, and that was why I flipped through the dust-covered novels on my bookshelf, trying to sort my feelings by reading distant, unrealistic stories of life and passion.

Maybe I should start with last night, or yesterday morning, or the morning before that, even a week ago, or a month ago, because it was precisely the existence of a daily routine that made last night so vivid and enriching. If it hadn't been a tragedy, I'd say even more valuable, more precious. It was much like Joyce's story "The Dead." There, if not for the lengthy and tedious description of a dinner party, how could the subtle theme of love come across with such power and appeal?

But the theme of last night's event escapes me. I witnessed it and felt it intersect the path of my life, but I don't yet understand it. To me, it was like a melody with no lyrics, rising abruptly in the symphony of my life. I can experience only my personal life — its mundane appearance, its ceaseless inner disorder, and the tenuous balance between them. In days past, I could find harmony between them with Liang Fen's help, but now the habit of maintaining the balance has gradually become instinctive.

Yesterday, even as late as last night, I was still able to maintain that balance. Admittedly, yesterday wasn't exactly like all other days — a planned talk had, in the end, disturbed me somewhat, and while not very important, in retrospect this talk had fundamental similarities to last night's event.

Yesterday morning after class, I called a student to my office to tell him to stop writing letters to me. They were long letters written on large sheets of white paper in cramped but neat handwriting. Of course, I was very gentle with him, for I know just how sensitive and fragile a twenty-year-old can be. He was a simple and unaffected boy who quietly followed me to my office without asking any questions when I stopped him after class. As a matter of fact, I'd noticed him the first day of school, even before he began writing to me. He had an unusually intense look on his face and a brightness in his fixed gaze born of natural passion, which set him apart from the other students. At the time, I interpreted this expression as a sign that he was used to being a loner. Several weeks ago, when I received the first long letter, with a poem enclosed, I immediately guessed who had sent it, even though it was unsigned. I wasn't at all surprised. Naturally, I didn't reply. But then, more letters came to the office, to my house even, and I figured it was about time to bring this to a halt.

It wasn't the first time I'd dealt with this kind of problem, so I knew exactly what to do. After preparing in advance what I wanted to say to him, I'd called him to the office at noon, when all my colleagues would be out to lunch and the office empty. I'd taken everything into consideration, including how to preserve his self-esteem, but I hadn't expected that, ultimately, I'd be the one who felt unsettled. I sat across from him, telling him, not entirely disingenuously, that I knew he was experiencing a young man's longing for purity and absoluteness and the resultant conflict between him and the world. I said I was grateful for that trust, but simply couldn't accept the way he expressed it, and that the incessant letters had become a disruption in my daily life. He was quiet the whole time I was talking. A large window behind him opened onto bright, dazzling sunlight. Against the backdrop of stiff, barren branches under a wintry sky, he looked especially young and helpless. I was probably only eight or nine years older than he, but at that moment, I was very much aware of the disparity in our ages. I'd shown all his letters to Liang Fen; we understood him, but he could not possibly understand us. He was able to feel, but not comprehend, life. His heart was like a flag, snapping in the slightest breeze as if caught in a thunderstorm. He treated everything as a sign; a phrase I used in class might instantly become a revelation, an instruction, or a beacon in his life. Even though we could see our former selves in him, when I looked at him, I felt not so much sympathy as pity. Would he be able to come through this stage in one piece? Could he accept the complexity of life without becoming hardened?

And what about me? Have I become hardened without knowing it? Has last night's event touched me that deeply? If not, then why had I needed to read novels all night long to prolong the excitement that had flared up briefly, like someone who can't stop pouring hard liquor down her throat? Here I am, writing and recording, instead of shedding tears or screaming. Is that because my body is so frail it can no longer withstand any strong emotion or action?

Nonetheless, despite the problem, whatever it is, I know I have a firm grip on my current situation and am capable of resolving the problem with a clear head; at this very moment, for instance, I am writing in order to come to grips with a threatening event beyond my ability to comprehend. I am secure; I am closely connected with life through my marriage, my job, and my daily routine. I am already far removed from the danger that was once very close at hand — the temptation to willingly surrender myself to self-destruction.

Yesterday, I believe I saw the same temptation on that pale, young face. Across a desk strewn with books, students' homework, and a variety of notices from the school, I noticed his nervously twisting fingers, so out of step with the daily life of this material world. He listened to me quietly, almost too quietly, reminding me of his subdued bearing in class. But at the same time, in contrast to his calmness, I could imagine the extreme anxiety and impulsiveness concealed beneath his silence. The act of writing to me showed that he was being propelled by his own desire. He had absolutely no intention of gaining an understanding of the complexity and weight of life — a heedlessness I had gone through myself as well. He could not help but know that an impregnable wall awaited him up ahead, but it was precisely the desperation born of this obstacle that made his flight so wonderful.

He thought I didn't understand what was going through his mind. So when I rose from my chair and picked up some books due at the library, quietly indicating that our talk had come to an end, he looked at me with surprise, as if he couldn't believe that people could deal with each other this way — talk about things so close to the heart, then dismiss them as easily as wrapping up a conversation. I doubted that he understood what I was getting at; I hoped only that he would regard this talk as a routine teacher-student discussion and stop writing to me. Although I understood him far better than he realized, I neither intended nor had the energy to get involved in his life. I knew I had the ability to ease him through this period with a minimum of pain and help him see the reality of life, but that would mean risking an interruption in my normal life. This was an excitable boy, and even though there'd be no misunderstanding on Liang Fen's part, I didn't want to attract my colleagues' attention. I took out all his letters from my handbag, came around my desk, and gave them back to him.

It's as if I could see him sitting there, head down, short dark hair falling softly across his forehead. When I handed him the pile of white envelopes, I gently patted him on the shoulder to show that I was being friendly. His shoulder was thin and angular, his shirt collar snowy white. He wasn't quite an adult, yet at that moment, I suddenly felt bewildered, as if it were he, not I, who needed to be comforted, as if what I'd just said were self-righteous, empty words, in stark contrast to his silence, which was truer and carried more weight. That kind of feeling displeased me enormously, but now that I'm finally able to put it into words, I can begin to understand it. I wonder if he would be more capable than I of comprehending and conceptualizing a tragedy like last night's event — in some ways, he seemed stronger than I.

Liang Fen hadn't left for work when I came home from school yesterday afternoon. Since he's been working the late shift these days, I try to come home early to spend more time with him. We made an early dinner together, just as it was getting dark outside. Looking out from our high-rise apartment window, we saw lights snapping on in neighboring buildings. Except for the meeting with the student, I can't recall what we talked about during dinner — probably just some small talk about what we'd done that day. After all, we've been together for a long time, and don't need to discuss serious subjects anymore. Right now, all I can think about is the window. Our dining table sits by the window, but the chair directly under it has never been occupied. So when Liang Fen and I sit across from each other at meals, by raising our heads slightly, we can see out the large metal-framed window. In the daytime, it is filled with sunlight, and, at night, it is not closed off by a curtain until it gets dark. Liang Fen doesn't want me to keep the curtain open. He picked out the ivory-colored linen curtain himself; he likes to imagine there is no window, for a room surrounded by ivory walls gives him a tranquil, comfortable feeling.

Liang Fen must be finishing the last hour of his shift in the hospital ER about now. He is probably staring at blood, a wound, or a dying patient breathing his last. And here I am, at this early morning hour, seeing the same window as last night at dinnertime, a clean pane of glass with the curtain open. On that clear, cold winter evening, we were staring at the crimson sunset and the pale gray outlines of concrete buildings. Golden lights came on at about the same time in buildings near and far. Our neighbors had just started to make dinner, the smell of fried green onions mixed with strong, fresh winter air wafting in through the slightly opened window. The room was lighted by a hanging lamp with a colored glass shade, which enveloped us in a golden aura like that of an oil painting. But the painting immediately lost its luster when we looked out the window. Even though it was dusk, and winter at that, the evening sky was still magnificent beyond description — although it no longer sparkled, its radiance, like a handful of diamonds set against a dark gloomy background, had a brightness that shone through everything, all the way to our hearts. Last night certainly wasn't the first time I'd noticed all this, but the window that existed then has been emblazoned into my memory and will never be forgotten.

But what exactly happened last night? I have dutifully recorded everything I saw, described every detail that I committed to memory. But does that mean I can understand and experience everything in the same way I experienced the window at dusk yesterday? My feelings about the window were like a sea of clear water washing through my body. Someone died last night. People die every night, but that person died only inches away from me. His death occurred right before my eyes; his body passed by my window. This death dropped into my life like a shooting star, and I knew clearly that I should be shaken by its weight; I have been waiting for the imprint left behind by its fall, but nothing has happened so far.

Only the window has changed. Behind the closely drawn ivory-colored curtains, the glass has been shattered, splintered by the person who plunged to his death from the roof of the building. It was about eleven o'clock; Liang Fen had already left for work. I was in the room making some tea, when I suddenly heard noises like tree branches brushing against the window in the wind, which immediately put me on my guard. We live on the tenth floor, and I knew there were no trees outside the window. The noises could only have been caused by someone flinging something hard against the window. I was mulling over the thought that this too was virtually impossible, since there is no balcony for anyone to stand on, when, all of a sudden, came a loud crack. It was the sound of the window shattering. Immediately, before I could react, perhaps even at the same time, I heard a long scream that hardly sounded human.

That was all that happened. At that moment, I knew that the person was dead for sure. I stood there motionless for quite a while, feeling my fingers, which were still holding the tea pot, turn icy cold from the shock, and hearing the blood rush to my ears. I didn't walk over to the window to check it out even after my heart stopped racing. Whatever happened had already happened; I was outside of it and there was nothing I could do. Even the phone call I made to the police afterward was a means of fulfilling an abstract obligation, because I knew that anyone who fell from a ten-story building would, with absolute certainty, be killed. Unless I could somehow stop the person's fall, anything I did would be a perfunctory gesture, an act to satisfy myself.

Nonetheless I did everything expected of me. Following the principles of normal life, I made all the phone calls I should make, asking neighbors who were startled out of their sleep to come look at my broken window. At the same time, the shrill sounds of ambulance and police sirens quickly materialized on the street below. My next-door neighbors, Dr. Wang and his retired wife, insisted upon staying with me the rest of the night. They also suggested that I call the hospital and have Liang Fen come home early — I didn't yield to their kindness on the latter. It wasn't me who fell from the rooftop, so why not leave Liang Fen's life undisturbed. I poured some hot tea for them, sat at this table with them, and listened as the event that occurred, which had taken only seconds, was gradually turned into a full-fledged story. Another neighbor named Chen, who ran downstairs immediately after it happened, breathlessly returned to give an excited report on what he saw. Under Dr. Wang's sympathetic gaze, I begged Chen to stop. I guess they thought that was because, as a woman, I was frightened and weak. I saw them wink at each other to show their understanding; after all, it was a scary scene, for the deceased was all bloody and unrecognizable. Chen pulled Dr. Wang over to the window, where they had a whispered conversation as they opened the curtain again to examine the broken glass. Chen, heedless of the danger, even stuck out his head to look up at the rooftop.

I guess he must have felt the cold air when he stuck his head out. A wind had started up outside, chilling the room inside. The unobstructed late night flowed in like water before it freezes in the winter, carrying with it all the foreboding of an imminent snowstorm. Could he see the deceased on the ground? Every light in the building might have been on by then, and the open space on the street must have been crowded with people: doctors and policemen, and neighbors who jumped out of bed and ran outside to enjoy the spectacle with fur-lined coats over their pajamas. I poured another round of hot tea for Dr. Wang's wife, and as I did, creamy white steam billowed out of the crimson spout of the purple-sand teapot, reminding me of a person exhaling a deep breath. Chen might have said something, after a prolonged silence, but no one heard what he said, nor did anyone understand him; only his breath, a sign of life, showed when he spoke. That was due to the cold, for on winter nights any trace of warmth is precious. The teapot was the very one I'd been holding, the object I'd gripped tightly at the moment the death occurred. Its tangible warmth and weight now put me in a daze. The moment when death flew past my window should still exist in it, just as the moment has remained in my body, my clothes, my books, my rooms — but nothing changed, nothing was touched, except for the open window with its shattered glass. These thoughts sent a chill deep into my bones.

I went to look for a heavy wool coat. But it wasn't warm enough, and I had to turn up the collar. The woolen texture carried a rough tenderness, caressing me like a hand and surrounding me when I moved around. It has an unconditional, everlastingly loyal sense of caring. I don't think I could ask for more, and in reality, I have never asked for too much — I have always treated the warmth of this sort of life as the only reality. Wearing my warm, comfy coat, I breathed, I walked around, and I lived, but at the same time, I imagined how the deceased's face was likely flattened against the icy cement and felt no loneliness, no chill, and no pain. At that moment, for some reason, I suddenly thought about my hand resting on the student's shoulder earlier that day. And I was aware of how insincere the gesture had been, for my hand could bring him neither warmth nor consolation, just as the phone call I'd made to the police a while ago and all the attention paid to that death were powerless to touch the tragedy itself. My hand did not provide the warmth of clothing, nor did it have the coldness of the ground.

Now I'm writing, describing. Now I can express and comprehend. But at the time, I felt no excitement, only a sense of turmoil — even this turmoil was calm and dispassionate. Police came upstairs to investigate — a meticulous and tedious process — then reporters started knocking on doors. Once again, the newspapers had found a hot local news story. I suppose editors working the night desks had already come up with eye-catching headlines about this death, such as "Mysterious Fall."

The police said they weren't sure if it was a suicide. They found two halves of a rope, one tied to the rooftop railing, the other looped around the waist of the deceased. When connected, the two halves were long enough to stretch from the top of the building to my window. Why had someone intending to commit suicide tied a lifeline around his waist? But, according to the police, the rope was too flimsy, clearly not strong enough to support the weight of a grown person. Naturally, it snapped in two when he began lowering himself. It must have been at that moment, the instant when he felt the rope part, that he kicked in my window. Then again, the rope could have given out under the strain of his attempt to crash through my window. Maybe it wasn't a suicide attempt at all; he might have been a thief, whose plan to break in through the window had been foiled by inadequate preparation. Yet, I think that no matter what he was trying to do, deep down he exhibited a death wish when he chose to tie a flimsy rope around his waist. On that late night, he stood in the bone-chilling cold on the rooftop; some of the windows must still have had their lights on, mine included. I imagine how the deceased, under the dim light, tied the thin rope around his waist, trying to conceal his death wish from himself. The police said the absence of a suicide note on his body also made them doubt that he had taken his own life. They didn't even find any identification. But I don't think that proves anything. In the end, everyone said, whatever the cause, it was a terrible death. People who saw the body said he was very young.

Finally, at two o'clock in the morning, I saw everyone to the door. I didn't go downstairs, although even Dr. Wang's wife went down to take a look, a sigh on her lips. I stayed in the room the whole time, sometimes looking up from the novel I was reading to visualize how people communicate and commiserate in fictionalized life, how they are able to shed genuine tears when facing death and tremble when they experience true love. The printed pages danced lightly in the wind in front of my eyes.

I opened the curtain a while ago, so now I am face to face with a gray early morning sky that is slowly turning light. The sky is as clear and magnificent as the one I saw yesterday evening. It's the sort of morning that makes me doubt that anything at all had happened. My troubling thoughts throughout the night were probably caused by excessive worry. I didn't have any reason to feel out of sorts. A dead person who brushed shoulders with me couldn't change me; only death in the novels has weighty lingering echoes. I will no longer write anything in this notebook; in fact, I have already sensed that these words are as meaningless as all those novels. Liang Fen will be home soon; I'll hear him opening the door any minute now. Our life will continue as before. It will consist of this kind of morning, will consist of responsibilities that we must assume in broad daylight, will consist of the waiting I'm experiencing now, waiting for a familiar body, a familiar voice — Liang Fen is home now, I can hear him unlocking the door — Let me just write a little more. I have to make breakfast now. Besides, Liang Fen is urging me to read the newspaper he brought back — he says there's some news that will surprise me regarding last night's deceased. But wait just another minute, let me write a bit more in this blue notebook. On a normal morning like this, even though the newspaper, curled up on the table and carrying tragic news, is waiting for me, even though there's no smell of disinfectant on Liang Fen, who is sitting across from me, even though this notebook in front of me reminds me of a sleepless night, I know I'm still contented. Sunlight is shining down on me through the broken window. I know nothing will disturb this life of mine. I feel calm and warm.

She closed the door, shutting herself into a tranquil space that could neither be seen nor heard. In so doing she realized that she had also forced open a tranquillity within herself. She sat down at the table, took a pair of scissors from the drawer and began carefully cutting open the letters. Meticulously, she spread the letters on the table in a specific order — according to the prestige of the university or academic institution. Her reading glasses forced her to maintain a certain distance from the words and the punctuation marks on the paper. This required a lot of patience. Then she took out a thick notebook. It was a good quality one with a hard silk cover and slightly yellowed pages. Although it was years old, clearly it had been well looked after. Liver spots had not fully concealed the scars and calluses which, like fish scales, covered her emaciated hands. She carefully numbered and recorded the letters as though noting excerpts of them for an essay. For the whole of that gloomy morning closely-packed but delicately neat characters flowed from the old nib of her Parker pen.

A fresh coat of paint covered the old paint on the chair which had worn smooth. The fresh paint had now also fallen into a similarly sorry state of repair. Like a vow sworn over an abyss, it was a symbol of endurance. She sat in the chair for hours on end. The days struggled their way out of the darkness, and then inevitably retreated into the darkness again. The trivia of daily life often heralded a momentary darkness which renounced the bleak melancholy of it all. It was a memory she didn't wish to disturb. She rarely went out: a feeble old woman swaying between the curvaceous figures of young women, who seemed like tender bamboo shoots. The passage of time had only left in her a bone-gnawing hatred. The yellow soil had risen past her chest and was aiming straight for her neck. She didn't feel sorry for herself in the slightest, and concerning herself, ventured no hypotheses, not even cautious ones.

The goldfish swam leisurely in the glass tank. Their eyes were like ill-proportioned lanterns hanging from their heads. Streams of bubbles were thrust from the opening and closing mouths, brushing past the lanterns as they dissipated. Droplets of water hung on the rim of the bowl. Some condensed into larger drops and fell back into the water, only to be swallowed by the goldfish. Perhaps there was once a pond, whose misty vapor seeped through the green forest and gathered high in the clouds. A strong man who is bogus, or a weak one who gains respect: who would understand? Now, at least the thin door to the room could afford her safety, freedom, and even joy. Every hazy afternoon would be spent re-reading her notes. Sometimes she would look up an old letter using her reference system. A fleeting comfort would brush past her wrinkle-lined face. Occasionally some lively images would leap out of the officialese on the page. Her eyes then became as bright as ice. All of this pointed to an omen which she had long suppressed. Her shriveled chest brushed the edge of the table as she dealt out the letters one by one, as though they were the treasured cards of a magician.

I.

Following eight years of hardship and destitution, the people returning in victory to Shanghai sighed upon realizing that the metropolis was as bustling as it had been in former times. On a certain day I happened to be forcibly urged by a friend to visit the Carlton Ballroom. Gentlemen and ladies in beautiful attire danced the fox-trot under dazzlingly colorful neon lights. The sidelong glances of the ladies rendered one enchanted. My vision was wholly occupied by the scene. The friend suddenly pointed to a beauty dancing elegantly across the floor and pronounced: Do you know that this is none other than Yu Hong, the famed lady of occupied Shanghai? Her writings are resplendent, and coquettish, and while she appears truly talented in belles-lettres, she is fabled for her unconventionality in life. Indeed, she so resembles her writing in all aspects that one may conclude she is both talented and beautiful. The friend moreover stated that after victory the Shanghai Nationalist Party Committee had sought to make a case against Yu Hong for her relationship with the collaborators. Contrary to expectations, the Party decreed Yu Hong a comrade who had carried out meritorious deeds for the underground. Her case was therefore allowed to rest. Alas, that such a *femme fatale* should come into the world in response to troubled times! The times continue to be troubled. One cannot but worry upon whose head she will bring misfortune.

2.

The darkness approached her casually, but still she did not turn on the light. Gradually, the moonlight appeared to insert itself in the gray wall like a knife. The tightly drawn curtains were unable to keep out the distant stench of evil. A small child could be heard crying next door. It sounded more like laughter, rendering the hard shell of the alley that much more real. She no longer feared the dark as she once had. Lying on the bed, she leisurely recalled the words in the letters. They were like thousands of sores and wounds, yet still exuded the fragrance of fresh ink. A sense of satisfaction clumsily entered her pitiful mind as she settled down to sleep. The problem was that she was too easily roused from sleep with fright. The cogs of dream and reality crunched their teeth together. Her pale, weak face lay hidden in the silken gray threads of hair disheveled across the pillow. Time was not about to retreat. It advanced stubbornly in one direction only, and she was unable to stem its icy flow.

It was on a bone-gnawingly cold day in early spring that someone knocked on the door.

She was curled up in bed like a statue built by a second-rate sculptor. She refused to dream. Yet a dream thumbed its way through the remnants, gently gathering what it pleased, unwittingly forming her into a tightly clenched, alert fist. She could see herself all too clearly, yet at the same time did not want to. There was another knock on the door. She stirred. It was not that she did not deign to welcome the visitor, more that it took her ages to warm her icy feet in bed, and she did not want to be dragged out of bed by the uninvited guest on such a cold spring night. A damp, musty odor permeated the room, reminding her of the prison farm. She had been young then, and could withstand pain one hundred times sharper than the cold. She stopped at the corner between her tiny kitchen and the room she used jointly as a bedroom, study, and sitting room. She looked back at the simple, old furniture in the room. The walls were bare, like those of a cave. A bunch of withering osmanthus flowers emerged from the dark shadows. Just over on the other side of the bed, a parting song whispered in the creases of the flowers. She was baffled by her own subconscious. Tonight was somehow special.

A young woman was standing at the door.

II.

In an article published in *Oriens Extremus*, Professor Cyril Bert of the University of California, Berkeley, an authority on research concerning Chinese literature, expounds the position of Yu Hong in literary history.[7] The article contends that modern Chinese women writers are infinitely superior to their male counterparts, whose intelligence is frequently congested by worrying about mundane affairs or constricted by practical political manipulation. Women writers of the post-May Fourth period such as Bing Xin, Lu Yin, Gan Nüshi, Ling Shuhua, Zhang Ailing and Yu Hong created a naturally flowing style and were more concerned with the renaissance of the Chinese language than male writers. Professor Bert expresses his delight that the Chinese literary world now regards Yu Hong highly. He writes that when C.T. Hsia praised Zhang Ailing in the late 1950s, the reverberations failed to reach China for twenty years. His praise of Yu Hong has only required two years to precipitate a veritable "Yu Hong craze." This represents a fortunate new attitude in Chinese literary circles.

3.

He picked up his umbrella and left the bench without saying a word. He walked a couple of paces and then cast a disdainful glance back at me. He seemed so unfamiliar. Only then did I realize that he had been avoiding me. It was just as Manyu had said. The sandalwood fan Manyu left behind last night smelt like the fairy-like aroma given off by her body. It is right and proper that women should be more lovable than men. Even if a woman has one or two little imperfections, she is still ten times better than a man...

"Why do you insist upon driving me mad? You've laid a trap and are luring me in step by step. Yesterday I had to travel alone by rickshaw to the banquet. You turned up late, pulled away my dancing partner and lost your temper with me in front of everybody."

"Huaiyue," he woke me up from a dream. My white silk nightdress had been pulled open. He was gently kissing my tear-drenched neck...

The girl recited the passage from memory almost without a single mistake, saying how much she liked it. The lamplight shone on her thin scarlet jumper. She was wearing a silver necklace around her slender neck. Her features were remarkably similar to those of a certain person, but she lacked her melancholy eyes and her slender fingers. Of course, she did not have a face straight out of a Botticelli painting. Oh, the Botticelli, with layer upon layer of painful, almost moribund, colors painted over and over again. From where does the swirling water originate and to where does it return?

For instance, just now as she tried to fathom the girl's words and actions, the girl insisted on helping her sit down on the solitary armchair, herself choosing to sit on the bed. She was evidently trying to create an atmosphere suited to their conversation. She still had a rather casual look in her eyes. Casual, but not careless, rather an admiring look exuding both intimacy and freedom.

"The goldfish is really cute. It swims so beautifully," the girl added in mid-sentence. She also said that next time she would bring some water fleas to feed it. The childlike purity of the smile on her face drew her into a world of reality she wanted to explore further. It suddenly dawned on her that once upon a time she had also made friends among the young and beautiful. Her head grew heavy with confusion. She was more comfortable receiving letters than she was receiving guests, for letters did not demand an instant reply. Guests, on the other hand, were much more trouble. She could not tell whether her deep amnesia should be put down to a skill honed by time or deliberate error and confusion.

That evening, as she leant against the chair, she realized she was the sort of person who was entirely unwilling to engage in conversation with anyone.

Fortunately, there were not many people who found their way directly to her door. Maybe one a year. The old friends she used to know had long since scattered. Some had died and could no longer speak. Others were still alive, but there was too much resentment. They had turned their backs on each other and had made their own way in life. The youngsters who were so loud in the office had no idea what her name was, let alone caught sight of her. When she left, the publishing house was still called The Violet Star Press, but now the name, the bosses, the colleagues and even the address had gone through several changes. The remains of the old place lay silently hidden beneath flowing waters. Who could still recall that rainy morning when she was taken away in an army jeep? Fear had naturally accumulated in that dying void, only to be blown to the surface year after year by the spring breeze. Only the gatekeeper who redirected her mail and the cashier who sent her wages knew her present address from the pension records.

The girl produced from her large denim bag an old photo album with a black cover. She didn't open it, but raised her head to look at the old woman and said gently: "You've got her photo, of course?"

She was not in the habit of replying to specific questions like this. Moreover, the girl's natural expression and the name she had mentioned pushed her at once into some unwelcoming waters. She had to get out of there, but realized that she had to conceal herself before she could rid herself of that sense of wetness.

"No, I haven't," she said, coldly, without hesitation.

The girl was able to take the hint that she was struggling. She apologized, said she had forgotten that they all said that all the material she had had been completely lost. Only then did she open her photo album, laying it on the arm of the chair between the two of them.

Through her glasses the old woman could make out an unfamiliar face floating into view. The veins bulged under pale skin. It was almost as if one could grab hold of them, as if they were attesting to a subtle expression of her eyes, a soft voice, the make-up, the hairstyle and the stirring youthfulness of those bygone days. Time turned back an entire half-century through that yellowing photo on the arm of a wooden chair that should have been thrown away years ago. This movement backwards in time was too fast, too easy, and too thorough. She had been caught unawares and felt as though she were going to faint. However, the habits of half a century directed her intellect.

"I'm not really sure. Look at the photo mounts, I've only just renewed them." The girl's voice buzzed in her ear like an insect. She took off her glasses. The tight-fitting silk *qipao* decorated with intertwining blue and purple flowers and the curly black hair became blurred. The girl stopped turning over the pages, her fingers with light rose-colored nail polish rested on the yellow page like ivory brooches, pinning her down. Her breathing became erratic. The dim lamplight in the room seemed to be deliberately avoiding her, leaving her at the mercy of the creeping darkness.

III.

In the opinion of most modern literary historians, Yu Hong belonged to the "New Neo-Sensualist School" in that she continued to write the urban fiction to which writers such as Li Na'ou and Mu Shiying devoted themselves. Professor Chen Zhishan from the Chinese Department of Shanghai Normal University has recently put forward a different opinion. He claims that Yu Hong's fiction is well-knit, with rich color and magnificent language, and that it does not shy away from decadence in its sexual description. It is very close to the style of writers from Nationalist areas, such as Xu Xu and the one called Anonymous. Moreover, the pupil has surpassed the master. Yu Hong's most famous novel, *Neon City* (1945), takes as its background love and political intrigue in the dance halls of Japanese-occupied Shanghai, but it is only a kind of historical "anchoring." Xu Xu's *The Soughing Wind* and Anonymous' *Beast Beast Beast* are both love stories set against a background of the political activities of the day. They are truly representative of the general mood of the time. Yu Hong should be seen as the last radiant splendor of the Shanghai School of novelists.

4.

The white tablet contained within it the tenacious force to drive away yet another sleepless night. Two young girls stared at each other like two mirrors facing each other, their silhouettes joining together. She hid behind the effects of the sleeping tablet, pretending not to see. The gentle white house transparently returned that summer evening to its proper place: Oh, it's you. Great! She was roused from her sleep by the sound of the door being opened. She had been ill and was lying on the bed. The elegant fragrance of osmanthus flowers floated in the air. Your voice was sweet and smooth. You said you had taken great pains to buy the osmanthus. It reminded me of the first time you came to the magazine offices with your bashfully melancholy eyes. Actually, what touched me was not your obstinate worship of me, your fervent love of literature, or your intelligence, but that face straight out of a Botticelli painting — the fatal face of a goddess born from the waves.

The two goldfish were playing with each other in the glass bowl. You cried as you watched them. When I told you my fiancé was not a problem you needed to worry about, I actually meant that he was never an obstacle to you. Okay, he left me and you came.

Shanghai nights, Shanghai nights
You stole my heart...

Was it all because of you, or was it something else?

All of it — like all of you. The tender tones of a song stroked those clasped hands: the special language of two women staring at each other. Loneliness lessened its volume, guiltily casting light on the fish in the bowl. She muttered the following words to herself: Why should such a beautiful and sentimental time have to come to an end?

The midday sun shone down. The musty smell in the room stubbornly lingered on her clothes, the quilt, the shoes, the furniture, and the floor, attaching itself to her flabby skin. She was almost seventy. Among the aging editors there were many old hands who knew everything, but experts were hard to come by. The first thing required of an expert was to "possess all the historical material," and on that count she was worthy of the title. Others found it hard to surpass her, yet her reticence left the literary world puzzled and guessing.

She changed her posture, closed the book, and sighed. The deep fishtail wrinkles on her cheeks tunneled tenaciously inwards. Two gray sideburns clung to either side of her head like dried hemp. She waited in terror. The sound of rapid footsteps emerged from the darkness. The sunlight in the musty air exacerbated the unbearable sense of oppression. The footsteps stopped outside the door. She wanted to prevent her real self from joining the image in the mirror. She almost succeeded in doing this. What if it was the girl? Oh, if only it wasn't her. Why every time she thought of her, her stomach twitched involuntarily, and a bad taste rushed into her throat.

The girl carefully spooned fish food into the bowl. The goldfish darted back and forth as though celebrating some festival. "I've brought you my grandmother's diary," the girl turned and said excitedly, putting down the spoon. "Just think, I had forgotten what my grandmother looked like. Now, suddenly, I know so much. From her diary I found out that you and she were once more than ordinary friends."

A sharp awl was closing in on her, forcing her to raise her arms in surrender. A mouthful of false teeth tore at her gums. However, once the girl had opened a silk-covered notebook and had placed it in her hands, her heart merely quivered. She looked beyond the notebook, beyond the girl, beyond herself. Gently, she closed the book, placing it on the edge of the table. She hoped the girl would know what this signal meant. She was genuinely sorry. She was this courteous to everyone.

"You didn't keep in touch after that? What a pity!" She failed to answer the girl's question. "Maybe as a wife and a mother she had to cut herself off from this experience. That's sad!" The room was quite dim.

The girl stood up and looked at her probingly. She realized that the woman would rather turn her back on this part of history. She remained weakly yet stubbornly silent. "It was you. You gave her all those things that men weren't able to. In the years that you knew each other...."

She knew she could no longer remain silent. She opened her eyes, cleared her throat, and said as distinctly as possible: "I don't know what you mean."

At last she had pried open her mouth! The girl was ecstatic and grew very talkative, saying how her grandmother had been grateful for the old woman's protection all these years. First, she had been accused of being a traitor and then suspected of being a spy — these crimes were too much for her to bear. Although she had endured many hardships, her grandmother continued to have a hard time of it during the Cultural Revolution. The local Red Guards managed to find something incriminating from who-knows-where, claiming that her grandmother had wept for three days following the Japanese surrender. Moreover, she was a promiscuous socialite, the wife of a capitalist, and a secret counterrevolutionary. She was "struggled against" in the alley every day.

"I didn't protect anybody. I wouldn't know how." Her voice was old but now very clear. "What do you want? Stop beating around the bush and come out with it."

For a moment the girl did not know what to say. She flipped through the silk-covered notebook. There was a newspaper cutting inside. It was a group photo from a "tea party." Of course, she stood in the middle looking extremely graceful and uncommonly beautiful. The girl handed her the newspaper cutting. She pulled the lamp closer to herself. The fear she knew only too well now appeared in the girl's eyes: her eyes were deeply sunken and two knife scars crossed her neck with a wisp of cold wind. It was all very clear. Then she raised her hands; they were rough and disfigured, her left hand almost totally crippled. She could no longer straighten her constantly quivering fingers.

That's not me. Do you understand?

The girl shuddered. "Can you honestly say that you didn't know my grandmother?"

A smile returned to the girl's face.

IV.

In an essay entitled "Feminism in China," Professor Yue Daiyun, director of the Institute of Comparative Literature at Capital University, points out that writers embodying a modern woman's consciousness in modern Chinese literature were comparatively few. Most of the women writers continued to write so-called "boudoir literature." Zhang Ailing was the most successful of them. Ding Ling was the pioneer of a feminist literature; unfortunately, however, she turned too soon to genderless revolutionary writing. Yu Hong's early works, such as the short story collection *Incomplete* (1942) and the novella "The Wind between the Two Doors" (1943), emphasize the free spirit of the modern woman — so much so that for a long time they were considered pornographic. Professor Yue points out that only the most broad-minded of women writers could aspire to this standard, laying a fertile soil for the feminist spirit. In recent years, more information on Yu Hong's life has continued to be unearthed, and this has assisted in an understanding of her writings.

5.

She turned her head away in fright. What the girl had brought was not a beautiful projection of the past, but a sharp weapon, one which pounded relentlessly through a fragile shell at an unspeakable root.

It was not merely that the past was excessively heavy, it was actually that she was a person with only a past and no present. She felt that before her was a dead end. Human history was like that: from the very outset every misunderstanding was the result of a previous misunderstanding, and in that way the whole of history appeared to have a foundation.

Men are merely embellishments, but women are the bones in the flesh. You said you weren't leaving, your eyes wet with the moisture of a rainy day…. It's not possible, nothing is possible any more. These unshakable resolutions came from within her. She had to hold out to the very end. If she changed the same blue blouse which she wore year round for some slightly more colorful clothes, if she applied some moisturizing cream to her face or two lines of pale lipstick to her bloodless, flaccid lips, then would she still be able to recognize for herself the continuation of history?

The girl sat back down on the edge of the bed and started talking. She said that writing her thesis on a computer was both speedy and convenient. Then she mentioned some trivial things about her grandmother. What she said did not appear to be marching towards an overall theme, but the direction was clear.

"I understand your thoughts," the girl said. "You helped create a beautiful legend. When you first parted, there were perhaps painful struggles, and despair over the fact that you had to each get on with your own." The girl took hold of her thin, bony hand. The girl was enchantingly gentle, a gentleness which flowed along her terribly dilapidated veins, launching an attack on her icy bones. Was she still afraid that her blood would never get warm again? "You suffered a great deal for the name Yu Hong," the girl said understandingly. "History has pushed Yu Hong into a black hole and you're not about to pull her out again. I can understand that. Why don't I structure it along these lines: Yu Hong — an eternal riddle?"

What the girl imagined was actually not far from the truth. That most helpless moment was etched onto her memory, and it had never faded away. There was, however, a great discrepancy between what the girl — and others — had guessed and the truth. We never said we would be together until death us do part. We didn't even say a single word when we parted. You hurried off in a huff. The stifling summer of 1945 and the mushroom cloud of the atomic bomb cast their shadows on Shanghai. You judged the hour, sized up the situation, and rapidly entered into marriage. Afterwards, the summer sank without a trace into pitch-black rainwater. You knew that not a single scent would last, and you were right. She smelt the sweat of the dozens of bodies who shared a room with her — sweat mixed with the stench of open chamber pots. The prison farm might have been able to change your thoughts and feelings, but it could never change the sky above your head. When she suddenly awoke that morning, she wasn't sure why she still remembered the glint of the diamond ring on that person's finger. So, do you want to turn the page? Oh, that would be the cruelest joke in the world! The sound of the rain resounded inside her body.

V.

The article "New Evidence on the Life of Yu Hong" was published in the fourth issue for 1991 of *Historical Data on Literature*. In response to an invitation from the Research Department of the Chinese Writers' Association, the Records Section of the Shanghai Public Security Bureau released the following data from Peng Fei's confession, to be published in the journal.

Shortly after Liberation, Comrade Peng Fei worked as director of the Propaganda Department of the East China Bureau. In 1953 he was implicated in the now exonerated Pan-Yang spy case and imprisoned. He died in prison in 1965. When the War of Resistance against the Japanese ended, Peng Fei was working for the Communist Underground Cultural Committee in Shanghai. The title of one page from Peng Fei's confession was "About Yu Hong":

"In the autumn of 1946 the Underground Municipal Committee decided to persuade those writers who had returned from the Resistance areas to stop criticizing the writers in the occupied area. Misunderstandings had to be eliminated in order to establish the widest possible unified front. They decided to let newly emerging writers on the literary scene from the occupied area like Zhang Ailing, Su Qing, and Yu Hong take part in progressive magazines such as Li Jianwu's *Renaissance* and Ke Ling's *The World*. I asked Professor Zheng Zhenduo to go and make contact with these writers, and he carried out the task well. However, he came to see me once, telling me how surprised he was not to have found anything out about Yu Hong. He asked the Communist Underground to help clear things up. He went to the Violet Star Press, the publishers of Yu Hong's works, to seek out the editor-in-chief Chen Wenren. Chen was young and beautiful, and spoke incisively. She said that Yu Hong was only a contributor and that she had never met her face-to-face. Zheng asked Chen for Yu Hong's address. Chen took out *Violet Star* magazine's accounting books and showed him the address to which the remuneration had been sent. It was a post office box number. Zheng Zhenduo reported that Yu Hong's literary style was peculiar and that her subject matter was decadent. The plots of her stories seemed to have vague political implications and therefore some people thought they were the works of a traitor or a spy. However, the stories could not be taken as evidence by themselves. I reported what Zheng had said to Comrade Yang Yong of the Municipal Committee to refer to the Security Section, asking that the matter be investigated. Comrade Yang Yong never told me how this matter was concluded. *Violet Star* magazine was, politically, right of center as it flaunted pure literature. I seem to remember that after Liberation Chen Wenren was employed by the Municipal Publishing Bureau."

Wu Fuhui, editor of *Historical Data*, annotated the article with the following: "There have been numerous rumors about Yu Hong's life for many years, but none of them has been proved. This article contains the only true material published to date and is therefore very valuable. In response to an invitation from the literary world, the Public Security Bureau has selectively published records of more than forty years. This is both unprecedented and heartening."

6.

She opened her weary eyes. Dazed, the goldfish swam gently to the surface, turning over and over again. Its yellow scales glinted through the glass, tugging gently at her heart. She put down the scissors and the letters. There was a large pile of opened and unopened letters on the table. None of them had been put in order or recorded. She hadn't re-read any of her old letters for several days. The knocking at the door was nothing more than an absurd cycle. She pretended not to hear it. There were several tiny signs which indicated that she had climbed some of those steps which had been hidden behind a veil of cruelty. She had skillfully avoided those clear-cut steps for decades. The smile merely annotated her face more painfully. For the first time in several decades she wanted to see what she looked like. However, there was no mirror to be found in the house. She bent over at her old waist and picked up an enamel wash basin. Having half-filled the bowl with water from the kitchen tap, she then topped it up with boiling water.

Looking into the bowl of clear water, she could see an illusory figure constantly quivering in her hands. She removed her hands from the rim of the bowl, but the water refused to still itself. The clamor of passersby resounded in the air. She put her hands back onto the bowl, wanting to plunge them into the water. She then lifted her eyes and gasped loudly. Tears streamed down her cheeks and rolled away. Slowly, she took off her topcoat and put on a jacket decorated with interlocking black and red flowers. The red flowers were only vaguely visible tiny patterns. As she waited for the girl, she was filled with unusual feelings she had not experienced for decades.

Just as she had expected, the night climbed over the day, and had just unfolded its black cape of weariness when the girl arrived. The girl asked her whether she had been sick. As she inquired about her, the girl produced a beautifully wrapped gift, as she did on every visit. She seemed pleased with what the old woman was wearing, even though it was in fact not so new. The girl's words were sincere, and she didn't mention the last few occasions when she had been left out in the cold. So it wasn't necessary for her to explain.

The girl came straight to the point and said that she had found her grandmother's manuscripts. Apparently one of them was almost the same as one of Yu Hong's poems. She knew that there were only seven of Yu Hong's poems still extant.

She stood up, taking over to the table the photocopied page the girl had given her. After turning on the lamp and putting on her glasses, the graceful handwriting put her in mind of that face she swore always to treat as unfamiliar:

Afterwards

Choose a flower
Such as a lily
The faint scent lingers with the remaining fear
But everything I recount
Seems to have lost its meaning
When your hand rises
I realize
It is still dark

"You see, apart from one or two words, it's the same as a poem published in *Violet Star*. It hints at a few things both you and she knew about. I imagine it was a beautiful and perilous romance."

She interrupted the girl who, standing by the table, was just getting into her stride. "She copied this poem!"

"I've looked up the date." The girl ignored her irritated face, and continued to intone each syllable in a warm and clear way. "My grandmother's words were written before the poem was published in *Violet Star*. It had to have been her work. This is the conclusive proof that my grandmother was Yu Hong."

She was gently stroking the glass bowl with her hands. She would not have regretted it had she been the fish in the water. Yes, you're really something, you never leave me with any way out. She turned around to look at the girl. The poor light made the girl's eyes twinkle mysteriously against her silhouette. She had really been pushed to the limit this time. She could no longer keep a secret that had not been divulged, no matter what the threat, for decades. The girl was highly intelligent. She may as well play her trump card and stop wasting time.

"Okay then, since you're so convinced, I've got no choice but to tell you that there never was a person called Yu Hong."

"But what about my grandmother?" asked the girl naively and anxiously.

"Your grandmother has nothing to do with this. She wasn't Yu Hong. She just helped me copy down poems, that's all."

In an instant the girl's kindness completely vanished. She suddenly said angrily: "Is that really fair to my grandmother?"

Her trembling voice was still very clear: "It doesn't matter how you phrase it, it's still a fact."

"How can you be sure that what you say is a fact and that what I say is wrong? Couldn't it be that what you say is wrong and what I say is a fact?"

"How dare you?!" She floated down onto the chair like a thin piece of paper.

The girl moved closer to her, putting her hand on her crooked, shrunken back. Her tone was much softer: "People have been taking liberties with you for fifty years. How come you didn't get angry with them?"

She paused. The girl said she knew Yu Hong had come into being as a result of their special relationship. Had her grandmother still been alive today, they could celebrate together the fact that history had awarded Yu Hong her rightful place.

She didn't hear a word of it. The bright colors of the borscht on the plate were dazzling. They left their seats together and walked out of the elegant western restaurant, each wearing a *qipao* with a high slit. They had a lithe and graceful gait, and held their heads up high. Yes, both of them were very arrogant. Everyone — every couple — is only young once.

VI.

On 17 May Shanghai's *Wenhui Gazette* carried the following report: PERPLEXING MISTS OF HISTORY LIFTED AT LAST: A UNIQUE TALE PASSES FROM TALENTED GRANDMOTHER TO TALENTED GIRL

Yesterday afternoon, at an academic seminar in the Chinese Depart-
ment of Fudan University, the young woman poet Fu Hao presented a special
report entitled "Research on the Identity of Yu Hong." During the seminar, she
used slides of manuscripts, letters, diary entries, photographs and so on, in
order to prove that Yu Hong was the pseudonym of her maternal grandmother
Lin Yuxia. Her verification of the facts against the works of Yu Hong were
most convincing. Based on the large volume of material she has gathered, Fu
Hao is preparing to write the nation's first Biography of Yu Hong. Replying to
journalists'questions, Fu Hao, who has become increasingly well-known in
recent years through her poetry, claimed that the inherent literary atmosphere
in her family had helped her develop her own unique literary style and spiri-
tual pursuit.

7.

She was unable to record this news report about Yu Hong in her
notes. This was the only new material on Yu Hong's life about which
she knew nothing. Her notebook was locked in the drawer.

There wasn't much water left in the glass bowl. The fish, opening
its mouth to breathe, was a symbol of fragrance. She was flustered and
short of breath. She lit a cigarette and then put it out. The two of them
were leaning on the railings of the Garden Bridge looking at the
Whangpoo River. She asked perplexedly: "Why do you publish under a
pseudonym? Is it because you want to avoid trouble? Or are you just
having a laugh?" She shook her head. No one scent could outlast the
whole rainy season, but it is a different story when it entered another
body and lived on.

The crisscrossing paths of the secret were forever leading her astray.
History is heartless. If you hoodwink history, history is bound to turn
around and hoodwink you. She had suffered her entire life for nothing
more than a tiny name. The protest lingering in her heart had already
decided to give up the fight. The riddle originated from within her. When
she had decided how to deal with it, she realized she was still its only
master.

She tottered towards the bed and cautiously laid her own body on it. Pitch-black waters swept away the shattered fragments at the depths of her heart. They carried with them everything in her memory: the song of Shanghai nights, the morning floating amidst raindrops, and the face from the Botticelli Painting — everything seemed so vulgar. Life transmigrated back and forth. Everything remained the same, except the occasional exception. If it so happened that she should chance upon one of the exceptions, then she would be able to start life all over again. She would be a genuine woman, no pretense, no compromise. Give it a try. Yes, she should definitely give it a try. She resolved to do so and so she did.

On a rainy morning in late spring the postman walked past her door again.

He originally thought that the old woman would continue making his work more difficult, as he had to return a pile of letters every day. He never expected that the letters would dry up and, in fact, vanish almost overnight. Never again did anybody send mail to that person whose ashes nobody kept.

January 1994, London

YANG LIAN TRANSLATED BY BRIAN HOLTON

THE COMPOSER'S TOWER

1.

the wooden bridge's direction is the rotten direction of dead fish
rain   dyed black by a silver lake

stone   rotted to let roots clutch
loathing's roots that ivy stabs in flesh

spit out the sound of rainsummer like a moldy pelt
birdsong plunging into the starving trap of the ear

hearing   turned into a breach in the dawn
everything interred in the tower sounds out in music

a madman's sodden head floats to the surface
makes the sky fall apart again and again   frenziedly stirs last night

but last night will never leave   you
somber windows everywhere open only on someone's pain

2.

the battle is only between sound and silence
you hear the corpse opening the lid and struggling up through the soil

the final day has finally arrived at a pallid letter
time retarded   just enough to forget

declaiming in the novel accents of a blood-red bird
the dead are wakened only to lose to death again

you lose   to a life on a page of the score
like a wrecker   lectured by the clenched teeth of the dumb

write   every man-faced grass shares the winter's flow
flesh invisibly returns

flesh   has elapsed in composition   gone further still now
as negating light moves from note to note

3.

the door bangs shut   the inquisitor's rage metamorphoses
father softly explains himself   not at all like a father

there's an ear aged eleven in the tower
glued to the wall by all of its years

overhearing all the time   how sound dies in sound
like silence   making a stone of heaped silence

a child stands on top of the high tower
swallows the wickedness stuffed into his little hand by dark stars

the storm stuffs a silent stomach full
this June morning   pulls you back into the madman's yesterday

writing out the final whistle
a tower of aging skin   so easily blown away

BAI HUA   TRANSLATED BY YANBING CHEN

THE ENGLISH INSTRUCTOR AT
THE INSTITUTE OF AGRICULTURE

By the time I got married in October 1983, I was already teaching at the Southwest Institute of Agriculture. Although SIA was not as secluded as the Southwest Teachers' College, there was a huge Communist Youth League garden in the middle of its campus. It was bright and beautiful and tidy footpaths ran through it like well-constructed couplets. The two campuses were very close, at most a ten-minute walk from one to the other. Apart from teaching, I usually stayed at home at STC and seldom went over to SIA, dodging, as much as possible, the weekly political study sessions. I continued to reserve my rightful dissent on this last critical point.

I started by correcting graduate English assignments for an old professor, but I was soon at the podium myself. I still vaguely remember how the excitement made me both nervous and talkative, the numerous eyes that tried to draw me in — oh, how they took me for an innocent old hand. I had taught "continuing education" English classes made up of science workers at the Science and Technology Information Center, but the university was a different world all together. It was more formal and serious; teaching is, after all, a specialized profession.

The first class I taught was made up entirely of middle-aged faculty members from other departments. At the time they were all working hard on their English. In order to become professors and associate professors, they had to pass an English proficiency test. They were equally nervous and attentive. By the end of the long-awaited first class, my heart was beginning to calm down; what followed after was normal every day work and life, easy and pleasant. I accrued a good deal of free time, and with so much freedom I eagerly awaited and prepared for the geyser of poetry that would surely erupt at any moment; while at the same time enjoying the newly-obtained peace and quiet of domestic life. The painful quarrels had not yet begun.

Having abruptly left the muggy weather of Chongqing, I congratulated myself for my luck at ending up within the serenity of Beipei. I breathed in deeply and lost myself in this unusual "quiet," a "quiet" that was somehow like that of my boyhood. As time passed, however, a touch of loneliness crept up; the loneliness of estrangement and helplessness. Day after day it grew stronger, and family life alone was far from able to dispel this hint of sadness triggered by an idealist's melancholy loneliness. It was as if the red-hot iron of youth had been suddenly dipped in ice-cold water. The ghosts of poems floated in midair, unable to land. Anxiously, my young heart awaited: a new friend, a fierce struggle. . . .

Domestic routines temporarily dispersed my secret angst. Weekend afternoons or Sunday mornings, we strolled along the refreshing streets of Beipei, watching glitzy fashions and the thin streams of pedestrians. Happiness floated like a gentle breeze over the small city, and we, too, were happy. She would pick a sweater for me and buy a new dress for herself, and for that we would be overwhelmed with joy for the entire day. One weekend evening, we sat on a bench in a street garden. The crowd thinning in the sound of dusk, returning home or reuniting with someone. . . . Night approached, and I whispered, as much to myself as to her, "I'll live here when I'm old, thinking or sorting through my youthful writings. This is a good place for a writer. . . ."

The home of a middle-aged geology teacher was our usual haunt. The quiet — which was habitual and therefore normal — attracted us. In this paradise of an ordinary family, I seldom spoke. As soon as I got there I would sit and leaf through newspapers and magazines until it was time to eat, and then, after the meal, pick up where I had left off. Oblivious to their conversation, I secretly enjoyed the atmosphere of beauty and harmony until it was time to say good-bye. Once, smiling, she said, "Look at him, every time Professor Huang comes over, he just sits and reads the newspaper." Everyone laughed. And I, embarrassed, laughed, too.

The loneliness continued. . . .

One afternoon in deep winter, the Foreign Language Department of SIA distributed oranges as bonus. Everyone was given a share. It was almost dark when the bustle was over. In the twilight, I carried home on my back a full basket of oranges. The lights in the dark distant mountains glistened, the smell of dinners seeped from the low barracks lining both sides of the street, swarmed in the air, mingling with the "Friendly News" broadcast on radios with poor reception. Suddenly tears filled my eyes. Tears of loneliness? Tears of happiness? I did not know. After the day's work, people prepared their suppers on warm evenings, following an ancient rule of life, while I, like a night traveler returning from a far-away place, hurried home. I was hungry, but the hunger, the winter night, the distant mountains, the streets of the small town, the basket of oranges, and the one who was waiting for me at home. . . . Life, ordinary and fleeting life, once more touched me and left me wordless. On a spring night six years later, in the beautiful city of Nanjing, I recalled this moment of deep winter in 1983:

> What should you be grateful for:
> this view, these details
> this earth attentive in her loving?
> What should you find,
> life, reality, or discrimination?
>
> Concentration, more concentration
> concentration is just lyricism
> when the way you plunge into happiness
> is just the way you sink into the moment
> when the night continues to darken
>
> . . . .

—from "Festival"

I felt my own image was changing, changing towards an unprecedented beauty; I felt I was enjoying life's bequest — the happiness of solitude. Even now, in the midst of the turbulent waves of economic reform, I still would like to revisit the short road home that night. Oh, how I'd like once more to carry home a basket of oranges in the twilight!

In my solitude, I made an absent-minded mistake — I incorrectly figured the grade of a good student, and ended up giving him an F. I could imagine the shock and suffering this meek and modest student must have gone through when he saw his grade, and how, in his self-flagellation, had believed it. A model student, he had trusted teachers since he was a child. When I found out about the mistake and told him the next semester, he stood with his head bent low, slightly puzzled and a little shy. Bravely, I confessed my mistake to him. Now it was my turn for self-flagellation.

One day on my way home after classes, I saw a young man of an imposing manner and peculiar features. He looked a lot like an East-European: deep, serious eyes looking straight ahead; a high nose with a sharp bridge that seemed to have been carved by a knife; the lips, a chiseled, unforgettable curve. His jutting lower jaw formed a perfectly acute chin; his hair was well-combed, every strand in place, exposing as much as possible his full forehead; and his thick but well-groomed black beard flaunted the charm of maturity. He had been afflicted with polio, and as a result had a lame left leg. Walking slowly, he nevertheless gave off a not negligible presence, and the air of someone who would be the center of any group. His whole figure and expression conveyed a combination of determination, suffering, and ideals. He brushed past my shoulder and continued walking.

We hit it off right away, quickly becoming friends. His name was Zhou Zhonglin. He was teaching himself aesthetics at the time. He not only had a rich collection of books and loved literature, but was also magnanimous. Our further acquaintance started with the poem "Shock." He did not write poems, but had his own set of critical standards. During that time, I read a paper on aesthetics and the drafts of a few short stories he had written, and learned that he had an esthetics teacher, Su Ding's father, Su Hongchang, the late Professor of aesthetics and the Chair of the Chinese Department at the Southeastern Teachers' College.

Zhou's parents worked at the Southwestern Institute of Agriculture, while his own job was typing for SIA at home. Later he did the typing for the first book of self-published poems by Zhang Zao and me, and it was this very collection that I had taken on my first trip to Beijing. His generosity, loyalty, and writerly manner attracted many poets, while he himself was also most willing to make friends with them. Apart from me, Zhang Zao, Wan Xia, Liao Yiwu, Li Yawei, and many others benefited from his selfless help and support.

So just like that, Zhou Zhonglin and his girlfriend, Xiao Hong (a student at SIA and the daughter of Ke Fei, a renowned Sichuan writer and the author of *Spring Rapids*), became friends of our family. Whenever we got together we always had a wonderful time with them. Unfortunately, Xiao Hong took ill and died shortly after her graduation. Zhou remained unbroken after this experience. He devoted himself to writing avant-garde fiction, and made a name for himself in literary circles, eventually becoming a well-known writer.

I soon found another good way of diverting myself from my solitude: amusing myself by revising the poems of students at Southwestern Teachers' College. I didn't realize at the time that this self-amusement would later grow into an eccentric habit — that is, the urge to revise other people's poems whenever I read them, with or without the authors' permission. This compulsive behavior was extremely offensive to some people. But after awhile, people wanting their poems revised began to form a line at my home. And a line of joy and happiness it was! I took special pleasure in revising poems by Li Heping and Chen Kangping — students from the Music Department. And Li, knowing of my addiction, took pleasure in feeding it by supplying me with poems day in and day out. He stood humbly at my side, eyes fixed on the manuscript, watching his disorderly passion being shaped. As he watched intently, observing the process of technical transformation, I enjoyed the immense happiness derived from my technical facility in revision.

In the inner ring of the poetic circles I hung out with at the time, mutual revision was a common practice. Zhang Zao was always eager to revise my poems, and I his, each perfecting the other while showing off oneself at the same time. What a wonderful but fleeting time that was! I am all for revision, and am more than happy to have others revise my poems. Zhang Zao revised the last stanza of my poem "Name," and Ouyang Jianghe the second stanza of my "Dusk." What's more, he made an important change in the second line of the first stanza of my "In the Qing Dynasty." My original line read, "The leisurely ambition deepens," he changed it to "Leisure and ambition deepen." The parallel between the two nouns was perfect. Fu Wei also made a change to one of the lines of "In the Qing Dynasty." Where the old version read "Reading the Grand Historian at night, fishing in the morning," he changed it to "Reading the Grand Historian at night, sweeping the floor in the morning," which emphasizes the overlapping rather than the fragmentation of images. In my "Air Keeper," he also came up with a breakthrough word for the whole poem. The line read "a dry and withered Taoist sits." He asked me tentatively, "would it be better to use 'adviser' instead of 'Taoist'?" The moment he said that, I had already decided on 'adviser,' and for that I have held him in respect ever since. To this day, I think shoptalk among poets is nothing compared to the hands-on experience of mutual revision. The best kind of revision, rather than forcing one's own system onto the other's, is one that takes place inside the system of the poet you are revising — which is not only the best exercise in technique but also a good learning experience. The best kind of revision is not amputation and transplantation, it respects what the poem says and improves it through being faithful to it.

Shortly before the Spring Festival of 1984, Peng Yiling and I made a quick trip to Chengdu. For him it was a revisit; for me it was the first time. Chengdu, a city five hundred kilometers away from Chongqing, which had made its presence felt in my college correspondence, enchanted us so much that we lingered on, forgetting to go home. Here, ferocious heat was replaced by coolness and chaos was overtaken by order. Time, as if out of instinct, slowed down and almost stopped. Time, here, pampered like a rich young man, strolled among the teahouses, wineshops, bamboo groves, birdcages.... The leisure in every small movement and gesture, the kind and intimate way people interact with one another, a small alley empty and quiet in the afternoon, a broad avenue pompous in its self-imposed dignity — a flavor of the past blended naturally into a taste of the modern. Two years later, I wrote "In the Qing Dynasty." What I really meant was "In Chengdu."

Around 1984, an air of poetic intoxication and magical blessing permeated the landscape, whereas nowadays it has already suffered some human destruction. The Riverview Park is just a miniature of such destruction, its quiet and mysterious atmosphere exorcised by gaudy vaudeville and variety shows. The unhurried outdoor tea-savoring of the old days is now packed into a two-story nominal teahouse, its purpose being more thirst-quenching and commercial display than leisured enjoyment. Tumbledown camels, cart-pulling goats, antique-style Panda Conservation paraphernalia, empty Sprite and Coke bottles, and carnival trains transformed the mood of "solitary walks on the fragrant paths of the small garden." The bamboo (for which the Riverview Park was famous), removed from the lyrical cloudy days, failed to communicate with us, to reconcile with us, while not too long ago they had still tremored in the cool breeze on a bright moonlit night, making believe that it was some villa in the old capital of the Kingdom of Chu — the mountain villa of Xue Tao perhaps?

Yet in spite of it all, Chengdu was already the Chosen City. It was destined to become the Holy City of Poetry. A long list of poets' names would be attached to it: Luo Gengye, You Xiaosu, Zhai Yongming, Ouyang Jianghe, Peng Yiling, Zhong Min, Zhou Lunyou in the early days, and Wan Xia, Shi Guanghua, Song Wei, Li Yawei, Liao Yiwu, Yang Li, Lan Ma, He Xiaozhu, Jimu Langge, Hu Dong, Zhao Ye, Tang Yaping, Ma Song, Pan Jiazhu, Sun Wenbo, Xiao Kaiyu later. Here was the birthplace of the three biggest poetic schools of China in the post-*Today* era: Mang Han (The Reckless), Fei Fei (No-no), and Han Shi (Han Poetry).

I was about to enter this city of landscape and poets.

As soon as we got off the train, Peng Yiling and I headed to the Propaganda Office in the Political Department of the Sichuan Military Area Command. We had hardly stepped into the courtyard when we bumped into Ouyang Jianghe clad in his army uniform. The gatherings followed like a storm. . . .

The group of us met that night at Zhai Yongming's home. There I saw You Xiaosu, the prince of poetry who was once all the rage on university campuses in Chengdu. A man of few words, he was the author of the poem "Black Snow." He had the typical look of the university students of the class of '77; his tall and slender figure gave a hint of his being a track athlete at school, while a certain shyness and fading vitality revealed his disposition as a lyrical poet. He, who was inclined towards gentleness, seemed to be entering a new phase of his life; I could no longer discern in him an irrepressible poetic sharpness. His "Golden Bell" — a poem that had been read and recited widely among university students — had left him behind; disappearing into the ocean of ordinary life. He would eventually end his career as a poet with a small chapbook of "Collected Poems." Luo Gengye, the slightly over-weight author of "Dissatisfaction" with an "old, weathered-look" listened with an absent-minded face, while Guo Jian talked on and on ... and another poet tumbled into a literary love affair right on the spot. . . .

It was then I noticed a young girl. Her beauty was sensitive and quiet. She stood at one corner of the room, close to the hostess. I could tell that she was an intimate friend of Zhai Yongmin and knew the place well, but the sudden appearance of so many people had unsettled her. Her large, dark eyes were now even darker and larger under the electrified light, brimming with a composed curiosity. With no need for intellectuality, she reintroduced me to the ways of Time.

And Time, on this winter night, at Zhai Yongming's home, was backtracking through this young girl — all the way to the 60s, or more precisely, to a certain day in the early autumn of 1965. An autumn night's drizzle had stripped the city of summer heat. In a classroom under the light blue sky and moist breeze, Xiao Hong changed her summer dress for her autumn outfit — a dark green corduroy. The teacher was recit-

ing a passage out loud from the textbook, "Autumn has come, the swal-
lows have left the north, and southward they fly. . . . Spring follows win-
ter, and the commune members work hard in the fields. . . ." My text-
book was turned to that lesson "Southward the Swallows fly," and there
was a picture on the page that I still remember vividly today: morning
at the Commune, the commune members are planting rice seedlings; a
line of swallows flies above them. A young female commune member
lifts her head and watches the swallows with a smile on her face, one
hand still holding the seedling she is about to plant in the rice paddy.
"Swallow," I remembered the word, as well as the teacher's description. I
thought about the way a swallow flies back and forth between the north
and the south, I imagined a morning at the Commune. But all I could
imagine was that mountain country on the other side of the Jialing River,
where our teacher had taken us on a school excursion. Late spring — a
crowd of children, a teacher, and Xiao Hong in her dark green corduroy.
Yet it happened that I did not see the Commune members planting rice
seedlings, nor the swallows flying across over the heads. I was just think-
ing ... then I saw Xiao Hong standing up to answer the teacher's ques-
tion. Her seat was in the second row next to the window, whereas mine
was in the middle (so that my hyperactivity was under the teacher's
continuous surveillance). I watched this girl from Shanghai answer the
teacher's question correctly in quick and standard mandarin just like a
little princess. One afternoon a week before, I had traded my *Spearing
the King of Liang* for her *Shadowing the Spy*. We sat on the edge of her
bed at home, against each other, pointing at and commenting on the
pictures over and over. She had on a black-and-white peasant-dress that
day and, eating candies one after another, read the picture books atten-
tively, whereas I, as it seemed, had already tasted the last strong fra-
grance of summer — the whiff of candies from her mouth. The long
summer came to an end a week later, skirts reassigned to the bottom of
trunks where they would stay until the colorful days next year. The cor-
duroy that had been stored with other autumn and winter clothes for a
whole summer, the dark green splendor, flashed out from a small trunk
that I could not see. I caught a scent drifting over from the front, from

Xiao Hong — the scent of candies and camphor balls, of her home-town, of her growing up, and of the picture books. I remembered the smell of corduroy, one you would never forget once you had smelled it. To this day I still remember how autumn had come to the classroom through Xiao Hong's clothing. The change of seasons, the passing of time, and autumn had all begun with a dark green corduroy dress that had been stored the entire summer. It looked a little worn. Its dark shine was mirrored, buffed, and kindled by the pale autumn light on that dis-tant day; far far away in the unrevisitable year of 1965.

Tonight, another corduroy girl stood quietly in a room filled with the excitement of a gathering of youths. The Xiao Hong of my child-hood had grown up. . . .

The conversations went on. Guo Jian was commenting on "A Lyri-cal Poem." A passionate poem illuminated a girl on a winter night. Time all of a sudden had turned mellow, and grown old, like a worn-out book of poems opened, read, being listened to, and recited. I heard a voice streaming by: "Autumn has come, the swallows have left the north, and southward they fly. . . . Spring follows winter, and the commune mem-bers work hard in the field. . . ." I began to think of the past, the melan-choly of my early youth.

I spent the entire three hurried days at Ouyang Jianghe's home. Two true fanatics of poetry, we stayed up all night long and talked. It was there that I first read the first part of "The Hanging Sarcophagus" which he had just finished. I was shocked by his uniquely strange, com-plex, and almost sublime way of writing. "After all, poetry could be writ-ten like this!" My intuition told me that this would be his successful debut, a poem that would catch the attention of many and start a fol-lowing. I said to him, "This poem has finally done it for you!" Those three days, however, were but the prelude to our frequent exchanges later on. He was a machine of perpetual motion in conversation, and his sharp, meandering, and profound remarks drew one in easily. In my recollection, there are only three poets who could draw me in through mere conversation: Ouyang Jianghe, Zhao Zao, and Duo Duo. These three were the rare Master Conversationalists of China. As disputed a figure as he is, I still think of Ouyang Jianghe as a poet. His early poems were not that great, but he kept writing, and step by step developed a new style of which he is the unquestionable master. He is also a calligrapher, a connoisseur of classical music, and a determined defender of modernist literature; as an omnivorous reader and a perspicacious and persistent poet, he developed very early on an influential theory for judging poetry using Western terminology.

One morning we made a trip to Sichuan University. In the dormitory, we met Zhao Ye, who was a student there at the time. While Peng Yiling had been corresponding with him and knew him well, it was the first time I'd met him. I had read his early poem "Capricious Thoughts" through Peng Yiling and thought he was very talented, even though he had yet to find a stable voice for himself. In the cramped, cold, and damp student dorm, a crowd of students headed by Zhao Ye geared up as if they wanted to resolve with us, in the shortest time possible, a number of critical issues — such as "to be, or not be." Numerous restless young lives surged in a cramped and agitated room. We were going to use whatever hot blood we had left to melt the merciless cold of winter, to defeat boredom with our ideals. They were ready to brave the future, and they longed for the day of the final "shoot-out." They were so eager that they were already impatient.

The only regret of the Chengdu trip was that we did not get to see Zhong Min. Zhong Min was editor-in-chief of the two earliest underground poetry journals in Sichuan. One of them was called *Subforest*, a journal beautifully designed and bound according to standards of the time. It had several black-and-white illustrations, and a plastic-wrapped hard cover. For the first time, an underground magazine attained, through his hand, a sense of physical beauty. (This passion for aestheticism and formalism reached a considerable height in the poetry journal *Xiang Wang* that he edited later.) This historical document of early contemporary Southern poetry, extremely rare and precious today, included the early works of poets from Sichuan, Guizhou, and Guangdong. From the selections that he made for this 1982 collection, one could already see his ambition, inclusiveness, and panoramic vision. It was through

Subforest that I first encountered him and Huang Xiang, and it was also through *Subforest* that Zhao Zao had gotten to know my work and that of Zhong Min. The other journal was called *Modern Foreign Poetry*, the earliest underground magazine devoted to the translation and introduction of modern poetry of the West. Through this journal one could sense both his editorial attitude and avant-garde inclinations, as well as which Western poets were favored by young Chinese poets at the time. Dylan Thomas, Wallace Stevens, and Sylvia Plath occupied many of its pages, and Plath especially was given a dominant presence. No doubt she had already made an impact on contemporary Chinese poetry. Zhai Yongming felt her influence, and Duo Duo once told me that he too was influenced by her and had even written a poem in her memory. I was no exception. Even today her influence still spreads like a hurricane of agony, sweeping through the prairies of China.

During those three days, I did not reveal my "unruliness." I maintained the image of an English instructor and poet from the Institute of Agriculture, an image willingly accepted by the public. Only at midnight, at Ouyang Jianghe's home, did my eccentricity flicker. As he reciprocated, we lost ourselves on a peculiar heated topic. Three days later, I returned, the image of a straight and clean-cut teacher, to fog-bound Chongqing, to the secluded Southwest Teachers' College, to the "Communist Youth League" garden of the Southwest Institute of Agriculture.

OUYANG JIANGHE

TRANSLATED BY
YANBING CHEN AND
JOHN ROSENWALD

OUR HUNGER, OUR SLEEP

1.

The feast rises, drooling.
All night, the waiters stood in the heavens
with no ladder to come down.
Alone, a pale candle flame ascends.
Apparently such heights are not fit for you
as you try to look at happiness from a higher hunger.
Happiness is a low whispering breeze,
audible only when you stoop to listen.

2.

The shadow crouches lower than the feast
waiting for the leopard to appear. The hunger of the leopard
is a spiritual condition,
it has the breadth of a family chronicle
but does not preserve the saw-shaped marks its chewing has left,
no digestion, no excretion
expresses animosity toward food
and the longing for an obsession with spiritual purity.

3.

It doesn't take sky for the bat to appear.
Bat, pressing against bat, comes flying —
this half-breed, camouflaged flying,
gets its features from a mouse,
but in other parts of its body
is no different than birds we see during the day.
Smearing sunlight on the negative, it deepens
our reliance on sleep and night.

4.

You invented some birds in your sleep
some pleasant trills, fluffy
white feathers. But they are only
the official account of flying.
The bat, however, has nowhere to live during the day,
its sky an underground sky,
whose visibility is less than that of a candle.
Blow out your candle, and let the night darken.

5.

Sleep covers sleep like a bat folding its wings.
You stayed where you were, that which stood up and left
was a leopard knocking on the door a thousand miles away,
its hunger the hunger of a prison;
the door of freedom opens on weapons.
In the morning the bat's sky disappears,
leaving the earth a deeply scratched insomnia,
polishing a key at the heart of darkness.

6.

As you fall asleep you hear the mysterious knock.
It is the dead knocking: what do they want?
Between two kinds of truths there is no door to push open.
So you remove your shoes and trade footprints with the leopard,
you take off your glasses and give them to the near-sighted bat,
you hand out coins of grief to the dead and let them spend.
Waking up you find the chains on your body
have grown into your flesh like the elegant pattern of the leopard.

7.

Those standing alone on earth,
are weighed down by those lying flat in the heavens.
Bodies laid flat are more or less alike,
their differences are like the pelts of other animals
glistening in sleep. A wool blanket
drops from the heavens, burning your night of happiness,
yet there is no bed on earth for you to lie on.
And you don't necessarily want to sleep in the heavens.

8.

For many years, we've been waiting for a supper in the heavens.
Those who come late climb
the old-fashioned stairs, but there're no chairs to sit on.
Food we see as mixed
the leopard sees as separate. This is a noble feast:
when ordering you must use the leopard's arcane language.
This is real hunger: you hardly
feel the hunger, unless it is given a little bestiality.

9.

Food rises, simple and clear. No one knows
how much salt you've put in our supper,
that's life's own secret.
Why do we feel thirsty at night?
After drinking up the water on earth, we drink water from the heavens.
The rain which lasts all night needs throats and eyes
to hold it, needs a faucet to hold it back,
as it tenderly streams toward the heart of shame.

10.

Water, gathered, cannot be poured out.
Oceans overflow yet our warehouses and glasses
are still empty. Look at this ocean,
what does it care if the body holding its water is gold
or rotten wood. Don't count on infinite happiness
to preserve your smaller happiness,
as small as black fillings in a decayed tooth,
touching the pain of many years.

11.

A leopard with a toothache: let it hunt for food any way it wants,
its broad stomach spreads like applause.
But all this is a product of our mind,
which moves toward our heart in the high form of violence,
as if hunger were an ancient art,
wearing time's immutable
face, using food as its mirror,
whereas we, led by our aging, stumble to this day.

12.

The bat's night is day turned on its head.
Seeing far in such darkness,
it sadly turns blind if faced with light.
In the bat, light is already blind,
it opens its eyes, human eyes,
looks at itself, its vision submerged in a different world.
As a bird, the mouse flies,
but as a mouse, the bird loses its sky.

13.

If we're going to supper, it must be in the heavens.
Pressing the buttons with both hands, we silently lift the garden.
But are our hunger and sleep really that high?
When the leopard, like grain, lives through harvest
and distribution, when the bat turns white on the wall.
The rain last night was the sunlight we sprinkled from afar.
The first ecstasy of the sun is a candle,
illuminating our bedroom and kitchen.

Completed, March 7, 1995

HAN SHAOGONG   TRANSLATED BY THOMAS MORAN

EMBERS

Fusheng went into the mountains to haul bamboo. The government had banned logging while they reforested, and there were roadblocks everywhere. If you wanted bamboo, you had to smuggle it. You went into the mountains during the day, found the village you were looking for, and made arrangements with whomever was selling. Then you waited for the sun to set and sneaked out with your bamboo like a thief. It was always pitch black when you did this. You had to travel at night, and you had to travel fast. If you got caught at a roadblock, they would bang gongs, set dogs on you, and maybe even start shooting, so you had to leave the main road and use out-of-the-way trails. Sometimes violence could not be avoided; the injured went home and treated themselves with herbal medicines.

Fusheng went with Qingzi. Qingzi's real name was Yuanqing, but according to custom he was called by his nickname, just like the other men.

Qingzi did not think much of Fusheng's flabby muscles, which made Fusheng angry.

"Qingzi, if I carry one ounce less than you, you can send me to live with the pigs!" To seal his vow, Fusheng hacked at a section of bamboo. The local people took oaths seriously, and when Qingzi saw Fusheng chop the bamboo in half, he shut up.

After a long silence, Kongzi said, "Well, maybe it's a good thing we brought a scholar along. He can write our self-criticism if we get caught."

There were five of them altogether. They had a bag of brown rice, and everybody had thirty cents for meals. Fusheng also pitched in a bottle of hot peppers in soy sauce. This was their food for two days and two nights on the road. Back then, soy sauce was scarce; only city people and a few village cadres ever got to eat it. To country folks, it was some sort of a myth. Qingzi tried some peppers. As sweat beaded up on his forehead, he wiped his mouth and said happily, "I bet Chairman Mao gets two catties of this stuff every month."

When they finished eating, the sun had gone behind the mountain. They were in a narrow valley, and it got dark in a hurry. A stream murmured, a mist drifted in, and the cold ran through their bones. A crow cawed. It was time for them to head down out of the mountains. Fusheng did not want Qingzi's beady eyes staring at him in condescension, and so when they were choosing their loads, he ignored Qingzi's advice and picked out two thick lengths of bamboo and tied them into a V. Despite their thickness, they only weighed out at eighty some catties. Fusheng tried to look relaxed as he strode off in the lead. He felt energetic and lifted the bamboo over his head like a barbell.

"One, two, one, two!"

Fusheng thought about gym class back in school. He felt so good he started singing. "We will liberate the people of Asia, Africa, and South America!"

Kongzi could hear Fusheng singing up ahead. He said, "I don't like foreign songs. No melody."

Qingzi said, "He's braying like a donkey. You wait. In a while, he'll be moaning like a cow."

By the time they climbed over the first ridge, Fusheng was not singing any more, and the others had lost sight of him. He was way behind, and the others had to take turns waiting for him to catch up. They stood in the pale moonlight, waiting for Fusheng to come staggering along. He was doubled over; the moonlight shone off the sweat that glued his shirt to his back. He strained to keep the carrying pole wedged under his chin. The others could not help laughing at him.

"Well, my boy, why did you stop singing?" Qingzi mocked him.

Fusheng tried to catch his breath. He could not get an answer out.

"Do you have bound feet or what? At the rate you're moving, you'll still be here at New Year's."

"I ... I think my asshole's bleeding."

"Hah. Is it that time of the month?"

"You're a bastard, Qingzi. These shorts are too tight. They're digging into my crotch."

"You call those shorts? Looks like a sanitary belt to me. Why do you wear them anyway?" Yuanqing finally had his chance to get in a dig at the school boy's basketball shorts.

Given the circumstances, Fusheng could not talk back. He was embarrassed. Plus his thighs were fat, and they were chafed and bleeding where his shorts rubbed them. His thighs stung so painfully that he decided he would have to take off his shorts. Luckily, there were not many people in the mountains, and even if he did run into some girls, it was dark and they would not be able to see anything.

With his pants off, his legs were cooler and more comfortable, but the bamboo was getting heavier and heavier. As he walked, the soft sound of his companions' footsteps moved out of earshot. Eventually, he came upon a vegetable plot. Next to it was a well. The road had disappeared, and Fusheng panicked. With a sinking feeling, he remembered a crossroads he had passed. He must have made a wrong turn. He cursed Qingzi and the others for not waiting for him. They had not even bothered to leave a sign for him to follow.

"Hey!" Fusheng's voice echoed lonesomely in the unfamiliar mountains. "Where are you?!"

A dog barked in the distance. Soon Fusheng could hear Qingzi's familiar footsteps coming down the road. Qingzi's left foot always hit the ground a little more lightly than his right.

"What are you yelling for? Are you trying to wake up the guys at the roadblocks?"

"I was lost."

"I told you to stick closer."

"Where are we?"

"We've only gone seven miles. This is only Battle Cry Field."

Fusheng collapsed.

"Get up! Get up!" Qingzi looked at Fusheng lying prone on the ground and kicked him hard in the ass. "You useless piece of garbage. I'll cut your damn balls off."

"I've got to catch my breath. Just let me catch my breath. Come on, please?"

"You think we want to wait for you?"

Fusheng pulled himself off the ground and tried to get his wobbly legs underneath him. He was covered in sweat and mud. He felt something on his face and reached up with his hand, which came away covered by ants.

Fortunately for Fusheng, it started to rain, and they had to stop. Qingzi knew the area, and he led them to a thatched shack next to a brick kiln. The place was deserted. Inside the shack there was a wok over a fire pit. They assumed that the man who worked the kiln had gone home to celebrate the Double Nine Festival, which was coming up. They dragged over two bundles of firewood that had been readied for the kiln and started a fire. They were soaked through, and they stripped and draped their steaming clothing near the fire to dry. They could see their dicks flopping around in the firelight.

Kongzi laughed and said to Qingzi, "I hear that thing of yours is so strong you can lift two bricks with it. True?"

Qingzi grunted and said, "When I was younger I could handle more than two! But I'm old now. And I've been under the knife." Qingzi meant he'd had a vasectomy during a government birth control campaign.

Kongzi looked down at himself and then over at Fusheng in amazement. "Why is yours so small? Your dick looks like a little red pepper! You mean to tell me that the reason you wear those jockey shorts is to keep that little thing under wraps?"

Fusheng tried to defend himself. "Hey, it's cold out."

Once they cooled down from their hike, they felt chilly. They gathered straw and pulled it around them to keep warm. Qingzi wasted no time falling asleep. He snored a few times, and then all of a sudden he was jumping up and down and shouting. His feet were too close to the fire, and one of his straw sandals had started to smolder. Qingzi kicked the others and woke them up. He said if they fell asleep they would get sick from the cold.

Qingzi said it looked like the rain was not going to stop and they would decide what to do after finding something to eat. Qingzi looked around and found a beat-up old basket in which there were a few earthenware bowls. There was some salt in one of the bowls but nothing else. He told the others to fill the wok with water and boil it; then he went out. He soon came back carrying a few heads of cabbage. There was mud on the cabbage. The others guessed that Qingzi had stolen it from the vegetable plot.

It was still raining. They could hear the rain falling across the entire mountain. The sound came from the distance in waves on the wind. They heard each rain drop falling on each leaf and each rock on the side of the mountain they faced. They heard the rain fall on the straw hats of scarecrows. The quiet night made their hearing acute. They could make out even the faintest sound. Thousands of sounds filtered through the night, each separating from the others, becoming clear and distinct.

Qingzi said he could hear deer. Two of them. One bigger than the other. He could hear them on the other side of the ridge.

Fusheng listened. He thought he could hear the soft sound of hooves from the mountain. He could even hear the breathing of the smaller deer. He heard it walking through leaves; he heard its hoof slip on a rock. He also heard something else. He heard the entire huge mystery of the mountains, but there was no way to express this. Fusheng knew that if he spoke, he would not be able to hear a thing.

Qingzi decided that the larger deer weighed at least twenty catties. It was big.

Kongzi said it would be great if they could shoot it.

Qingzi said they should wait until it got a little fatter. They would get it next time.

"You think you'll find it next time?" Fusheng was surprised.

Qingzi laughed, licked his lips, and took a drag on his cigarette. His laugh was confident, as if he believed every animal on the mountain was his. As if he had the venison on his plate and it was just a matter of deciding if he wanted it and when.

Steam rose from the wok. The smell of cabbage soup rose to their noses. They rubbed their hands in anticipation. They did not have chopsticks, and so each of them broke off a stick to eat with. They wanted to eat some of their brown rice, but Qingzi insisted on saving it until they reached Cao's Hollow.

Qingzi blew across the hot soup. He lifted his hand suddenly and looked up. "Somebody's coming."

Kongzi heard something too. "Somebody is coming." He looked out into the night and cried out, "It's a woman." When they heard this, the men who had taken their pants off to dry ducked into the shadows.

A lantern light swayed in the doorway, and a woman's voice spoke from outside. "Excuse me, sirs. Is there a Mr. Li Fusheng here?"

"Li Fusheng? I, uh . . ." Fusheng was surprised that somebody had come looking for him.

"I've finally found you." The woman's shadow came tumbling in from the outside and bowed down before Fusheng. He was so startled he jumped back. It was a middle-aged woman. Her hair was dripping wet, and she was wearing a copper earring. "Mr. Li, you can save a life, and that will earn you more merit than building a pagoda. You have to have mercy on us. Do us a good turn. You have to help us. We will set off firecrackers for you. We will burn incense in your honor and make sacrifices to you. We'll remember you for the rest of our lives."

"Slow down. Slow down. You must have the wrong person."

"Are you Li Fusheng?"

"Yes."

"They said you had a car we could use."

"What car?" Fusheng was more and more confused.

"They said the driver would take us only if you gave your permission."

Fusheng laughed out loud. In the first place, he did not know anyone around, and in the second place, he had never even dreamed of having a car. He did not even own an ox cart. "I'm from the city. I was sent here. I live at the new camp. Do I look like someone who gets to ride around in a car? Hey, I wish I could get the chance."

Desperation appeared in the woman's eyes. She took a tight grip on Fusheng's shorts. "Do a good deed. Do a good deed. The doctor says if we don't get Juhua to the hospital tonight, neither she nor her baby is going to survive. This is life and death. You have to do something." She began to cry.

Fusheng put his bowl down. "Look, ma'am, what do you really want? Just tell us. It's the middle of the night. We're too tired for your jokes."

Qingzi waved his hand in annoyance. "Beat it, you nut. These guys are all criminals. They'll give you a sound beating."

"Go ahead. If you don't let me use the car, I don't want to go on living anyway."

Qingzi lost his patience. "Shengzi, she wants your approval. Just give it to her."

Fusheng turned to the woman. "Okay, okay, okay. You can use the car."

The woman looked up joyfully. "Thank you. But it won't do me any good unless I have it in writing. Write me a note."

"You want a note?"

The woman insisted that Fusheng write a note giving her permission to use his car. Fusheng had to laugh. Fortunately, he had a pen with him. It was hanging around his neck on a sweaty piece of string. He had brought it in case he had to write a self-criticism. After looking around, he came up with an empty pack of cigarettes, which he ripped open and spread flat on his knee. He wrote a few lines and handed it to the woman. This did the trick. She tucked the paper inside her blouse, thanked Fusheng profusely, bowed to each of the men, picked up her lantern and ran off.

They all laughed and ran to the door, but she had already disappeared. "Come back, come back. We'll get an airplane for you," Qingzi yelled, but there was no response. They heard her footsteps move down the slope, across a bridge, and then slowly fade away. A dog started barking again in the village below.

Fusheng went back to his cabbage soup. As he drank, he could not know that he would never forget this bowl of soup. Nor could he imagine that years later he would come back to this very spot.

In the blink of an eye, it was once again mid-autumn. A company found a promising spring in the mountains and decided to go into the bottled water business. They needed to borrow money right away. Fusheng was now vice president in charge of loans at a bank; he accepted an invitation to come evaluate the enterprise as a potential investment. As his car left the provincial capital behind and crossed the county border, Fusheng grew wide awake with excitement. An expanse of pale yellow poured through his window from the deserted harvested fields and countless haystacks. On both sides, grassy hillsides sped by and slipped out of sight. Fusheng looked for familiar houses and faces but saw none. New buildings appeared along the route faster than he could count and got in the way of his memories. Young women he did not recognize stood alongside the road and greeted him with practiced smiles and gestures as they touted inns and restaurants. "Flat Tires Fixed" "Food" "Flat Tires Fixed" "Food" "Food" "Flat Tires Fixed" These signs, painted on brick walls, wooden fences, and bamboo matting, assaulted Fusheng's eyes. These were the only words of greeting and welcome to mark Fusheng's homecoming.

The spring water bottling plant was located in Battle Cry Field, only now the name of the place had been changed to something less colorful. The plant was nothing more than a few dilapidated buildings and a few country girls filling bottles at a pipe that ran down from the mountains. The plant director, Mr. Zhang, was elated to find out that Fusheng had lived in the area during the Cultural Revolution, and he kept calling him Shengzi.

"You're not kin, but you have ties to this place. It's pretty here, isn't it? We've got spring water. It just wouldn't be right if you didn't give us the loan."

Fusheng kept his mouth shut. He was concerned that spring water would have a market only in the summer. He was hoping Zhang would have a plan for the slack season, such as canning asparagus or making rice wine.

The factory director insisted his guests stay over. He fed them frog and civet, offered to take them fishing and hunting, and promised them a tour of a famous temple. He grew animated as he encouraged his guests to enjoy themselves. "Heaven is high and the emperor is far away. Once you get a few miles away from the county capital, anything goes. Just think of yourselves as Japanese troops on a rampage. Do anything you feel like! Would you like me to get some women for a little dancing?"

Mr. Zhou, one of the bank's section chiefs, was with Fusheng on the trip, and he loved to dance. As soon as he heard Zhang's remark, he said he felt lightheaded from the drive and his feet were bothering him. He suggested to Fusheng that they spend the night.

After nightfall, Zhou waited around still dressed in his suit and tie but Zhang did not appear. No women showed up either. A procession of men on bicycles brought oranges and peaches, which they said were gifts from Mr. Zhang. He could not say that Zhang was a bad host, but Fusheng was not entirely pleased with the ex-school principal turned factory director, and he was exasperated with the hotel that Zhang had put them in. The place was run as a sideline by the county's financial bureau, and they had done everything they could to make it fancy. There was an imported water heater, but it did not work properly on the local electrical current, and therefore there was no hot water. The bathroom was equipped with a modern toilet, but it was stopped up, and filthy water seeped steadily from the bathroom. The carpet was marked with a stain like a coastline on a map and it gave off a mildewy odor. The wallpaper was blistered and sagging. These urban flourishes did not survive transplanting to the countryside, and their ruins surrounded the hotel's guests. Everything felt strange and uncomfortable to Fusheng. He realized his past was eluding him. Even the oranges did not taste like they used to.

There was a phone in the room. Fusheng thought about calling his wife, but he was afraid that if he managed to get through, it would be a letdown. He was not sure if his wife would listen to him talk about oranges. She might start shouting and cursing at him.

Two misdirected calls reached his room.

"Listen, Cao, do you want me to leave a scar on your left leg or your right leg?"

"What? What? There's nobody named Cao here."

"Don't play dumb with me. My knife knows who it's after."

The phone on the other end slammed down.

Fusheng wondered who this might have been and who he might have been feuding with. He decided that it was fitting to get such calls in a room with a stopped up toilet and a fetid carpet.

Worse were the bedbugs. The itching kept Fusheng awake. He kept sitting up to scratch until he finally decided to get out of bed. He knocked on the door of Mr. Wang, the chauffeur. Fusheng had decided to make an immediate retreat to the provincial capital. There was no answer. He knocked on another door.

"Where did Wang go?"

"He drove to town."

"What for?"

"You're the one who told him to go." Mr. Zhou, who was drunk, stood in the doorway.

"When did I tell him to go there? The stuff he gets up to. I bet he's doing a little gypsy delivery service with our car." Fusheng was aware that wood and tea-seed oil were inexpensive in the mountains, which is why drivers liked making this trip. They bought cheap and drove to the city to sell. He was also worried that Wang might have gone looking for women. During the day he overhead Zhang boasting to Wang that the village was so poor that prostitutes were very cheap. You could sleep with them for two yuan. They would even take an IOU. But Fusheng did not mention this to Zhou.

Zhou stared at Fusheng. "Did you forget? Wang had a note that you wrote yourself."

Zhou went into his room and came back with a piece of paper. He said that just before he turned in, a woman came to the hotel with a note. She said that Fusheng had given his permission for Wang to drive a pregnant woman who was having a difficult labor to the hospital in the county town. That was why Wang had left. He handed Fusheng a flattened cigarette pack.

"Impossible. This is a forgery!" Fusheng had written nothing that day, he knew nothing about a pregnancy, and he had not met the woman with the note, whoever she was.

"Look carefully. The handwriting does look a little like yours."

Fusheng was surprised to find his signature on the cigarette pack. The writing was definitely his, but it was smudged and looked like his old handwriting. It looked like his handwriting back when he was imitating the calligraphy on old stone inscriptions.

"Bizarre!"

"That's your handwriting, no?"

"Yeah, it is. But when did I write it?"

Fusheng felt the hair stand up on the back of his neck as he recalled a night long ago. He could not believe that a note he wrote that long ago was still around. Even more incredibly, it was right there in his hand.

Zhou listened to Fusheng explain the history of the note and then laughed. "You sure are babbling on for someone who didn't have much to drink. I had two bottles of the hard stuff and I could still play that pinball machine."

"You can believe me or not, but everything I said is the truth. I think it's weird myself. Who would have a note I wrote twenty years ago? Look here. This is a pack of Tangerine cigarettes. Where are you going to find that brand today?"

"The woman was a ghost. She has to be a ghost!"

"I'm being serious."

"Has to be a ghost. Twenty years ago, one look at you and she knew you were going to be a big shot one day. And she knew that you'd be driving around in an Audi. If she's not a ghost, what other explanation is there?" Zhou started laughing again. He patted Fusheng on the back. "I'll give you some of my tea. Go make yourself a strong cup. It will sober you up."

The moon came out from behind the clouds. It had just rained, and the creeks were high and running fast. From the window, the moonlight made the mountain slope across the way look as if it had grown in size and moved closer. It pressed down on Fusheng and made him feel short of breath. The black silhouette of the mountain was familiar to Fusheng. After all the years, the same ridge rose up to meet the same sky. The skyline came down and mirrored the mountain in the same startling fashion. As the mountain came into clearer focus, Fusheng found the thread that could draw his memories back and untangle his confusion. This thread of memory brought back the smell of cow dung and the stinging of his chafed, bloody thighs. It brought back the sound of footsteps padding down the path. Fusheng thought he could even see the lantern light at the foot of the mountain. He did not know why, but there was always a light burning in that house.

"There's a kiln shack around here," Fusheng said with confidence. There was no response. Fusheng turned around, but Zhou had gone back to bed, leaving his box of tea on the table for Fusheng.

Fusheng was positive there was a kiln shack near by. He was sure of it. He distinctly remembered stopping there to get out of the rain. It was his first time in the mountains. The round-trip was thirty miles and it had almost killed him. He remembered he used a fishing line to steal a chicken. You stuck an insect on a hook and cast it out on a length of line. Then you waited for an unlucky chicken to take the bait. With a hook in its throat, the chicken had to follow along silently. Because the fishing line was invisible from a distance, nobody would suspect anything. Even if they did, they would think you knew some magic spell to make the chicken follow you like that. On his first trip to the mountains, Fusheng used this trick to steal a chicken. He broke its neck as soon as he got it out of sight. Qingzi was afraid that they were going to bring bad luck on themselves; otherwise Fusheng would have stolen a few more. Fusheng also remembered that the road back never seemed to end. He walked and walked and finally fell asleep on his feet. When he woke up, he was lying in water in a ditch. There was a funny taste in his mouth. He reached up and a tooth dropped into his hand. Bad luck indeed. His companions were practiced at sleeping while they walked, and they did not notice when Fusheng fell into the ditch. They were long out of sight by the time Fusheng came to, and it took him a long time to catch up. Just before dawn, they reached a village. It was early, and the inns were not open yet. They pulled their collars tight and settled down on the street under the shop eaves to sleep. At sunrise, the cold woke them. Frost coated their tattered padded jackets and crackled when they moved. The villagers were observing a holiday, and everybody on the street carried meat and wine. Fusheng and the others had to make do with bowls of rice that they paid for by swapping some of their dry grain at an inn. They had nothing to go with the rice, but they wolfed it down as they squatted outside on the street.

Fusheng walked out of the hotel, and a large bird flapped up in alarm from the roof and disappeared in the dark sky.

There was a broken-down outdoor theater by the side of the road. The wooden pillars were covered with insect holes, a crosshatching of knife marks, and a patina of green moss, which made it look as if the wood were growing new bark. The hewn columns of wood seemed not to be dead; they were trying to come back to life. A similar thing could be said of the bricks strewn on the ground near the stage; they were crumbling into pieces, trying to return to the clay.

Fusheng walked down the road. He could hear footsteps ahead. Most likely four or five people. He wondered who would be traveling this late at night. He had just had a cup of strong tea and was not going to be able to get back to sleep anyway, and so he continued to walk. He found a stone bridge that he remembered well. The third stone on the decking was still loose. It had not changed. On the other side, grass still grew up and brushed his shoulders. This had not changed either. He crossed a muddy expanse littered with pieces of broken bricks. He walked on and found the kiln. The shack was still there. It loomed larger and larger as he approached. He turned his flashlight on and looked into the shack. There was still no one there. Bundles of dry grass had been spread open as bedding. People had slept there. There was a wok in the middle of the floor. Steam rose from a puddle of soup in the bottom of the wok, and a cabbage leaf was stuck to its side. The wok was on bricks above the remains of a smoldering fire. When the breeze came up, the embers glowed red.

It was obvious that someone had just left. Men who had come to the mountains to buy bamboo had just left.

Five of them. Now he remembered. As he crossed the bridge, Fusheng had looked down and seen their reflections in the moonlit water as they walked away in single file along the bank. Five of them altogether. They carried bamboo lashed together in Vs that bounced as they walked. The last in line walked in an awkward, bowlegged fashion, keeping his thighs apart as if protecting his sore crotch.

"Hey!" His voice sounded lonesome in the familiar mountains. "Stop. Wait."

A dog barked in the distance. Fusheng hoped to hear the sound of footsteps coming back toward him on the road. Qingzi's footsteps. The left foot a little softer than the right. Then he would hear Qingzi cursing him. But the sound of the footsteps did not materialize. It never did. There was only a bright, moonlit mist. The footsteps had long disappeared into the mist. They were gone, and Fusheng had no way to bring them back. He did not know the way. He did not know how he was going to catch up.

"Thief!"

Someone was yelling at him from up ahead. A shadow appeared on the road. Fusheng could not tell who it was until he came closer. It was not Qingzi. It was an old man in a ragged padded jacket. He had a stout stick in his hand.

"Coming in here to steal firewood. Fucking assholes. You people have stolen all the firewood from this kiln. As soon as I hear that dog bark, I know what's up."

"I just came to look around."

"Do you have any idea what firewood costs these days?"

"I didn't steal anything. Really."

"If you didn't steal anything, then who were you just yelling at? Ghosts? You're all in it together."

"I'm with the bank. We are here to look at your spring water bottling plant."

"Spring water?" The old man pointed his flashlight at Fusheng and looked him over. "There's nothing good about that either. Ordinary water that our pigs and cows drink. You put it in bottles and sell it for what meat costs. Is that something any decent person would do? No wonder they call it spring water. Spring another fast one on the people. Are you going to live the rest of your life on water?"

The old man went into the shack and looked around with his flashlight. When he came out he was even angrier. "Fucking assholes. Fucking assholes. They broke my bowl. Why didn't they just smash the wok while they were at it?"

Fusheng remembered that Qingzi had broken a bowl by accident. It happened when he was arguing with Kongzi. He remembered that Kongzi put a curse on Qingzi. Kongzi vowed that Qingzi would die from a snake bite, which turned out to be true. Yuanqing had been catching snakes his whole life. He learned his methods from an old master. Qingzi never got bitten. Even if he did, the wound would not swell or fester, and all Qingzi had to do was spit on it to make it better. Fusheng heard that as time went on Qingzi got overconfident. His master told him to swear off dog meat, but Qingzi loved dog meat and figured it would be okay if he ate it just once in awhile. Not long afterwards, a snake no bigger around than a chopstick bit him and he died right in his own yard, leaving four little children behind.

"I'll pay for the bowl." Fusheng took his wallet out, but discovered he had no cash; and he had left his watch by his bed in the hotel. "You can have these shoes as payment. They're leather."

"Leather shoes give you blisters. I don't want them."

"Well, come back to the hotel with me and I'll give you money."

"Two bundles of firewood and one bowl. All I want is what they cost. Eight yuan."

The two of them walked down toward the hotel together. It was darker. Clouds covered the moon. Halfway there it started to rain. They ducked under the eaves of a house by the road. The rain came down fast and the wind bent the trees and broke branches. Falling leaves danced all around and the rain splashed and surged. Thunder boomed and rolled across the mountain. It sounded as if the trees were howling and rocks splitting and tumbling away. The sky seemed ready to fall. They could also hear a loud shouting sound, but they could not tell what it was or where it was coming from.

"That's a scary sound. Sounds like people yelling."

"That's nothing." The old man was hidden in the darkness. All Fusheng could see of him was the glowing tip of his cigarette. The old man said that in April, in this kind of weather, you could hear very clearly the sound of cannon, gongs, ox horns, and the clanking of swords and armor. You could hear the battle cries of thousands of men. He said this was the absolute truth, and if it was not, he asked, then why did they call this place Battle Cry Field? It was only in the last couple of years that the name had been changed.

Fusheng handed the old man another cigarette and lit it for him. The old man continued his story. He said that a long time ago a boy blessed by heaven and destined to rule had been born in Battle Cry Field. The boy was conceived by a blacksmith's wife who lay with an immortal who came to her in the form of a dog. The boy could talk as soon as he was born. As a child he could compose poetry at the drop of a hat. He became an official. He made ink with his urine, wrote petitions to the court with it, and won every case he argued. The emperor was afraid the boy would usurp his throne and he sent one hundred thousand troops to kill him. When the troops entered the mountains, the bamboo and rocks came to the defense of the boy and attacked the emperor's soldiers. Bamboo exploded and rocks rained down. The slaughter was such that blood ran in rivers. But in the end, the sheer number of the emperor's troops was overwhelming, and the boy was caught and taken back to the capital where he was boiled in oil. The old man said that ever since that day, you could hear battle cries in Battle Cry Field.

The old man said the emperor was a corrupt, fatuous, self-indulgent man with a jealous fear of people of ability. He said that had this not been the case, and had the miraculous boy from Battle Cry Field ascended to the throne, then China would not be in the awful state it was in today. Clear-cutting would not have destroyed the bamboo, and at the very least, you would be able to get all the fertilizer you needed without having to use shady backdoor connections. And China would have wiped out the U.S. a long time ago, of course.

Fusheng smiled.

At daybreak, Zhou came out of his room and saw Fusheng in the hallway cleaning his shoes. He asked Fusheng where he had been at night and why he had mud on his shoes. Fusheng lit a cigarette and did not say anything.

Their car was parked in front of the hotel. There was a glaze of ice on the windshield and hood. After Fusheng ate breakfast, he went to driver Wang's room, pushed his door open, and shook him awake.

"Did you get her there last night okay?"

"Yes." Wang rubbed his eyes.

"The baby okay?"

"Yes."

"Boy or girl?"

"Girl."

"What was the family's name?"

"I forget. Lin maybe? Or maybe…."

Fusheng was not really interested in the name, and if the driver had remembered, Fusheng would have forgotten.

"Get up and have something to eat. We're leaving. We'll get an early start while the weather holds."

All Fusheng knew for sure was that another child had been born. He knew that all babies are covered in blood at birth. He knew that baby boys were usually ugly. Their faces were wrinkled, and they looked just like shriveled old men.

HAN DONG TRANSLATED BY YANBING CHEN

MOURNING THE CAT

We buried the cat. We
buried sisters of the cat
We emptied the paper bag
We scattered dirt

We carried shovels
to the autumn hill
We moved rocks
ingratiated ourselves with the sun

We traveled
wandered into the Peace Mall
went further to the meat counter
among the transactions there's a dead cat

We informed you of this in our dispatch
We exaggerated the death, but
realized it only after
we'd recovered.

Dec. 15, 1993

THE DUCK PROPHET

Seventeen degrees below, means dropping
seventeen notches more, below the cold of
zero. He doesn't want to go south, where it's warm
or head north, looking for a winter stove, all because of
the two autumn sycamores still standing outside his window

The only work, the only work
is to alter the thermometer which hangs like a gallbladder
the only work is to keep the blood in the glass
from turning green. For this
he has burned his calories too soon

Imagining the South Pole freezes the poet's thoughts
on leaves scattering before his eyes
His inexplicable wounds display signs of frostbite
His eyes are burnt by the white wall due to a false perception
The air thickens, the conversation congeals in a cold silence

Excitedly he says to himself, "Seventeen below!"
then mimics in his fever the shivering leaves
Inspired, the sycamores shed their leaves, bare their branches
After a fire embellished with crackling twigs and crunched leaves
the charcoal sketches the prophet's image over the ruins

December 18, 1993

Huang Shi
TRANSLATED BY YANBING CHEN

FANG WAN'S PARADISE

Wednesdays are now their only days together.

After dinner, Fang Wan's wife Gao Xiang puts on makeup in front of the mirror. She first puts on the foundation, applies powder, and then starts to work on the details with brushes, eyebrow pencils, tweezers, and lipstick. Bending slightly forward, she peers this way and that in the hand-mirror, as if trying to decide whether the face in there looks like her own.

"I'm clueless," says Gao Xiang. "There are always more pimples a couple of days before my period."

"That's because you use cosmetics. Pimples are caused by the pores being blocked." Fang Wan is washing dishes at the sink.

"I didn't use any cosmetics last month, and did it get any better?"

"It's the hormonal imbalance before menstruation — it has to do with the internal system — you won't have any more pimples after you have a child," Fang Wan says, drying his hands on a towel.

In a little while, they are going to see a movie. Though Gao Xiang is upset because of the lush growth of pimples, she cannot go out without makeup. Whenever Fang Wan says that cosmetics are bad for the skin, she rebuts him with information from TV commercials. She loves using cosmetics, which are everywhere in their home, and has as clear a count of them as she does the goods in the warehouse she's in charge of at work. She also loves soap operas, snacks — her teeth have already been softened by desserts — and hip-shaking music and dances with strong rhythms. Together they form an inexplicable skin for Gao Xiang, distinguishing her somewhat from the other women in their small city. Yet for Fang Wan, Gao Xiang is not much different from the other women.

A woman's need for ingenious decoration and trivial fantasies, he tends to think, is similar to men's need for women. Like now, the soft lines on Gao Xiang's face have disappeared — in the blink of an eye, she is already sharp and clear, like some cold woman in a movie — the relaxed atmosphere is gone.

Normally it goes like this. Almost every week since they've been married it has been like this. Wednesday is the last day of their week — as if it were the weekend. After dinner, they go to a movie or to the dance hall, even though the thirty-year-old Fang Wan no longer has any interest in the stench of the movie houses and dance halls. Like an old couple, they go to bed as early as ten o'clock.

They make love using contraceptives — the twenty-five-year-old Gao Xiang insists on not having a child for the time being — and then sleep till dawn. If they have gone to sleep early and still have energy, they do it once more early in the morning. After daybreak, Fang Wan takes the bus to the outskirts of town thirty kilometers away. He works for a week at the scenic and secluded Cloud Pond Reservoir, goes home for a week on vacation, and then returns to the reservoir to work for another week. It has already been ten years since he started working at this small power station by the reservoir. For ten years, he has been running back and forth between the reservoir and his small city. Fang Wan used to be a rare playboy at the power station. Since his marriage, everyone says he has become a different person. Perhaps Gao Xiang's lonely nights at home every other week have touched his conscience, therefore every time he goes home he feels guilty for being absent. He has heard numerous tales of marital problems — traveling salesmen and sailors on over-seas duty — and therefore especially cherishes how things have turned out for him so far. He has acquired the patience to spend time with his dear wife, as well as homesickness and longing on sleepless nights at the power station. He likes to hold Gao Xiang while they are sleeping. A sound sleep is good medicine for driving away one's worries.

In the spacious duty room of the power station the electrical hum sounds like a drizzle. For Fang Wan and Ma Jianshe, however, the station is too quiet. After ten years, they are too accustomed to this monotonous sound to notice its existence. They are like watchmakers living in the midst of a hundred clocks, oblivious to the ticking of time. A room of a hundred square meters is indeed too big for two men who have not much to do. Outside, there is an open ground even bigger — the size of one and a half soccer fields. Standing on the balcony of the third-floor duty room, they have a broad view of the mountains, the reservoir, the long dike, and the rural landscape.

Fang Wan is working the same shift as Ma Jianshe this time. The two of them watch over a big stretch of open ground and the high voltage equipment. There is almost nothing to do except logging the galvanometer and voltmeter readings every hour. There used to be six of them at the power station. Besides Fang Wan and Ma Jianshe, there are now Wang Shan, Luo Shoudao, and Station Master Hou Xuejun; another one quit recently. He became the owner of a private enterprise, whose plastic products are now being sold in all the major cities of the north. The six of them were recruited together, graduates of the same high school class in a small city. Now, these five can only talk enviously about the other one's Volkswagen, high-class apartment, and mistresses. Both this parvenu and Fang Wan have families, while the rest of them are either at a certain stage of a relationship or looking for one.

At work, Fang Wan reads an abridged edition of *The Strange Tales of Story House*. He has been reading this book on and off on duty for more than six months, yet he can never finish it. He feels that he might never be able to finish it, for after about a dozen tales, he forgets all the ones he has read earlier. Dutifully, he starts over again. As a result, the plot grows between the tales and blurs the lines marking their integrity — to this day he cannot put together a complete story. To add to his irritation, Ma Jianshe, at the moment, is howling a song beside him, and from time to time mumbles something to him. Ma holds a grudge about the outcome of a recent bonus evaluation and can't stop complaining. That's the way he is, Fang Wan says to himself, a narrow mind and a big mouth, always thinking the worst. That is the unanimous opinion they've reached about Ma after years of working and living together.

Ma also gets nostalgic for no reason. It's possible to make it through a single day with him, but an entire week is unbearable. He takes every chance to gossip about the past, like the time he was given an award in high school. This spring, he ended one relationship that had been arranged for him and started another. Over the past several years he has had brief relationships with about a dozen girls, but none of them has developed into anything serious — one by one the girls all left. He is eager to get married, but lacks any good prospects. At the age of thirty he still guards his virginity like a piece of fine jade. For some reason he takes pride in this, and he hopes that his girlfriend will also be a virgin; on the other hand, his virginity is also what's behind his lack of confidence. With a touch of sadness, he says, "You can't find an innocent woman in this world any more."

"Don't be ridiculous! Give up the virgin hunt," Fang Wan tells him. "You're only making it harder on yourself. Would a virgin really know if you were one?"

"Oh, you're so experienced!" Ma feels even more uncertain about the future. As he stands up to log the meter readings, Gao Xiang calls from the warehouse.

"I'm OK ... We're just joking around," Fang Wan says. "Are you all right?"

"I just want you to come home earlier. Seven days are too long."

"Think of them as seven hours."

"I couldn't sleep last night."

"Lock the burglar-proof door and windows and you shouldn't be afraid."

"I'm not afraid of burglars. I'm afraid of being alone, afraid of the empty room."

"Leave the light on, the room will be smaller."

"Hey," her voice suddenly becomes softer. "You want to make love to me?"

"Don't…." He looks over to Ma Jianshe, who is pretending to be skimming a newspaper. "Is it raining there?" Fang Wan asks loudly.

"I don't know." Her voice is stiff.

They are both silent. Holding the receiver, he does not want to say anything to her in front of Ma. He visualizes the way Gao Xiang looks when upset, and feels a little nervous. In the end, Gao Xiang says goodbye coldly and hangs up.

"See how much fun it is?" Fang Wan says, putting down the receiver. "Better to be single."

The rain doesn't come as expected. There's been no sunshine for several days. The sky, as if an accomplice to the sun, keeps pulling a gloomy face. The two of them have been just as low and gloomy, wilting spirits. At night, Fang Wan and Ma Jianshe huddle around the TV watching one show after another. Educational movies about the revolutionary war are on every channel. Fang Wan has never figured out why so many scriptwriters and directors in the 90s waste money and energy making such low-IQ movies. Yet the TV stays on, and he imagines Gao Xiang watching the same program. TV is the only thing that links their physical spaces.

As soon as dusk falls, no one can be seen in the reservoir from the balcony. The sky and the few small hills bunched together above the water of the reservoir appear dim and low. The view, which resembles a faintly drawn ink painting with churning clouds, holds a certain sadness that makes one sentimental. Gao Xiang does not love the scenery here anymore. While they were in love, every Sunday, as long as Fang Wan was working, she would come all the way here and then take the bus back to the city to work early the next morning. She loved the limpid water in the reservoir, the sunshine, the lush green trees. Now she'd rather sleep late at home on Sundays, would rather stay at home scared than come to this solitary reservoir. She used to be a girl of inexhaustible energy. They would stay up all night, never running out of things to talk about. The place then seemed to be a reservoir for all their fantasies. Gao Xiang liked the outdoors, liked to indulge herself in darkness on the long dike, watching the low dim lights glowing in the distance — even a whiff of a cold breeze could excite her. One late night, they did it standing on the dike, not caring if anyone was watching. They found out only later that the mosquitoes were not their most polite admirers.

Now it's spring. In summer, men and women lured from the city by the crystal clear water flood into the quiet Cloud Pond Reservoir, bringing agitation and disorder. Their hot bodies cooling in the water, the intruders look like wanderers in paradise lost in bliss. The sun blazes in its splendor. It was one such afternoon in July three years ago that Fang Wan crouched on the slope of the dike like an indifferent guard of the reservoir, watching those playing in the water. Half a host, he watched over the scene with a professional seen-it-all manner. In fact he was enjoying himself more than the scene. He was not, however, entirely unaffected. When his eyes fell upon the body that had just emerged from the water, he knew immediately what to do.

That had been Gao Xiang. He admired and was obsessed by, her delicate but agile limbs. He watched her glistening soaked black swimming suit cling tightly to her body — a unique banner among the flashy colors. He saw the water dripping along her body, and her shoulders and legs flashing in the sun. At that very moment, Gao Xiang casually reached her finger under the lower edge of her suit and gave it a tug. The fabric rebounded. It was quick and easy, but this fleeting gesture stirred Fang Wan's desire to probe a certain secret. It was a discreet, tacit thrill beneath a clear sky and beautiful sun.

From that point on things developed in a quick and simple manner. For his part, Fang Wan displayed a matching audacity and perspicuity. She lied to her friends. The lie was clumsy, exposing more than it tried to cover, but it made no difference. So long as she let them know, nobody cared. She stayed after dark, solely to kiss a man, a stranger, on the long empty dike. She had never heard of the power station, and thought it was not much different than a guard post for the reservoir. Fang Wan suddenly realized that she was taller. He tried to glimpse her expression while kissing but it was too dark. Her tongue was clumsy and passionate, not giving him a chance to breathe. He barely managed to hold on to her waist with a single hand. At the time, he didn't know she had a boyfriend in the city (though he probably should have realized that it would be unlikely for a girl like her to be without a boyfriend) who was on a business trip in another city. But then things had not yet turned serious, neither of them had had a chance to talk about anything beyond passion — though on Gao Xiang's part it was a deliberate move. That night in the dorm, Fang Wan could not stop himself from talking. With the tone of someone who had been around for a long time, he told sensational stories of accidents in the reservoir. He dwelt on the details of the drownings in the reservoir every year, the 1959 capsizing of a cruise boat in which more than a hundred high school students were killed. "Everywhere you heard people crying," he said. "From this end of the dike to the other, there was not enough room for the coffins. The whole reservoir had become a cemetery."

At home, Fang Wan has more time to kill than he needs. He is a good and efficient cook. Gao Xiang, who has a good appetite, is satisfied and almost proud of this. Soon after they married Gao Xiang had an abortion. After that Fang Wan began doing all the household chores. Gao Xiang could not get over the abortion. In the operating room her legs were spread and tied high up like arms. Before the operation Fang Wan comforted her in the waiting room. "They said it's as simple as going bird-nesting." Indeed, the operation was simple, but the pain left her half dead. "It felt like something was blowing a cold wind into me down there, and then it sucked things out," she told Fang Wan. "They were not bird-nesting, it felt like something with talons was tearing my guts out." She also said she clearly saw the nurse toss the bloody stuff they'd pulled out of her into the basin. "They tossed a life into a spittoon," she said. From then on she would never again use the diaphragm (that was the cause of her pregnancy) and insisted that Fang Wan use condoms. She would not take the pill either, for one side effect of the pills, she learned, was pimples.

During the day when Gao Xiang is at work, Fang Wan imagines her sitting wearily through the long day in the dusty warehouse. Unlike other women who knit sweaters at work, Gao Xiang reads romances one after another. By the time she gets home she doesn't feel like doing anything. She gets up early in the morning. He can tell what she is doing by the sounds. Lanky Gao Xiang will probably never learn to be careful.

Reckless as a boy moving around in the small room, she knocks things over, if not a chair, then a glass. She is impatient and gets easily depressed. Her reckless speed only slows things down in the end. He hears the crisp sound of the spoon hitting the glass when she stirs in the milk powder, then the thundering noise of the toilet flushing (the way she sits unabashedly on the toilet is still very much like that of a young girl). In a long stretch of silence — the same kind of silence as before his mother went out when he was child — he can imagine how she paints her face, one stroke after another, until her eyes look as blue as those of a peacock. The bun of hair coiled on top of her head for sleep is now let loose, the comb works strenuously through the curls, the ones that snap scatter to the ground, impossible to recollect. But in the meantime a brisk, healthy image breaks out of the dregs of night.

In direct opposition to Gao Xiang's stubbornness, Fang Wan is patient and meticulous. He feels relaxed when absorbed in cooking. He has tasted the passion of doing housework, instilling calm and order in the messy chores. As a child, he was accused by his mother, Cao Qiufeng, of being careless and rash, but he inherited his mother's hot temper, and for that, often found himself under his father's fists. Now he takes everything calmly. So much so that even when he learned one day that Gao Xiang had lied to him two years before, he still kept his composure. Gao Xiang had insisted that she and her ex-boyfriend had never made it to bed. In fact, she had been living with her boyfriend all along before she met Fang Wan. Fang Wan knows such petty lies well, just as he knows her magnanimity and youthful, bursting desire, which once illuminated his life like a beam of sunshine.

But Gao Xiang does not want a child. She says to Fang Wan, "We barely have enough time together anyway, and it'd be worse with a child. Think about it, we live together only every other week. In fact, out of forty years, we'll only spend twenty years together." Therefore, as if to make up for lost time, they never leave each other's side at night. Sometimes, the monotony of sitting together too long leaves them feeling empty. Like a peddler, Gao Xiang lays out snacks on the side table and munches as she watches TV. Fang Wan smokes off to the side. When watching TV, she becomes completely dumb, almost a puppet. She never gets tired of those 20th Century Fox melodramas. Those eye-flirting, butt-twisting heroines keep her in a perpetual state of envy.

"Ah! Foreign women's legs are just longer than ours," she has said more than once, "and their breasts are so big you'd think they're fake."

Fang Wan said they must be the result of breast surgery or medical injections. "Who invented the phrase Meatballs?"

He doesn't like these raucous movies, but he watches them anyway. In the dim glow of the screen, Gao Xiang's face looks cold and fragile. She is innocent as a child. Fang Wan often considers, with some humor, the unthinkable incongruities she represents. She is resolute in dealing with things, yet she is afraid of dark nights and loneliness. The upper half of her gives one the impression of a mature woman (she likes all of the small adornments of mature women: scarves, hats, sunglasses, stockings, etc.), but her slightly drooping buttocks are round and tight, and she also has oval-shaped kneecaps like those of a baby. Though such a mismatch between her upper and lower halves is a minor defect, it arouses Fang Wan's curiosity and pity, as if she had taken both abundance and sadness on to herself.

Once a month Fang Wan changes the propane tanks for his parents. Except for that he rarely visits them. He tries hard not to be alone with his mother so that there are no unpleasant exchanges on the topic of Gao Xiang. His mother never liked that tall lanky Gao Xiang, and has always thought it was just a brash moment of foolishness that made Fang Wan marry Gao Xiang. She is a small woman, but has a big voice. Her slightly overweight body has lost quite a few pounds since her gallbladder operation. She is a woman of fortitude, gets easily excited, and is always preaching to others. Before she retired as head nurse, her routine tongue-lashing of her patients approached the level of absurdity. As a child, Fang Wan had an innate fear of her. Even now the polished, dust-free furniture surfaces still preserve her stern features of days gone by. The first time Gao Xiang went to see her mother-in-law, she had long polished nails. As soon as Cao Qiufeng saw her, she said, "Long nails are not good for work, and not hygienic, either."

When Fang Wan gets home through the rain, Cao Qiufeng is sitting on the sofa knitting a sweater. She cannot stand being idle after the operation, so she busies herself with knitting sweaters one after another. "When you can no longer move, it'll be too late," she says. As Fang Wan takes off his soaked jacket, the sight of the sweater he's wearing — a work of her own from several years ago — sparks her temper. "Don't know what she does day in and day out, doesn't even take care of her own husband's clothing," she says.

"She gets back pains knitting," Fang Wan says.

"But thrashes like a dragon when she's dancing."

"The gas company says the gas will be forty *yuan* a tank next month," Fang Wan says. "Where's dad?"

"He's so busy he thinks he's the President." Cao Qiufeng is more upset now. "Price hikes everywhere. You'll know what good planning means when you have children. I thought you were like me, but now I see you're more like your father — he worries about nothing."

So much dissatisfaction, spinning out like a hymn from his mother's mouth. In the old days — when the tone of such hymns was sterner — mother and severity used to be synonyms. Fang Wan now finds the inhibitions in intellectual families anachronistically naive and vulgar. Through Gao Xiang, Fang Wan has rediscovered in his mother the nature of woman. They all have the songbirds' urge to sing, but that does not interfere with their sensitive defense mechanism. So whenever Fang Wan starts to shout, Cao Qiufeng becomes silent. But now it is just the ever-present rude gossip of his mother — how it makes him want to laugh in secret — that has kept the home from being dead silent. A laboratory technician, Fang Wan's father has been a person of good nature and few words all his life, so much so that his presence bears almost no relevance to others. Sometimes, Fang Wan himself deliberately provokes petty arguments. "What's there to worry about?" he says, "It doesn't change a thing — besides, we don't want to have children yet."

Cao Qiufeng has just finished a sleeve and is measuring it against her own arm. "I just don't understand. She thinks she's still fifteen? At her age, I was already dragging one in each hand going off to the night shift. If you ask me, she just doesn't understand how life's supposed to be."

Fang Wan comes to Gao Xiang's defense, "I should be happy enough that she doesn't complain about my working at the reservoir."

"Happy! Watch out, Fang Wan, the way you pamper her! What are you going to do, you fool? I'd say you have a child right away. It's not good for a woman to have children when she's old."

Her reprimands have lost the pure singular weight they used to carry when he was a child — her excessive seriousness now brings him more amusement than anything else. Looking at the solid, firm lines of Cao Qiufeng's face, Fang Wan ponders the childish skulking under her stubborn bones. "Fine. Can't you just be quiet?" he says.

At night, a fierce rain strands them in the room. Gao Xiang is obviously anxious. At dinner she turns to look out the window several times. She indifferently rushes through her dinner, a distressed look on her face. Fang Wan knows what she is thinking, but he keeps on smoking, oblivious in his feigned unawareness. There is a wet patch in the ceiling with water seeping through the cracks in the roof. He wonders whether the water will collect and drip through.

"Hey," Gao Xiang says, "I think the North is better than the South. At least it won't rain endlessly like this in the North."

She was in Beijing and Xi'an as a teenager. At this moment she is doing her home aerobics at the foot of the bed. It's been a long time since she's done aerobics, just as it's been a long time since she has been away from the city. Perhaps it's wearing her aerobics outfit again that has made her think of the North and the past. She used to swim a lot, but she hasn't gotten near water since the abortion. Yet she still manages to do the splits without too much difficulty.

"It feels like I never recovered from the abortion," she says, kneeling on one leg and propping up her elbows. "I ache all over sitting at work."

"The body gets healthier after childbirth, they all say," Fang Wan says. "My sister-in-law is now plump and white."

"I don't want to be any more plump!" Gao Xiang protests.

Kneeling on the floor, she flips the TV channels anxiously, but there is not a single good program. From the side, her body seems thin and sharp-lined, so much so that he wants to caress it, but at the same time, he is worried about her chaotic mind. Fang Wan knows that Gao Xiang's irritable temper and chaotic mind have to do with the noisy and cluttered family she was brought up in. He remembers how, one day in front of Hou Xuejun and Wang Shan, with whom he was playing cards at the time, she dragged him home. From that time on, he has never played cards with them again in Wang Shan's room. He thinks about his colleagues downstairs as well as Hou Xuejun's short girlfriend, whose fickleness is etched forever on the Station Master's pale face. Wang Shan's even funnier when dating, rushing off every night as if performing some duty, while he and the pigeons he raises, by comparison, appear to be in a more proper kind of love affair. Ma Jianshe's just clueless, and as a result, the girls have left him one after another. We're all fools in the theater of marriage, Hou Xuejun said once at work.

"Want to play cards?" He sees her sitting there, close to despair. She's changed back to her normal clothes, dark brows knitted, eyes glued blankly to the screen. "No, I've got a headache," she says.

When Fang Wan tries to feel her forehead she pushes his hand away. "I don't have a fever. It just feels like there's a band squeezing my head." She ignores him, shuts off the TV with a click, and crawls into the nest of quilts.

"You want some aspirin?" he edges over to her and asks.

With her back to him, she keeps silent. He calls her name, and says, "Are you really OK?" He repeats it once, but she's still silent. The light illuminates one side of her face, the stiff lines show that she's awake. Sometimes Fang Wan feels like she's unreasonably stubborn, just like her knock-knees. Are all women like this? He shuts off the light, lies down beside her, and cautiously reaches for her shoulder. He knows he's just asking for disappointment and she remains untouched.

He's almost sunk into sleep when Gao Xiang hooks his neck with her arm and stretches her leg on top of him. All of a sudden she starts to cry, wiping her tears on Fang Wan's face. He's baffled by this curious move, but nevertheless holds on to the leg on his belly, as if grasping on to his marriage.

"It's funny to think that two of us six might never get to work on the same shift before retirement," Station Master Hou Xuejun explains to Fang Wan — strange ideas pop into his head from time to time — as Fang Wan looks at a newspaper photo reprinted from *Vanity Fair*: an ad of Elizabeth Taylor holding a condom. Why don't you cut this out and give it to your girlfriend, he teases Hou Xuejun.

The two of them used to be quite close, because they are both poor wretches with quick minds. To hide his squint, Hou Xuejun wears glasses. He tries to make a joke out of everything. As a worker, he is impulsive and lacks persistence. The burden of women only adds to his doomed expression. Nevertheless, he seems quite content with his own haggard look. He is the best at bantering among the six at the power station. He and Fang Wan are like a pair of standup comedians, their hilarious remarks break the boredom and cheer everyone up.

According to the schedule, Fang Wan should be working with Ma Jianshe this week, but Old Ma's face was slit by someone in a fight several days ago. "That's just like him, getting into a fight every time he plays Mah-jong," Fang Wan says. "I knew it would happen sooner or later."

"That's because he got dumped," Hou Xuejun says. "He's been dumped again, and now he's angry with all women." He moves his cane chair onto the balcony. "It says in the newspaper that there are 100 million people falling in love everyday, but I'm sure there are at least 200 million falling *out* of it."

"I really can't figure this out, in the past thirty years we should've fallen in love hundreds of times. According to your estimate, we've been in and out of love ever since we were in diapers." Fang Wan moves his chair onto the balcony. "And marriage doesn't necessarily count as love."

"I've decided to get married in 1997. Would it be cheaper to go shopping in Hong Kong then?"

"By the time you get married I'll be divorced. Only Luo Shoudao seems to have any confidence."

They put their feet on the balcony railing, languid as two old men sunning in a nursing home. The reservoir is right under their eyes. The palm-shaped reservoir is connected to the water system of five counties. If it ever bursts, the flood will cover the entire city. In a month, the summer scenery and cool water of the Cloud Pond Reservoir will make those who come from the city stay put for a few days, drunk and entranced, while oblivious to the unknown power station. Hou Xuejun often fantasizes about a flood. "That would be spectacular," he says. Yet last summer it was a flood that had ruined his first venture into business, costing him a whole truckload of persimmons he had hauled back from Shanxi. Early this year he tried to get it back with a deal involving tropical fish, but the cold currents of winter again shattered his dream. His brief stints in business have become a running joke at the power station, something close to the comedy of a failed first love.

At night, they grind time away on the chessboard. "Thank goodness we're going home tomorrow." As Hou Xuejun speaks, a few muffled rumbles distract their attention.

"That's the first time we've heard thunder this year."

Though not swept away with joy, Fang Wan is nevertheless stirred. He knows that it won't rain yet, and the thunder is nothing but an empty gesture. Even so, the rumbles linger in the distance, as if somewhere a hill has collapsed; the sound reverberates in the valleys, disappearing only when touching the face of the water. The conversation about thunder fades. Hou Xuejun turns on the TV — he's lost his patience long before the end of one game — and watches the commercials. The one about a lotion for athlete's foot has lost its humor. In the silence, the two of them are lost in their own thoughts. Hou Xuejun yawns endlessly — no doubt thinking about his short girlfriend again. He goes back to his room shortly after nine, saying he's tired.

Fang Wan is also tired, but for some reason he can't fall asleep. Without Gao Xiang, sleep does not come easily. He tries hard not to think of the worried faces of his colleagues, the obsequious look on Hou Xuejun's face when answering calls from his girlfriend. Gao Xiang didn't call him this week — she's taken a second job working as a waitress at a nightclub. Now she no longer holds her nightly vigil of stupefaction, eating snacks and chatting with her equally stupefied girlfriends about fashion and movie stars. He misses her, misses her slightly overweight breasts and sharp shoulder blades. The pain of longing intensifies at night. The sound of ducks quacking at a nearby duck farm agitates him. The storm has not come. He cannot gather his strength, as if he has already strayed far from this duck farm of a clamorous world. The night is still young, but he's already waiting anxiously for the dawn of farm noises and bird chirps — anxious, but with no good reason. Only in his laughable fantasies can he achieve such a moment of mysterious joy as described in *The Strange Tales of the Story House*, indulging in pleasures with the fox fairies, and catching himself just in time to get out. Who knows, there just might be a happy fairy living in the deep forest near the power station.

The cold expression on Gao Xiang's face makes her look just like any other fairy. The layers of cosmetics get thicker and thicker. At dinner, she rushes through her meal, swallowing the food as if swallowing hours of boredom. Her meticulousness in her dress and make-up — as if she were going out on a date — makes Fang Wan's heart sink. The nightclub closes at midnight, so Fang Wan sits up to wait for her to go to bed together. But when he cautiously approaches her under the quilt, he is rejected.

"I'm exhausted and I have to get up early tomorrow morning," she says.

He doesn't actually feel any desire. He was only lifting the rubber band of her underwear when she brusquely pushed him away.

"What's the matter?" he says, "We haven't done anything for two weeks."

"Really, I'm tired."

"We used to do it several times a week when I wasn't working."

"Can't you see I'm working two jobs now?"

"Nobody forced you." He raised his voice. "You always complained I spent too much time at work. Now *you* don't want to stay at home."

"Don't yell at me. You can think whatever you want."

She pays no more attention to him. Though her eyes are closed, Fang Wan knows she is awake. He's mad at her attitude. He wants to slap her in the face, but doesn't dare. (Once after he hit her, her hysterical screams scared him out of his wits. A few days later he told her, "It felt as if it were me that was hit, and I was as helpless as when I watched my parents fight as a child.") He feels satisfied that he can tolerate Gao Xiang's rude behavior. Early in their marriage, he was full of hopes and dreams about their life together. He was intoxicated in the luxury and radiance of Gao Xiang's body. He imagined a world of passion and mutual respect. A paradise. But now his bowels are aching again.

He cannot stop Gao Xiang from going to work at the nightclub. Self-respect requires that he keep silent, but it does not prevent him from feeling depressed. It's not so bad during the day, when he can read *The Strange Tales*, cook, or walk along the street, but at night time slows down. It was never this bad before. Now occasionally he begins to miss the power station and reservoir while at home, but at work, he again thinks of home. Even his mother has learned about Gao Xiang's working at the nightclub. Cao Qiufeng has always been sensitive about his son's relationship with his wife, and she's read in a glance everything from the tense expression on Fang Wan's face. Unlike Fang Wan she doesn't pretend to be calm, and launches into a long passionate chastisement of Gao Xiang.

Gao Xiang, on the other hand, is displaying an unprecedented youthfulness and energy; as if she's gone back to her maiden days. Fang Wan can imagine the way she looks — happy and excited — at the nightclub. She now works tirelessly.

"I've never felt so good, like I never had the abortion," she tells Fang Wan, "and I seem to have an endless amount of energy."

"That's because you're spending less and less time at home."

"It's funny you said that, Fang Wan." She turns around abruptly from in front of the vanity mirror, her half-painted face strange and unfamiliar. "You sound exactly like your mother."

"That's the way it is. You complain about being tired in bed, and as soon as you get up, you're full of energy."

Fang Wan thinks of the Gao Xiang with the strong, insatiable desires, who swallowed birth-control pills like she took cold medicine. She was never the shy and bashful type; sex was a game that surprised and amazed her. Before their marriage she would change her sanitary napkins standing in front him, as if he were a close friend of the same sex. But now she seems to have suddenly awoken from her indulgent sport; cold and in full seriousness she guards her chastity like a nun. She leaves without hesitation. It seems almost absurd. Not too long ago she was still complaining, sweetly and tenderly, about being left alone; now it is Fang Wan who is the sentimental one at home every night. Their roles have switched. He can't figure out how it happened. All that's left of their marriage is an outline of their eating and sleeping together, the rest has all been omitted. The world's face has been distorted (he thinks of the slash on Ma Jianshe's face); a dogged slave of petty family life, he (like Hou Xuejun, Wang Shan, and the others), dreams a sweet, cozy, but fragile dream ungraspable by others, while the city is caught up in a money-making frenzy.

Pain seems to permeate the air. Wang Shan and Ma Jianshe are working this week. Hou Xuejun must have scurried over to his girlfriend's place. Luo Shoudao moved in with his girlfriend's family some time ago. Outside, the thunder thrashes. The pouring rain did not stop Gao Xiang from going to the nightclub. He keeps watch over the empty building by himself. The rain always reminds him of his childhood, of mud, of the dreamlike shadows in a black-and-white movie. Though the weather has turned warmer — summer has come suddenly — he often feels a stream of cold air moving in the room. The scene is black and white, but Gao Xiang resides in a world of colors: she wears shiny, intangible clothes, her black hair haloed in red light, her delicate features look as if they were a colored ink painting with extremely fine brushwork and meticulous detail.

Hou Xuejun's face is twisted, which makes him look like a guy named Victor in the English language program on TV. Wang Shan's expression, on the other hand, resembles the shell of a walnut. In the harsh fluorescent light — which Fang Wan initially took as daylight — things have lost their shape. He says, "How come you two are soaked?"

He tries to concentrate, pulling himself from his dreams back into reality. Wang Shan, a man of few words in normal circumstances, is speechless, like he's just been beaten up. Hou Xuejun is more agitated, and he tells him what happened during the night.

"Old Ma?" Fang Wan tries to say something, but a bitter taste in his mouth paralyzes his tongue. He wonders if he has heard it right, but no, it is Ma Jianshe. Several hours ago — he'd fallen asleep on the sofa — Ma Jianshe was electrocuted. Fang Wan imagines how, in the rain, Ma Jianshe walked in a daze over to the high-voltage equipment, and how, as he stepped across the safety line, the equipment discharged toward the flashlight he was holding.

"I'm afraid he's going to lose an arm," Hou Xuejun says. The rain has blurred his face.

"It was really terrifying," Wang Shan says, having finally calmed down. "It never occurred to me that he would go out on an inspection in such a storm. I thought he was just going to the bathroom."

Outside, the rain is still pouring down, but they don't hear any thunder. To Fang Wan, the past few hours feel like an entire season, and it is already so distant. It's two o'clock in the morning. One of their old colleagues has had an accident, and the rest of them have gathered in the middle of the night, talking about it — the scene seems unreal. Several years ago, they often gathered in someone's dorm room, talking into the night, but there was never this sense of absurdity. Women have effected profound changes in them; it's as if it were they, not the women, who have turned from young girls into wives. They are now enfeebled, secretive, and androgynous. Maybe it is because he has just woken up,

Fang Wan still fails to grasp the meaning of what has happened — that Hou Xuejun and Wang Shan have come in the middle of night to inform him of the accident seems like an exaggerated scene in a movie. The way they are talking about Ma Jianshe smacks of a conspiracy, of a rebels' meeting after a failed revolution. In the midst of the rain, the chauffeur at the reservoir guard post, a man with a warm heart, has driven Ma Jianshe to the hospital. Poor Old Ma, he's finally made himself into a one-armed man. Lost love, the wound on his face, the arm bandaged, the images float and circle in the night air.

After Hou Xuejun and Wang Shan have left — they hurried back to the power station on the reservoir bus — Fang Wan is alone again. He suddenly realizes that Gao Xiang hasn't come back the entire night. Outside, the rain seems to have stopped. The air at daybreak must be especially fresh. He's surprised at his own indifference to his wife's staying out all night. The fluorescent light is still on, separating his room from the rest of the world, as if he were the only one awake at this moment. He's not the least worried, and he even feels a hint of joy. At this unhurried moment — everything in the room is in order; there's not a single speck of dust in the details of the furniture — he thinks of nothing. He only wants to be immersed in a state of plenitude that's been latent in him for a long time; he is imperturbed, invulnerable. Everything will be all right. The dawn will come as it does every day, and he will remain his old self.

What else could he expect? Nothing prevents him from entering his dreams. In them he sees Ma Jianshe covered in bandages, leaving only a hole for his gaping mouth — all of his hair has fallen out. At the same time Fang Wan finds himself standing at the window and sees, down below at a dark corner of the building, Gao Xiang is talking with a man, a stranger in a leather jacket. He turns around and sees his colleagues at the power station gathered in his room, talking and laughing. But these scenes bore him quickly, and he goes back into the past and vaguely sees his father and his silent tenderness toward his mother. He is in the midst of a well-ordered world, as if he has gone back to the good old days of boyhood. A time when worries flamed then went out like a match, and happiness churned like a hungry stomach; spurring him to grow, so that he would never become frail.

In his dreams, Fang Wan has no fear, no worry, no jealousy. There, nothing is unsatisfactory. He may do whatever he likes, and shall always overcome.

AUTHORS

BAI HUA was born in Chongqing in 1956 and graduated in English from the Guangzhou Foreign Languages Institute in 1982. He studied Comparative Literature at Sichuan University and is currently working as a journalist in that province. He has published two collections of poetry.

BEI DAO (ZHAO ZHENKAI), born 1949, is the founding editor, with Mang Ke, of the original *Today* magazine. Bei Dao was crucial to its revival in 1990, and continues to act as its chief editor. His collection of short stories, *Waves*, was published in English in 1987, and he has several collections of poetry in English translation, *The August Sleepwalker* (1989), *Old Snow* (1992), *Forms of Distance* (1994), and *Unlock* (2000) all published by New Directions. Bei Dao's forthcoming book of essays *Blue House* will be published by Zephyr Press in late 2000.

CHEN DONGDONG works in the resource room of the Shanghai Association of Industry and Commerce. He was born in 1961, and graduated from Shanghai Teachers' College in 1984. His poems have appeared in numerous journals, including *Modern Chinese Poetry* and *China*.

DUO DUO (LI SHIZHENG) is a prominent young poet and prose writer associated with Bei Dao and other members of the 'Misty' (*menglong*) group of poets. Before leaving China he worked as a journalist. A collection of his poetry, *Looking Out From Death*, was published by Bloomsbury, London, 1989. He has also been widely published in Holland where he lives and works.

GAO ERTAI was accused in the 1957 "Anti-Rightist" campaign and sentenced to labour camp where many of his fellow prisoners perished. A well-known aesthetician, painter and writer, he went to work in the Dunhuang Art Research Center upon his release, but continued to be persecuted throughout the Cultural Revolution. Even in the 1980s, he was subject to repeated campaigns of criticism, and was arrested again in 1989. He now resides in New Jersey.

GU XIAOYANG, essayist and film-maker, was first active in film criticism in China, and, in recent years, in film-production. He was born in Beijing in 1956, and after secondary school served three years of military service. In 1982 he graduated from the People's University, Beijing. For some years he worked as a journalist on *The Art of Film*. In 1998 he went to study in Japan, and in 1990 travelled to the USA. He now lives in both Beijing and Los Angeles.

HAN DONG was born in Nanjing in 1961, and graduated with a degree in philosophy from Shandong University (Ji'nan). He now teaches in Nanjing and has published two collections of poetry and a number of short stories in magazines.

HAN SHAOGONG is one of the best representatives of the young generation of fiction writers who emerged in the post-Maoist years. *Maqiao Cidian*, his novel of 1997, won critical acclaim. He is now based in Hainan Island.

HU DONG was born in Chengdu, Sichuan province and graduated from the Department of History at the university there. In 1982 he joined the modernist poetry movement. He later moved to London, where he continues his writing of both poetry and fiction.

HONG YING (CHEN HONGYING) was born in Chongqing in 1962. She started to write poetry in 1981 and fiction in 1988. She has published four collections of poetry, three collections of short stories and a novel. She moved to London in 1991.

HUANG SHI is a poet and fiction writer who lives in Zhejiang Province, China. His work has been published in many literary magazines. His short story *The Song of the Grasshopper* appeared in the Chinese anthology *Selected Short Stories of the New Era*.

JANET TAN writes and publishes fiction, essays and poetry in both Chinese and English. She has studied at St John's University in New York and received her MFA from Brown University's Creative Writing Program.

LU DE'AN was born in 1960. He has published two poetry collections and now makes a living from portraiture in New York state.

LU DONGZHI is a poet, fiction writer, and collector of Chinese antiques. He lives in Beijing.

OUYANG JIANGHE was born in 1956. He was 'sent down to the countryside' in 1975. In 1986 he was demobilized from the Chinese army and joined the Institute of Literature in the Sichuan Academy of Social Sciences. In 1992 he went to the United States, and now lives in Washington D.C.

SHI TIESHENG, a celebrated Chinese fiction writer, was born in 1951. He joined the *Today* group in its earliest years, quickly becoming its major fiction writer. He has been widely regarded as one of the most distinguished writers to emerge from the 1980s. Paralyzed from a disease when he was labouring in the remote mountainous regions, he now lives in Beijing with his wife Chen Ximi.

SONG LIN currently lives in Singapore. He was born in 1959 in Xiamen (Amoy) but spent his childhood in the countryside. He was a graduate of Shanghai Normal University where he stayed on to teach Chinese Literature for eight years. He was imprisoned for nine months in 1989 and left China for France in 1991.

SUN XIAODONG is a fiction writer and essayist. She studied at Berkeley, and is now a Ph.D. student of anthropology at Princeton University. Her collection of essays is currently being published in China.

WANG YIN was born in1962 in Shanghai. He studied literature at East China Normal University, where he started writing poetry.

XI CHUAN (LIU JUN) is a poet who graduated from the Deparment of English, Beijing University. Later, he worked for the Xinhua News Agency and now teaches at the Beijing School of Fine Arts.

XU XIAO was born in 1956 and studied physics in university. He started to publish poetry in 1977 and fiction in 1983. He moved to the United States in 1991, and currently lives and works as a freelance writer on Long Island.

YANG LIAN is another prominent name associated with the 'Misty' (*menglong*) group of poets. He has been widely published and translated, including the Bloodaxe Books collection *Where the Sea Stands Still* (1999), and the forthcoming *Yi*, to be published by Green Integer.

ZHANG ZAO was born in 1962 in Changsha. He studied English at Hunan Normal University and Sichuan Foreign Languages Institute. In 1986 he went to Germany to study for a Ph.D. in literature at the University of Trier. He began writing poetry in 1977, and has published two collections of poetry.

ZHANG ZHEN was born in Shanghai in 1962, and studied journalism at Fudan University. She continued her education in Sweden, Japan, and the USA, and received her Ph.D. from the University of Chicago. She currently teaches in the department of Cinema Studies at NYU.

ZHU WEN spent his childhood in northern Jiangsu Province. He was born in 1967 in Fujian province, and studied engineering at Southeast University where he began to write poetry, turning to fiction in 1991.

TRANSLATORS

H. BATT is a free-lance translator of Chinese literature. His collection of Chinese fiction on Tibet is forthcoming from the University of Minnesota Press.

JOHN CAYLEY is a poet and literary translator as well as the founder editor of the Wellsweep Press. A collection of his tranlsations and original poetry was published as *Ink Bamboo* (Agenda & Bellew: London, 1996).

YANBING CHEN was educated at Fudan University, Beloit College, The University of Notre Dame, and The University of Iowa. His translations of contemporary Chinese literature have appeared in numerous magazines and *Abandoned Wine,* the previous English anthology of *Today.* His short story "Genghis Khan" was published in *The Notre Dame Review* in 1999.

HOWARD GOLDBLATT has translated the stories and novels of several writers from China and Taiwan, most recently Mo Yan's *The Republic of Wine, Please Don't Call Me Human* by Wang Shuo, and, with Sylvia Li-chun Lin, Chu T'ien-wen's *Notes of a Desolate Man.* He teaches at the University of Colorado at Boulder.

DUNCAN HEWITT currently works as the BBC World Service correspondent in Beijing.

BRIAN HOLTON teaches at the Universities of Durham and Newcastle. His translations of Yang Lian's collection of shorter poems, *Non-Person Singular* was published by Wellsweep Press, and *Where the Sea Stands Still* by Bloodaxe.

GREGORY B. LEE lives in France. His book, *Troubadours, Trumpeters, Troubled Makers: Lyricism, Nationalishm and Hybridity in China and Its Others*, was published by Duke University Press in the USA, and C. Hurst & Co. in Europe.

SYLVIA LI-CHUN LIN, winner of the 1999 Liang Shih-ch'iu Translation Award, translates Chinese fiction and essays for publications in Asia and the West. She is the co-translator of *Notes of a Desolate Man* by the Taiwanese novelist Chu T'ien-wen. She teaches at the University of Colorado at Denver.

MAO LIANG graduated as an English Major from Fudan University, Shanghai, China in 1992. He continued his education at The University of Oregon and The University of Illinois at Urbana-Champaign, where he received his M.A. in East Asian Languages and Literature. He is currently a Ph.D. candidate in Classical Studies at Johns Hopkins University.

THOMAS MORAN has a Ph.D. in modern Chinese literature from Cornell University and is Assistant Professor of Chinese at Middlebury College inVermont, where he teaches Chinese language, literature, and film. He has published translations of stories by Han Shaogong and Shi Tiesheng and a play by Wang Peigong. His research interests include Chinese prose nonfiction, including reportage and travel writing. He has recently written for publication two short essays, one about Lao She's novel *Camel Xiangzi* and one about same-sex love in contemporary Chinese literature.

JENNY PUTIN completed a doctorate in Chinese literature at the University of Oxford, and currently works in the United States.

JOHN ROSENWALD is a poet, translator, and Professor of English at Beloit College. He is also on the editorial board of *The Beloit Poetry Journal*.

DESMOND SKEEL is a free-lance translator of Chinese literature. He won his Ph.D. degree in Chinese literature at the University of London.

SU GENXING earned his B.A. in English from Fudan University, Shanghai in 1991. He worked for the Xinhua News Agency 1991-1994, and received an M.A. in Peace Studies from The University of Notre Dame in 1995. He is currently a Ph.D. candidate in Comparative Literature at The University of Arizona.